The Shadebinder's
Oath

I0646031

Jeanette Cottrell

www.dragonmoonpress.com

The Shadebinder's
Oath

Jeanette Cottrell

The Shadebinder's Oath © 2004 Jeanette Cottrell

ISBN: 978-1-896944-31-9

Dragon Moon Press
www.dragonmoonpress.com

Dedication

Despite twenty-six years of living with a nut, my husband Michael still seems happy to help me apply reality to my flights of fancy. He even found me a map of the perfect island with the perfect harbor as my model of Ailsandia, and explained how best to defend it! Thanks, love.

Thank you also to my son Kevin, who helped me design and fly a dragon, and to Kate Windstar for critiquing my early manuscripts, and giving me benefit of her perspective.

Lastly I wish to thank Glen Ray Crack for his extensive website on the ancient Bayeux Tapestry (www.hastings1066. com) which was the inspiration for Queen Ailsa's tapestry.

Chapter One

D avid flattened himself against the wall of the King's
Stable. He bit his lip, glancing at the shadows along
the rear of the cottages. Most of his friends loitered
there, waiting to see if he really had the nerve to do it. Of
course, it all hinged on the apprentices, those few hiding in
the stable loft. If they hadn't snared the latch open, no one
could blame him for not stealing into the stable. If they'd
done their part, he was stuck for it. David, the eldest son
of High Captain Vance Heronlys, couldn't back down in the
face of their stupid superstition.

He sidled around the corner, braving the torchlights that
spilled pools of dull flickering light along the wall. Three strides
carried him to the door. He tested the latch, felt the give, and
grimaced. He couldn't be that lucky. Coins jingled in too many
pockets; bets hung on his success or failure. He pressed the door
ajar, straining his ears for a moment before slipping through.

Gods, if only he could wake up, and discover himself in
bed, wedged between the other cavalry juniors. The warm,
horsy scent filled his lungs. He firmed his chin, glancing
quickly from one end of the barn to the other. He'd snuck
in without alerting guards or grooms. He could do this, no
question. Shades weren't real anyway.

There were no such things as shades, he reassured himself. No such things as shades, no such thing....

The hair rose on the backs of his arms as he suppressed a shudder. The Shadebinder lurked inside the haunted stall, halfway down. In that stall, years ago, the Princess' horse had gone mad, possessed by a demon. David had been seven then, but he'd never forget the tale. The gelding berserked, stomped on his groom, splintered the door, and drove his hoof through the wall. He'd leaped, stumbled, and crashed through the wooden paneling. By the time men dashed in with ropes, blood gushed from a hole in his chest, and his left foreleg flopped uselessly. The horse thudded to the floor, his eyes clouded before they managed to drag his groom from the wreckage. Workers rebuilt the stall, but people shied away from it unless they had compelling reason to work nearby.

Tonight, rumor had it, the Shadebinder demanded 'permission' to house his horse in that stall. The moment they heard, the boys huddled together, jabbing dares at each other. Their suspicions were confirmed. If the Shadebinder selected it especially, it must be haunted. Imagine the spells he'd cast this very night. David sneered at the idea. The Master wouldn't allow the Shadebinder to conduct rites in his stable. He'd never put the King's horses at risk. The moment David opened his mouth, he regretted it, but it was too late.

He had to prove himself and salvage his reputation. At this moment, apprentices in the loft awaited David's signal. If he didn't get to the stall and rap on the beam, they'd brand him a coward.

Lanterns hung on every other post along the aisle, but they didn't dispel the shadows draping the stalls on either side. He steeled himself and slunk down the aisle. He edged past a groom, asleep on the floor. After the Princess' horse had gone mad, grooms slept in the aisle, not in the stalls.

He counted the half-doors, his heart pounding painfully,

and stared at the fourth on the right. No light crept from it; no sound or movement hinted at activity. Demon raising, huh. And with all these grooms about, sleeping. Obviously, they were scared to death. David peered into the light, glimpsing the shape of the Shadebinder's horse. If the man himself were here, he must be asleep.

He grinned at his fears. All his terror, for nothing. With light feet, David crept the final steps, slipped the stick from his belt and stretched as high as he could to rap the beam running from floor to ceiling. Three raps, and he was out of here.

A shadow seized his arm, hauling it behind his back. Demons. Fear seized him. His throat closed, choking off the air. A hand clapped over his mouth, rough fingers denting his face.

"What do you think you're doing?"

The words rumbled over his nerves, scraping them raw. David twisted his head around. Not a demon, thank the One, but a man. His panic ebbed, surging again as his captor's face shifted out of the shadows.

"Don't yell," said the Shadebinder. "You'll startle the horses."

David croaked something, but the words jammed in his throat as his spit dried. The Shadebinder had been waiting for him. Somehow, he'd known David was coming. His legs wobbled under him and he sagged against the burly arms. He nearly fell as the Shadebinder released him, spun him around, and grabbed his shoulder in an iron hand. The stick fell from David's nerveless fingers. The Shadebinder caught it, twirling it lightly.

They stared at each other. The man's eyes pulled at him, demanding something of him. David's heartbeat pounded, skipped a beat, and thumped more slowly. The Shadebinder nodded slowly, and David understood. If he yelled, he'd wake the grooms too, as well as the horses. The Shadebinder knew it and didn't care. He didn't intend immediate violence.

David drew breath more easily. At worst, the man would turn him over to the Stable Master for punishment, in which case, David would go hungry tomorrow and sling dung by the cartful. Of course, the Shadebinder might have a score to settle, but David could deal with that another day.

His fear faded, and he slid a glance to the loft where his accomplices waited for his tap. Damn it, now what? He'd gotten here, but they'd never believe him. They'd rag him for days. He had to give the signal.

"Why the stick?" The Shadebinder shook him by the shoulder. "Scare a horse or two? That's a despicable game."

David bristled. "No. It was a dare, that's all. To get to this stall."

"Why?"

No one could read the Shadebinder's face. The Shadebinder rejoiced in tragedy, and glowered at celebrations. In years past he'd avoided the castle, as a hawk avoided civilization in favor of fields overflowing with rabbits. Now, he soared in daily, hovering over people, and the human rabbits shrank under his gaze. Did hawks think? Did they plan? Did they care what their prey thought of them?

The Shadebinder raised an eyebrow. David cleared his throat. "Um. No reason."

"Because of me?"

"No. Well, partly," he added. "I guess."

"You're welcome at my home any time," the man said, his words crackling like thunder in distant clouds. "But confine your stable visits to daylight."

David eased backwards. "Sure."

"Look at me." The Shadebinder grabbed his chin and forced his head up. "Answer me truly. Were you planning to hurt anyone or anything?"

"No."

The Shadebinder dropped his hand. "Ah. Go, then."

David paused in mid-step and scowled. "You believe me?"

"It's the truth. Go."

"Umm." David toed the straw at his feet, and glanced at the ceiling. The apprentices would hear the voices, but that just proved he'd been caught. Which was the greater danger, really? The Shadebinder, or the loss of his reputation? Should he run? Or grab the stick, rap the pillar and then run?

"What's the trouble? This dare of yours?" Amusement threaded between the words.

"I'm supposed to rap three times on that beam," David said in a rush.

"Hmm." The Shadebinder raised the stick and rapped, one, two, three.

David heard a muffled yelp in the loft overhead. He let out his breath, flashing the Shadebinder a grin. "Thanks. Bye."

He slipped out the stable door, shoved it closed, and ran for the corner where his friends stood. A scream cut off in mid-breath, as the boys scrambled out of the shadows, bent over strangely as they scattered in all directions. David slowed to a halt, glaring after them. Now who were the cowards? Not the High Captain's son, that was for sure. He'd braved the Shadebinder's lair and escaped. David snorted, stuck his thumbs in his belt, and sauntered slowly to the barracks.

Back in the stable, the Shadebinder growled softly to the shadows. "Did you have to scare them to death? I'd almost convinced him...That's nonsense. They didn't wake you up. You don't sleep. Just cooperate for once in your afterlife. A boy runs in on a dare, and you smite all his conspirators so they vomit their guts out. He believed me, damn it. And the others would have believed him. Now all the stories will roil up again."

The Being radiated his anger in stiff-legged silence. A groom stirred in the straw, turned over, and slept. The Shadebinder stroked his horse's flank, his gentle hands a mute contrast to the rage evident in his bunched shoulders.

He turned his back on the Being in the corner, analyzing this episode and its effect on his plans.

☙

Gods, he could swim in his own drool.

The Being crept closer, his mouth watering, his eyes riveted on the intruder. She couldn't hear him, naturally. Mortals were deaf. Blind, too, even with the full moon glaring overhead. He swallowed his slaver and planted his feet more firmly as he studied the creature. Curiosity flickered, grudgingly.

Why the hell was a peasant girl ransacking the King's garden? Coarse gray woolen stuff shrouded her to the teeth, hiding her in the darkness. Weren't there guards or something, to protect the King's property?

He shifted stance, silently stamping a forefoot. To hell with mortals. He only had to turn around and cough twice, to find another castle or a city reducing the countryside to a rubble heap. Humans, for the gods' sakes. An entire generation of the critters could vanish into memory during the slightest flick of his beard. Oh, granted, they were amusing. Occasionally, their frantic little lives entangled him, but even the most entrancing entertainment rarely lasted for long. The moment he got attached to one, it went and died on him. An odd coincidence, really. Doubtless, this latest young man, sulking in the stables, would do the same.

He hadn't meant to get involved. It was the Demon's own luck that he'd been sucked in by his euphoric memories, drawn by that one, undeniable, unscratchable itch. In one single sphere of knowledge, only one, humans mastered the universe: Food.

Deft human fingers toyed with roasts, herbs, and heavenly aromas, tempting the Beings from their lofty pinnacles. Oh, if the Others could see him now, wistful and greedy, lurking just outside the King's garden, like a common thief. Wouldn't they sneer! Was he a sniveling brat or a true Being?

Oh, but buttery cheeses melting on the tongue, delectable sweets delighting the eye, and tender roasts trapping his nose with their warm succulence. Oh, for *those* he'd suffer the occasional company of hobgoblins, if need be. He'd sacrifice a little dignity for the sake of the vast rewards awaiting the true gourmet. And so he'd graced the King's garden with his presence, only to discover a thief in the night, poaching on his territory.

He glowered up at the castle wall. The feckless guards should be scaring off vagabonds instead of swaggering along the perimeter wall, hunting out places to raise a leg and piss. Meanwhile that girl, that dastardly girl, stole the King's green beans. More importantly, *his* green beans. Kings were here today, gone tomorrow, but Beings were forever.

By the Hills, she had quick hands. She skittered through the garden like a starving doe. What a greedy little thing! Just look at all that stuff she squirreled away in those great apron pockets.

She pulled something from a leather pouch at her belt. Moonlight glinted on the blade of her belt knife. She dropped an object into a newly dug hole, shoving the dirt over it with one bare toe. As she rose, she nipped off a firm red tomato and bit into it with avid pleasure, half-closing her eyes to savor the taste.

"Don't they feed you?" he rumbled to her unhearing ears. Unwillingly, he studied the bones on her wrists and the hollows under her eyes. Her bony face looked like underground crystal, pale, rigid, and sharp-edged. He bit off a tomato and ate it. Her delight struck him as a trifle extreme.

From overhead, hobnailed boots struck the walkway on the stone wall. The girl shrank into a grape arbor's shadow. The guard strolled along, glancing away towards the city.

Apparently, his priorities did not include the King's garden. He vanished around the curve and his footsteps faded into the distance.

The girl eased out of the shadows. She slid an item from her pouch, blew on it, buried it with quick, neat movements, and slipped down the row. The Being flicked in behind her, whuffling at the freshly turned earth. He prodded the dirt heap.

"What are they?" he said. "What are you doing?" Why couldn't he break himself of expecting the deaf to answer? She'd dashed into the orchard already, where she held something high in the air, and tucked it onto a fork in the tree limbs.

He flicked in behind her, rose onto his hind legs and balanced against the tree trunk, sniffing. Frustrated, he snorted. "Hurruff!" He stamped his forehoof against the tree, irritated as it slipped through the bark and into the wood. He yanked it free, leaving the bark unmarred beneath it.

"Girl," he snapped. "Answer me. What is that thing?" To his astonishment she paused, resting a hand on the nearest tree. Her eyes passed over, through, and beyond him. With a small shrug, she swung up onto a branch.

Girls in trees? Times *had* changed. He dug into his capricious memory, extracting the King's name from half-remembered tavern talk. Gerritt. King Gerritt and Queen Ailsa of Ramsvalt, with twin sons and a daughter or two. He'd seen the boys once, at the Emperor's court, unless he had the wrong century. They were fostering there, over the sea, with the Emperor Theo-somebody-or-other. Emperor Whosit, and his wife, Empress Whats-her-name. Huh. Such impressive names for creatures that died in a few decades.

In fact, he'd wandered this way partly because the name attracted him. Ramsvalt. It sang to him. At least it acknowledged its debt to a Being, even if it was the wrong one. So here he arrived, after meandering for a few months. Or was it years? No matter. Time was for mortals.

Plums. She found plums. If only he could fly, and just hop to the treetop, and cram them all down. Oh, to eat a ripe plum, the juices sweet, dripping down his beard. They were nothing like those disgusting windfalls, so sour to the lip and sickeningly overripe. *Gods, it's so unfair.* He groaned. *All those plums out of reach. Why can't I fly? I demand to fly.*

"Girl! Girl, you up there. Give me those."

The girl's darting hands faltered with three plums in one hand and two in the other. A black braid fell free of the hood, dangling over one shoulder.

"That's right, I'm talking to you. Make yourself useful, and drop me a plum. Better yet, drop them all."

She blinked, her dark eyes glittering in the nighttime, like deep caverns trapping the firelight.

"Are you deaf?" Of course she was. They all were. He could *burst* from the frustration. He dropped to all fours and slammed a forehoof against the ground. Slowly, deliberately, he enunciated the words, "Drop ... me ... a ... plum. Now!"

A ripe plum plopped to the ground. Greed swamped his astonishment. He leaped on it, slurping it into his mouth with a long tongue. "Nectar of the Gods. Another one!" She lay against the branch, unmoving. His temper flared. "Another one. Throw it to me!"

She dropped to the ground, picked up the plum he'd just eaten and held it out to him, perfect and whole.

"I can't eat that one again. There's no flavor left," he said impatiently. "Give me another." Thank the gods for his self-control, or he'd just gobble them out of her pocket. However, as she'd been polite, he'd be polite as well. In his own way, of course. "A plum, girl."

She held out a second plum, jerking her hand back as he snatched it. The plum hit the ground with a heavy, juicy thud and fresh sweetness perfumed the air. He lunged at it. She raised the first plum to her lips and bit into it. A puzzled look crossed her face briefly, leaving behind it the calm, glassy look of a pond after the ripples have ceased. She sat on the ground, poured the plums from her pocket onto the grass. He tore through the lot, moaning with pleasure. As he finished each one, she set it aside, eating several herself, storing the pits in a small leather bag.

"They taste all right to you?" he said, in mid-munch.

"They're fine," she said.

"Aha. So you can talk after all." He threw back his head, shook it wildly, and broke into a gallop through the garden. "Hurruff. Damned good fruit, girl, great stuff." He skidded to a stop, the turf remaining undisturbed behind him. "Do you have a name, girl?"

"Riss."

"Caprio, caprine apparition." He shook his head again, his beard spiraling beneath him.

"Caprine apparition. Why would a goat be a ghost?"

"I am not a ghost. Or a shade, or a spirit. Or even a goat, come to that."

"You *look* like a goat."

"Correction," he said sternly. "Goats look like *me*. I am a Being. Ghosts, shades, and spirits were all mortals who died. Beings aren't mortal. We simply exist. We're gods, really." He nosed at the fruit pile, his tail wriggling furiously as he tried to find one he hadn't eaten before. "Any more of these luscious things?"

"If I take more, they'll notice. If they set a guard, I'm out of luck. Have a tomato instead."

"I've three more stomachs for tomatoes, peas, and beans. Fruit's harder to obtain," he said, gazing at the fruit dangling far overhead. A small flash of movement arrested his gaze. A bat swirled around a tree and swooped after a firefly. "I've never seen one so brave around humankind before." Caprio jerked his head towards her. "You should be screaming, girl.

16

First me, then a bat. Don't you have any normal reactions?"

"I knew it would come. I called it."

"Ha. Is that what you hid in the tree? Some kind of charm? And those other things you've been hiding everywhere?"

"Yes. They summon ladybugs, praying mantises, and bats, or chase off gophers and moles. Just little magic things. Nothing big."

"Well cut my horns and call me a carrot. You're a charm maker?"

"Oh no, no, no. The cook gave them to me. I work in the kitchen." She fumbled the remaining fruit into a pile and scrambled to her feet.

"So the cook gave you charms to put out in the dead of night." He snorted skeptically. "Uh huh, right."

"I have to put them out at night. Magic is, I mean, I could lose my job if they find out." Riss poised to flee, like a mouse trying to fool an owl with stillness.

"Hurruff. You're in no danger from me, girl. Sit down." He pawed the ground. "All right, *don't* sit down. See if I care. Come on, run with me."

"Run?"

"Run, run, run. Race me to that tree." Caprio bolted. After a moment, Riss lifted her skirts and trotted after him. Caprio tore around the target tree twice, waiting for her to catch up. "Slowpoke! What's the matter with you?"

"Nothing." She breathed heavily, clinging to the tree trunk as she staggered. "I'm not used to running."

"You need to eat more." Damn it, what did *he* care if she ate enough or not? It wasn't his business. "Why can't you smile? Snort, scowl, grimace, and laugh. Show you're *alive,* why don't you? I'm more alive than you are, and I was never born. Here, now, don't run off, girl, I don't mean anything by it. Get back here. That's better. Sorry I offended you," he added gruffly.

She measured him with a glance, from four dancing hooves, to shaggy gray hair and beard, his floppy ears flicking constantly. "You really are a –an apparition? I mean, you're not alive? People don't see you?"

"Fools can't see me. In my experience," he said, thrusting out his nose, "most people are fools. I never make friends with fools. With non-fools, occasionally." He cocked his head at her.

"A friend," she said, testing the words for hidden spikes.

She was just like a rabbit, invited into a wolf's den for company's sake. Suspicious creature. "Or not," he added carelessly. "I don't suppose I'll stay long. The world's too wide to be stuck in such a damp bit for long."

Her mouth quirked.

"Humph. Call that a smile? Looks like you painted it on. Never mind, girl. Some of us can smile, and some can't. One last race? I've places to go and stomachs to fill. Just to the wall, let's say. Keep *up* this time, can't you?"

Caprio dashed for the wall. Riss ran after him, one hand outstretched as if to catch his tail. Caprio hit the wall, his white tail lingering for a split second as his transparent figure faded through the stones. Riss caught herself against the castle wall, grazing the palm of her hand. She leaned back against the wall, breathing hard.

The garden's stillness soothed her soul. A second bat flitted in crazy loops around the first, hunting insects. The other charms would toil away secretly, hidden in the greenery and dirt. The garden had produced a bumper crop this year, despite the gardeners' disinterest. Royal gardeners loved ornamentals, wondrous flowery displays, or geometric greenery plantings for the visiting nobles. The farmers took huffy pride in grain fields, snarls of squashes and tubers, and their beast herds, providing wool, milk, and meat. Fruits and vegetables were an afterthought, a rich man's whim.

Bonnara, the royal cook, had the garden planted yearly so she had additions for stews and some savories for the table, but beyond that, no one bothered much. Except Riss, of course, who snuck in at night, planting seeds garnered from previous years, weeding, thinning, selecting, and eating, her stolen garden protected by castle walls and the King's unwitting connivance.

A revolting surge of nausea swept through Riss' stomach, erupting to the front. Caprio danced under her nose, beating the air with his front hooves.

"Ha! Gotcha, girl. Scared you, didn't I? Admit it!"

Riss gasped, her hands clutching her stomach. The cold vanished, replaced by unaccustomed warmth, spreading through her body and mind.

"Now, *that*," said Caprio, triumphantly, "***that's*** what I call a smile."

Chapter Two

Denys strode across the farmyard, casting covert glances at the gleam on his boots. His grin burst loose again and his stride lengthened. Tomorrow. He could almost smell the hot saddle leather baked under the sun, feel the horse's power beneath him, or reach for the cross bolts strapped across his back.

He scanned the farmhouse with impatient eyes. His grin faded. He couldn't help it. He still looked for Aunt Nan in the doorway every time he passed. He forced the grief down. At least her two-room house was still here, sandwiched between the tiny stable and Farren's workshop. The three-in-one building conserved heat from winter fires and family bodies. He listened in vain for Nan's goats, the small sharp hoof thuds, and the occasional bleat as they snatched mouthfuls from each other. Farren must have taken them to the King's herdsmen already.

He cupped his mouth to shout. "Farren? Brother!"

A response, more grunt than words, drew him around the last corner. Farren bent over his workbench, engrossed in some incomprehensible task with small wooden strips, pegs, frames, and bowls of water and oil.

"Farren. Look at me, for the gods' sake."

Farren straightened. Denys stepped back, as startled as ever at his little brother's long, lanky form. Farren looked like a loose-jointed wooden toy. Unkempt brown-black hair hung over his blue eyes. His hooked nose and the heavy bristle on his chin fitted incongruously with the smile lines near his eyes. He was twenty-one and he'd done a man's work for the last ten.

It turned Denys' stomach, the way people watched his brother from the corners of their eyes. Even after all these years and the beatings and abuse he'd taken, he still couldn't keep his mouth shut. Not that it mattered, really. Either he kept silence and people suspected his strangeness, or he spoke and they knew it. While Aunt Nan lived, she'd buffered him. Half the world had loved Aunt Nan, and tolerated her nephew for her sake. Once Denys left, what would happen to Farren?

Farren glanced over him, head to toe, noting the gleaming boots, the brown-black leather vest with the King's insignia on the left side, and the squared shoulders. "Denys, you did it. You passed the trials for Second. I knew you would." He clapped Denys on the back.

"So did I," he boasted. "Terrell didn't have a thing to do with it, either. The Commander didn't know we were brothers until afterwards. Terrell's still off with the Western."

"And you'll be what? Rimlands Patrol?"

"I'm a Second with Southern Patrol." Denys straightened his vest.

Farren turned to the bench and set down the curved wooden slat. With exaggerated care, he aligned pegs on the bench, ranking them according to size. "You? You get seasick in a row boat."

"I was a kid then."

"Uh huh." The words bumped heavily over hidden boulders. "Wonderful news, Denys, I couldn't be prouder. Nan says the same."

Denys' lips tightened. God, only two sentences spouting from his mouth and already he sounded cracked. "It's a great opportunity, Farren."

"No need to tell me that." Farren's neck muscles stood out, and his shoulders looked like rocks.

Denys considered and discarded several speeches. "Look, Farren, I'm off tomorrow."

"That's fast."

"Well, you know how it goes. We have to patrol the whole route before the Progress, and that's only three weeks away. They, I mean we, we've got to be sure the passage is safe before the court sets out. The near areas should be fine, but security's a problem further down. After all, it's been seven years since the last Progress." Denys bit his lip. Damn. He'd walked into that one.

"I remember."

"Damn it. It's not going to happen again. You can't *possibly* think a disease is lying in wait to hit me the minute I set foot on the Island. I'm not saying it's easy, going to the Island, since mother died there last Progress, but I'd be a fool to give up this chance just because I was afraid."

The Progress was an exhilarating blend of family reunions, craft hall competition, and international commerce. The royal family, many of the Valtiris nobility, and highly placed representatives from every Valtiris guild attended it. Emperor Theomedon sent representatives and merchants, and so did every member nation of the Empire. As a newly fledged Second of Southern Patrol, Denys couldn't have asked for a more prestigious assignment.

"You don't need to tell me. I know." Abruptly, Farren bent over the waist-high railing into the holding pen that comprised the workshop's southwest corner. He glared into it and commanded, "You stop that."

Denys looked over Farren's shoulder. Aunt Nan's prized

nanny goat lay on her side in the infirmary pen. The skin shone pinkly along one leg, exposing jagged red rips in the flesh. Several lines of Farren's meticulous stitching laced her up again. She lifted her scarred head and nosed Farren's hand.

"Lovely girl, Felicia," he said. "You rest now. This ruffian will let you be, if he knows what's good for him."

What ruffian? Denys shifted to his other foot. "I thought you handed the goats back to the herdsmen."

"All but Felicia. She tried to jump a fence, but ran through it instead. Our Felicia, always the acrobat. I've got to fix her up before I take her back the herdsmen, or they'll throw her onto the spit or in the stewpot. Aunt Nan would have a fit."

"Too bad," said Denys. "Look, Farren—"

"You," Farren said, pointing into the pen. Felicia wriggled uncomfortably. "Leave Felicia alone, you hear me?" Felicia relaxed onto her side.

"Farren. There's nothing in there but the goat. Damn it, stop changing the subject. Talk to me, will you?"

A long moment passed. The tension faded from Farren's shoulders as he leaned back against the bench, studying his brother under lowered eyebrows. "On the last Progress, seven years ago, evil struck."

Temple-like words, spoken in a common, matter-of-fact tone. That was so like Farren. "Not again," Denys said. "Please don't go on about that again. It wasn't evil. It was a fever. Mother died and so did a dozen others. Aunt Nan was crippled, the Queen nearly died, too. A disaster, I'll grant you, but it wasn't evil, and it's over."

"It's not over, Denys. I'm telling you, I've seen the shades. They're clustered around the castle, just waiting for the Progress." Farren's strain wrenched the words out of shape. "There's something going on and it's building up fast. Aunt Nan can't tell me what it is. She hasn't been watching as long as I have, so it doesn't look strange to her."

"Aunt Nan's dead!" The shout ripped through the workshop. The brothers stared at each other. "Look, I'll agree with you on one thing. There's something strange going on at the castle. Do me a favor, would you? Eat dinner there while I'm gone? You're entitled, you know, it's King's work, every bit of it. Even the goats are his, and all this." Denys' sweeping arm encompassed the stacks of selected woods, chosen for different hues and shimmers, the shelves filled with stains and oils, the tools hanging on the wall rack, and the large chest of tiny drawers and cubbies which rested on Farren's workbench.

Denys' eye caught on the box. "Who's this for?"

"The Princess. It's a travel case for the Progress. Holds her jewelry, scarves, things like that."

Denys stifled an automatic curse. "Nice work." He traced the wood inlay along the case's lid, patterned in subtle reds, browns, and blacks. Steep mountain slopes descended into ocean waves. A seagull flew over the water. He threw a sidelong glance at Farren. "You designed it?"

"Yep."

"She doesn't even know you're alive."

"She doesn't need to."

Denys shook his head. Aunt Nan had filled Farren's head with all those stories, and now look at him, wasting his time on fancy woodwork for that cold-hearted bitch. "Promise me you'll eat at the castle."

"Why? You've got to mollycoddle the crazy little brother? Make sure he eats? Makes friends?" said Farren, an edge to his mild voice. "How can he ever meet a nice girl if he hides himself away? I get enough of that from Aunt Nan, alive or dead. I don't need it from you."

"You're not crazy. If you were, I damned sure wouldn't ask you to eat at the castle so you can keep an eye on my girl."

"Your girl."

"Trissi." Denys' eyes dropped, then lifted. "She works in the kitchen. She's a true Island girl. She's got that long black hair and the most gorgeous dark eyes." Denys' voice firmed again. "You'll know her when you see her. She's been edgy lately. She won't tell me why. It bothers me, her working there, but I can't marry her until I've been Second for at least a year." He paced back and forth across the workshop. "Whatever it is, she'll be okay once Progress starts. With the," he checked himself, "the royal family gone, things'll be calmer. Will you keep an eye on her for me?"

"Sure."

Denys' relief died as Farren turned to the pen, shaking his finger sternly at the air. "She needs her rest, you demon. Leave her alone, you hear me?"

Of course he'd be fine, Denys fumed. He lived in delusion, talked to things that weren't there, and couldn't step into the town without half the population planning to lynch him. Yes indeed, he'd be just fine.

"There's nothing there, Farren," Denys said with forced patience. "Just the goat."

"How can I *make* you?" Farren addressed the empty air. "Is that a challenge? How about a deal instead? Leave her in peace and quiet, and I'll give you an apple. No, I don't *have* two apples, only the one. I have to trade for them, you know. They don't grow here. One apple and an oat bag. All right then. Out you come, and mind you leave her alone today. Deal?" Farren held open the pen door and glowered at a patch of nothingness as it passed by him. "I'll be back in a minute."

Farren left the workshop. Denys shifted uneasily. Perhaps, after all, a shade lurked there, smirking at him. "If you're there," he said, with joking bravado, "you leave my boots alone."

"He only likes boots if they're half-rotten," said Farren, re-entering with a feedbag and an apple. "Here you are, Caprio, you demon. Mind you keep your side of the bargain or I'll get one of the Guardians out here tomorrow. Sure, you scoff if you like, but Brother Andreas can make things warm for you, and don't you forget it. So, Denys, got all your gear together?"

"They'll issue me the standard kit," said Denys, stumbling over the change in topics. "No need to wear down a horse with needless comforts. So, all I need is Brolin and I'm gone." The previous year, the Western Patrol had flushed out a bandit lair. Terrell had claimed the horse for his younger brother, still in training. The Captain, after a judicious glance, approved. Even malnourished and limping badly, the horse's lines spoke of strength and speed.

"Brolin? Oh, no."

"Farren, stop it," Denys' dignity deserted him instantly. "I've got to take Brolin, that's the whole point. Terrell got him for me, so I could take him on Patrol."

"He's not ready to go yet."

"He's perfectly fit. I took him out yesterday for a couple of miles. You'd never guess he was a breakdown. Terrell was right on the money there, wasn't he?"

"Uh huh."

"Farren, I'm taking him, and that's that. He's mine. You can't stick me with a Patrol horse. The seniors always take the best ones."

"No."

Denys grabbed Farren by the arm and dragged him out the door. He flung an arm towards the pasture adjoining Aunt Nan's farmyard. Brolin, tail streaming behind him, galloped easily across the King's enclosure. Denys' breath caught in his throat at the animal's smooth mile-eating stride. Technically, the Stable Master looked after Brolin. Denys knew better. The whole business about shades stuck in his craw, but it had an advantage or two. Farren lived and breathed on the edge of life itself. When he worked with animals, he seemed to divide life from death, and health from ill health, and shove a creature a little more firmly onto the correct side.

"God, he's fantastic," murmured Denys.

"Hmmm."

"I'm taking him."

"Hmmm."

Denys rolled his eyes and prayed for patience. Farren watched the horse with a slight frown. "Tell me *why*, Farren. At least tell me why I shouldn't take him."

"He's not ready."

"He *looks* ready." Silence. "Damn. Look, Farren, can I have him by Progress? You can send him down with Wolton. Promise me?"

Farren looked at him, affection glinting in his eyes. "At Progress. I promise."

"Okay, then. And keep an eye on Trissi? She serves at dinnertime. If you eat there—"

"Oh all right. But only because Aunt Nan's after me too, mind you."

"Farren, listen to me. Aunt Nan is dead."

"I know that, Denys," said Farren, as though talking to a small child. "Of course I know that."

Denys sighed. Conversations with his brother seemed to slip under him, like loose sand under his feet. They never seemed to be talking about the same things. He wished to the gods his mother's efforts had worked, but even the Guardians of the One And Many had failed to shift Farren. He hadn't changed his mind at all. He'd just stopped talking about shades outside of the family. "She's dead. You can't talk to her and she can't talk to you. Farren, don't do these things. Don't draw attention to yourself, you hear me? Brother?" Words failed him. Again and again, he'd told Farren, about Aunt Nan, about their mother and father, about dead dogs and cats, and the cemetery. "You've got to stick with what's real, Farren. Especially while I'm gone, when I can't protect you from people who cry witch or sorcerer." *Or Shadebinder.*

Farren turned away, staring into the pasture. A muscle jumped in his jaw. "It's like being in a cage."

Denys strained to hear him. The look on Farren's face struck him to the heart. Sometimes he wondered who was sane and who wasn't. He laid a hand on his brother's shoulder. "Okay then. Go to the castle for dinners and keep your mouth shut." His voice roughened. "I don't want you burned at the stake while I'm gone. Promise me."

"Sure."

"That's two promises. Brolin and Trissi."

Farren balled his hands into fists, raised them as if to strike the fence railing. The muscles in forearms bunched and released. He stretched out his fingers a time or two, and laid them on the railing. "Two promises."

"And there's nothing in that workshop except Aunt Nan's white goat. Got that? Just remember it. Nothing but one goat."

"Nothing but one goat," said Farren tonelessly.

Denys gripped his shoulder and shook it. "Good-bye, brother."

Farren shut his eyes tightly, turned and grabbed Denys in a rough embrace. He thumped Denys on the back. "Good-bye."

With a wave and a laugh, Denys bolted down the path. Farren moved to the workshop doorway and leaned against the frame. Denys leaped puddles like a ten-year-old boy. For years, Denys had ached to join the Patrol, and his triumph couldn't be dimmed.

Dry-eyed, Farren stared after his brother and the ghost that ran close behind him: their murdered father's shade. Da had trailed Denys off and on for years now. Farren hadn't told Denys. He wouldn't have believed it anyway. Which had come first? Denys' ambition, or their father's shade? He couldn't recall.

Farren turned back to the workshop and the Princess' travel kit. The workshop held only Farren and Aunt Nan's goat.

And the Being presently eating oats from a pan.

The gulf between Farren and the rest of the world had yawned early. He'd been in the cottage with Mam, straining his three-year-old muscles to "help" turn the straw-filled mattresses.

"Mam? Mam!" Terrell popped his head inside the doorway, his words tripping over each other. "The players are here!"

Denys ducked under his arm. The freckles stood out in his flushed face.

"Farren, come on! There's tumblers, too! They're going to the Castle Green."

"I'm coming, wait up!" What were tumblers and players? Farren bolted out the door after Denys and Terrell.

"Farren!" called his mother. "Farren, wait for me! Terrell, we'll be there, you go ahead. Oh, I wish your father were home, too."

Pipe music sparked the air, tickling Farren's ears. Dancing with impatience, he waited for his mother, his feet raising their own cyclone of dust amid the cluster of neighbors walking on the road. Their neighbor, Sylvys, fell into step beside them, settling her baby on one hip and grappling her small daughter's wrist.

"I thought they weren't coming," Sylvys said. "It's been over a year!"

"They wouldn't skip Castle Ramsvalt," Mam said, half-laughing. "They're not stupid! They must have come through the town first. It looks like most of the townsfolk are on their way."

"Hurry, Mam," Farren urged, tugging on her hand. "They're almost at the castle! Look, they're on the drawbridge already. We'll miss it!" He squinted at his brothers. Denys ran backwards in front of the piper. Next to him, two players flipped in the air, landing on their hands, their feet, and their hands again. One more flip, and the castle gate swallowed them up entirely.

"Come on, come on, Mam!" He dragged at her hand, his feet slipping on the hard-packed road. "Hurry up or we'll miss it!"

When they reached the Castle Green, many scores of people milled ahead of them. Farren clung to his mother in a moment's shock. Even on market days, he'd never seen so many people. Denys and Terrell waved from the front of the crowd, where they stood splay-legged, saving room for their family. Farren dropped to the ground at Terrell's feet, his eyes glued to the dancers winding a joyous jig around the pipe player. Farren sucked in his breath as the piper stepped closer and waggled his eyesbrows at the boy. The music threaded sweetly through his ears, his throat, and his tongue.

"This is just the fore show. We're in good time," whispered Mam. In ones and twos, other players snatched their attention, offering tantalizing glimpses of the main performance. The neighbors settled in place in a noisy hum of anticipation, calling to those behind them. Only when the crowd grew large enough would the players be tempted into their full performance.

"Oh, look at the dog!" yelled Denys. Eagerly following the pointing finger, three-year old Farren saw three dogs circling their trainer. A dog staggered on three legs, shattered yellowish bones jutting from its hip. A brown dog with matted fur struggled to its feet, the jagged rips in its flesh wet with blood. The laughter caught in Farren's throat. The pipe music soured, punctuated with strangled moans. All around, his neighbors, young and old, laughed and clapped in time with the thrumming in his head.

"Mam, stop that man! He's hurting them!" His mother didn't hear him. Denys and Terrell shouted their approval. "Mam! Do something!" He yanked on her skirt.

The brown dog heaved itself onto its hind legs, only to collapse, jerking in spasms of agony. A red gash erupted in its side and hot blood gushed onto the grass, the salty scent blanketing the air. A high pitched yip of anguish stabbed Farren's brain. His stomach heaved.

"Stop it!" he screamed, scrambling to the stricken animals.

His mother snatched him back and cuffed him on the ear. "Farren, behave yourself! Stay put and enjoy the show."

Terrell glared at him. Farren flinched and swallowed hard. How could they let that man hurt the dogs? How could they laugh and shout while the dog died in front of their eyes? He wriggled out of Mam's grip and ran away, dodging through the forest of legs. He slid under a farmer's wagon, snatched up an empty feed bag, and curled up tightly, dragging the rough folds around his head. He chanted Mam's favorite lullaby, trying in vain to block his ears to the tortured animals' shrieks.

"Farren! What are you doing?" Although she panted for breath, his mother's voice drowned out every other sound. "Can't you just enjoy the players with everyone else?" With hands both brisk and gentle, she hauled him from under the wagon. "You're missing the show, Farren, and you're making me miss it, too."

"But mother, those poor dogs, he hurt them—"

"There's just one dog, Farren, with spots. It's perfectly well and he never touched it." She picked him up, bracing against his weight, and carried him back to the Green. "It takes a lot of work to teach a dog to balance a ball on its nose. Ah, look, see? It jumps through a hoop, too!"

The music twisted and dropped like snakes around his ears. A sudden chill choked his protests. His stomach roiling, he stared at Denys and Terrell, exultant and whooping their delight. The knowledge burst upon him. No one else *saw* the two slaughtered dogs. They only saw the third dog, the spotted one, leaping around its master performing tricks. Even more baffling, no one but Farren saw the demon leaping from the man's eyes, or the craven terror billowing in waves from the spotted dog.

By the time the dog climbed a ladder and jumped into a water pot, Farren's uncontrollable sobs and frantic lunges had attracted tart comments from all sides. His mother's cheeks flamed as she marched him home before the main show, tight-lipped, angry, and disquieted.

That night he overheard his parents talking in the main room under the loft where he slept.

"It's so unlike him," his mother said. "He's such a happy little mite. It's a shame you couldn't have watched, Brandt. Just think of teaching a dog to do such tricks! But he kept going on and on about there being three dogs, and two were crippled. The man only had one dog, Brandt. I saw it myself. A dog with spots, doing tricks."

"I won't have a liar in the family. He knows the difference between truth and stories." The steps on the loft ladder creaked.

"Brandt, no, Brandt! Leave him alone, he's only three." The steps paused, and retreated. "I just—" Her voice broke.

"What is it, Maari?"

"What if, what if he really saw three dogs?"

"How could there be three dogs, when there was only one?" At the darkness of his father's tone, Farren grabbed his blanket and hid in the loft corner behind strings of onions hanging from the sloped ceiling. "How could there be? Maari, say it, straight out."

"I just thought, maybe..." Farren strained his ears. "...Shade..."

"No!" yelled his father. "No son of mine is a demon-raising Shadebinder!"

"Brandt, I'm not saying—"

But the pleading voice had no effect. The footsteps hit the loft ladder at a run, and Farren's tears took another course thereafter.

It was hard for a three-year-old to figure out things. Avoiding pain, shame, and family dishonor, Farren did his best. There were things other people could see, and things that they couldn't, and death was the difference between them. Seeing dead things was wrong. Farren must go to Guardians' temple with Mam every day, and pray, pray, pray, that the One fix his eyes so he saw only half the world, like everyone else.

Meanwhile, people stared at him and warned their children away. He clung to his family, especially Mam. Mam knew lots of things. She could read. She'd served Queen Ailsa of Valtiris in her youth, maintaining Her Majesty's wardrobe. Maari sometimes regretted giving up her work when she married Brandt, a Second in the Castle Guard. Unearthing her lofty education, she taught her three sons to read, write, and figure.

When Farren was five, Denys earned his apprenticeship with the Stable Master, as Terrell had done three years before. With only one child at home, Maari returned to the castle a few weeks at a time, whenever the Queen joined King Gerritt on his sojourns at Castle Ramsvalt. Maari brought Farren with her. It would be good for him, his father said. If the boy hung about at home, he'd never learn to live in a man's world.

At first, Farren ran about the castle, running errands for the cook, hauling bags of tubers, and turning the spit over the fire. Without his brothers' protection, other boys victimized him with steadily more vicious undercurrents. Adults teased, disapproved, and admonished him for his strangeness. His peers sniffed out his essential differences in a flash, and made him pay. After Maari patched him up for the dozenth time, she released him from palace work, and let him spend hours with Sylvys in the fields, picking stones and chopping weeds.

Three or four times in a month, if he were lucky, his brothers dashed home in their free hours and Farren went mad with joy. Denys, Terrell, and their friends played tree tag, swarming from branch to branch in the woods, climbing on the fences, or playing target practice with slings and knives. His brothers' friends, Aston, Wolton, Callindis, and Goffree, accepted him off-handedly, shielding him from others with gruff kindness.

One day Denys came home, his face torn with anger and grief. Aston had drowned in the river. Denys moped around the cottage and Farren trailed glumly behind him. Farren's grief evaporated the following Sunday. Walking soberly to the funeral with Denys, he saw Aston run from between the cottages clustered along the castle wall.

"Hey, Denys," yelled Aston. "Hey, squirt. Let's play tree tag. Bet I can beat you both."

Farren laughed, but Denys didn't pause in his step. Wide-eyed with puzzlement, Farren followed his brother. Denys smothered a sob.

"What's the matter?" Farren asked.

"Aston, you moron," snapped Denys. "He's dead, and I'll never see him again."

"But he's right here," said Farren blankly. "He wants to play tag."

Denys knocked him down and ran away. Farren watched, grief for his brother's abandonment overwhelming his grief for Aston. "I'm sorry, Aston," he said. "I can't play with you, either. Denys would get mad." With a quivering chin, he left the dead boy standing by the roadside.

A year after that, his mother's friend Sylvys died from the

fever. Almost in a trance, Farren watched the same drama played out, as Sylvys hugged Mother while Mother remained sorrowful, oblivious to her friend. And so he learned.

It could be tricky, figuring out who was dead and who wasn't. The soldiers on horses were usually alive, but if they were missing both legs, they generally weren't. He could see through dead people, but not through the live ones. The dead could walk through things, and their actions rarely had a lasting effect. If a shade ate an apple, a living boy could eat it after him, and be glad to do so. A bed filled with spirits still had room for Farren.

His father Brandt had risen to the Castle Guard through his stable work, which was the first stepping-stone for the impoverished. If a boy worked hard, he could join the Guard and perhaps earn the ultimate honor of land ownership or even, the people whispered, a title. When Farren turned eight, his father negotiated his apprenticeship to the Stable Master as he had for Denys and Terrell. Farren objected with rising hysteria, knowing that his father would scorn the only reasons he could give. If he said, "but the Stable Master is a thief and a cheat," his father would beat him.

His father's righteous rage exploded. Stubbornly, Farren bore his father's belt and his fist. His father's pride hauled him in one direction, and his own determination not to work for a thief hauled him in the other. After the third confrontation, pain and despair drove him from the house and he cowered behind the woodpile.

Why did it matter so much? Why couldn't he just give in, and do what his father said? But he knew he couldn't. The Stable Master's deceit lurked in his eyes. The man's putrid colors blared at Farren, dark and threatening. If he faced that silent betrayal throughout his apprenticeship, he was bound to speak out, if only by accident. No one would believe an apprentice's word against his master, and such lies were punished harshly. He suffered nightmares about the branding, the searing heat, and the smell of burned flesh on his shoulder. Fear congealed his will into solid stone.

His mother's voice sounded from the yard. "Brandt," said Mam. "What if you apprentice him to the Stable Master and he runs off? What then?"

"He won't run. He's my son, Maari. He's not a coward, and he's not afraid of hard work."

"Brandt," she said, her voice strong and certain, "he will run."

His father slammed his fist against the cottage wall. Mud flakes flew to the ground, melting into the puddles in indistinguishable globs. Brandt swore violently and stalked away.

Mam stepped around the woodpile and pulled Farren to his feet. With a rag dipped in a water bucket, she rinsed off the blood. She pried his mouth open with her thumb and looked inside. "It's about time those teeth came out anyway," she muttered. She cupped his head in her hands. "Stubborn as your father, aren't you? But not a coward. You have a choice, son. Either you take the apprenticeship your father's arranged, or you find one for yourself. An honorable one, mind you, or he'll see you picking stones in the fields for the rest of your life." She grabbed his ear and shook his head lightly. "Goodbye, Farren. You have no home here, until you find your own place." And she drove him from the house.

Farren spent the night in the King's goat shed, his stomach grumbling about the raw turnips snatched from the mangers. Shivering in his drafty corner through the long dark hours, he weighed his plight.

The One and the Many had not heard his pleas. Either They chose not to forgive him for his unknown sin, or They wanted him to see shades. In either case, it was out of Farren's hands. The alternative was to snatch every advantage that his peculiar Sight lent him. The thought steadied him.

Systematically, Farren found every artisan, churchman,

or upper servant in the castle and scores more in Ramsvalt's sprawling city down the hill. He listened to the shades congregating around the shopkeepers and traveling merchants. He hid in corners until he saw each man's eyes, with their betraying glints of kindness, cruelty, shiftiness, or godliness. Once a man gave him an errand, tossing him a squash in payment. Another time he earned half a loaf of stale bread from a baker. Most people ignored him. One or two recognized him as the strange little boy who saw things only demons—and the ancient Sorcerer King Elizar—could have seen. They said nothing, but their eyes glimmered with fear and their thoughts shrieked at him: *Shadebinder.*

As the fourth day closed, he tackled Master Pardell, the King's cabinetmaker. After a trial of two days' unremitting labor, little sleep, and continual suspicious glances from the Master's other apprentices, Farren and Master Pardell sealed the bargain. Boy and Master, they'd found his father and signed apprenticeship papers, for the same stiff fee the Stable Master had demanded.

The lights in Master Pardell's eyes flared with impatience, quick rage, and humor, but through every mood and whim, the clear shining lights of truth and tolerance never wavered. Master Pardell might be scathing over any shoddy job, but his acceptance of his new apprentice never slipped, even when he fully understood Farren's Sight. The ache in Farren's heart lessened, and his trust in his captious master deepened into passionate loyalty and affection. Master Pardell was the only constant in a world of variables.

When Farren was eleven, bandits riding fast horses raided outlying farms. The Castle Guard responded and two guards were slashed to death, one of them Brandt, Farren's father. The Stable Master disappeared immediately thereafter, with several fine horses. The King's Guard insisted that they captured and hanged him at Selefrevalt, eighty miles north, but Farren doubted it. Most shades returned to their hometowns for a few days after their deaths, as his father had. The Stable Master had not.

Brolin sidled sharply, yanking at the tether that bound him to Farren's belt. Farren let down the handcart, discarding his memories.

"Settle now, little one," he murmured. Sweat streaked the shining bay hide, but compared to the rivers of lather of a week ago, Brolin's improvement astounded him. "Such a fine fellow." Brolin shoved his nose into the crook of Farren's arm, and stood there for a long moment, his hide quivering as though suffering an onslaught of horseflies. Brolin hated crowds, town roads, and men in armor. He squandered his energy in nervous fidgets, reducing the vital staying power essential in the courser Denys wanted. "All right then, let's try the next bit, shall we?"

Farren trundled his handcart down the road inside the castle's perimeter wall. Brolin pranced behind him, shying at the sight of a running apprentice who panted under the weight of a basket of scrap metal. Brother Lawrence's shade drifted down the road. Brother Andreas followed with his measured tread, and nodded to Farren solemnly, fanning his fingers in the blessing of the Many. Was it a blessing or was he warding off evil? Probably a little of both, Farren thought. He paused frequently, calming the horse and keeping his cart, with its precious burden, out of the path of both shade and living, from castle servants to stable lads, a long-dead baker, three guards, and the King's falconer.

Farren's choice of profession might have been based on Sight rather than logic, but his hands loved the work. Wood molded itself to the designs in his mind, flowing into color patterns, soundless hinges, seamless joints, smoothly sliding drawers, and cleverly hidden compartments. His apprenticeship had ended seven years before, just after the last Progress. When his Aunt Nan retired from the castle nursery and took her pension, she made their home a mile outside the castle gates. Farren continued working for Master Pardell as a journeyman.

A flock of boys huddled at the Green's edge, darting quick glances over their shoulders. Farren dropped a quick hand to his belt, fingering the leather strap that secured Brolin's halter.

The boys' mob rustled furiously and a single boy flew out, like a melon seed spat into the dirt. The boy darted out, tagged Farren with a rough slap on the arm, and escaped with good speed. "Shadebinder!" the boy taunted.

Brolin snorted and reared, but Farren pulled him down by his tether. The horse stood stock-still, his breathing coming hard and fast. "Now, now, little one, don't tell me their opinions matter? Not to a fine creature like you..."

The boys' laughter echoed with equal parts derision and nervous fear. Farren felt his body stiffen and forced himself to relax. A quick look assured him that the daring boy of the midnight stable raid wasn't among them. That was good to know. His eyes lingered on the boys, one at a time, as they fled into the crowds. He would remember them.

Two grooms staggered across the road, bracing a wild-looking sorrel horse between them. Its muzzle frothed and its eyes widened with fear. Farren pulled Brolin's head forward over his shoulder, feeling the warm breath gust along his cheek. He crooned softly. Brolin tossed his head, buffeting Farren painfully on the ear.

The stable men, Wolton and Vorest, wrestled the horse across the roadway towards a wooden framework. With experienced hands and a slap, they startled the sweating horse into the frame and latched the gate behind it. Vorest poulticed the horse's swollen left fore hock while Wolton stood at the horse's head, grunting soothing noises.

Wolton waved Farren past. Wolton's eyes lingered on

Brolin and his eyebrows shot up. "That Denys' courser, the one Terrell got him?" he called.

"Yes," Farren said. The less he said, the better, he'd found.

"Nice work, Farren. Nice work." Wolton jerked a thumb in the air in approval. "Denys said you're coming to supper now he's gone, that right?"

Farren stifled a sigh. "Yes."

"Listen for the gong. Look for me once you're inside, right? Denys told me to look out for you."

Farren had eaten at the castle daily for his seven years' apprenticeship. He knew the process. He knew Denys' concern as well: the 'Shadebinder' showing up at the castle again on a daily basis. His brother's weighty affection dragged on him like a yoke of granite. "All right. Thanks."

The great stone wall loomed overhead, dividing the elite royal artisans and favored courtiers from the common herd of the town populace down the hill. The royal artisans plied their trades in shops planted inside the wall, like so many mud-covered boxes shoved against a barn. Drellford, the Master's second journeyman, lived over the shop, guarding the shop's equipment and finished work. The shops were plain and wart-like, but nevertheless inspired envy from the craftsmen relegated to the town warren down the hill. Personally, Master Pardell considered the location a double-edged sword. Flattery was sweet, but it didn't feed the family.

Master Pardell's inspired cabinetry filled the King's castle, and routinely accompanied other royal gifts to the Emperor's Court. In faithful imitation, Ramsvalt's highest nobility vied for the Master's services. During the last May Festival, the Earl of Danneminton even ventured inside Master Pardell's shop, rather than sending a retainer or commanding the Master's presence. Still, the Earl's promised table would have to wait.

The bulk of the Master's fees came from the town down the hill. The Master, his wife, five children, and three apprentices lived in town, where his large house could accommodate them. Mistress Catherine, the Master's stout and energetic wife, dickered with traders as she kneaded bread and swatted rowdy apprentices. The traders, in turn, plied the rivers and traversed the dusty roads, collecting commissions from wealthy townsmen and landowners along the way. Their orders offered less prestige, remarked Mistress Catherine, but considerably more in gold coins, decent clothing, and good, nourishing food. Valtiris nobility hadn't amassed its hereditary fortune by paying its bills promptly.

Farren stopped in front of Master Pardell's shop, flanked by the stonemasons' guild office, and the glovemaker's shop. The wide doorway gaped open, allowing carts to load and unload. Farren set down the handcart. The horse nosed at the shop's wall, flaking off bits of mud.

"You don't want to eat that. It's just wattle-and-daub. Mud on sticks. Wait for the pasture." He ran a hand over Brolin's glossy neck, and called through the doorway. "Master Pardell?"

"Ah, Farren." The Master's mouth twitched as he glanced at Brolin. "Did you get it done, Journeyman?"

Farren lifted the canvas from the barrow, and hoisted the chest onto the bench just inside the door. The workshop's nutty scent of fruitwood, the spice of cedar, and the sharpness of pine blended into a heady brew. His fingers itched to rasp the rough edge from the partially completed table on the third bench. Drellford's work, he saw at a glance. He leaned against the doorframe, folding his arms to make them behave.

"Well, well." Like Denys, the Master's fingers traced the carved island and sea waves. "Just with the natural wood grains, too. The waves are rising high," he mused, his voice rich with reverence. "Just as they do before an April storm.

41

My word, that's a fine piece of work. I'll swear I can feel the wind blow."

Abruptly, his delicate touch roughened. The Master flicked his fingers contemptuously. He heaved himself onto a high stool, and gestured to a second. Farren hitched Brolin outside and joined his Master. "There was no need for all that," grumbled the Master. "It's far beyond specification. Why'd you bother with it?"

"It's for the Princess Mericia of Ailsandia. It seemed right."

"Princess of Ramsvalt."

"Of Ailsandia, Master, the Great Island. Isn't that what the Progress is all about? Every seven years, to her birthplace, to her mother's heritage, to the place where she'll be Queen. This," his gesture dismissed the artistry, "seemed little enough to do, when she's going so far from home, perhaps forever."

Master Pardell peered out from under his heavy brows. "After what she did to your brother?"

"Stop testing me, Master."

Master Pardell thrust out his chin, shot a glance at Farren, and rolled his eyes. "All right, all right. It's high craftsmanship, but no more than I expected. I did wonder, a little, if you could throw your soul into it, after Terrell. I should have known better."

"Terrell applied for the Captain's post in the Princess' Guard. She chose a man with greater seniority. That's her right."

"Humph. That's a bare bones description," the Master snapped. "She told the King that Terrell had an unreliable eye, and she'd do better with a man she could trust. Unreliable eye, my foot. Did the miners think he was unreliable when he risked his neck in that cave-in? What about that caravan stranded on the mountains after the avalanche? He's got more guts than the jackasses jousting in her blessed tourneys. She slaughtered his reputation."

"Hardly that. He's still a First in the Western Patrol."

"All right then." The Master slammed a fist onto the bench. The box quivered. "You'll do your best work, whether for a farmer or for an ice princess, though neither understands your gift. I thought it, I tested it, and you've proved it." The Master eyed him moodily. "See any shades about, boy?"

Farren grinned. "Only the usual, Master."

"Humph. That old curmudgeon." The Master glanced at the corner bench. While he couldn't see his grandfather's shade working there, he had no doubt Farren was right. When Master Pardell had inherited the shop from his father, he'd discovered his long-dead grandfather's peculiar tools. Unable to make heads or tails of the strange configurations, he'd laid them away until his self-selected apprentice forced his way into the shop. Matter-of-factly, he'd organized a three-way conversation with his dead grandfather and brought several of the tools back into use. He also barred Drellford and his apprentices from working at the corner bench.

"See here, Journeyman," growled the Master, thereby changing the subject.

Farren chuckled. The Master said 'journeyman' the way another man would say 'fool.' *Fool, not to try for your Master's pin.* Farren's skills far exceeded most Masters in the guild. With Master Pardell's advocacy, obtaining his Master's pin would be a simple matter. Unfortunately, it required a formal audience with the Guild council, without Master Pardell's paternal eye. Farren did not intend to embarrass his Master through his inability to rule his own tongue.

"It's all very well to laugh, boy, but I've a plan or two concerning you," said the Master, reading his pupil's mind without effort. "The Master's pin is essential."

"There's Master Cintellay in the town."

The Master flushed and pressed his lips together. "Master Cintellay," he said in careful even tones, "is an excellent craftsman."

"Yes, Master," said Farren, eyes dancing.

The Master snorted. "I don't need your impudence, you young hellion. I don't know why I put up with it. I've a perfectly good journeyman here, and apprentices coming out of my ears. Master Cintellay is completely capable of any work I send him."

"I completely agree, Master." The key was not to send Master Cintellay any job more complex than constructing a plain wooden box to hold apples.

Master Pardell erupted from his seat and drew back a hand to cuff the young man. He gave Farren a dark look, dropped his arm, and paced the floor. "Look, Farren, it's about time you moved back in, don't you think? Drellford's dying to move away from the shop. He's got a town girl on the string. You'd be doing him a favor. You'd have privacy here, just like at Nan's."

"I'm fine at the farm, thanks."

"But you won't be. Your Aunt got that tenancy as part of her pension. Guilt money, if you ask me."

"She got the same care as the Queen herself."

"Once they found her, unconscious in her quarters. Why didn't they notice she was gone? She was a Nanny, for the gods' sake. She hovered over the princess like a hen with one chick. Once the plague struck, she'd have been all over the girl. But no, she collapsed unconscious twenty feet from the princess' bed, and not one person thought to open the damned door to see if she was alive. Not the guardian, the chamberlain, the housekeeper, or that snooty Lady Lelori."

"Master—"

"Why are they even *planning* another Progress at all? It's beyond me. Last time, seven years ago, the royal family fell ill unto death, and half their staff as well. The Queen deafened and her wits addled, your mother dead, and your Nan, the Princess' own Nanny, damned near died before they found her. Now they're set to do it all again, maybe kill the Queen for good and all. Royals! You'd think they had a death wish. Your Nan," he said, waving a threatening finger, "got the farm, and the King loaned her enough goats to support herself. Now she's dead and the tenancy's over. It's only a matter of time before the King's Steward tumbles to it and reassigns the farm. So I'm telling you, Farren, turn the goats back to the King's herd, and leave the farm before they throw you out. Come back to me, and—"

Farren chanted with him. "—Take your Master's pin."

In spite of himself, the Master chuckled. "If you get your Guild mastership, there'll be no more of that Shadebinder nonsense. The Cabinetry Guild doesn't tolerate such insults to their Masters." His anger dimmed into a resigned glare. "Well, just remember, I've got rooms waiting for you."

"Actually, I've already returned the goats. The last one went today. I'm getting Brolin used to the stables, or he'll be no good to Denys. The Stable Master lent me a stall for a while."

"And you've been sleeping there with the horse. Boy, boy, boy...."

"Master, Master, Master. What have you got for me to work on this week?"

Chapter Three

F arren, over here."

Farren stared into the Great Hall, one foot frozen in mid-step. The Hall was packed, teeming with moving figures, light and shadow, heads thrown back in raucous laughter, faces glowering in menacing threat, figures running, walking, standing on tables, scrambling over the floor and floating overhead.

"Farren." At the far left table, Wolton waved his arm.

Farren wiped his boots in the rushes. His racing heart slowed and his eyesight shifted into dual perspective. Only a third of the crowd was alive. He'd eaten in the Great Hall countless times and never seen more than a dozen shades at a time, the faces changing gradually every month or so. This time, a hundred shades or more crammed the hall from floor to ceiling. It was unreal. He caught himself in the midst of the thought and laughed silently. Unreal, yes indeed. For once, he agreed with everyone else.

He wove his way through the room, avoiding both the living and the dead, trying to make his wandering travel seem natural, and failing as usual. Servants backed away from him; guards and craftspeople shifted hastily out of his way. Still, what could he do? He hated walking through shades. Their clammy feel made the hair rise on the back of his neck. Most shades didn't notice him, a fact he always found ironic. Shades attached themselves to particular people or situations, and were blind to everyone else. He'd as soon keep it that way.

He circled three farmer shades pontificating on the harvest, and avoided eye contact with a belligerent journeyman leatherworker who was very much alive. He nodded to Wolton and ducked his head at Vorest's breezy greeting. He slipped into the empty space on the bench, allowing the shade of a flirtatious maidservant to get past him.

"You all know Farren?" Wolton stuck out his chin, regarding their tablemates through narrowed eyes. "Younger brother to Terrell and Denys? Brandt's youngest." One by one the grooms, servers, and a few guards looked his way. Most nodded. A couple opened their mouths, registered Wolton's challenging look, and turned their attention to their food. "Right. Okay then. Here you go." He handed Farren a crusty bread bowl filled with stew. "When you're done, hand it back for seconds."

Wolton and Denys were old pals; Wolton and Farren weren't. The capable horseman had little tolerance for the unusual, and Farren scaled the heights of the unpredictable.

"Thanks," Farren said.

"You eat your fill," Wolton said. "No one goes short here."

Farren got on with dinner, which was much the same from one day to the next. A hearty stew filled the crusty bowl. Some kind of meat rubbed shoulders with whatever tubers were on hand. There were turnips today, parsnips and a carrot or two, engulfed in onions and meat sauce. Mounds of bread loaves hid the table's center. Farren drew his belt knife, hacked off part of a loaf, and ate from his knifepoint.

"Great news about Denys." Vorest said, raising his mug.

"Deserved it, too. He's got Terrell's way with a short sword." A gray-haired groom grinned, revealing more gaps than teeth. "Here's to them both."

Farren raised his mug with the others, smiling acknowledgment, trapping a response behind his teeth. The conversation turned to High Captain Vance Heronlys and his arrival with the King's Guard elite. Vorest waxed lyrical over the High Captain's destrier, while Wolton and his other neighbors bent eager ears.

Farren allowed his eyes to drift over the ghostly congregation. On a table near the room's center, three buxom women flitted in a scarf dance among the platters. Shades of shoemakers, sewing women, weavers, and herdsmen squeezed together, shoulder to shoulder with the living and often overlapping. They clapped for the dancers, shouting the songs in boisterous disharmony. Ghostly servitors scurried past the benches, delivering cauldrons and bread platters. Child spirits threw sticks to each other and leapfrogged between the tables.

Farren's knife moved mechanically from bowl to mouth, slowed down and finally stopped all together. He'd known, in theory, the number of shades he'd see. How could he not? Still, knowing it was one thing, while seeing—and hearing, smelling and touching—was another. Even when the plague dropped people by the scores, he'd never seen so many shades gathered in a single place. They weren't unhappy, angry, or sullen, but they were *there*. Even the King's table attracted its share.

Surprisingly, the King's table bore a spotlessly white cloth. Silky rugs engulfed the dais under the ornate chairs, replacing the usual rushes. Behind the table, the two fireplaces blossomed with cut flowers in huge pots. Farren tapped Wolton on the arm, indicating the royal table with a raised eyebrow.

"Founding Day," Wolton said, and turned back to his conversation.

Huh. A man lost touch when he lived alone. He'd forgotten about Founding Day, the day the long-ago King of Valtiris had completed the Ramsvalt watchtower, precursor to the present-day castle. He'd built it in a hell of a hurry, too, just one jump ahead of Sorcerer King Elizar's advance. After a mighty onslaught, Valtiris rallied its countrymen who'd cast Elizar the Shadebinder back to the Great Island. His charms temporarily ensnared Ailsandia's Queen Merentil, but eventually she'd recovered her common sense and slew him with her own hand. Those were glorious days, the minstrels cried, but to Farren the history was infinitely depressing. Elizar's shadow lingered today. Farren's ostracism was proof. Legend had it that Elizar danced through the nights, harnessing the winds, the stars, even the fluffy white clouds, as fuel for his shade bindings. As a result, Farren drew suspicious whispers if he even glanced at the weather.

A brief commotion signaled the royal family's arrival. Benches screeched. A rustling noise spread through the room, as all present, living and dead, stood in the King's honor. When the King's vassal lords came to court every May, they crammed the royal table from edge to edge. Today, the High Captain of the Guard, Vance Heronlys, was the only guest. The high table looked nearly deserted. The only occupants were Queen Ailsa, King Gerritt, Princess Mericia, Lady Lelori, and lastly, Captain Heronlys sitting between the King and Queen.

Farren's glance lingered on the Queen. Addled, Master Pardell had called her. She didn't look addled. She looked magnificent, every move attended by grace and dignity. Her gloved hands manipulated a complicated array of cutlery. The only odd note was the ceaseless wrist movement, as the Queen conveyed food rapidly from plate to mouth, as though stoking an inner fire.

When Farren had eaten here as an apprentice, the twin princes, Kellian and Randall, had invigorated the atmosphere with their cheerful high spirits. It pained him to see their buoyant attitudes supplanted by Lady Lelori's icy dignity. The Lady had returned with the family from the last Progress, attending the Queen and the Princess after the deaths of of several servants.

Two ghostly dogs flopped at the Princess' feet. A transparent servant tended the Queen, who ignored her completely. Seven or eight shades roamed around the Guards' table. Three more, scruffy and scarred, circled the High Captain. Two floated over the high table, nodding agreement to the Captain's remarks. At the Guards' table, three shades took turns ripping chunks from the roast at the Guards' table, matching the mortals' ravenous hunger.

"Ha! There you are, boy."

Farren jumped, pretending to rub out a leg cramp to hide his chagrin from his tablemates. Caprio swaggered down the tabletop and nosed Farren's tankard.

"What are you eating?" the goat demanded. "Anything good?"

Farren leaned back and stretched his arms, letting Caprio sniff at his bread bowl.

Caprio snorted in disgust. "Goat meat. Think I'm a cannibal, boy? The pickings look better at the Guards' table. Roast pig, it looks like. Maybe a boar." Caprio sauntered down the table, heedless of where he put his feet. One hoof planted itself through Vorest's mug. Farren watched fixedly as Vorest raised his cup, and drank deeply, with evident pleasure.

"Thirsty?" Wolton said. "Give me your tankard." He passed the tankard down the line for a refill and returned it.

Farren nodded his thanks, sealing his lips closed with difficulty. In such mixed company, he could easily respond to the wrong comment.

"My sweetling," caroled a voice across the hall.

Involuntarily, he splashed ale from his tankard. Aunt Nan was here, parked at the King's table. Well, it made sense that she'd take a shade's advantages and visit her 'dear nursling' again. At least now, visiting the castle couldn't make her deathly ill, as it had after her retirement. The recurrent and violent illness had nearly killed her twice. Eventually, she'd stayed at home. Bonnara, chief cook to the Castle, bustled out to visit every month or so, bearing the latest gossip and food baskets filled with dainties.

Aunt Nan beamed at the princess, murmuring maternal advice into the deaf ear. Princess Mericia resembled an austere statue, as she listened to her father's conversation with the High Captain. The King said something to her. She lit up with a radiant glow that made Farren catch his breath. The King patted her hand and turned back to the Captain. Her shoulders slumped, animation dropping away like a blanket fallen underfoot.

Nanny stroked the long black hair with a proprietary air. The frothy silver scarf emphasized the princess' glossy black hair and her pallor. Nanny whispered fiercely into the girl's ear. Nanny reached for something on the platter, and exclaimed angrily as her hand sank through it. With sudden decision, she rounded the table, faced the princess and shook her finger. Despite her flailing arms and excited admonitions, the princess ignored her. Nanny threw up her hands, and flounced off towards the kitchen.

"Problem?" asked Wolton. He followed Farren's stare and snorted. "Her, huh? It's beyond belief, that she'd do a thing like that to Terrell." He punched Farren lightly. "Don't let her bother you. Have some more stew. Hey, Vorest, fill this up for our boy here. He's down-in-the-mouth about Terrell, after what the ice bitch did to him."

Vorest ladled out stew with a lavish hand. "Hey, look at it this way. She turns twenty-one in mid-September, right? So they'll take her to the Island on the Progress, and if we're all really lucky, they'll leave her there. She's supposed to inherit anyway, right? Let's just hope it's sooner rather than later."

"Well," demurred the graybeard, "wouldn't want the

Queen to die. It's her holding, you know, not the King's."

Vorest waved the ladle. "They can keep the Queen, too. I wouldn't want to deprive the princess. Small loss to us."

Uneasy chuckles subsided under the heavy disapproval of a man with sagging jowls and spiky red hair. "It's not a fit subject for jokes, young Vorest. It's the Queen's island and thank the gods for that. Best harbor in the Empire. Maybe the Princess will move down permanent-like, but that's for the King to decide."

"And for us to hope," muttered Vorest, irrepressibly. His neighbor glowered at him. Vorest waved a hand in apology, and turned the discussion to a wrestling match.

Farren's head jerked back to the royal table as Caprio slurped loudly from the High Captain's wine cup. Caprio sampled the Queen's wine, then skipped to the next table, stepping daintily down the line, moving from cup to cup. A guard, a Second in the Western Patrol by the insignia, lifted his cup to drink just as Caprio reached him. To Caprio's indignant protests, the guard drained the cup, wiped his mouth with the back of his hand, and slapped the cup back on the table. Caprio took a workmanlike stance and pissed in the man's stew. Farren pressed his knuckles into his mouth to hide his grin as the guard ate heartily.

Ah, there was Aunt Nan again, shooing along a very mortal maidservant. Now how on earth had she managed that? The maid, looking harried, stepped between Lady Lelori and Princess Mericia and placed a platter on the table.

Wolton elbowed Farren in the ribs, and indicated the serving girl with his tankard. "That's Denys' girl, you know."

"Trissi?" Farren said involuntarily. "Is that for real, the two of them?"

"Hard to say. She works in the kitchen mostly, but the cook's got her on a short leash. She can't get away from the castle as much as Denys would like. Quite a looker, isn't she?"

"I suppose so," said Farren.

Princess Mericia turned on Trissi. She flicked at the plate with her fingertips, dismissing it. Trissi curtsied, shook her head, and gestured towards the open door. She whirled, her long hair swinging behind her, and fled, leaving the platter on the table. Lady Lelori glanced at the platter with polite disinterest and returned to her own plate.

Over the hubbub of a hundred eaters, Nanny's words spiked the air.

"... Enough to keep a sparrow alive, so *eat*, my little love, my darling. You love cheese, you've always loved it, and these cunning little radishes..."

Princess Mericia stared at King Gerritt and the High Captain, hanging on His Majesty's every word. The King turned to her, raised an eyebrow at the food platter, and asked something. The princess shook her head.

"...You've always had such a precarious appetite, my love, but you must *eat*."_Aunt Nan's voice grated shrilly. The shades gradually ceased their hubbub, hunting for the source of the irritation. "You really must, or you'll be sick again. My darling, you're entirely too thin—"

The shades hooted.

"That's telling her, old woman."

"Get some meat on your bones, flesh up those boobs."

"Shut up, woman, we're trying to eat."

Caprio stamped a hoof and bellowed. "You there, girl. Eat your food before that woman screams us all deaf." The Princess didn't move. Enraged, Caprio flicked away, reappearing at the high table. "*Eat!*" he thundered.

And oh, so absently, the Princess' hand stole out and picked up a cheese wedge.

"Don't stop," he threatened, "if you want to sleep tonight. Stupid girl. You, woman, quit your belly-aching and let us get back to our food."

Nanny's voice subsided into insulted huffing. Caprio grazed his way along the tables. The ghostly fair continued their antics. And back in the completely mundane world, the workers at the back tables dispersed, as Wolton slapped Farren on the back and wished him good night.

Farren lingered, resting his chin on his hands, his eyes fixed on the King's table. Absent-mindedly but steadily, the Princess ate, first the cheese, then the 'cunning' little radishes, the fruit slices, and in fact everything else on the platter.

Brolin cocked a foot and drowsed. It was his fourth night in the stable. He still objected to strangers, and to the weaponry with which Farren had lined his stall, but he'd begun to adapt. Hopefully, the pranksters would give them a rest tonight. Farren stretched out in the straw and opened his Sight to the fullest, watching and listening with every fiber of his being. Eventually, he nodded to himself and pulled up his blanket. Just before dawn, he woke to the sound of low voices in the stall next to him.

"....Transfer?"

"No way. Leave Southern Patrol, during Progress? Ha! You're jealous, Duran. Chance of lifetime, this is."

"Chance to get killed, you mean. Damned right."

"It's not that bad. Hand me those. Thanks." The Southern guard seemed to be packing his horse.

"With Irandis as Captain? You're mad."

"Irandis is captain of the Princess' Guard, not Southern. He's an ass, I'll grant you, but he won't do us any damage."

"He's not just an ass. He's a bumbler. Royal Guards outrank Patrol captains in a fray. If he louses up during Progress, you guys are going to get flayed."

"There won't be a fight," Southern said blithely, "because we're in charge of preventing it. I'm delivering instructions from the High Captain himself to my Captain, and they're no fools."

"No," grumbled his friend. "Damn it all, if only Terrell—"

"Then you'd have lost him as your First." The stall door unlatched. Soft, heavy hoof thuds marked their movement down the passageway.

The Western guard laughed. "True enough. Well, off with you. Watch your ass, okay? Remember last Progress."

"That was disease, not bandits or insurrectionists. Quit being a mother hen, will you? Nothing's going to happen, and if it does, I hope I'm in the thick of it. Turn down a good fight? Not me."

"Well, stay the hell away from Irandis, then." The voices faded, still wrangling amiably.

Farren rose, leaning against Brolin's warm hide. Irandis. Men always thought commanders were fools, but perhaps he should look into the matter. He'd heard Irandis' name a few times from the shades, but none of them seemed to hold grudges against the man. Denys was safe enough, surely. The High Captain wouldn't let a girl's whim affect the safety of the entire Progress.

He wished he could see Irandis, eye to eye. He'd know by the man's colors, wouldn't he? No, perhaps not. Emotions flared through the eyes, but intelligence and experience took closer acquaintance to read. That left him with witness testimony. It was damned hard to question shades who couldn't see him. He could force them to see him, but it wasn't worth the risk. He'd have to go on meddling in sidelong fashion, at least for now. He sighed.

Why on earth had the Princess rejected Terrell? An unreliable eye? Or was someone guiding her choice? Someone who wanted Terrell's sharp eyes elsewhere, and a fool in charge.

Which left a large question: who'd want a fool in charge of the Princess' Guard during Progress? And why?

Chapter Four

The Princess Mericia, Her Highness of Ramsvalt, fourth in line to the throne of Ramsvalt, and Heir Presumptive to the Throne of Ailsandia, gazed into the bronze mirror.

"Thank you," she said.

Trissi, the kitchen maid, brushed at the goose pimples on her arms. She looked over the Princess' shoulder into the mirror, stepping back a pace to avoid her own reflection. The Princess' black hair gleamed like an obsidian helmet. The brown-black eyes, the only color in the marble face, glimmered like agates on an Island beach. The Princess gazed past her, untroubled, a statue without a trace of life. If someone touched that skin with a finger, would it crease? If there was a soul behind the face, it never surfaced.

The room reflected the Princess, as surely as the mirror did. The bare stone walls sucked in cold all winter long, and steadfastly radiated their clammy chill for the rest of the year. King Gerritt said Emperor Theomedon repelled the cold by draping his palace in heavy silk tapestries. He'd offered to do the same for his family, regardless of the cost. The princess could have lavished the room with tapestries and rugs, or piled the bed high with cozy furs and down-filled bedding. The glistening bowls might be mounded with profusions of sweets and flowers. Comfort and pleasure could have embraced her.

Instead, the room sparkled with crystal and precious metal. Empty silver vases rested on an ivory inlaid table. Crystal bowls and goblets caught the light, cascading it to the floor, but remained barren from year to year. The great wooden bedstead and the wardrobe gleamed with beeswax, and the brass handles shone unsmudged. Every item in the room demanded reverence and admiration.

"Did you have a further message?" said the Princess.

The agate eyes in the mirror met hers. "No, Your Highness." Trissi curtsied and slipped through the door.

After a long moment, Princess Mericia withdrew her attention from the mirror. She walked down the hall, past two doors, up five steps, through a narrow hall and down six more steps into Queen Ailsa's Tapestry room. The Queen spent virtually every waking hour at her needlework in the Tapestry room. It wasn't even a real tapestry, just miles of wool embroidery thread pulled through linen with expert stitches.

Mericia's mother, Queen Ailsa of Ailsandia, looked every inch a Queen, from the regal set of the coif binding her black hair to the tips of her gloved fingers. She floated through public occasions on the attentive arm of King Gerritt. Her guests understood that her deafness precluded conversation. Nonetheless, her kindly smiles charmed lords and ladies, entertainers and servants. In the privacy of her tapestry room, the façade crumbled into dust.

Lady Siree plucked at her left sleeve. Siree had attended the Queen since her illness, striving to uphold the image of the Queen's perfection. She looked up at the Princess' entrance.

"Welcome, Your Highness." Siree's heart slumped into her cloth slippers as the princess approached. The girl was a living snowdrift if ever there was one. She shivered as an imagined draft of disdain sliced through her defenses again. But she'd *had* to call for help. What else could she do?

The princess gazed at the rectangular tapestry frame. Siree cast an anxious glance at it, but nothing seemed amiss. She'd rolled the completed section of the linen panel around the side bar so the Queen could work unhampered on the last stretch of this panel. Six completed panels lay forgotten in the linen cabinet, rolled up and protected from moths. The Queen lost interest in each panel the moment she set the final stitch. In a few more years, Siree would need another cabinet.

"I've ordered the linen for the next panel." She bit her lip, feeling stupid. Two sentences, and already she was rambling. Siree felt like a beetle, waving its antenna for attention. A tired flicker of resentment flared and died, leaving ashes of resignation behind it.

"You requested my presence to advise me of this?" the princess said with an elegantly arched eyebrow.

"No, no, Your Highness, not at all. I beg your pardon for disturbing you, Your Highness," Lady Siree faltered. Her hands fluttered over a platter of untouched food. "But Her Majesty hasn't eaten a *morsel* since the Founding supper the night before last. I had a most dreadful time getting her to the supper at all. And now, I can't persuade Her Majesty to eat a single thing. I've tried, I truly have. She just slaps my hand away. She hardly even sleeps now. All she does is stitch." Siree remembered to breathe, and threw up her hands only to let them fall. Two days without food. At her wit's end, Siree had considered trapping the Queen in her room until she ate, but she didn't have the nerve.

In the early years, on a physician's advice, they'd dismantled the tapestry frame. The Queen tore at the locked door to the storeroom, and beat her hands bloody on the stone walls, sobbing soundlessly. When she tried to leap from the tower window, Siree and Trissi barely managed to drag her to the floor. They'd hung onto the struggling Queen until a maid heard them call for help. She ran to the Steward who retrieved the frame, and ordered it set up under the Queen's eyes. The King ejected the physician from Court.

The Queen never spoke, never listened to a word, never sang, never read a book or a letter, and never wrote to her sons, whom she hadn't seen in seven years. Except when forced into public view, she devoted her life to pristine lengths of linen, expertly embroidering mountains, hills, houses, and creatures. Every figure was couched, laid in, and surrounded by neat pipeline stitching, miles and miles and miles of it.

Lady Siree dropped into her chair and raised a hand to her quivering chin. It was pointless. What could the princess do? And would she even try? The girl had no normal feelings at all. She'd once watched a tourney knight speared in the chest, and continued to eat grapes with complete unconcern. Besides, Siree admitted, even if the princess jumped up and down, tore her hair out, or waved her hands in front of her mother's face, the Queen would take no notice.

Exhaustion swamped Lady Siree. She dropped her arm limply. "I can't—she won't— Oh dear. Trissi tried and tried, and finally suggested I call Your Highness, but honestly, Your Highness, if Her Majesty won't eat, it will mean calling the physician, and the last time he came Her Majesty was frantic. He gave milady a tonic, and she collapsed for days on end. And I keep thinking to myself, her heart can't stand this strain—"

"I understand," Princess Mericia said. Lady Siree's words choked off as though the narrow hands had closed on her throat. "Will she drink?"

Siree coughed. "Sometimes, if I hold the cup to her lips. Not today."

"I see."

The Queen's rapt gaze fixed on the plum tree growing beneath her fingers, stitch by stitch. She spiked the needle into a cushion perched on the tapestry frame and retrieved a second, threaded with two-ply red wool.

The Princess lifted a strawberry from the plate and raised it to her own lips. Lady Siree swelled with indignation like an enraged dove. Well, wasn't that just *like* the Princess? Imagine, eating her mother's food, when she should be begging her mother to eat. The girl didn't know the meaning of compassion or love. Only Lady Siree's extreme attachment to Her Majesty had driven her to ask for help. That, and the knowledge that however repellent the Princess might be, Lady Lelori was vastly worse.

As though the wayward thought had prompted her appearance, Lady Lelori entered the room. Her tall figure stood as straight as a rod of iron. Her gray dress fell unbroken from her shoulders to the floor, with only the suggestion of a figure beneath it. Her green-brown eyes reminded Siree of a murky tide-pool. The filmy stuff of her cap completely enveloped her hair. Siree cherished an unworthy hope that the woman was bald.

"Your Highness," said Lady Lelori, her voice both musical and compelling. "His Majesty asked me to convey a message. His Majesty requests that Your Royal Highness attend him in the library in two hours' time. High Captain Heronlys has requested counsel. Something to do with maps, I believe," said Lady Lelori, faintly disapproving.

"I will," the Princess said, "assist the King, my father, to find the best resources to answer the High Captain's concerns."

"Pardon me," Siree said stiffly. She glared at Lady Lelori. Like twin snow angels, the other two turned to stare at her. She shrank back in her chair, then stiffened her back. "I believe the Queen's needs outweigh those of High Captain Heronlys."

"Naturally," said Lady Lelori.

The entire castle could crumble into dust this instant, thought Lady Siree, *and that woman wouldn't lift a finger.* Her voice sharpened. "The Queen hasn't eaten in two days."

"Her Majesty is eating now," said the Princess.

Lady Siree's eyes bulged. The Queen set a strawberry hull on the table and picked up her needle. The Princess lowered her hands to the tapestry, setting down an array of brightly colored fruit on a towel just beyond the Queen's brisk hands.

The Queen paused, needle poised to take a stitch. She picked up a second strawberry and held it to the light, the length of red wool dangling alongside. For a moment, the dull thread sparkled with the glow of the berry. The Queen drove the needle into the linen and popped the berry into her mouth.

"Color appears to be the key to her appetite at present," said Princess Mericia. "Her artistic nature, no doubt. I will discuss the matter with Cook. Thank you for bringing the matter to my attention, Lady Siree."

Princess Mericia sailed out the door without a backward glance, leaving Siree sputtering behind her. The Princess descended the tower steps, her feet automatically bypassing the slippery spots. She crossed the Great Hall, entering the passageway to the kitchen wing. Above the kitchen were apartments for the Steward and other high ranking retainers, as well as the long lofts shared by the lower servants. She passed the stairwell without a glance and paused at the archway to the kitchen.

"Bonnara," said Princess Mericia.

An iron ladle clattered onto the stone table. Bonnara straightened, ladle in hand, cheeks flaming. Bonnara had been the castle's head cook for twenty years. The King called her a treasure rarer than any in his vaults. Bonnara clenched her jaw and scowled. Most people quailed under her frown, and even the King had been known to rephrase his requests. It never worked on the princess, though, or the Lady Lelori. Bonnara knew it.

"Bonnara, please see that the Queen's private meals contain a lesser proportion of breads. More fruits and vegetables."

What was the ungrateful twit complaining about now? She'd sent a wonderful breakfast to the Queen, sausages, a fresh egg dish with spices and herbs, and lovely flaky pastries. "Her Majesty has never been fond of vegetables," Bonnara said firmly.

"Her Majesty," said the princess with deceptive gentleness, "has eaten nothing since the Founding Supper. No doubt her appetite is at fault."

"I'm sorry to hear that Her Majesty is ill."

"She is not ill. She is simply not hungry."

The implication hung in the air. She was not hungry for the things Bonnara had chosen to send. Bonnara flushed a deep unattractive red. She'd served her Queen for two decades. She knew her tastes to the last dot of butter on broiled trout.

"I am certain this is no reflection on your abilities," said the princess.

Why say it, then? Bonnara mustered enough civility to respond without obvious sarcasm. "What dishes would Your Highness recommend?"

"Fresh fruit, strong tea, and some of your magnificent ham."

"Her Majesty has never overly cared for ham."

"We'll try it anyway, shall we? And if you would take a little time to set a pretty tray, with nice color contrasts, I'm sure she'd appreciate the attention."

Bonnara's breath came in short, sharp jerks. "Yes, Your Highness. Should I send up an additional tray with Trissi?"

"Yes. As soon as possible, if you please. By the way, your

efforts in preparing savories for the Founding feast were laudable. However, for future reference, the King prefers a sampling of meats and pastries served at the high table."

Well *that* was a slap in the face. Bonnara had only bothered with them because Trissi had made such a fuss about the princess' lack of appetite. She'd taken trouble to please the selfish creature, and got a thumb in the eye as a reward. Well, it would be a decade or two before she troubled herself again. The guards could take bets on it.

Mericia passed through the main kitchen towards the storerooms, glancing from side to side critically. After a moment's struggle, Bonnara stumped after her.

"You've retained sufficient extra staff to handle the preserving?"

"Yes, Your Highness." Why bother to preserve it? Nobody ate the stuff. The King hated preserves with a passion. Some sweets on the pastry now and then and the occasional bit of ripe stuff were the extent of his tolerance.

"Last year, we had insufficient stocks of pickled goods, despite the bountiful harvest. I trust that will not occur this year."

"No, Your Highness." Of course not, your bitchiness. Certainly they needed tons of the junk around, so the servants could steal it all through the winter to feed their pigs.

The moment the princess left the kitchens, Bonnara exploded. "Riss!" She slapped together a tray for the Queen, managing not to break anything. "Riss? Oh there you are. Here, take this to Lady Siree for the Queen. The—," Bonnara discarded the first several epithets that came to mind, "Princess," she spat, "demanded them."

Trissi headed up the tower for the fifth time that day. Bonnara punched the bread dough viciously, imagining a pale face on the table beneath her poised fists. The Princess' interest in foodstuffs was entirely unnatural. In most lordly households, the ladies didn't know where the kitchen *was*.

෨

Princess Mericia slipped into the front pew of the empty family chapel. Brother Andreas wouldn't arrive for several hours, so she'd avoided his reproachful look once again. Members of royalty were not subject to the Brotherhood's approval, although her father sought it frequently as a matter of policy. This was unnecessary pandering, so Lady Lelori said.

Princess Mericia would be a Queen Regnant in due time. Her actions were inspired directly by the One, so there was no need to seek the Brotherhood's approval. Even the Many had no authority over royalty. The important thing, Lady Lelori said, was to maintain a correct attitude at all times, cultivating the serenity, duty, and leadership qualities one owed to one's people. Royalty should not bother the One for His approval of every trivial decision. Such dependency was a sign of weakness. So Lady Lelori said.

Dear Lord forgive me, she prayed, *for all my sins. I must have sinned, or You wouldn't have cursed me.* Her exhausted mind circled endlessly in her prayer of the last seven years. She couldn't deny the blame. She could only bear the burden of her guilt, and drag herself from day to day, slogging through the muck and mire of other people's hopes and dreams. No matter what Brother Lawrence said, she knew what she'd done. She just didn't know *how* she'd done it, or which of the many gods she'd offended.

Few girls celebrated their fourteenth birthdays by murdering people they loved.

As though it were yesterday, she heard Brother Lawrence's earnest baritone, and saw his warm brown eyes fill with sympathy. "The One does not work that way. He's filled with love and mercy. He doesn't take a young girl's sins, and use them as an excuse to strike down others. Tragedies strike in any life, but not through the One's connivance."

So many of them, dead or injured, she'd thought, stricken with fresh heartache. Her mother, her Nanny, the lady's maid who'd given her piggyback rides, the groom who'd taught her to ride, the two girls who'd taught her to swim, most of them dead, the others reduced to fumbling wrecks.

"Besides, my dear, what could you possibly have done to cause such misery?"

As his words sank in, her fledgling hope died unborn. He offered blessed reassurance with one hand and snatched it away with the other. If the One didn't do such things, why would Brother Lawrence wonder if she'd caused it? She understood. The long list of deaths and disabilities could all be laid at her door.

Her mother, Queen Ailsa, recovered her life, but not her health or her wits. Nanny regained enough health to return home and retire honorably. Her Nanny's sister, though, had died. Mericia had loved Maari. The lady's maid told Mericia stories of her own children, of pranks, jokes, and lively games. There were fourteen deaths in all. One for each year of her life.

Only once, in seven years, had Mericia gained her mother's complete attention, and that only for a few minutes. Again and again, Mericia reached out to her mother, to no avail. Mother brushed her away with total indifference. Hurt by her mother's rejection, she implored Nanny to visit as often as she could. But somehow, every time Nanny visited, she fell prey to wracking illness. After a while, she stayed at home, outside the Castle gates.

Bereft of comforters, Mericia clung to old Brother Lawrence. She strove to accept his words and forgive herself for sins she couldn't recall. Then one day the Castle Guard entered the grounds at a gallop, and trampled her dog to death. Her father, greatly sympathetic, imported another dog, a long-legged elegant thing, all eyes and legs and glossy brown fur. The new dog loved exploring the countryside as Mericia rode her dappled gray horse through the hills for hours at a time.

One night at dinner she'd been delightfully surprised by the savory stew. Bonnara was an artist at the cooking pots, her dishes rich with fat and flavored with onions and herbs. Turning to Celli, she asked appreciatively, "Is this venison liver? It tastes wonderfully good."

"Oh no," said Celli, smiling in response. "It's horse. There was a horse killed by accident today."

"Really?" She took another bite, savoring its richness. "I didn't know there'd been a hunting accident. Was the rider hurt?"

"No, no. There was no rider. The horse just went mad in its stall. It kicked down the stall, killed itself, and crippled one of the grooms. Bonnara said it was a shame to waste the meat, especially the liver. A lot of people don't like horse meat, but Bonnara is so good, she could bring the flavor out of an old boot."

Mericia's stomach turned. "Which horse was it?" she asked faintly.

"That dappled gray palfrey, a gelding."

Mericia put down her knife. Her horse. Her horse went mad in its own stall, and killed itself. Shivers ran through her body.

Her horse had killed itself, rather than belong to her.

Since then, she'd never eaten meat except seafood and poultry. Fish had to be brought overland through the mountains, from the Great Island or one of the smaller ports. Fish was always preserved, either dried, or packed in salt or oil. The King did not favor it at table. The King was fond of game birds, and sometimes Mericia managed to eat her fill of pheasant and quail, but more often, red meat was the only choice, the gravy slurped over them all, making even vegetables inedible.

Mericia tried to convince her stomach that she'd never been fond of a pig in her life, and ham didn't resemble much of anything else. Meat carved from a deer's carcass couldn't possibly be horse, or a goat like those Nanny kept, or, heaven forbid, a dog. Her contrary stomach refused to listen.

Her father was already distraught over her mother's instability. Rather than add to his troubles with her foible, Mericia picked through the offered courses, and staunchly pretended a lack of appetite that spanned many years. Winters were the worst, with four months of meat, bread, and hunger, made worse by the constant pretense. In self-defense, she'd developed an interest in food preservation which no doubt puzzled Bonnara exceedingly.

She watched the new dog with fearful eyes as the pattern continued. If Mericia climbed a tree, hugged a maidservant, or laughed out loud at a buffoon's antic in the Great Hall, her dog developed a limp or drooped about in whining distress. On the day her second dog died in a frenzy of vomit, she ran to Brother Lawrence.

"I *am* cursed. Everything I love dies."

"Now, now, my dear, that's not true. You're sixteen now, and there are changes." His face reddened, and she knew he meant the womanly changes in her body. "Things like this, they affect the way you think about things. In a year or two—"

"No, Brother, I'm cursed. The One despises me. Help me, help me." Sobbing, she'd thrown herself at his knees. He'd stroked her hair and listened as she poured out her heart. Together they had prayed long into the night, for peace, acceptance, and faith in the One. In the morning, she felt much better, with a new hope sprung from the old man's belief.

Her maid Celli, dressing her hair, beamed at the transformation. "So nice to see you smiling again, Your Highness. Though there are sad things in this life, I have to admit. I'm afraid you'll need to brace yourself for a little upsetting news. The guardian, Brother Lawrence?"

Mericia stared at Celli's face in the mirror. The blood drained from her cheeks.

"He was such an old man, you know. He died in his sleep last night."

The world stilled into a numbing silence, and Mericia stared at her own mirrored eyes, dark and aware. Cursed. She'd dared to confide in the old man, and so he died.

"I don't feel well, Celli," she managed to say. "I think I'll stay in my room this morning."

All day, she thought of the risks she spread around her, a trail of misery and death tracking her every move. Unintentionally, she threatened Celli with every smile. The gods obviously didn't like it. She couldn't put Celli in danger. She couldn't put anyone in danger, not any more.

Taking Lady Lelori as her guide, she invented a new Princess Mericia, a sterile cold creature without personal bonds or affections. She carved from her speech and actions every vestige of emotion, whether positive or negative, striving to emulate Lady Lelori's distant nature. When an envoy of the Emperor presented her with a parrot, she gave it away. Dogs presented in a similar manner were given other homes. She stopped riding. She no longer smiled, joked, ran, or skipped.

She buried her energies in music for a time, singing the old ballads, and learning to dance. Her proud father hired a musician, Master Orino, to instruct her in dance and the art of lute playing. Her tremendous emotional relief sang joyously though her songs. Then, after several months, Master Orino disappeared, never to be heard from again. *At least he's not dead*, she thought, hoping it was true.

Brother Andreas replaced Brother Lawrence. Mericia kept him at arm's length, and was pleased to find that he didn't die. She shunted Celli's services to Lady Lelori, and took a new maid with whom she enforced a chilly relationship, feeling a bleak reward when Vinita's health remained uniformly excellent.

In time, Mericia saw a benefit to her cultivated indifference. A queen could rule more justly if she loved her country rather than the individuals in it. Her soul shrieked at the loneliness, and her unremembered dreams were fraught with tears, but from one moment to the next, she conquered it. This was the only safe way to live. The gods decreed it.

If only she weren't so hungry. If she stole from the kitchen, the servants were blamed. She ordered for the dinner table, and to an extent she ordered what she could eat, but her father snorted at vegetables, and rarely even touched fruit. More than anything else, she wanted to spare him anxiety. His sharp eyes watched her, perhaps looking for signs of her mother's madness. She couldn't possibly tell him of the curse and her distress.

Thank the One, she was permitted to love her father. Set beside that single freedom, her troubles seemed minor. It was only a matter of a little hunger.

Perhaps the huntsmen will catch a pheasant today, she thought forlornly.

She vowed never to own a pet bird.

"Your daughter has great talent, Your Majesty," said the High Captain.

"Yes, indeed she does." King Gerritt touched Mericia's hair. Mericia warmed inside and leaned briefly against his hand. "Still, Captain, you'll need to develop other resources in time to come. As, indeed, will I." The King shook his head and sighed.

Mericia shaped a miniscule piece of clay, referred to the map beside her, and added it to the structure under her hands. Contentment soared through her. She felt useful in the library with her father. Perhaps the gods understood that even a princess must love someone. Was her father subject to the same curse? She paused to look at him, her index finger crowned with a wedge of clay.

The King looked his age, fifty-six last January. Silver frosted the famous rust-red hair of the House of Valtiris. His face sagged in deep lines on either side of his nose. Mericia wished she resembled her father, but she'd inherited her dark coloring from her mother and countless generations of Islanders.

She deeply appreciated her father's willingness to share his political experience. The Great Island, which would be hers, had only two ethnic groups, and they had been at peace for three generations. Countless tribes of surly temperament lived on the mainland of Valtiris. Raids and organized banditry were rife. King Gerritt gritted his teeth, commanded, mediated, and dealt justice as evenly as possible. Any sort of preferential treatment rebounded on those who were favored.

In fact, it was much like her own situation. To protect them all, the King must hide his own preferences, and be even-handed to all. A constriction around her heart eased, as she relished the parallel. He must find his life every bit as difficult as she did hers. If he could bear it, so could she.

"The Emperor insists that she marry soon. I suppose he has a point. I should at least provide the opportunity for her to meet suitable young men, eh, sweetheart?"

"You do provide the opportunity," she said. "You hosted jousts and tournaments, and entertained countless young men during the May Festival. None of them interested me, that's all."

"Well, well, maybe next year. Though mind you, sweetling, the Emperor will persist. He doesn't care to lose his influence over the Great Island."

"And its harbor," she added tartly, throwing a glance at the High Captain.

The Captain nodded. "The Emperor's fleet relies heavily on the Island's port. It's his primary staging point for all points south. A perfect harbor."

The kingdom of Ailsandia had passed from Queen to oldest daughter for countless generations. Three generations before, the Emperor's grandfather acquired the Great Island, though maintaining the ruling house, as his own great-grandfather had done with Valtiris. The Emperor had been delighted with the love match between Gerritt, King of Ramsvalt, and Ailsa, Queen of Ailsandia. As the throne prepared to change hands again, Emperor Theomedon strove to consolidate his resources by getting Mericia married off safely.

These days, the islanders were philosophical about their annexation. Their prosperity had increased dramatically, and they'd largely kept their independence. The islanders' restiveness had a different cause. With the Queen's illness, she'd ceased her lengthy stays at the Island, and the King had served in her stead. Ailsandia chafed at being relegated to a vassal state. Mericia had reluctantly agreed to shoulder the burden her mother could no longer handle. This Progress would combine her twenty-first birthday, coronation as Princess Regent, and a permanent move south.

"I will miss you greatly, my daughter," her father said. He tucked a strand of her hair behind her ear.

Tears stung her eyes. "I've always valued our closeness."

A half-chuckle forced its way through the King's lips. "You sound like a Queen already. I love you, too, my dear. It comforts me to know that Lady Lelori can stay with you, if indeed you must remain in Ailsandia after Progress."

"Just be sure you visit more often than every seven years." Mericia teased.

He barked with laughter. Pleased, Mericia returned to her work.

The High Captain hovered over her studying the paper map and her relief map, of clay hills, mountains, roads, and valleys stretching across a wooden platform. The Captain showed a puzzling fascination with Mericia's maps, though they were far too cumbersome to transport on Patrol. The paper maps showed the same features, with lines indicating elevation at key points. She referred to the map and created the same features to scale, in three dimensions.

"Amazing," said the Captain, his finger poised over a point behind the Khonsellin mountain pass. "You're certain about this outcropping?"

"It's right there on the map," said Mericia.

"Yes, but—" He shook his head. "It's just the curvature, and that line running along the back slope."

"Perhaps I'm wrong," said Mericia, taking another look at the map. She treasured the ability to speak, person to person, without the cumbersome formal modes. Here, in her father's library, her cage walls retreated.

"No, no, trust yourself, Your Highness. You've made many a map for me, and you've never been wrong yet. This explains that surprise attack two weeks back. They had an access point I never suspected. Odd that the locals never thought to mention it." He chuckled cynically. "It was all too convenient, the stores and animals stolen, and no one injured. Ha."

The Captain tapped her shoulder approvingly. At the King's burning glare, he pulled back his hand as though scorched.

"Thank you very much, Your Highness, Your Majesty. If I could just have access to the map once Her Highness is done, I would be most grateful."

"Yes, indeed," said the King, rigid with disapproval.

Mericia shifted uncomfortably.

The Captain glanced at her almost imperceptibly. "I did have a request, Your Majesty," he said.

"Indeed?"

"If it would not inconvenience Your Majesty, might I put off the Castle Guard review until tomorrow? This is such a fleeting stop. I haven't seen my wife and children yet, and probably won't again until after Progress."

"Ah." The King's voice softened. "Yes, that would be acceptable. Your oldest is in the cavalry juniors, isn't he? Perhaps you would like us to include your family in the Progress?"

"That would be most kind," said the Captain. "Chandra would love to attend the Weaver's Guild conference on the Island. I believe David's already scheduled to go. The younger ones aren't apprenticed yet, so there'll be no problem at all with them. They'll be over the moon."

"It's no problem," the King said, rocking back on his heels with a benevolent air. "Lady Lelori will see to it. She's overseeing the domestic side of the Progress, with Her Highness' assistance, of course."

The Captain bowed deeply and departed. King Gerritt leaned over Mericia's map, and traced the line up the back of the hill.

"He's right, you know. It's obvious, now I look at it." The King picked up the map roll and frowned at it. "And it's right here on the map. How very strange. You have an excellent eye. The Captain is right. It's a gift."

Mericia worked a curve into the clay, almost glowing with contentment. The King ran a finger over her cheek.

"No more bad dreams, dear?"

"It wasn't a bad dream," Mericia protested, laughing a little. If it had been a bad dream, she wouldn't have told him. "On the contrary, it was a beautiful dream."

"A dragon, living on the northern cliffs of Ailsandia?

Hungering for human flesh? A beautiful dream, indeed!"

"He wasn't hungering for human flesh! Well, at least," she chuckled, "not *my* human flesh. Just evildoers, of course. It was as though he frightened all my nightmares away."

"You have nightmares?" he said sharply.

"No, no, of course not!" She waggled a finger at him "Because he scares them away before I have them!" They both laughed. "That's why it was beautiful. I've been a little worried about moving to the Island, I suppose. It made me feel I'd be protected, even when you're not there."

The King sighed and dropped into a chair next to her. "My dear, are you sure you didn't meet anyone interesting at the tourneys? I would be only too delighted to invite back any young man who took your fancy."

"No one at all. Truly father, I'd tell you."

"I don't want you to be alone all your life. Your mother is ill now, but the years we had together were happy beyond compare. Are you certain?"

A face appeared in her mind, with challenging eyes and crisply curled chestnut hair. He carried a shield decorated with a lion rampant. His horse danced beneath him as though they were one creature. She'd overhead Trissi whisper his name to Vinita: Lord Ranilth, eldest son of the earl of Danneminton. Ranilth, she'd thought, testing the name. He leaped onto his horse and charged into the joust. His horse faltered and a spear caught him in the gut, throwing him to the ground with a clatter of armor. He sprawled, unmoving. She lifted a grape to her mouth and made a light remark to Lady Siree. The One was appeased, and the man recovered, though he'd probably never ride again. She'd understood the One's message. She would not risk her affections on an innocent.

"Absolutely certain," she said firmly.

Chapter Five

Farren craned his neck, staring up at the night sky. He framed the crescent moon in the curve of his fingers, brushing the distant starfield with the palm of his other hand. Almost, he felt the tingle of a multitude of lights, each distinct and pure. Each might be an angel, shining in the heavens. Perhaps when shades completed their journeys, they became stars. If only he could climb a ladder into the world's loft. If only he could clamber into the midst of those sparkling eyes, escaping the turmoil of his life.

A shooting star seared the night. His hand darted after it and fell as it vanished. His eyes stung and he swallowed hard. His feet remained rooted on the path between the yew trees, those closely packed sentinels guarding the center of His Majesty's hedge maze.

The Goat's head poked through the branches. "Are you *still* here? Hurry up, will you?"

"I'm sorry. I know I'm slow."

"I'd think you'd hurry yourself," the Goat scolded. "Not that she looks like much. Now that Felicia, there's a female with a tail worth shaking."

"I'm sorry," said Farren, "but I can't just barge through—"

The Goat vanished through the hedge maze without a rustle.

—the hedge wall again, Farren finished. If he broke a tree limb, someone would have a fit. He understood Caprio's urgency. If the King's staff discovered Caprio's nanny goat friend, she'd be in the stew pot in short order. Still, his little rescue mission wouldn't cut any ice with the King's gardeners or the Steward. Poachers paid with their hands.

Ah well. He'd been a fool a thousand times. Despite their distrust, neighbors had often knocked on Master Pardell's door, and later Aunt Nan's, to borrow the 'boy.' He'd stitched up torn udders, removed porcupine quills from the nose of an enraged bull, and extracted stillborn pups from a beloved hound. In nighttime forays, he'd scurried after guides to perform more dubious services. He'd cut an arrow from a poacher's leg, stitched a drunkard's throat after a dispute with his wife, and delivered a frightened girl of her bastard son.

When daytime came, the same neighbors dragged their children from his reach, and watched his every move. The injustice rankled Denys deeply, but except for the sourness in his stomach, Farren dismissed it. Denys didn't see the wounded colors of those who slunk to Nan's house. Their agony flooded him, a mute reproach to a man with peculiar vision and quick fingers.

To his left, a shifting movement caught his eye. A man and a maiden, shades dressed as castle servants, twined arms and drifted through the side of the hedge maze. Lovers liked a bit of privacy, even shades. Perhaps Denys and Trissi had met out here, too. Denys and Trissi. Had that been going on for long? Why hadn't Denys told him? He grimaced. Well, that was no mystery. Farren had never had a girl, and probably never would. What girl would put up with a babbler like him, spouting nonsense about shades and colors?

Enough of this. It was time to get on with the job. He needed to traverse the maze without injuring it. He visualized old Kottel, the gardener, talking nonstop at the dinner table, spewing spittal everywhere. He bragged often enough about the hedge maze, waving his arms to illustrate. How did the turns go again? Left turn, left, left, and right. Or was it one right, and then four lefts? Farren studied the fork in the path. Left. It was definitely left.

"What are you doing?" the Goat exclaimed.

"I'm following the trail."

"She's not *in* the maze, you dimwit. She's in the orchard."

"The *King's* Orchard? How am I supposed to get in there?"

"The guards won't give a damn, if that's why you're fretting. They're gabbing over their ale in the south battlement. Follow me," the Goat commanded. "Mortals," he added, with a snort.

Farren forced his head between two hedge yews, the stiff branches spiking into his neck, their damp, sharp scent filling his nostrils. Fifteen feet above, the guards' walkway nestled against another four foot wall that provided cover in case of attack. The two guards leaned in the south battlement's sheltering nook, swigging their ale, and wrangling over the odds on a dogfight.

"Move it," fumed the Goat.

Farren edged through the trees and took cover against the wall, prowling around the shrubs until he passed beyond the guards' earshot.

"Gods, what an ungrateful fool," said the Goat. "I've given you day after day of my selfless attention and assistance, and when I offer you a tiny challenge, you mope." The grumbles took on a martyred tone. "Night after night I've sat nursing your neurotic horse—"

"Two nights, total, and you didn't help a scrap."

"Two. Two nights? What about last night, and the night before that, not to mention my vigil with that lovely little—"

"I haven't seen in you in a week. And that lovely little doe, if you mean Felicia, has been running with other bucks for days, and I'm glad of it."

"A week? Nonsense."

"A week. Not that I mind. Go do whatever you want, it's nothing to me."

"But I distinctly remember last night—"

"A week. I've been sleeping in the stables for ten nights, trying to give Brolin a peaceful night in the stables. That's me, hopelessly optimistic."

The Goat looked hard at him. "You mean I've been gone for a whole week, and I didn't know?"

"Hmm."

"Well, I'll be a horsefly's dung heap. I wonder where I've been." He leaped in front of Farren, dug his hooves in the dirt, and fixed him with a beady-eyed stare. "Do you know?"

"How would I know? Ah, there's the orchard. Where's this goat that hurt her leg?"

The starlight painted the garden in drizzles of green, black, silver, and gray. Farren circled the Goat, and picked his way around the staked beans towards the fruit trees. Caprio loved fruit, and Aunt Nan's goats had been a menace to the neighbors' apple trees. Perhaps this nanny goat had escaped the King's goat shed, and gone hunting for windfalls.

"A whole week. I wonder how I did it? I think," Caprio stamped a decisive but silent hoof, "I'll try it again."

"Where's this nanny goat? I don't see her."

The Goat was gone.

Farren shifted from one foot to the other. Try what again? Disappearing for a week? Damn it, wasn't that just *like* Caprio? Lead him on a merry chase, and drop him in a muckheap. However, somewhere around here huddled a wounded goat, due for the morning stew pot. Unless, naturally, Caprio saw her last week, and had only just got around to telling him.

"Here, girl." Farren uttered the wordless whuffling noises that Aunt Nan's goats found irresistible. Not the faintest bleat answered him. Strange. Goats didn't suffer from guilty consciences, especially over gardens. "Don't be afraid, little one. A friend of yours sent me to help you."

The futility of it struck him. What was the point? One more goat, more or less, wouldn't save the world. He glanced up, his gaze drawn by the starlit brilliance. The night sky's aloof radiance shrank him to nothing, a pebble on a mountaintop. He was alone. His closest family were shades, or on patrol miles away. And a shade might love him still, but it had its own concerns. Like the stars overhead, they were visible but distant. The longer a shade existed, the more its focus narrowed, as though the effort to remain left little energy to spend on the living. Aunt Nan's present warmth towards him would fade, as his parents' had. Denys and Terrell would be on patrol for the next dozen years, at least. He'd be lucky if he saw them a handful of times. In fact, except for Master Pardell, Farren's lifelines had disintegrated. The rest of the world regarded him with suspicion. At best, he was a tool for healing and woodworking. At worst, he was a nightmare of demons and sorcery.

"Little one?" His voice cracked. He brought himself back to earth with a jerk. Enough maundering. He'd best get on with the task, or start the long trek back to the stable and Brolin. "Come on, little thing. If you're out there, let me help you."

A dog's shade darted past him, flying like an arrow to a shape crouched next to an apple tree. Was that it? No, it was probably just another shade. Goats didn't crouch. Just in case, he hummed a light reassurance, holding his hands in view, so she could see that he wasn't carrying a rope. Two shining spots resolved into eyes, reflecting the soft sheen of moonlight. Farren stopped dead.

"Female, he said." He fought an impulse to flee. "Not a goat. Um, are you hurt?"

The wary eyes tilted like an Islander's. Denys' girl, Trissi, had eyes like that. So did the Queen, the Princess, and dozens of transplanted Islanders in Ramsvalt.

He cleared his throat. "A, er, friend of mine said someone was hurt. Is that you? Or was he completely wrong? It wouldn't surprise me. He wasn't even sure what day it was."

"What friend?"

He scarcely heard the voice over the thrumming in his ears. The girl shrank back from him. Instinctively, he dropped to his knees, hanging his hands loosely in front of him. "He has a beard," Farren said. "And four feet."

"And horns?"

"Like a demon." His voice steadied. "Sorry, forget I said that. Just a friend of mine, who saw you here." He waved behind him, hoping she'd assume he meant a guard on patrol.

"He likes plums," she said. "He kept after me, so I climbed the tree to get one for him, and I fell."

"That sounds like him." He revised his first opinion. If she'd seen Caprio and not descended to hysteria, then she couldn't be the timid sort. "He planned to introduce me, but he got sidetracked."

"That sounds like him, too."

Only his family and Master Pardell looked at him like that, straight on, as though he were human and not a changeling. A small warmth kindled inside him. "How badly are you hurt?"

"I wrenched my knee. But I'm not supposed to be out here."

"I can imagine." Farren glanced at the half-open sack at her feet, with its hoard of fruits and vegetables.

"I fell over there," she said, indicating the plum trees fifty feet to the west. "I managed to get this far. I can get the rest of the way, too. If I get to the castle, I'll make up a tale about falling downstairs." She sagged against the tree.

"Let me help. My name's Farren. I'm not a complete stranger," he said, searching for something to make himself familiar. "Maybe you know my aunt. Aunt Nan used to work here. She took care of the princess years ago."

"Nanny's your aunt?"

"Yes. She died a few weeks ago."

"I'm so sorry. I hadn't heard." She wrapped her arms around the tree, and pulled herself into a one-footed stance. Her long black hair caught on the bark. She jerked it free. "I'm sorry to hear that. Bonnara talks about her a great deal. I'm Riss. I work in the kitchen."

Without conscious thought, he checked the colors flickering from her eyes. Emotion shed colors through the eyes, and had in every pair since the first man walked upright. A sensible man made use of his small advantages. Riss had told the truth, but only part of it. That was nothing new. People who skulked in forbidden territory were a mite economical with facts.

He slung her bag over one shoulder, and slipped his other arm around her waist. She tensed, and humiliation stabbed him. People couldn't help their suspicions. But it hurt.

"Perhaps you knew my mother," he said. "Maari, lady's maid to the Queen. She died on the last Progress, though, so it might have been before your time."

After a moment, she gripped his shoulder and leaned into his arm as she limped towards the castle. "I remember Maari," Riss said. The stiffness of her voice echoed her limping gait. "A nice woman. She had three sons."

"Yes, you've met my brother, I think." He smiled to himself. Well, Denys had wanted him to look after Trissi. He just hadn't figured to meet her like this.

"Yes. He's a fine man."

At the pain in her voice, Farren glanced at her. Of course, she'd be missing Denys as badly as he was. "Are you all right? I could carry you, if you like. It might be easier."

"No, I'm fine."

"Sure," he said, disbelief heavy in his voice. She shot him a glance, and stared at the ground ahead of her. They reached the tool shed and took partial shelter from the breeze. "Hang on for a bit. Eat something out of this bag of yours. Don't they feed you at the castle?"

"There's lots of food. Bonnara's a wonderful cook. This is, well, it's not all for me. It's, I can't talk about it."

"You're too thin," he said, handing her a green pepper.

"I beg your pardon," she snapped.

He grinned at her. "Where's the best entrance? The kitchen?"

"That side door would be better."

"Need help up the stairs? Do you have a friend I can call for you?"

"I'll manage," she said. She glanced up the castle to its towers. She demolished the green pepper, seeds, and all, and began another. "I left a lantern at the foot of the stairs."

Riss froze, her hand halfway to her mouth. Farren followed her stare to the top of the castle's keep. The keep and the watchtower up the hill anchored opposite ends of the inner castle wall. The keep was the largest tower in the castle complex, the most central and protected. Traditionally, the lord's family took shelter there during battle.

On the roof of the keep beneath the night sky a woman danced dreamily, her hands lifted towards the stars. Her long dark hair swept about her with every move.

"Come on." Riss pulled at him. "We've got to go."

"What's she doing?" There was something poignant about the woman's stance, as though she were pleading with the night sky for her freedom, a lark with clipped wings. A deep recognition took hold of him. In just this way, he clung to the stars himself, yearning for their all-seeing vision, and their unattainable beauty. The strains of a celestial harp seemed to float on the breeze. He strained his ears, but it was gone. He heard only the sighing of the breeze as it drew clouds though the river of stars.

"It's just someone who can't sleep," said Riss. "Come on."

"That's the Queen," he said.

"It can't be. She's asleep, and anyway, you couldn't tell possibly tell. It could be anyone."

His eyes were riveted on the swaying figure. He hunted for matter-of-fact words, trying to hide his sudden feeling of kinship with the woman on the keep. "Maybe she's sleepwalking. I hope she's all right."

"Of course she's all right," said Riss sharply. "Forget it, I'll get myself to the stairs." She pulled herself from his grip and struggled up the slight incline. "It's not the Queen."

It was, though. Farren recognized the ghostly figure dancing along behind her. Maari, the lady's maid. Maari, his mother, dead these seven years.

A shooting star split the night, streaking through the sky to the Queen's hands like an eagle to its nest. She dropped her hands, seeming to tuck the star into a pouch at her waist. As he watched, she swayed into her dance, hands lifted to the stream of pinpoint flames. Behind her, in faithful mimicry, his mother's figure followed.

Riss staggered a step or two, teeth clenched.

"I'm sorry, let me help," he said, catching up to her.

She leaned against him gratefully. "I'm sorry. I shouldn't have snapped at you. It couldn't be the Queen, you know. It's probably Lady Lelori. She keeps late hours."

He knew she lied. "Of course," he said. *Goodbye, mother*, he thought to the figure dancing behind the Queen. *It's good to see you again, after all these years.* A ghostly kiss sailed to him on the breeze, and his heart lifted.

"Ha," bellowed the Goat, bounding out of nowhere. "I did it, didn't I? Another week gone. What are you doing out here again, you fools?"

Riss jumped and grabbed her knee, trying to ease the pain.

"Twenty minutes," said Farren.

"Twenty—? Nonsense. I've been all over this castle a dozen times. It can't have been twenty minutes. Scared a night watchman, and met a few interesting fellows in the dungeon."

"Dungeon?" said Riss. "It's empty, isn't it?"

"Of course not, filled with mortals. No friends of mine, though. A little surprising, actually."

"He means shades," Farren interpreted, hiding his exultation. She actually saw Caprio, and heard him, too. Had she told Denys? Perhaps Denys would finally believe him, and understand what Farren really saw. And if not, if Denys thought Riss was delusional, then perhaps— A sudden hope flared in his heart. He squashed it firmly. Riss was his brother's girl.

"I do not," said Caprio. "Well, a few of them, maybe, but the ones in the dungeon are completely alive, poor buggers. Still, I heard a lot of good stories in there. What's in that bag? Any plums in there?"

"No."

"Liar," said Caprio, sticking his nose through the bag and munching heartily. "Hmm, oh, I like these carrots of yours, so fresh. Bet those poor bastards never get any. Not that it would do them any good. No teeth, you know, not after the guards are done with them."

Riss gasped. Farren broke in fiercely, "Keep that kind of talk to yourself. I know most of our guards. They're not vicious."

"All right, all right," said the Goat, willing to concede a point. "So it wasn't the guards. Happy now? It wasn't the guards who sliced off the ears and nose off that slob in the Little Ease, either. No, of course not. Can't imagine why they'd do that. He wasn't *that* bad a singer. Little off-key, maybe, but you'd expect that after—"

Riss cried a wordless protest.

Farren slammed his arm through the Goat, enduring the stinging cold. "Get away from us. She helped you, and all you can do is torment her." He swiped the Goat backhanded.

"*She's* helped *me*?" the Goat spluttered. "Who got help for her, I'd like to know, as if I were a little errand boy!"

"Who nagged her into climbing a tree until she fell out and hurt herself?"

"Oh," said the Goat, taken aback. "Well, I apologize. There, is that good enough?" Huffily, he stalked at Farren's side. "To prove my sincerity, I shall sing you a little song to ease your weary footsteps."

Riss hobbled on, supported by Farren's arm, her jaws clamped shut.

"I'm sorry," Farren told her. "There's not much you can do with shades when they get this way, or Beings, either."

"*When the wings of the mountains,*" warbled the Goat, "*brush the soul of the sea—*"

"No!" cried Riss. "Where did you hear that?"

"I told you," said the Goat, with exaggerated patience. "From the living carcass in the dungeon's pit. Now, to continue: *When the two and the many—*"

"No!" Riss flailed her free arm at the Goat, lost her balance and twisted into a heap on the ground.

Farren grabbed her and swung her off her feet. "Shut up, you," he said to the Goat. "What is it, Riss? It was just a song."

"Not *that* song, not from the dungeon." Tears streamed down her cheeks.

"Not that song?" Farren exchanged a bewildered look with the Goat, shifting her slight weight into a more secure position. Her head fell against his shoulder. "Riss, it's all right. He won't sing it any more. Right, Goat?"

"I suppose," said the Goat, aggrieved, but intrigued. "Why? I didn't think the song was that bad."

"Apart from your horrible voice, you mean?" said Farren, trying to jog a smile out of Riss. His small attempt failed. He walked up the rise towards the entrance. "Riss?"

"A friend wrote it," she mumbled. "I haven't seen him for years."

"Well, now you know why," remarked the Goat.

"Shut up, Caprio. You don't know it's him, Riss. This man probably just heard the song somewhere else, years ago."

"Absolutely," said the Goat, chuckling.

Farren shot him a look. The Goat was more trouble when he agreed than when he argued. "Don't worry, Riss. The songwriter left long ago. You said so." Encouraged by her silence, he continued. "He must have sung it to many people. It's a lovely tune. It's only natural someone remembered it."

"No," she said. "He hadn't finished it. He never sang his songs until he'd perfected them. He only sang it to—," she hesitated. "To me."

"Maybe he sang it after he left here, before he died."

"He's not dead yet," noted the Goat. "Probably wishes he were, but he's not." He skipped away as Farren aimed a kick at him.

"Wait," said Riss. She lifted her head and stared at the goat. "Please, how much of what you said was true? Did you really hear that song," her voice broke, "just now, in the dungeon?"

"Yes."

"From a man who—"

"Had no nose or ears? Hmm. My advice is, if you don't want to hear the answer, don't ask. Well," said the Goat cheerfully, "glad to see you're all right. That's my good deed for the day. See you around." He disappeared.

"Riss." Farren stopped at the door and swung her to her feet. The blood-red aura of pain enveloped her like a fog. His heart clenched. "Wait, Riss. I'll look into it. Caprio doesn't always understand what he sees."

"You couldn't get into the dungeon. It's been locked up for years."

"No, but I can talk to people who do." Her pain lashed him with its intensity.

"So can I," Riss said.

"Riss, please, just let me do it. What was his name? The songwriter?"

"Master Orino, the princess' dance master. He disappeared four years ago."

"Well, then, he'd hardly still be here, would he? In the dungeon? Caprio got his facts mixed up. I'll check into it, but don't worry, all right?"

"Caprio knew the song. Master Orino only sang it to me and to the princess. No one else. He wrote it for the Islanders, to sing on the next Progress."

"Riss—"

"He was kind to me, when I was a little girl. He *listened* to me."

"Riss, just let me talk to some people. Don't do anything until then, all right?"

She looked at him, her dark eyes direct and unyielding. "That's all I'm going to do, too. Just talk to some people. Farren, thank you for your help. I really appreciate it. You're a fine man, just as your mother said you would be. She talked about all three of you a great deal."

"I know Denys thinks a lot of you."

"Poor Denys. Well, thank you. I can manage now. Can you get back to your home?"

"No problem." He smiled.

"Take care," she whispered, as the door closed behind her.

"Take care," he echoed. He backed away from the door, turned, and walked away, heedless of the guards' indolent patrol. The image of a mutilated man engulfed him, a battered wreck caged in a small cell in the dungeon. It sickened him. Gods, what a thing for Riss to hear, especially about a close friend. It was a pity the Goat chose this moment for his little announcement.

Farren slammed a fist into his other palm. He almost wished the Goat were mortal, just so he could *make* him a shade.

Chapter Six

Books by the dozen, and maps by the score, lined the walls in ordered rankings. Mericia's pot of clay and her work table sat side-by-side with the Lady Lelori's study table. Mericia dabbed a bit of clay into a curved coastline on her relief map of Ailsandia. The knots in her spirit loosened their grip as she worked alongside Lady Lelori. Her curse couldn't strike Lady Lelori. The Lady smothered emotion like a wet blanket over a blaze. Lady Lelori floated through any disaster, ever rational, distant, and predictable.

Mericia rubbed a wad of clay between her fingers, relishing its smoothness and the promise of its pliability. The clay could be anything. She only had to shape it with her fingers. Nowadays, she couldn't touch a living thing without risking its life. Clay helped fill the void. Childhood's mischief with mud pies and sand castles had jelled into a passion for sculpture. Over the years, hundreds of clay animals, people, plants, buildings, roads, and mountains had sprung, fully formed, beneath her hands.

Lady Lelori sat bolt upright, her spine six inches from the back of the wooden straight chair. The History of the Dannevalt Empire, Volume IV, lay open on the table. Lady

Lelori touched a page with her left forefinger and penned a note on the parchment to her right. The Lady's face reflected the preoccupation of a cat considering a nap before a stroll through the garden. So did Mericia's. She'd mastered the Lady's full repertoire of expressions and postures, practicing in front of a mirror for hours at a time. Now, she could lock an expression onto her face, and be certain it would never betray her.

"Lady," said Mericia, "I have a question about the Island's harbor."

"Yes?" The Lady glanced at her.

"I see a freshwater river flowing into the channel. Topsoil erosion must be a problem on the slopes upriver. Doesn't it silt up the harbor?"

The Lady tilted her head and extended a long-fingered hand to touch the table between them. Mericia bent her head over her map, hiding her pleasure at the Lady's rare gesture of approval.

"A good point. Yes, that is so. Once in a number of years, eight or ten, the Merchants' Guild arranges the dredging of the river mouth. Most fortunately, the second channel to the harbor does not contain a freshwater outflow." The impromptu lesson expanded to include dredging methods and the use of fresh water to kill barnacles. Lady Lelori had tutored Mericia for years. Although never a match for Nanny in kindly common sense, her inexorable logic and intelligence had made its own appeal.

Mericia's studies centered on Ailsandia. In years past, Queen Ailsa had lived in Ailsandia six months out of every year, while her husband paid frequent visits. All three children reveled in the island freedom, learning to swim, sail, fish, clamber over mountains, debate local issues, and wrap up skinned knees with equal exuberance. Now, the Queen's neurotic fixation had stranded the King amid island controversies. King Gerritt openly thanked the One for Lady Lelori's knowledge of Ailsandia politics, and Mericia strove to match it.

Mericia pressed a river channel into the lower cliff-side of the dormant volcano. "This crater bowl is virtually inaccessible. Splendid place for a dragon to live, don't you think?" When she reviewed Minister Rogitas' latest reports from the Island this morning, she'd been surprised at the scarcity of fish on the northern side of the Island. With secret amusement, she'd wondered if her dream dragon was responsible.

"A dragon." The Lady's blank look erected a wall between them.

"My levity is inappropriate," said Mericia, mentally withdrawing to her own side of the wall. "I read some of my mother's notes last night, and they reported legends of sea serpents. From there, I just," she met the Lady's uncomprehending gaze, "drifted to the thought of dragons."

"There's no such thing as a dragon. Or a sea serpent," the Lady added for good measure.

"Except through sorcery."

The Lady was silent, her hands frozen on Volume IV. "True, though your mention of it surprises me."

"I'm well aware of Elizar's sorceries. My mother does not believe in hiding from history. The only way to prevent such horrors is to understand them."

"Yes." The Lady stared at her, never blinking. "If you're interested, I suspect the chronicles in Volume III would cover the period."

"Elizar's not in there. My great-grandmother had the volume re-written. My mother's information came from the Island's oral history. There hasn't been another Shadebinder in Ailsandia since Elizar's time, or a sorcerer capable of seven-year sorceries, which is the only known way to generate a mythical beast. I apologize for the digression,

Lady. As I worked on the map, I thought of Elizar's green dragon, and wondered where he'd housed it. The crater seemed possible."

"Ah," said the Lady, unbending a trifle.

In the first years of her mother's seclusion, Mericia had kept jealous watch on the Lady and her father. Nowadays, Mericia marveled that she'd ever worried. The Lady's attitude ranged from chilly disapproval to tepid encouragement, whether she spoke to the King or to Mericia. In fact, the King garnered less of her approval than did his daughter.

"Does your research advance satisfactorily, Lady?"

The Lady compared her notes with a second parchment. "I believe, Your Highness, that you might consider a barge for the Coronation. It would permit greater participation among the populace, at least visually."

Mericia's stomach tightened. She'd learned how to mitigate the curse's effectiveness here in Ramsvalt. If she replaced her mother, she risked the lives and sanity of hundreds of people as she felt her way into her new position. The Lady appeared to read her tension accurately and withdrew to her book.

With a clay-stained finger, Mericia smoothed the terraced slopes on the mountainside. When she'd visited the island last spring, Masterfarmer Eolin insisted that she admire the imported citrus saplings, now sinking their roots into the newly-built terraces. Citrus trees throve in exotic lands hundreds of miles further south, but Eolin had wrestled the Guild into supporting his experiment. The mountain's shelter from prevailing winds would, he proclaimed, protect them from chill. Minister Jonsel, minister of agriculture, ridiculed the attempt, bellowing that the island climate and the salty air completely demolished any possibility of success. Well, this winter might prove Jonsel correct, or another ten years might vindicate Eolin. By then, they'd have pounced on another cause for feuding. Regrettably, the Islanders' volatility drew the Emperor's attention far too often.

The Dannevalt Empire engulfed a dozen nation-states surrounding the Merolian Sea. Ailsandia, the Great Island, sat in the mouth of the Merolian Sea as it adjoined the ocean. Ailsandia neighbored Ramsvalt to the west and Catiffar to the east. The entire Empire depended on the sea for shipping and large-scale fishing. Ailsandia's magnificent harbor was its key commercial pivot point and the Empire's first bulwark of defense against invasion.

Ailsandia required an active ruler to maintain its semi-autonomous state. Queen Ailsa's interests had shrunk to her tapestry. King Gerritt, an outlander in islanders' eyes, lacked time and credibility to cope with its internal debates. Mericia must control Ailsandia, or the Emperor would. Once lost, Ailsandia's autonomy would never be regained. A flawless plum never remained on the tree.

The door opened. Trissi limped in and attempted to curtsey. Mericia forestalled her with a raised hand. Trissi caught herself on the doorframe.

"Your Highness, Bonnara wished to know if you'd prefer luncheon served here?"

"I think not." Trissi should quit climbing stairs and let Bonnara send someone else on errands. Reflexively, Mericia dismissed the thought. Even in her own mind, it wasn't safe to express personal interest. Besides, no matter what anyone said, Trissi wouldn't take it easily. Mericia recalled certain incidents of childhood with exceptional clarity.

"Trissi," the Lady said, "you appear to be in pain." She looked from Trissi to Mericia. The suggestion of a line appeared between her eyebrows.

"I'm fine, my lady," said Trissi. "I just turned my knee on the stairs last night."

"Curious."

"Lady Lelori is surprised," Mericia informed Trissi. "It so happens I twisted my own knee last night. Tower stairs can be slippery. Rather a coincidence."

"I trust you're feeling better, Your Highness," Trissi said.

"Yes, of course. However, I believe I'll skip luncheon today." Inwardly, she cringed as the gnawing in her stomach dug a new hole for itself. Still, if she ate, either she or Trissi would climb more stairs: Trissi to deliver luncheon, or Mericia to go to a lower level to keep Trissi *off* the stairs. Either way was unacceptable.

"I will be lunching with Her Majesty the Queen this noontime." The Lady had recovered her detachment. "If Her Highness changes her mind, she will join us. Lady Siree will attend to the details."

Lady Siree's maid served meals at midday. A flush of gratitude warmed Mericia's cheeks. She turned her head to hide the unwelcome color. "That seems a feasible solution."

"Very good, Your Highness."

A note in Trissi's voice forced Mericia's head up to face her, eye to eye across the room. Trissi's face resembled her own. She'd seen it in the mirror: thin, hollowed faces, dark eyes, and long, black Islanders' braids. Mericia wore a many-hued blue brocade gown, shining with silver threads. The gorgeously feathered cage impeded movement and deep breath. Only her hands and wrists remained free of constriction, so she could work with her clay. Trissi's coarsely woven gown was plain and unstylish, but its simple grace freed her limbs for her work.

A spark lit Trissi's eyes and flew to Mericia's. Mericia paled, nodding almost imperceptibly. She fixed her eyes on the annual agriculture reports as the door shut behind Trissi.

"Lady." The words forced their way between her teeth. "I'm concerned about law and order. Here in Ramsvalt, most crime is dealt with by the city councils, and not by the King's Court. Is it the same in Ailsandia?"

"For the most part..." The Lady embarked on a detailed explanation, most of which Mericia already knew. "... does not concern the Royal House, as a general rule."

"Except, of course, for dungeon maintenance."

"Dungeons?"

"Yes. This castle has a dungeon, under the watchtower on the mound."

"It has been empty for many years."

"No, it's in use now. Father told me so." The lie burned.

"You must be mistaken." The Lady's emerald green eyes reflected her customary indifference. "Dungeons are only used for political purposes, such as incarceration of purported spies, pirates, or men who've threatened the King or his family. Ramsvalt is not prone to such unrest. Khonsvalt, possibly, has its dungeon in use, but not Ramsvalt or Selefrevalt."

"Have you seen the dungeon recently?"

"Naturally not. Why should I visit a dungeon?" The Lady closed the Dannevalt History. "What reading have you done to expand your understanding of Island culture?"

Persistence was pointless. When the Lady closed a subject, it was bolted, jammed, and nailed shut. "I have read a little poetry."

"Poetry has promise. One can learn a great deal about people from their forms of artistic self-expression. Do you recall any examples?"

Master Orino's songs counted as poetry, didn't they? Mericia spoke the lines from memory, instead of singing them. There was no need to force too much 'artistic self-expression' at the Lady at one time.

> *"When the wings of the mountains brush the soul
>   of the sea,
> When the two and the many are one,*

*When illusions of freedom encircle and flee
Then the threads of the challenge are spun."*

The Lady nodded. "Interesting, if uninspired doggerel. Local legend or prophecy of some sort, woven into poetic form."

"Yes, that was my impression." Encouraged by the Lady's unusual broad-mindedness, Mericia drew breath to sing, straining against the confines of her gown. In a clear alto, she strove for the wavering tones of Master Orino's hypnotic melody. "No matter the dream, or the steps you may stray, Our lives entangle your net—"

A chair overturned with a crash. Mericia's eyes flew open wide. The Lady stood, her smooth face hardened into granite, her teeth bared in the gash of a serpentine mouth. Her glare stabbed through Mericia.

"How *dare* you." The words shot out like cannon fire.

"L-lady?" Mericia stammered, paralyzed. She beat back her sudden terror, edging her chair around the corner of the table.

The crazed glare faltered. The Lady drew a ragged gasp and stared down at her hands, clutching at the table edge. The bones and tendons of each finger stood out, striving to dent the oak table. A long moment inched past, marked by the thudding of Mericia's heart.

With slow, deliberate care, the Lady set her chair to rights. The cracks in her composure mended, replaced by a façade of calm. Abandoning her book, papers, and notes scattered on the table, she left the room. The door shut with a decisive click. The last notes of the refrain still lingered in the air.

Mericia dashed away a tear, leaving a smear of clay on her cheek. Her left hand convulsed on the clay mountain, mangling it into a twisted mass. What in the name of heaven had just happened? The Lady was *never* angry. The calm and elegant cat had sat at the table, reviewing her notes, and then, in an instant, a tiger had bared its teeth and snarled.

Still staring at the door, she worked the clay. Lady Lelori's hand emerged from it, grappling something invisible with predatory fingers, as though ripping the life from it.

"But Farren, dear boy, I don't *like* talking to shades. I've always disapproved of your doing so. You can't possibly think I've changed my mind?"

"Aunt Nan, I just thought—"

"Well, you thought wrong, young man. Really." Aunt Nan's wispy figure drifted through Farren's workbench. "For heaven's sake, people might think I was a—"

"Shadebinder," suggested Farren.

"Exactly. The very idea! As if I'd encourage that sort of thing."

Her hand rested on his arm and slipped through it. He bore the sudden chill with equanimity. Aunt Nan hadn't quite adjusted to being dead. "There's something so nauseating about Shadebinders. I mean, really, the *very* idea of imprisoning the soul of dying person, and enslaving it—"

"I'm not a Shadebinder."

"Of course you're not, dear," she said. "None of my nephews is so lacking in good manners."

"I just talk to shades, that's all."

"Oh no, no, no. I wouldn't, if I were you. Such nasty creatures."

"But Aunt Nan, I talk to *you*."

Aunt Nan gave him a withering stare. "I am *not* a shade, Farren. I am a spirit, the soul of a person who belongs to the One. I could ascend to the heavens at any moment. I simply don't choose to do so at the present time."

"No one could possibly doubt that," Farren said. "You have a beautiful soul."

Aunt Nan nodded with stately acquiescence.

"I thought of you right away, when I heard the dreadful

tale. Aunt Nan, I thought to myself, would be the first spirit to call if some poor soul were being tortured in the dungeon. With your crusading spirit—"

"Cut to the chase, dear."

"Do you remember Master Orino?"

"The princess' dance master? Only vaguely. He was from the island. He came to Ramsvalt a few years after I retired. So many changes." She sighed. "People dying right and left, like your dear mother, and even our poor Queen so sadly disabled…"

"Yes, yes." He'd heard much this same speech from Aunt Nan for seven years, both living and as a shade. No, *not* as a shade, as a spirit. "But you know who he is?"

"Oh, naturally. Rather a peculiar young man, given to spouting weak poetry and singing odd-sounding tunes, but an excellent musician. He sang in the Great Hall at the Founding Feast once, about four years back. Don't you remember?"

"Would you know if he'd died?"

"He's not buried in the church yard."

"I know, but he disappeared a few years ago. He might have died somewhere else. Would you know?"

Aunt Nan rubbed her upper arms, uncharacteristically silent.

"Aunt Nan? Would you? I talked to Trissi, the kitchen maid. She's worried, and she thinks the princess is, too. It might settle her mind to know the truth."

Aunt Nan clutched her god star necklace, and paced back and forth through the workbench. "He's not dead. I don't know where he is, or where he's been, but he's not dead."

"How—"

"Hush. Sweetheart, if this is so important, can't you ask someone else? I don't like dungeons, and I can't see living people very well any more. My eyesight seems to have deteriorated since my death. I can't think why."

"That's pretty common," said Farren. "Most spirits can't

97

see me, either. Master Pardell's grandfather can sometimes."

It bothered him, seeing her flit through the bench. For years, she'd driven him mad by cleaning his workshop, sometimes 'organizing' his tools, and burning wood scraps which weren't scraps at all. Even as a shade, she fluttered nearby, expostulating at the mess that enveloped him. Watching her now, pacing through the grime and disorder, heedless of the iron vise holding a table leg and the mounds of filings, he knew she was profoundly disturbed.

"Him," she snorted. "I remember that old coot. Never a pleasant word for anyone."

"Even mother doesn't seem to see me now, most of the time."

"We're attached to the people we worry about, dear boy. She's worried about the Queen, perhaps, but she's confident that you can manage your own life."

"I'm glad she's not worried about me."

"I am," she said.

The words struck him with jarring force. "Aunt Nan, there's no reason to fret about me."

"Of course not, dear."

His conscience twinged. Aunt Nan still wore the drawn look she'd worn for years before her death. The lines in her face hadn't blurred into youth, as usually happened after death. For some reason, she'd clung to her illness even after death. The plague, still? Or was it his fault, binding her with worry about him. *Binding*, he thought. No, it couldn't be. He couldn't have bound Aunt Nan, not without knowing it. He'd never hurt her so.

"The princess," he said, "wouldn't want you to worry about her, either. Forget it, Aunt Nan. I'm glad Master Orino's alive. That's all I needed to know. I don't want you to put off your trip to the heavens because of me. If anyone deserves it, you do. I won't be a burden."

"You've never been a burden, Farren, my dear. You're as

close to being my own son as could ever be." She waved a finger under his nose. "I'll leave when I choose to, and not before. I've a few more things to do first, that's all."

"All right. Thank you for your help." He rested a hand along the side of her face. "And for your love."

"Of course. Perhaps—" She frowned. "Perhaps I could ask around a little. Just with another spirit or two."

"No, no. Just rest."

"*Perhaps*, I said." Sudden mischief glinted in her eyes. "There's Loquerile, you know, such a nice man. You remember, the King's Steward before this one? He died several years ago. Perhaps he'd know something."

Farren found himself alone, his hand poised in mid-air over the iron vise.

The Steward's office held pride of place on the ground level of the main castle's east tower. Slots in the ceiling gave access to the guardroom above, for shouted orders, warnings, and the occasional loaf of bread. Next to the outside door, a tall narrow window overlooked the kitchen yard. The Steward had an excellent view of the watchtower on the hill and part of the barracks nearby. For a man keeping his finger on the pulse of the castle, the location couldn't be bettered.

Farren paused on the threshold and stifled a sneeze. A damp, moldy scent pervaded the cramped room. In fact, like Master Pardell's shop, its disadvantages nearly outweighed the prestige of its location. Dampness crept from the ground and seeped from the tower above, streaking the inner walls with mold. Ancient cabinets crammed the corners, and the desk squatted over most of the floor space.

Farren scuffed his boots on the threshold. "Sir?" He took in the room at a glance. Obviously the Steward was gone, but intended to return. He'd left the main door open, despite the importance of his records. An inner door was also ajar, barely visible between two cabinets. It must lead to the kitchen hallway and the stairwell. Perhaps he'd stepped in there. "Steward Archibald?"

Farren inspected the ancient pine furniture. It certainly wasn't Master Pardell's handiwork. Perennial damp warped the wood. Several of the cabinet doors hung askew, wedged into place by chunks of wood, or propped shut with old boots. If the Steward stored his ledgers here, they'd be on the road to ruin. The solid-looking desk was deeply scarred, and told of generations of men pinning maps to the desktop, and repairing countless bits of leatherwork.

The inner door thumped against the cabinet. Steward Archibald shuffled in, his shoulders and neck rigidly erect. Farren's jaw dropped as the Steward removed a tankard from its perch on the top of his head, and plopped it on the desk with shaking hands. The Steward's hounddog jowls sagged as he closed his eyes, as if the sight of the tankard sickened him.

Instinctively, Farren backed out of the door and stepped to one side. Courtesy urged him to close the door and let the Steward recover himself in private, but curiosity consumed him. What on *earth* was the man doing? Practicing acrobatics?

An odd humming noise, faint and discordant, insinuated itself into Farren's head. He twisted a finger in his ear, trying to relieve it as he peered through the window. The Steward opened his eyes, and with a look of loathing, reached for the tankard again. Caprio stood at his ease in the corner, chewing contemplatively on a spare boot.

"What are you doing to him?" Farren hissed to Caprio.

The Steward jumped violently and threw his hands behind his back.

"Er, I'm sorry, sir," said Farren, "I hope I didn't startle you. I, er, came to discuss my aunt's pension?" He glowered at Caprio, but the Goat just smirked at him.

"Your aunt," said the Steward, his voice hesitant.

"Yes, my aunt." Farren recalled himself and smiled at the man. The Steward backed up, wedging himself into the corner behind the desk.

"I've been training this idiot," remarked Caprio. "I've got him performing some complicated little tricks, juggling and so forth. And to think Scorpion insists mortals are untrainable. Ha! Wait'll I tell him. He'll turn puce, the old reactionary."

"What Scorpion?" said Farren, without thinking.

"*The* Scorpion, fool. The Beings, the gods, you fool, like me, like the Plowman, the Twins—"

"My aunt Nan," Farren told the Steward. Belatedly, he dragged his eyes from the Goat. "She's been receiving the King's pension, but she died. You'll be wanting to stop the allowance now. I've turned in the goats that were loaned to her, and I've moved out of the house."

"You've handed the goats over to the King's herd," the Steward repeated mechanically, "cleared out of the farmhouse, and I should stop the pension." He fumbled with the tankard, balancing it on one finger, and then another. Ale sloshed and dripped down the side.

"What did I tell you?" said Caprio. "Perfectly trainable." The keening pitch rose, and the Steward stood on one foot.

"The pension wasn't in money," Farren said, through his teeth. "Foodstuffs, bolts of cloth, provisions. I just wanted you to know that she wouldn't be drawing anything in the future."

"Oh," said Steward Archibald, putting down one foot, and holding the other in the air.

"For your records," prompted Farren. "So you could reassign the farmhouse."

"Oh."

"You're not helping!" Farren snapped at Caprio.

The tankard tipped off the Steward's finger and plummeted to the floor, splashing ale across the Steward's tunic. Farren lunged at the falling tankard, and snatched it halfway to the floor. He offered it to the Steward, who backed away from him. Great. Now another story would go the rounds! The Shadebinder shows up, and the Steward goes mad. Farren set the tankard on the desk, and wiped his hands on his thighs. "Er, sorry about that. Sir? Are you all right?"

"Yes, I'm sure. I mean—" Archibald dropped into a chair, and picked up a ledger from the desk. "Your aunt, you say." He opened the book randomly, closed his eyes as though he were in pain, and pushed it away. "I'm afraid," Archibald said, "you've caught me at a bad moment. I keep getting this feeling..."

A feeling, huh? Farren glanced at the Goat. "Quit it, you fool," he said in a low voice. "Leave him alone."

Caprio gave him an offended look. "You wanted into the dungeon, didn't you? I'm getting you there. Mortals! Try to help them, and all they do is complain."

Farren's hand flew to his ear. A faint, discordant sound emanated from the Goat, of whistling high notes mixed with the distant sound of thunder. Half music, half threat, the inaudible vibrations engulfed the hapless Steward.

Archibald stood up, his quivering hands cradling his head. Words streamed from his mouth. "There's this, well, a feeling of impending doom, so to speak. I suppose it's just because of the Progress. So many changes, you know." The music careened into an anguished screech. Archibald fell into his chair again, clapping his hands over his ears.

"Would you lay off him?" shouted Farren, beyond caring whether the man heard him or not. "It's cruel to badger the poor man like this. He'll be afraid of his own shadow soon, afraid to step out the door."

"That's it!" The Steward sprang to his feet and pointed out the window. He glanced at Farren, and tucked his hand behind his back. "That's it, you know! Outside the door." His voice deepened into a groan. "Disaster is coming."

"It's pointless brutality," Farren snapped.

"Really?" said the Goat. "Think it through, blockhead."

If Farren had a Shadebinder's legendary powers, he could drive Caprio away in the blink of an eye. Unfortunately, Farren got the blame for being a Shadebinder with none of the benefits. He could talk until he was blue in the face, but Caprio wouldn't budge unless it suited him.

Besides, the Steward was right, although for the wrong reasons. There *was* disaster in the air. The shades themselves were no bother, and even the Goat was only a nuisance. Still, the oddities accumulated: a congregation of shades, a mischievous Being, a prophesying dance master tortured but not killed, and everything coming to a head just before a Progress celebrating an ascension to Ailsandia's throne. Farren felt a growing certainty that this time trouble had a human face.

Aunt Nan, for all her chiding, had gossiped mightily with the former Steward Loquerile. Archibald, trained at the slower-paced Khonsvalt, was now drowning in the sea of demands from the Lady, the King, the senior castle staff, the Guard, and the tenants of the King's property. Yesterday, the King had returned from a two-week sojourn in Selefrevalt. Lady Lelori had met with him immediately, and her accusations of flagrant incompetence spread like wildfire through the castle retainers. Archibald had good reason to be a worried man.

Archibald sighed, and shuffled back to his desk. He extracted a roll of parchment from a shelf and flattened it on the desk. "Princess' Nanny," he muttered. "Two acres? Five? Ah yes, here we are. Is that it?" He looked up.

Farren studied the man's blood-shot eyes for guilt or deceit. They flickered with good intentions, self-distrust, and an unhealthy share of dread. He slumped with the permanent exhaustion of a man who'd been stretched to his limits trying to perform duties he barely understood.

"Young man?" said Archibald. He tapped the map. "Is this it?"

"Yes, that's it, sir."

"Nice little spot. Thanks for letting me know." His eyes roamed the room. "You needn't move out right away. There's no rush."

"Thank you, sir, but Master Pardell offered me the rooms over his shop. It's more convenient to my work."

Archibald rerolled the parchment, one end tight, and the other a loose coil. "Ah."

The Goat arose with a graceful deliberation. The haunting music intensified.

Archibald swallowed hard and burst out, "I don't suppose you know anything about castle construction, young man? No, no, forget that. Stupid question."

"Is this about the watchtower?" asked Farren, turning a sidelong glance to the Goat.

Caprio tossed his head. "It's about time you tumbled to it. I was most kind, and lent a hoof in your little investigation."

Archibald jumped to his feet, eyes ablaze with excitement. "Yes, the watchtower! That's it, exactly. Why the watchtower? Come on, now, you had a *reason* for mentioning the watchtower."

"Well, no reason really," said Farren.

Archibald grabbed him by the arm and towed him out the door. The Goat followed with a self-satisfied "Harruff."

"There *was* a reason. You feel it too, don't you? Every time I look at the watchtower," Archibald threw out a shaking hand towards the tower, "I get this —aahh!" Fascinated, Farren watched the Goat rear up, and swipe a forehoof down the Steward's spine. "I get these horrible shivers," finished Archibald, shuddering.

"About the watchtower," said Farren. It really shouldn't be funny, but oh how he wanted to *laugh*. He ached to share the humor with someone, but everyone he knew was half-blind. Irresistibly, his sense of mischief swelled. He shrugged mentally. Perhaps the Goat's plan wasn't so bad after all. He turned a grave face to Steward Archibald. "Actually, sir, I have been wondering about the tower's foundation."

"That's exactly it. I have this terrible feeling that it's not stable."

"Well, sir, it's possible that the foundation has suffered over time." Farren held out his hand, angled against the distant image of the tower.

Archibald gasped and grabbed his hand. "Look at that, look at it! It's crooked!"

"The tower's crooked?" Farren attempted to straighten his hand, but the Steward grappled it, sighting on the tower feverishly. Farren glared at the Goat.

Caprio stamped a hoof. "Oh, all right. Ask your questions, and I'll leave him alone. I'll even reward the poor sucker."

Farren nodded to the Goat. "Umm, well, sir, it does seem a bit off. I wonder whether the ground could be settling. Perhaps an underground stream weakened it." Caprio grunted his approval. "If so, the foundation could be at risk."

"Oh damn," said Archibald, his shoulders sagging. "What about the rest of the castle?" He spun around as though expecting it to crumble into heaps before his eyes.

"No, sir, I haven't noticed a problem anywhere else."

"Ah, that's good."

"Unless," Caprio suggested, "the problem spreads."

"That is," said Farren, "unless the problem spreads."

"Spreads..."

"But it depends on the cause. An underground stream would be bad news, but if it's just been undermined some-how, it could be shored up."

"Undermined? How?"

"Oh," Farren waved an arm, "any number of ways. A support in the cellars might have weakened with the last earthquake. Or perhaps something has tunneled under it."

"Tunneled," Archibald muttered. He slapped the roll of parchment into his other hand, once, twice, three times. "Tunneled."

"Anyway, I'm sorry to bring it up. I'll tell my Master you're on top of the matter. When, er, if any of the other merchants brings it up, he'll allay their concerns. Good-bye sir, and thank you for your time."

"Wait. You work with Master Pardell, you said? Quiet man, keeps to himself, right?"

"Yes, that's true."

"And you work with wood?"

"Cabinetry, fine woodworking, yes, sir."

"What about beams? Pillars?"

"Oh no, I know nothing about masonry. You'd need Master Geoffrey for that. Although," Farren added, "he might be in Khonsvalt right now. I know his journeymen are here. I saw them gossiping at dinner. They'd help you out. Thank you again, sir."

"But you and Master Pardell, between you," persevered Archibald, "could at least determine if there's a problem? I don't want to bother Master Geoffrey over nothing, especially as he's in Khonsvalt."

And especially as his journeymen gossip. "Well, yes, I'm sure Master Pardell could give you an initial opinion."

After several minutes of earnest talk culminating in a hearty handshake, Farren watched the Steward head for his office. Farren pointed at the Goat. "You said something about a reward for the poor man?"

"All right, all right," said the Goat. "I'll take care of it." He vanished and reappeared in the office doorway. The Steward walked through him and shuddered.

Farren grimaced to himself and headed back to Master Pardell's shop. Now, how to break the news? The Master would not be happy.

In his office, Steward Archibald collapsed in his chair, wondering what else would go wrong with this day. Ah, the girl had brought his midday dinner, meat, bread, and ale. He reached for the jug.

He sucked in his cheeks, watching mesmerized as rich red wine tumbled into his tankard, the thick sweet perfume encircling his weary head. Such stuff never came his way, except by the meager half-glass in the King's presence twice a year.

His stunned disbelief slithered into delight. He inhaled deeply, and ventured a sip. Heaven. And a whole jug of the stuff! What if the maid discovered her mistake and came to retrieve it? He snatched up the jug and stowed it under his desk, barricading it with dusty ledgers. Only then did he lean back in his chair, close his eyes, and savor the delight that had come out of nowhere.

"Thank you," he breathed, with deep gratitude. Which of the Many had spared a moment for the Steward's ale jug? He had no clue. It was best to make his prayer general. "Dear lord, thank you!"

A distant voice made him open his eyes and search his empty office.

"No problem," it said.

Chapter Seven

You're Nan's boy, aren't you?" Bonnara said, slamming her cleaver through a mutton knee joint. "Maari's youngest."

"Yes, ma'am," said Farren.

"I don't allow followers in my kitchen, Farren," said Bonnara. The cleaver hit the block with unnecessary force.

"I'm just delivering a message."

"She's had it already, if you mean a letter from that rascally brother of yours. Not Terrell, the other one. What's his name? Denys."

Farren hid a smile. For all her disdain, Aunt Nan's old friend had their names down pat. "He asked me to give her something. Should I leave it with you, ma'am?"

Bonnara pursed her lips and threw a look over her shoulder. "She's over there."

The windowless kitchens tunneled like linked caverns underneath the castle. Aunt Nan used to spin tales about new servants, lost for days in the kitchen labyrinth before they staggered out, wan, exhausted, and extremely well fed. More than once a stray waif had simply moved in and begun running errands, everyone assuming he belonged to someone else. The kitchen servants roasted from everburning fires, dripped with sweat, and ran headlong under Bonnara's constant instructions. Not one of them ever left by choice. Bonnara might be irascible, bossy, and judgmental, but her kind heart embraced anyone who wandered into her domain. Her staff ate well, slept soundly, and laughed while they worked.

Beyond the main kitchens lay the fish room, the meat room, and privy kitchen. The first was crammed with barrels of fish preserved in seaweed; the second, with meats both smoked and freshly slaughtered; and the last, with the complicated tools and ovens used to dress food for the King's table, including sweets and savories. Tucked inside the privy kitchen was the so-called King's Pantry, with its heavily locked spicery. On the other end of the kitchen labyrinth was the boiling room, in which fifty-gallon vats boiled the daily stews, scenting the humid air with meat and onions. The massive baking operation occupied a huge warren all its own. The support facilities were in detached buildings: the slaughterhouse, grain storage, and smokehouse. In their daily effort to feed over four hundred people, a multitude of servants rarely moved slower than a trot.

Despite the flurry of movement, Trissi presided over a huge table mounded with green and yellow squash and sacks of broad beans. Several large baskets sat behind her, lined with heavy cloth. Trissi wielded her knife with speed and skill, splitting a squash, scooping seeds into one basket, chopping the rest into hunks, and stowing them in a second basket.

"Make yourself useful," Bonnara told him, gesturing towards a basket of early nuts. "Crush the shells. Don't interrupt her work, and don't let her stand up. Stupid girl twisted her knee on the stairs a few nights ago, running around in the dark. What your Denys would say, I don't know."

"I'm sorry," said Trissi. She ducked her head in pretended penitence, her eyes sparkling with mischief.

"Humph." Bonnara let fly the back of her hand at Trissi's ear, missing her head by several inches. The cook stumped away, handing water buckets to two chattering kitchen maids, and shooing them out the door.

Trissi gave Farren a speculative glance as she chopped vegetables into uniform hunks. He picked up the bag of nuts and looked around helplessly. A small chuckle escaped her.

"Pour some in that coffer, grab the mallet, and hit hard," she instructed.

As the nuts rattled into the open crate, a blonde girl, her hair bound up at her neck, swooped up behind Trissi.

"Gimme that, Riss," she caroled. She grabbed the corners of the cloth in the basket, and hauled up a load of squash chunks. "Ha! I got you! You were about to lug it off yourself, weren't you?"

"Thanks, Karina," said Trissi.

"And who's this young man you're flirting with?" She arched an eyebrow, smiling.

"He's Denys' brother, you fool!"

"That's what you'd *like* me to think!" Trissi's mouth quirked and Karina laughed. Karina disappeared in the direction of the boiling room. Trissi pulled a heavy cloth from a stack on the floor, and tucked it into the basket.

"Um," said Farren. He stole a glance at Trissi. He picked up the mallet, and smashed nuts. After a few whacks, he shifted into a steady rhythm. "Denys sent me a note. He wrote to you, too?"

"Yes." She kept her eyes on the table, her laughter gone.

Farren dropped the mallet and slung the leather pouch off his back. "He asked me to give you this." He withdrew a small travel box, no larger than a loaf of bread. He set it on the table, picked up his mallet, and concentrated on battering nuts.

The oak box sported inlays of three woods, outlining a fruiting plum tree. Trissi brushed the top with reddened fingers. She lifted the lid and sucked in her breath. The box opened into three levels, each rising to a different height. He'd lined the partitions of each compartment with scraps of brocade from Aunt Nan's treasured rag box.

Trissi closed it, tracing the pattern of the plum tree with one finger. Her hand stilled as she saw the ghostly tracings of a goat's head in the clouds overhead.

A plum tree and Caprio.

"This is from Denys?" she asked, her voice doubtful.

"It is. He asked me to make it before he left. The design's mine, but he'd approve if he'd heard about your garden exploit."

Her eyes were watchful. "And will he? Hear about the garden?"

"Oh yes," said Farren cheerfully. "As soon as I see him, unless he's gotten my letter first."

Trissi laughed, her eyes alight. "Or mine."

Farren grinned at her. "You *can* laugh. Now there's a surprise. I thought you didn't know how."

"I smile when there's reason to smile," she said. Her eyes danced. "Denys told me about you."

"Good." He wrapped the box in a white cloth and set it nearby. "I trust nothing too frightening."

"No, not that." She attacked another squash with her knife. "He wanted me to understand, I think. *Not* to be frightened." She gave him a quick look.

"I'm not a—"

"I know. But you see them, don't you? Shades? Lots of them."

"Not shades," he said. "Spirits, my Aunt Nan says. Spirits are bound for heaven. She was most pointed about it."

"I can just hear her saying that." Trissi shook her head. "I still miss her. She was such lively company. Even after she stopped visiting, Bonnara sent me to see her sometimes."

Baskets of special foods had magically appeared in Nan's house on a regular basis. "You're the one who brought the baskets. I didn't know that."

"That's how I met Denys." Her cheeks turned pink. "It seems odd that I never met you."

"I stayed in my workshop when visitors came."

"Oh."

"You see shades too, don't you?" he said.

"Oh no." Her eye caught on the box and Caprio's form. "Well, just the one."

"He's not a shade. He's a Being, whatever that is. He's hard to miss."

"Boy, that's the truth." she said fervently. "But it's not the same. It must be very hard for you. Oh all right, I can see you don't want to talk about it. But if you don't mind, there's another thing. Denys said that you see colors in people's eyes, and know all about them?" She let a moment pass, and continued thoughtfully, "That could be a very uncomfortable trait."

"In a brother-in-law, you mean."

The glint in Trissi' eyes acknowledged the hit. Suddenly, they were old friends. "I think you've mashed those nuts enough. Pour them out into an empty bag and start over. Someone else will pick through them. It's the muscle work we need done."

Farren obeyed. "I'm going into the dungeon tomorrow with Master Pardell. It's official, too. I don't have to sneak around about it. I can explore a bit. You don't need to take any risks. I figured you'd be safe for a couple of days, with your knee hurting. How is it?"

"A lot better, but I don't think I'll be dancing any time soon. That's why Bonnara's got me on chopping detail." She eyed the basket of squash chunks and threw another cloth over the top. She picked through the remaining squashes, selected three, and slit them lengthwise. "She won't let me climb stairs, either," she said, exasperated. "And there's so much to do right now, with the King back, and the runners here from the outlying Patrols. Though it was nice getting

Denys' note from the Southern runner."

A scullery maid staggered across the kitchen with a basket of meat scraps. Karina popped out, grabbed the basket's other side, and they hauled it into the boiling room.

Trissi lowered her voice. "I got some gossip on the dungeon. Bonnara's got a feud going on with the guard captain. She says he's always demanding more food, enough for twice the number of guards." They exchanged a significant look. "It started years ago. At first, she wouldn't do it, said they were greedy wastrels, and useless tubs of lard. The Steward complained—that's the old one, not Archibald. She wouldn't listen, but eventually Lady Lelori took it up with her. She's still seething, years later. Oh, she was just savage about it! The Lady's an interfering bitch, a calculating besom, and a lot of things I'd never repeat to a man." She grinned. "I learned a few new words, too."

"A lot of extra food," Farren mused.

"Hmm. She gets around it by sending stale stuff, leftovers, scraps that burned. It's funny, though. They never complain about the quality."

Their eyes met. "We can guess who's eating the bad stuff."

"Yes," said Trissi. "Farren, would you hand me that bowl of butter? And a clump of grapes? And pick me out a few handfuls of those nuts. Thanks." Trissi jabbed small holes into the squash and nested grapes inside them. "I can't believe you've actually talked your way into the dungeon legally. How did you do it?"

Farren told the story, enlarging on Caprio's assistance.

Trissi choked down her laughter. "Oh you rat! To think I missed it."

"I was lucky to catch the Steward alone. Usually, people mob him with questions."

"Poor man. Bonnara doesn't like him much. She says he's incompetent." Her voice dropped into Bonnara's sharp staccato speech. "And she can't think *how* he got the job, even if he *was* Loquerile's nephew." She stifled a giggle at Farren's look of appreciation. "But even she's sorry for him now. Poor old Archibald, he's never handled a Progress before, but he did the best he could. He arranged for stopping points at various manors, sent on supplies. But, he didn't realize that the roads were in terrible shape, and couldn't manage all the carts, and he forgot to order half the carriages, so they haven't even been built yet."

Farren winced. "Poor man. He should've read the old ledgers. Steward Loquerile must have documented everything."

Trissi rapped his hand with her butter spoon. "Ah, but last time the royal family left from Selefrevalt. They didn't used to live here, remember? Anyway, he sent out all his assistants, snatched up every able-bodied man he could, and has them out rebuilding the roads. He was out there himself until he got word of the King's return. They'll probably still be fixing the roads as we bump our way over them."

"You're going on Progress?" asked Farren, surprised.

"Oh yes." Her eyes twinkled, and dropped to the line of halved squashes on the table as if she were embarrassed. Farren understood. The Southern Patrol would be at the Island, and so would Denys. From what he'd seen of Trissi, she'd manage whatever she chose, including joining the pack of servants going on Progress. She'd probably manage Denys himself, too. Ah well. He could imagine worse fates.

Bonnara's sharp voice rang across the kitchen. "What on earth are you doing, Trissi? You're supposed to be chopping squash for the stew."

Trissi set her chin stubbornly, dotting the line of squash with nuts, butter and a drizzle of honey. "Lady Siree requested a special dish for the Queen."

"I know, I heard her," snapped Bonnara. "Strong colors, of all the foolish ideas." Worry deepened her wrinkles. "Her

Majesty's getting worse, the poor dear. She's notional. Lady Siree says she was up on the keep in the middle of the night trying to catch falling stars. I ask you!"

"The Princess brought her down," murmured Trissi.

"Humph. And tumbled down the stairs herself, crippling her knee as badly as you did yours. I'll swear you two are twins, although," she patted Trissi's shoulder, "you're much the nicer. My word, you've fixed enough for the Rimlands Patrol. None of these louts will even *eat* squash unless we throw it in the stew."

"The Princess and Lady Lelori are dining with the Queen until the King's return."

"Still, that's no reason—"

"Lady Lelori would notice if the servings were small," said Trissi primly.

"That woman," exploded Bonnara. "Don't get me started on her. She's got Steward Archibald thinking the King will have him up for treason, all for want of a stupid carriage or two. I suppose you want these baked, as if I hadn't enough to do." Bonnara stalked off, tray of squash in hand, still fuming.

"So tell me, Farren, when you look at my eyes," Trissi teased, "what do the colors tell you?"

Farren recovered his wits and glanced at her eyes. "Strong loyalties."

"That's all?" she said.

Damn it, he wanted to grin at her. *She's Denys' girl*, he thought, *not mine.* "And," he added recklessly, "you lie, when the truth won't serve you."

Her anger flared, and dissolved into silent laughter. "And if you looked into a mirror at your own eyes, what would you see?"

Farren stopped pounding nuts and stared at her, caught offguard. Reluctantly, he chuckled. "Exactly the same thing."

Trissi balled a fist and struck the air. "One hit for me!"

෬

"I greatly appreciate your help, Master Pardell," Steward Archibald said, craning his neck over his shoulder as he climbed the hill. "Of course, the watchtower's primary function is precautionary, but one never knows what's around the bend. If the fortifications should prove faulty... I'm so glad you agreed to inspect it."

Master Pardell ignored the Steward's remarks. His glower singed the ears of his unruly journeyman. The Master clamped his hands behind his back as he strode after the Steward.

"The dungeons have very little use these days," the Steward said, "as you'll see, only a couple of occupants for the most dreadful crimes."

"Extortionists, no doubt," grunted Master Pardell.

The Steward winced, but Farren knew the shot was aimed at him. He slowed his step, letting the Steward get ahead of them. He regretted pitting two honest men against each other with lies and subterfuge. He'd told the Master the whole story, striving to explain his urgency over a story that sounded weaker every time he considered it.

"I'm sorry, Master," said Farren. "I have to know the truth. I didn't know a better way."

The Master grimaced as though he'd bitten into a maggot. "You owe me, boy."

"Yes, Master."

The Master shot him a glance, satisfaction flaring in his eyes. "All right, then." He lengthened his stride to catch up with the Steward.

Farren sighed. So, the Master had finally gotten his way. He'd been after Farren for months to join the Progress with the other royal artisans, insisting that his inflamed hip joints barred him from making the journey. Obviously, he hoped to goad Farren into applying for his Master's pin at the Guild's convocation. In the last weeks, he'd redoubled his efforts. The moment the Guild saw the travel case Farren designed for the princess, the Master maintained, it would rush to award him the pin.

At first, Farren rejected the idea. For a suspected Shadebinder, hell itself couldn't be worse than weeks in the company of suspicious strangers. Yesterday, though, the vision of a pair of dark brown eyes danced before him. Perhaps, just perhaps, he should go after all. Trissi might need him, and he'd promised to watch out for Denys' girl.

The Master's stride lengthened, no longer hindered by exaggerated ailments. The Master knew he'd accepted the bargain: travel on the Progress for a faked inspection of the tower.

The grass massed thickly over the mound, bald only on the worn path to the kitchen yard, and in the circle of beaten earth around the tower and adjoining barracks. Guards leaned against the barracks, cleaning their crossbows and leathers. Three sat cross-legged, throwing dice on the ground. Shades mingled among them, their jests carrying over the casual talk of the living.

The tower guard moved aside, with a nod for the Steward. The Steward stepped into the guardroom, closely followed by Master Pardell. The guardroom had an iron door on either side. One was propped open. Through it, Farren saw the stairs leading up to the tower. The other door was shut. The Steward inserted a key, the great lock clanked, and he stood back allowing them to enter.

A peculiar tingling ran over Farren's shoulders as he entered, as if he'd jumped through a thin sheet of flame or ice. He quick-stepped out of its path, almost landing on the Master's heels. His head felt muffled, as though shrouded in burlap bags. He touched his ears and his eyes, but the haunting sense of being blind and deaf persisted. Stone smothered him, shoved down on his shoulders, and weighted him to the floor. He lifted a foot, and then the other, aware of his foolishness. Of course he could move his feet. Nothing glued him to the flagstones. He could run, if he chose.

The Steward pulled the door shut, locked it, and started down the narrow stairway, leaving them to follow.

"What's the matter with you, boy?" hissed the Master.

"Nothing."

"Then stand up straight, you fool." The Master made his way down the narrow staircase.

Farren lingered for a moment, wondering why the Steward had bothered to lock the door. The dungeon was empty, right? Farren forced his feet to follow and tried to shake the cobwebs from his brain. This was just a watchtower, like hundreds of others. The thick stone wall was centuries old, warmed by the sun on the outside, cool on the inside. Their footsteps scraped in the darkness. The glow of the Steward's shuttered lantern blinked on and off as it descended, disappearing behind the continual curve of the stairwell.

The walls seemed to hug them closer. He dragged in a deep breath. How would it be to live here for years, imprisoned in pitch-blackness? Would his eyes stop working after a year or two? What about his limbs, ears, and nose?

Gradually the smell of damp mold mingled with another stench far less appealing.

"Very rarely used," mumbled the Steward, shooting a surreptitious look at the Master. The lie shouted from his eyes. Even a blind man would have seen it; a deaf man would have heard it. The dungeon might be empty now, but it had been in use as recently as yesterday, and would be again tomorrow. The sharp smell of urine and the sourness of human excrement nearly swamped the more subtle scents of decay and despair.

Farren stepped forward hastily, touching the Master's back. The Master pulled away from him, swung around, and cuffed Farren on the ear. The wordless accusation stabbed Farren with shame. The Steward said the dungeon was unused. Therefore, the King said the dungeon was unused. Not even an artisan of Master Pardell's eminence dared accuse the King of a lie. Such unnatural restraint trampled the Master's beliefs into the mud.

The cuff was more reassuring than painful. Farren was accused and forgiven in a single blow. "I'm sorry, Master," he whispered.

"Here we are. This is the bottom level. There are extra lanterns on that rack." The Steward unshuttered his lantern fully, and raised it high above his head. "I'll unlock all the gates. Watch out where you step—rats, you know. No men in here these days."

The lie echoed through the shadowed room. There were no shuffling feet, hoarse coughs, or moans of pain. Prisoners had been here, very recently. But where were they now? Farren's gut twisted. The guards could have executed them, or marched them away to the mines, Master Orino included, and he'd never know.

The metal gate clanged against the wall. The Steward disappeared into the next stone cavern. His voice wafted behind him thinly, "No instruments of torture, you see. Ha ha."

The Master walked along the edge of the room in stiff-legged offense, holding his lantern rigidly before him.

"Master—"

"It's the dishonesty of our pose that I object to," the Master said, keeping his voice low.

"I know, I'm sorry."

"Nevertheless, there's an intriguing mystery here. The King has every right to keep prisoners. Why should Archibald deny it? It's a pointless lie, and stupidly obvious." He indicated a corner of the room, caked with feces. "Fresh," he said succinctly. "Don't shudder like that, boy. You obviously expected something like this."

They passed the gate and entered the next room. Master Pardell stopped short and Farren walked into him. Farren followed his gaze to the opposite wall. The stones were different here, larger, more carefully cut.

"Foundation stones," Farren said. "It must be an exterior wall. Master? What's wrong?"

The Master pointed to the floor in front of the wall. Hollows sank in the stone, left by countless footsteps over countless years. The wall itself shone strangely. The Master held his hand to the wall. Farren did the same, cool dampness coating his palm.

The Master made a strangled sound. "They lick the walls for water, for the seepage. It's criminal." He turned on his heel, in pursuit of the Steward.

"Master? Master, look there."

The Master hesitated and bent to look. A murky shift in shadow marked the bottom of the wall. Farren knelt in front of it, resting his hands on cold vertical bars. The stone wall jutted out into a small rectangular pit behind the grate. A storage bin?

"Little Ease," said the Master, the words dropping like stones. "The pit. They stuff a man in there."

"How could they? There's not room."

"Not enough room to sit, lie down, or stand. It's passive torture, but it is, most definitely, torture."

"They leave men in there overnight?"

"They leave them there until they die. It takes weeks or years, depending on whether someone feeds them. Can't you see?"

"See?" said Farren numbly.

"The shades, boy. The shades of those who've died here."

Farren straightened, turning his head from side to side. His obtuseness shocked him. "There aren't *any* shades here, Master. You're right, there should be. That's a good sign, isn't it, Master? They must be fed all right, reasonably well-treated." He flinched at the Master's pitying look, and recalled Trissi's remarks about the food. "Okay, you're right. Men've died here, probably a lot of them. Why aren't their shades here? What am I missing?"

"Later, boy. Check the blasted walls, and keep an eye out for a body or two. I'd wager they moved the ones that could walk, and carried the others. If there's anyone left, you'll find him chained to walls or stuck in a pit. And don't bother calling out for prisoners. If they left anyone, you can bet they knocked him unconscious. Besides, Archibald would hear you."

They followed the Steward through several interconnected caverns, joined by imposing metal gates. The Master made a show of thumping the walls and peering at cracks in the floor, distracting the Steward with a flow of technical jargon. Farren trailed along behind them, surreptitiously poking into shadows and kicking at mounds of debris. He discovered two more Little Ease cages and a deep pit in the floor, all covered by grates, and all empty. With every step, the ceiling loomed closer, the crushing weight driving the air from his chest.

As if from a great distance, he heard Master Pardell speak. "Steward Archibald, I believe we've seen all the foundation walls. That's sufficient for my purpose. Of course, for an expert opinion, you'd need Master Geoffrey."

"Ah," said the Steward.

"It looks good to me. The foundation's probably secure for another hundred years anyway."

" Really?" said the Steward hopefully. "What about the watchtower's tilt? I looked at it again this morning, and it seemed far more pronounced."

The Master tightened his lips, glancing sidelong at Farren. "The tilt," he said, "has not changed noticeably in the last twenty years. We've got to expect some settling. I'm certain you carry out routine maintenance inspections on an annual basis."

The Steward coughed. "Oh, naturally. Annual basis."

The Master walked back towards the entrance. "No doubt you'll attend to that while the royal family's gone on Progress."

Farren's lantern shed a pool of light, surrounding him with an illusion of safety. He fought the urge to speed up and studied every inch of the floor and wall as he went. His sense of failure grew as the miasma of despair overwhelmed him with its own distinctive odors. Stale vomit, cheap wine, rancid cheese, rotting carcasses.

His steps slowed, as though he were walking through a marsh, and bogged down entirely. There was something—just a wisp of a thought. He turned, raising his lantern, and looked into the darkness of the cavern behind him, and the rusting metal gate slung back against the wall. He took a few steps back, resting his hand on the gate, and opened his senses, looking for shades, rats, movement, anything. His nose gave him the answer.

Sour wine. Behind the gate, against the wall.

The rumbling voices of the Master and the Steward, two rooms beyond, offered scant comfort. He set down his lantern and lifted the end of the gate, swinging it forward inch by inch, straining his muscles in his effort to make no sound. The Master's light receded, and he fought the urge to run after him. It was stupid to hang back like this. There'd be a battered tankard behind the gate, with small drops still clinging to it. No doubt guards smuggled the stuff in for the scraps of money the prisoners squirreled away. Even as he scoffed at himself, a sense of urgency consumed him. He angled the gate two feet from the wall and let it settle to the floor. He held his lantern into the pitch-black triangle beyond and flinched.

A dark hole gashed the wall, barred with rusty iron. A Little Ease. Inside crouched a battered wreck of a man, still breathing. The man huddled, half-sitting, half-standing, arms curled between his knees. On the shoulders sat a lump of something. Farren saw it, rejected it—this couldn't be a man, not this mangled blob of flesh. Knotted scars took the place of ears. The face was a random oblong of awkward lumps, with a slash across the base where the mouth should be. The few teeth jutted at strange angles. In place of a nose were slits, mere holes in scar tissue.

Oh gods, great and small, no, this can't be...

"Master Orino?" Farren breathed.

The thing in front of him took a rattling breath. A wash of wine-laden air took Farren in the face. Filled with sick pity, he drew back. In his dreadful state, the drunken slumber was a blessing.

A sickeningly practical thought hit him. Why hadn't they knocked the man out with a mallet to the head and dragged him with the others? A moment's glance at the bars delivered the answer. There must have been a lock once, or jailors could never have shoved him in, but the lock was gone. The grate was welded in place, its rust and dirt offering mute evidence that it had lain undisturbed for years.

Four years. It had been four years since Master Orino disappeared. Four years of this hell. Why hadn't they killed him? And in this torment, why hadn't he simply died?

"Farren," the Master called.

The Steward would come back for Farren, if he didn't hurry. The Steward might be a well-meaning man, but he knew about the prisoners. He knew about this pit with the human wreck inside. He must have known. Silently, Farren replaced the gate, closing the man into obscurity.

"I won't forget you," he whispered. "I'll do something, I promise."

He forced himself to think rationally. If the Steward knew, the King knew. If the King knew and wanted his secret kept, it would *be* kept. If a stupid journeyman threatened his little secret, there was another Little Ease available for his eternal resting place. And another for the Master's. *Oh God, the Master.* He snatched up his lantern, and strode to the others.

"My apologies," he managed to say. "Thought I found a spot where the stone leached away. No, no," he waved away the Steward's sudden look of alarm. "I was wrong. Just one of those old pits." His voice broke down.

The Master gave him a sharp look. "Steward Archibald, I do have something to say."

"Master," Farren interrupted urgently. "We mustn't waste the Steward's time. I'm sure he has a thousand things to do before Progress."

The Steward's vague doubt degenerated into the look of a man facing a pack of hungry wolves. "Er, yes, I'm afraid so. As long as you're sure about the foundation?"

"The foundation's fine," snapped the Master. "But I've a question about water." He scowled. "I am the King's man. Let there be no doubt of that."

Oh gods, he was going to mention the wall, licked by hundreds of men for moisture. "Of course not," Farren overrode him swiftly. "Master Pardell has always been the King's man. That's why he wants you to double-check the mound for water seepage and underground streams. The stonemasons can give you the name of an expert."

The Master glanced at him sharply and snapped his mouth shut. After a moment's indecision, he grunted, and headed up the steps. Farren followed him, hearing the screech of the gates behind him and clank of the Steward's key in the lock. They waited at the top of the stairs until the Steward hurried up to let them out. Farren passed the threshold, enduring the horrid itching sensation a second time. Sight and sound rushed over him in great waves. He stepped out of the guardroom onto the hill, and sighed in relief, shading his eyes from the sun's glare. A ruckus down the hill bombarded his ears, but it was only a couple of boys, fighting in a whirlwind of dust, surrounded by cheering spectators. Four shades in guard uniform marched down the hill towards the stables. His glance rested on them gratefully. Never had he been so glad to see shades.

"Thank you very much, Master Pardell." The Steward clamped his hand around the Master's and shook it heartily.

Farren shut out the Steward's fervent thanks and promises and stared back at the tower. He was wildly glad to be free of it, and guilt-stricken at the thought of Master Orino, still wedged into that poisonous rattrap. A tug on his elbow brought him back to the present. He and the Master walked down the hill.

"You found him," stated the Master.

"Yes. He was—" He drew a shuddering breath. "Yes. I did. Master, why? Why would anyone do such things? Even for treason or murder? They should kill him and be done with it. Death would be kinder." The foolishness of his words jarred him. Kindness was irrelevant to those who buried men in dungeons.

"You can think of most of the reasons yourself. One of them, you should know better than anyone else."

"The shades? But there weren't any shades, Master. All over the damned castle there are shades, shades in every corner! But not in the dungeon. Not a single one."

"And why not? Because someone prevented them. I'm betting those prisoners have secrets. If they die, and they're shades, an enemy could bind them and extract those secrets. All it takes is a Shadebinder."

"What?" Farren gasped.

The Master rapped his shoulder. "You're not a Shadebinder,

Farren, I know that. But if such a sorcerer exists, what then? Think about it. If he could seize your worst enemies, bind their shades, and recruit such an army against you, wouldn't you fear?"

"You think there's a real Shadebinder, acting against the King?"

"Unlikely, but you never know. Emperor Theomedon usually has a sorcerer or two at his court, never very good ones, mind you. Not in Elizar's class at all. But if the King feels at risk from the Empire, matters are well beyond our scope. You and I couldn't do a thing about it. Not a thing." The Master's mouth twisted. "We can't even be sure those poor wretches get water, instead of having to lick the damned walls." With a violent oath, the Master doubled his stride in his haste to return to his shop.

As they passed the kitchen yards, they passed Trissi leaning against the wall, watching. Farren didn't notice.

Chapter Eight

The sorcerer Hesselin brooded from his third floor window. From this height, the harbor lay before him like a perfect jewel, a double-pear shape, joined at the stems. The busy docks and warehouses were as much a sign of prosperity as the palace itself. Ailsandia was a gem, rich and lovely. Elizar himself had yearned for it, and clung to it when his other ventures failed. Hesselin, like Elizar, had an eye for beauty and power. Ailsandia had stirred his covetous heart from the moment he saw it, a decade ago.

If Elizar had lived, had killed his wife before the bitch killed him, he'd have legitimized his only son. Then, with Ailsandia's matrilineal line broken, its royalty would have reverted to common-sense tradition, from father to son, down through the ages. In time, Hesselin would have been king of Ailsandia. His parents had told him the story, with a sort of limp-willed wistfulness. It meant nothing to them, a mere fluke of history, slightly amusing. In a flash of insight, Hesselin had understood it all, that sense of seclusion and superiority he'd felt since infancy. He wasn't the son of farmers, but the direct descendant of a mighty king and sorcerer.

Ailsandia, this bright, bustling, vital land, was meant to be his. Ailsa and her get had no right to it. She and her forebears had offered the Island to the Empire as a gift, while clinging to their palace and titles with simpering self-satisfaction. Well, their loss was Hesselin's gain. Blinded by their trust in the Empire's might, they'd let Hesselin's cagey manipulations go unchecked. The time was near. Ailsandia would shake off its sloth, and exert its power once more. He would see to it.

"Master," Serpe whined. "I've completed my task."

"And?" he turned towards her, half impatient, half tolerant. The poor, weak fool wasn't worth the searing agony he'd suffered to bind her, but she was proof that he was Elizar's heir. She was useful in her way, and he had Durgas for his real work.

"I caught him near Reledorn, on horseback with half-a-dozen of his men. I frightened the horses and they—"

"The horse didn't throw him? If you've killed him—"

"He's alive! The horses bolted, but he kept his seat. I wouldn't kill, Master, you know I wouldn't kill."

"Yes, once was enough for you, wasn't it? Just remember, Kogyr's of no use to me if he's dead."

Something about the woman's shifty-eyed cringing seemed a little different from usual. He hesitated, then flicked his fingers at her. Whatever she hid from him, it wasn't likely to be important. "Leave now. Be back at nightfall."

She flitted through the wall as he closed the window shutters. He unlocked a cupboard, lifted a shelf out of place, and opened the false back. The globe gleamed in the darkness as he drew it from hiding. Two firelights glittered within, the binding powers for Serpe and Durgas. The globe misted and slowly cleared. He saw Kogyr, his face flushed with fury, riding up a mountain, no doubt hunting for his men. He watched the awareness of his presence grow on Kogyr. The man drew up his horse and glared at Hesselin.

"Just another month, friend," said Hesselin, keeping his

tone conciliating. "Another month, and you can do as you will. Until then, keep your rampages for the tourney field. Agreed?"

Kogyr's mouth opened, no doubt streaming with invective. Hesselin's patience snapped. "Pull yourself together, man. You know the consequences if we fail. Restrain yourself!"

Kogyr's horse sidled under him, responding to the bunched muscles. After a long moment, Kogyr nodded. He turned his horse, and cantered after his men.

Hesselin dismissed the image, his hands trembling, and sweat pouring down his face. The damned displacement spell was taking everything he had. Seven years of ironfisted control—it was no wonder Elizar finally slipped.

Kogyr mustn't know his vulnerability, or the leash would break entirely. Crude the man might be, but he'd been a pirate ship's captain for good reason. His men would follow him into hell and back without the least question. Together, Hesselin and Kogyr would master Ailsandia and the surrounding seas.

Hesselin bit his lip and decided to risk another Sight. He kept his touch easy, so his subject couldn't detect him. Lelori sat at a table, yet another vast tome open before her. Did the woman do nothing but read? He tried to banish his uneasiness. He wanted Ailsandia whole and prosperous, not a shattered wreck it would take years to rebuild. Yet, if he moved against Lelori, he'd lose half his advantage. Obstinate though she was, he needed her, at least for a week or two.

Then, of course, the secrets would be out in the open. He could release his enchantments on Ramsvalt tower and on the creatures he no longer needed. With that drain gone, his power would resurge a hundredfold. At last, reinvigorated, he could reclaim the throne that was rightfully his.

He sensed movement on the stairs. With swift hands he stored the globe, the two fireflies gleaming fitfully as their lights vanished behind the cupboard wall. He opened the shutters and by the time he heard the knock on the door, he was staring out the window.

"Minister?"

"Come in," he called, with hearty cheer. "And what can I do for the good guildmaster today?"

Mericia leaned against her father's arm as they gazed out of the window. Blue skies touched the top of each battlement tower. The dark greenery of the hedge maze formed a backdrop to the fruit trees in the orchard. The very colors of the world brightened at the sound of her father's footsteps.

"So, what's new with my favorite girl?" he said, hugging her. "I'm sorry I didn't have more time with you yesterday. Come sit with me, and give me your news."

Mericia glanced down at the passageway below them. Trissi stood there, staring up at her. Mericia's heart skipped a beat. She moved away from the window.

"Just studying," she said. "Tell me about your trip to Selefrevalt. I haven't been there for months. Everything all right?"

"Passable. I've missed you fiercely, my dear, but I had to pick up a shipment of selefrony for my daughter. Children are nothing but trouble." He mock-glared at her and twitched an eyebrow.

"Why did you bother? I don't go through it that fast." Selefrony was the trade name the Selefrevalt Artists' Guild gave to the clay Mericia favored for her hobby. It remained pliable all day, even unwrapped, and didn't cling to her hands. The composition was a craft secret.

"I thought you might want an extra barrel on hand. Selefrevalt's a considerable distance from Ailsandia."

Mericia's stomach flip-flopped. She loved the Island and the freedom she enjoyed there, with boats to sail and mountains to climb. If only the move didn't put so many people at risk of her curse. She sank down into an armchair next to his.

"Thank you, Father. I'm glad you thought of it."

"Lady Lelori tells me you've been studying very hard, history, culture, commerce, and shipbuilding. She says your questions are insightful, and that you show true promise as a ruler."

"You're exaggerating. She didn't say that. It's not at all like her."

He frowned, considering. "Let's see, what were her exact words?" He took on a mincing precision of speech. "'On occasion, Her Highness' interest in extraneous matters leads her astray from the essential studies, but on the whole her insight is to be commended. I believe we may envision a peaceful transition as she gains experience in her life role.'"

Mericia laughed, relishing the freedom to do so. "*That* sounds just like her."

"For the Lady, that is praise indeed, my dear. What are these extraneous matters, may I ask? I can never tell what you're thinking!" He chuckled.

"Hmm, let me see. The latest were harbors, barnacles, and mountain goats."

"Mountain goats?"

"Whether they could interbreed with domestic goats. And I asked about courts and dungeons." Mericia's hands lay poised in her lap. Her father covered them with one broad, square-fingered hand. The warmth of his hand soaked into her bones.

"Courts and dungeons? What about them?"

"Our laws divide into three categories," she said. "The town magistrates deal with crimes of violence and property, such as theft and murder. The royal court deals with national laws, like damaging public waterways, or refusal to pay taxes. The King's court handles crimes against the King or the nation, like treason, spying, or attempted assassination. Only the

King, Queen, or delegated official has the right to judge those cases. Ailsandia abides by the same category divisions."

"Right so far."

"Penalties are exacted by each court, and include physical punishments like lashing or the severing of a hand." Her father patted her arm. "Or serving a sentence performing extra labor, or paying a fine. The King may also impose the death penalty. And so can the Queen."

"I'm sorry, sweetheart, of course as Regent, you'll need the practical details. If you wish to attend trials, I will be glad to arrange it. I should have done so already." He sighed. "I suppose I meant to protect you."

"It's all right, I know that. But I wanted to be sure that I understood about dungeons. Only the King can place someone there, right? Or his delegate?"

"Yes, though I can override my delegate's decision. The delegate only holds such authority during the ruler's absence, and can't impose the death penalty. When you are Regent, you'll need a delegate of your own. One of your three ministers, perhaps. Sendillon, Jonsel, or Rogitas, any of them would be an excellent choice."

"Sendillon, perhaps. I don't entirely feel comfortable with Minister Rogitas. But is it truly necessary? Lady Lelori says the dungeon here is no longer in use."

"But—?"

"But it is, isn't it?" She held her breath, not knowing what answer she hoped he'd give. Would he tell the truth, or lie to protect her?

"Yes, it is."

She took a moment to control her feelings, equal parts pride, and painful loss. He trusted her with the truth, and she was proud that he recognized her as an adult. Still, it hurt to grow up, to feel the subtle withdrawal of his sheltering arms. Soon the gulf would widen further. When she was sure her voice would be steady, she said. "Who's your delegate here when you're gone?"

"It used to be your mother." The lines in his face deepened. "I am her delegate in Ailsandia. Nowadays, Lady Lelori acts for me. She finds it little trouble. Ramsvalt, in fact, all of Valtiris, is relatively free of treason. Banditry is another matter. Of the four dungeons, in Ailsandia, Ramsvalt, Selefrevalt, and Khonsvalt, only the one at Ramsvalt is currently in use, as this is the official Royal Residence. It used to be at Selefrevalt, until we moved."

"How many people are in the dungeon right now?"

"Four. Two of them are spies for the Emperor. We don't always agree on Valtiris' duty to the Empire." The King's eyes twinkled. "The Emperor knows I'm holding his men, and he knows I know he knows. It's a political game. I visit them occasionally. They share an apartment, and have grown frighteningly good at chess. I haven't won a game against Tanaxus in several months.

"The third prisoner is," he paused, turning it over in his mind, "an impetuous young man. He tried to shoot me with a crossbow several years ago, not once but three times. I grew to doubt that they were all hunting accidents. I should have had him put to death, but his father is a noble, and a fine man. I don't choose to jeopardize his loyalty by killing his son. His living conditions are less—kindly. So are the living conditions of the fourth man, whom I suspect of being a large-scale pirate. He claims royal blood of a country to the south. I turned his men over to the magistrates at Ailsandia, who confiscated his ship. I kept him, pending further investigation."

Mericia met his eyes. "I hate the idea of prison, but I do see the necessity."

He nodded. "As a ruler, you must protect your country. When the disputes to be settled involve other nations, only a ruler can safely deal with them."

"But—torture?"

"Some say it deters people from committing crimes. Your mother and I aren't convinced."

"So, it's not practiced in Ailsandia, either."

"Not for several generations. My word, Mericia, such a serious subject. What a way to welcome your father home."

She pulled his hand to her cheek and leaned against it, closing her eyes in relief. There were only four prisoners, and her father would never stoop to torture. She tried to shake off the niggling doubt. No, her father wouldn't torture a man—but Lady Lelori? The image of the Lady, consumed by rage, her fingers like claws, made Mericia shudder. The Lady was her father's delegate. Did her father actually *know* that there were only four prisoners? Did he visit the dungeon, apart from the apartment with the chess players?

She sat up, releasing his hand. "Remember Master Orino?"

"To be sure I do. He knew Island music even your mother had never heard. That's why I lured him up here a few years ago. I rather hoped," he said, his smile fading, "that he could rekindle your mother's interest in her country, but my hopes were unrealistic. I was sorry when he left us. A wonderful musician. I envy the Emperor his service, I can tell you."

"The Emperor?" she said.

"Yes," he said, with mild surprise. "That's where he is, now, didn't you know? For goodness sakes, surely I told you. He turned up there a couple of years ago. I got word in one of the twins' letters."

They stared at each other. Relief flooded her body. She felt limp. "Really?"

"Really. I'm amazed they didn't mention it to you. They wrote to you a few weeks ago, didn't they?"

"No, I haven't heard from them since the May Festival. They didn't mention him then."

"He might not be there any more, of course. Still, you

should write and ask immediately. I wish I still had the letter to show you, but it's been quite a while since then. My poor dear, what did you think happened to him?"

"I don't know. It just bothered me, when he left so many things behind—"

"He took his musical instruments, though, didn't he? For a musician, that's the most important thing. They weigh heavy, and he probably didn't want to carry a lot." Her father frowned and slammed a fist on the arm of his chair. "It was unforgivable of him to worry you. I'll have a thing or two to say to him if he turns up here again. It's unconscionable."

"I don't mind, Father, not any more." Mericia smiled at him, her heart free again.

"Well, then, shall we drop this dismal subject? Come play chess with me, and I'll show you a move Tanaxus taught me."

Mericia lingered on the window seat in her bedroom, snatching her peace while she could. The Lady had disappeared to harry Steward Archibald, while her father met with the Guard. Early afternoon sun lit the watchtower's south face. For a few horrid days, it had hulked through her nightmares, an embodiment of evil, peopled with spectres and phantasms. Now, once again, it stood as the bulwark of Ramsvalt's defense, symbolizing alert warriors standing guard over the countryside.

How *dare* Master Orino ramble off without even a song warbling behind him on the people's tongues, telling her he was safe. A sense of ill usage sparked and died. Finally, Master Orino rested easily in her memory. The shroud of her heartache had lifted: fear that she'd cursed him, and dread for his suffering. Thank the One, he was safe. More than safe, he performed for the Emperor these days, unless his wanderlust had seized him again.

Her brothers, Kellian and Randall, had never been reliable letter-writers. They wrote to their father at their tutors' insistence. On rare occasions, they tucked notes inside for her, but she hadn't gotten one since May Festival when they told her about two knights of the Emperor, due to attend the Ramsvalt tourney. She wished they could attend her Coronation and her twenty-first birthday. Their own fifteenth birthdays had passed last June. She'd sent them a flotilla of clay model ships, perfectly scaled, and painted: the Emperor's state vessel, pot-bellied merchant ships, the andisailles all three of them enjoyed sailing, and a galley, complete with twenty rowers on a side.

Her fingers paused in their kneading of the clay. Was the Emperor, perhaps, holding her brothers as hostages, as courteously as her father held Tanaxus and Zirron? The clay stretched, growing faint outlines of stones and mortar. She shook her head, and balled the clay into a glob.

Master Orino sang at her fourteenth birthday celebration, his joyous trills lifting the hearers so their feet nearly left the ground. When her curse struck, its vicious arrows had struck him down, along with everyone she loved, with spiteful exactitude. Even her father had trembled on the verge of death. All her youth, her mother had enchanted her children with her flights of fancy, infecting their rambunctious spirits with the urge to explore. Now, her mother's fixations doubled and trebled with every year. Her mother had lived, but her soul had died. Mericia's crushing grief still floored her whenever she visited her mother.

Only once, in seven years, had the Queen given Mericia her full, undivided attention.

After Mericia's horse berserked and killed himself, Mericia had despaired. Her feet dragged boulders behind them, her stomach revolted against every offering, and her eyes saw only the looming threat of her mother's madness, the darkness of Trissi's eyes, and the shattered lives of those who dared to love her. Apart from dragging herself to the garderobe to deal with the disgusting side of life, she lay in bed, staring out the window. One morning, when boredom battled depression, she stumbled to the Tapestry Room, and fell into a chair, staring at nothing.

The day passed by unnoticed. Lady Siree bustled in and out on myriad pointless errands, her blathering nonsense a distant comfort, like a caged bird singing to itself. In mid-afternoon, Siree exclaimed over a stain on her gown. With babbled apologies, she left to change her clothing and find the laundry maid.

Gradually, Mericia became aware of her mother's stare.

"Mother?" she said. But it was too much effort. She'd tried so many times to get her mother's attention, and had failed every time. She dropped her face into her hands.

Something plucked at her sleeve. Mother stood next to her, her gloved hand resting lightly on Mericia's arm. With dawning hope, Mericia stood.

"Mother, are you better?"

Mother took her arm and led her to the tapestry. Mericia pulled back. She detested the tapestry, which absorbed every bit of her mother's remaining mind. She raised her eyes and stopped, transfixed by the mystic light in her mother's eyes.

Mother drew off her gloves, and took Mericia's hands in her own. The long narrow hands, so much like Mericia's, spread out her daughter's fingers. One by one, she touched Mericia's fingers to the embroidered stars in the tapestry's night sky. She raised Mericia's hands to her lips and kissed them, first the right and then the left.

"Mother? What—?"

The Queen tucked her hand behind Mericia's head, and kissed her on the forehead. Tears started from Mericia's eyes, in a flood of bewildered hope.

"Mother—" she began gladly.

But her mother walked away. The Queen rounded the tapestry, seated herself, put on her gloves, picked up a needle, and continued to sew with single-minded intensity.

"Mother? I don't understand." She ran to her mother's side and fell to her knees. "Mother, please, come back to me, Mother, I need you—" After fifteen minutes of fruitless agony, Mericia flew to her room in a torrent of tears.

Now, sitting in her room, Mericia steeled her heart. Once, in seven years, her mother had recognized her. It would never happen again. There was no point in expecting blood from a turnip, a blossom from a stone, or love from her mother. Mericia instructed the maids for her mother's comfort, and looked in on her daily, much as she would do for an obnoxious pet dog. If she expected nothing, she could not be disappointed. For affection, she had her father. For normal human relationships, she had none, since Master Orino departed.

Dear gods, how she missed him. He'd brought the island to life in the songs he'd taught her. So many experiences unfurled before her when he sang. The tenderness of a mother with a new baby; the terror of a sailor in a high sea; the raucous humor of the farmyard; the grace of a deer bounding through the woods. She should have known better than to share his song with Lady Lelori. The Lady preferred order and calm to the thrill of human experience. Of course, her taste in songs would be similar.

Mericia glanced at the clay in her hands. She'd formed a lute, with its squash-seed shaped body and a straight neck, lightly scored with four delicate strings. She set it on the window ledge and worked with a second clump of clay.

Master Orino would have known how she felt about leaving her father for Ailsandia. He understood loss. He'd written a lament on the death of her grandmother, Queen Merellia. The tune and the words were simple, but together they still touched her heart.

Sea waves wash the grief from our hearts,
Scattering pearls behind on the shore....

If only she knew that her own grief would end, that her isolation had a purpose. If only she could find the pearl in her curse.

"Help me, Master Orino," she whispered to the lump of clay in her hands. "I wish you were here. You could help me understand."

Master Orino had never finished the prophecy song. The One and the Many hadn't written the future yet, he said, laughing. No matter. He'd written better lyrics, but never a more compelling melody. The tune carried it, lifted her soul into a whirlpool of longing.

A wave, almost of dizziness, swept through her. A band of tightness wrapped around her forehead. She picked up the model of the lute in her left hand and held the small clay model of Master Orino's face in her right. She cupped them in her hands, and without thought raised them and blew gently. She closed her eyes, and sang:

"When the wings of the mountains brush the soul
of the sea,
When the two and the many are one,
When illusions of freedom encircle and flee
Then the threads of the challenge are spun.

No matter the dream, or the steps you may stray
Our lives entangle your net
As you leap to the skies, or dive to the sea,
Our hearts must follow you yet.

When the wool and the flax meet madder and weld
When the stars cease their tumble to flare..."

As her voice faded on the inconclusive note, the last of the words he'd written, she heard something. Not from her ears, not through the window, or from the watchtower, but through a dream, half-waking, half-sleeping, for her ears alone. Master Orino's tenor voice picked up the song with a bitter certainty.

When the wool and the flax meet madder and weld
When the stars cease their tumble to flare
When hidden desires refuse to be quelled
Then treachery seeks to ensnare.
A face floated before her, maimed and ruined.
 Only the eyes were alive with warning, as the
 refrain bent into notes of sorrow.
No matter the captive, or the heart that now sleeps
The world is caught in your net
As you soar to the clouds, or plunge to the deeps,
Our hearts are torn with regret.

With a great gasp, Mericia tore herself from the fog, staring at the clay in her hands. She dropped the figures onto the window ledge, and her eyes darted to the watchtower. No. It couldn't be. Master Orino was safe in the Emperor's court. Her father said so.

"No," she said aloud. With horrified fascination, she looked at the rejected clay figures. Before her eyes, the lute, still warm and pliable from her hands, crumbled into dry dust. She caught her breath, and picked up the figure of the Master's head.

Its ears were gone. So was its nose.

Nice little birdie, Lady Siree thought tiredly, watching the Queen stitch. *Nice birdie, stay put, don't make me chase*

you all over the castle again. The apt comparison seeped into her mind. Birds had their own agendas. They sang when they pleased and ambled on their perches, but once disturbed they'd beat themselves insensible in the effort to escape their cages.

The kitchen servant set down the last tray, her veiled insolence trailing behind her like bog mist. Some people worked for a living, the look implied, while others clung like barnacles to the Queen, and got waited on hand and foot. She scanted her curtsey and left, leaving the door ajar.

Lady Siree wilted under the scorn, tears of exhaustion welling into her eyes. If only that girl knew! Lady Siree hadn't slept well in years, always fretting, always fearing she'd wake to discover that the Queen had escaped again.

She'd tried bolting the bedroom door and hiding the key. Later she'd had Trissi lock them in at night. That hadn't worked either. How *did* the Queen get outside? She couldn't be climbing out the window, not four floors up from one roof, and two below the top one? She didn't have wings! Mentally, Siree threw up her hands. She just hoped, fervently, that she could find the Queen every time she flew the coop.

Once or twice a week, Siree embarked on the quiet hunt, one hand carrying a shielded lantern, the other feeling her way along the stone walls. If she managed to locate Trissi, the job was halved, but sometimes, finding Trissi was as hard as finding the Queen. Lady Lelori refused to help in the midnight searches. Well, she didn't refuse, exactly, and she wasn't overtly rude. Some things went without saying. One could bother some people at night, and not others. Lady Lelori was the most 'otherly' person she knew. Siree couldn't possibly pester the King, and the Princess was nearly as unapproachable as the Lady. When Siree had first come, the Princess was a lively, bouncy little thing. Nowadays, she glided through the castle, the perfect princess, always polite, always cool, and completely untouchable. Since the girl couldn't have her own mother, she'd apparently chosen Lady Iceberg as a model.

The Queen pulled the short green wool through the linen. Siree unrolled the green skein, snipped off a length, threaded it through a needle, and laid it on one of the eight pegs on the wool board. She cut several other lengths, and stretched them across the spare pegs. The Queen's artistry astounded her, considering that there were only eight colors throughout. Lady Siree had never picked up the Queen's expertise with dyeing, though she'd certainly helped often enough. The Queen dyed all her own colors: brown, gray, black, red, yellow, green, blue, and purple. Often, Siree found her in the dye room when she disappeared in the night. Sometimes she'd be on top of the keep's tower, where Trissi had found her last week. Sometimes, Siree searched for hours, only to discover the Queen sound asleep, back in her own bed. A nice little birdie, flown back to its nest.

Princess Mericia entered. As usual, she looked like a porcelain statue, moving by magic, every strand of her braided hair carved from black stone. Her lips barely moved as she spoke.

"Good day, mother. Good day, Lady Siree."

"Good day, Your Highness. Her Majesty ate well this morning." Lady Siree glanced anxiously at the tray. "She ate the ham and the melon, but I still can't get her to eat bread."

"I see. Lady Siree, would you be so kind as to do me a favor."

The 'favor' was an order. "Delighted to be of service, Your Highness," said Lady Siree with an inward sigh.

"The Queen appears particularly interested in colors of late. Please go to the garden and obtain two live butterflies."

"Butterflies?"

"Different colors. More if you can find them. Also a live grasshopper. I will stay with my mother while you are gone."

The Princess closed her mouth. Clearly, she did not intend to explain herself.

After a moment's disbelief, Lady Siree shut her gaping jaw, heaved herself to her aching feet, and headed for the door. Butterflies. How did one catch them? Did one have to climb trees? In a dress? Butterflies, indeed. And a grasshopper. Like mother, like daughter. Both of them were a length short of a full skein, if Siree was any judge.

As the door closed behind Lady Siree, the steel in Mericia's spine dissolved like a guttering candle.

"Mother. Mother, I need your help."

The Queen's hands stitched rapidly. The wall around Ramsvalt Castle rebuilt itself, laid on stone by stone with gray wool.

"Mother—" Mericia's voice broke. Mother wasn't here, not her real mother, just the wax doll with moving hands. Whom could she ask? She couldn't bother her father with this. He'd be certain she'd gone mad like her mother. But by the One, she needed help. She had to save Master Orino, had to free him, heal him, and restore him to his life. All she had to go on was a dream. A peculiarly certain dream, with bitter new verses, but only a dream. Not magic. She wasn't a sorcerer. After Elizar, Ailsandian royalty shunned sorcery. She *couldn't* have seen it. But she had. It couldn't be true, but it was.

In the back of her mind, she heard Lady Lelori say dismissively, "There's no such thing as a dragon." No such thing as a dragon...except by sorcery.

How had Master Orino wound up in the dungeon, tortured, for four years? Why didn't her father know? The small voice in her mind whispered, *the Lady is his delegate. He trusts the Lady.*

She couldn't add to her father's burdens, especially just before Progress. Her heart sank as she remembered Lord Ranilth last spring. She'd watched him intently, and he'd been speared in the gut. She didn't dare share her trouble. Her mother wouldn't hear a word, and couldn't care less, no matter what she said. Her heart rate steadied. She'd only be talking to herself. That should be safe enough.

"You used to care about me," she said. "You played with us. Remember, at the Island? All those games about entering rooms, and playing we were nobles, or fishermen, or herders. Remember Kellian, pretending to be Lord Waspidell? I laughed myself—" into stitches, she almost said, glancing at the tapestry. "We'd laugh and laugh, all four of us. It wasn't just playing, though. You were teaching us etiquette, the people's worries, and their daily troubles. The boys, and Trissi and I, we just thought they were games. You were so much fun. I loved you so much."

The fingers flew on their way, expertly piping a line of stitching around the edge of the Castle gate. Mericia drew a shuddering breath, and knelt on the floor by the Queen's chair.

"You loved us all. I miss you so much. I miss the boys, too, but I'm glad they're not here. If they—" Her mother didn't know about Mericia's curse. It had struck after her illness. She finished the sentence silently. *If they were here, my curse would strike them down.* "I've lost so many people. You and the boys, Maari, Barton, and Dyllis, and dear Nanny. She only just died, but it seems like she's been gone forever. And Master Orino. Do you remember him, mother?"

Mericia couldn't bear to watch her mother's intent stitching. She settled onto the floor, leaned her head against her mother's thigh, and closed her eyes.

"He came to Ramsvalt a few years ago, but we knew him before that, on the Island. It's not the same without you, when I visit the Island now. He taught me a great deal, singing, dancing, and playing the lute. He was bursting with Island stories and legends. I used to look out my bedroom window, and dream of his mermaids, sprites, and flying horses.

"And then, all of a sudden, he left, with no warning. He just took his lute and his pipes and he left. I was so scared that he'd—" *been cursed because I loved him* "—that bandits killed him, or that he'd drowned, and I'd never know what happened to him. I thought maybe he left because he didn't like me.

"Father thinks he went wandering, and went to the Emperor's Court. Which is funny, now I think of it, because the boys have been trying to come home for a visit for years, and every time they take ship, the waves drive them back. Ships make the transit all the time, unless the boys are on it. That's strange, isn't it?" She toyed with the notion for a moment, but it drowned in the image of Master Orino's battered face. She clutched the clay figure in her hands, and sat upright.

"Mother," she cried. "Mother, won't you look at me? It's your little Riss, don't you remember? Would you know the twins if you saw them? Oh dear gods in heaven...."

The Queen put the needle, trailing gray wool, on the wool-board. She selected a needle with green thread and turned back to the tapestry.

"Mother, I can't take this. I think I'm going mad."

With steady sureness, the Queen added another yew tree to the hedge maze.

"He's in the dungeon, Mother. Master Orino is in the dungeon. Father doesn't even know he's there, and I don't know what to do. They cut off his ears and his nose. His nose, mother." She stared at the clay figure in her hands. It blurred. She wiped away a tear, and discovered a steady stream. "I was in my room, making little images. The lute crumbled into dust, and this one—I put his ears on it, I *swear* I did, but now they're gone."

It sounded insane. Mericia heard the rising pitch of hysteria in her voice. She bit her lip, tasting blood. She slumped, leaned her head against the living flesh of what used to be her mother, closed her eyes, and sobbed.

At first, she ignored the slow movement overhead. She felt a slippery touch on her hand. Her mother's kid glove touched Master Orino's face. Mericia straightened, like a child trying not to frighten a bird. She held the figure out, and her mother plucked it away.

Disbelieving, Mericia watched her mother set the figure on the tapestry, and remove her kid gloves. Mericia gasped. The fingers were scarred and the flesh warped.

"Mother," she whispered, "what happened to your hands?"

The Queen lifted the fragment of clay. A long still moment passed. The Queen looked her daughter full in the face, running a finger over the mutilated clay figure. Her eyes glistened.

"Mother, you understand. You believe me." She waited eagerly for a nod or a word, but none came. Only the eyes lived, glistening.

"Why won't you talk to me? You can hear me, can't you? You're not deaf. Mother? Mother, don't, please don't—"

The Queen placed the small image back in Mericia's hand, and pulled the gloves over her white, pitted hands.

"Mother, please."

The Queen lifted the green-threaded needle.

"Mother, don't leave me!"

The Queen's hand shook as she took a stitch on the yew tree. It went awry, and she picked it out again.

"Mother." Mericia rocked back and forth on her knees, waving Master Orino's figure in the air. "Mother, help me. He's in there, and in such agony, I can't bear it, I can't bear it. I loved him. He was so good to me. How can I help him? Tell me, please tell me."

The Queen captured her eyes. Mericia fell silent, trying to pull meaning from the dark eyes over hers. Her mother took her hand, lifted it, and kissed the fingers. She turned Mericia's hand, revealing Master Orino's face. With a movement both gentle and certain, she drew the line of green thread over him.

"I don't understand, Mother."

Queen Ailsa pulled softly, dropping both image and hand on the tapestry. On the yew hedge. She laid the green wool over the top, and pressed Mericia's hand with her gloved one. A chill ran down Mericia's back. Yew was poisonous.

"Mother, no. Please, no."

Her mother pulled Mericia's head closer. A light kiss brushed her forehead. With sweet pain, Mericia felt something shatter in her heart. Her eyes met her mother's, identical in their brown-black hue, silvered with tears.

"It's the only way to free him?"

A tear streaked her mother's face. Mericia's eyes brimmed, and the tears spilled.

"All right, mother, if you're certain. I will."

Chapter Nine

S uch a temptation, dear, to just say, 'I want two squirrels, a ripe melon and a raccoon in my bedroom by noon.' Or something else ridiculous like that."

Farren stuck fast between two yew trees, and hung there. "And *you* did that when you were in the palace?" He regarded his aunt with a fascinated eye.

"Well, no. Not exactly," Aunt Nan said, brushing nonexistent lint from her sleeve. "Except for the peacock, of course, but Maari said— Anyway, that footman was an overbearing snob. He had it coming. But what I mean to say, dear, is that while it's not—not strictly *nice* behavior, the temptation can be irresistible. I suspect she got it from me."

"Like snooping?"

"I was not snooping, my dear. It was merely, when Bonnara muttered about the Princess sending Siree to look for butterflies, I thought I'd check into matters, and of course, there they were, staring at the hedge maze out the window."

Personally, Farren was getting tired of the hedge maze, especially at night. The stiffly upright trees with their red berries were as much large bushes as trees. Spiders and crawly things swarmed through them, and all of them resented his passage. He plucked a branch from his sleeve. It sprang back and gouged him in the ribs. He shoved himself through the narrow gap, heedless of the ripping sound as his tunic gave way.

"But you didn't hear what they were saying?"

"Farren." Aunt Nan drew herself up, floating directly in his path. "I am not a spy. Really, my dear, how crass."

"I apologize, Aunt Nan," he said gravely.

"I should hope so." She flitted through another tree. "Besides, Maari wouldn't tell me a thing. She's so closed-mouthed, that mother of yours."

Farren hid his grin as he wriggled through another small gap in the hedge.

"I saw Trissi here this afternoon," she went on. "And then half an hour ago, she snuck out of her bedroom mumbling about the hedge maze. Imagine, in the dead of night," huffed Aunt Nan. "Incredible behavior. If I were alive, I'd have a word or two with that girl."

"And she wanted you to bring me here? Why not the garden, where we met last time? I don't understand, Aunt Nan. She can't even see you. I'd think she'd ask Caprio."

He recoiled as Aunt Nan whirled on him. "Don't you talk to me about that hell-born Goat. The trouble he causes in this castle! He's convinced the serving staff that the Great Hall is haunted, says there are shades dripping through every crack in the ceiling."

"But, Aunt Nan," he said, "he's right. There are hundreds of them."

"That's not the point. So what if a few guards and ladies hang about after their deaths? That's not haunting. There's no ill nature to it. It's just their home. Do you know what he did tonight? Well, I'll tell you. Sweet little Karina was delivering a kettle of stew to the Great Hall, one of those heavy things, where you lug it with both hands. And that demon Goat bolted right through her body as she reached the doorway. Well, of course, she didn't see a thing, just felt that hideous nausea, and she screamed. She scared the wits out of everyone in earshot. And then she thought Gareth did it, so she let fly with the kettle and bashed him one. He hit the wall, and knocked himself out. The stew splashed everywhere, and scalded her and Gareth both. Celli saw it all, and she knew Gareth hadn't done it, so she and Karina took care of the poor dear and cleaned up. Now they're all convinced shades are haunting that passageway, and they refuse to use it at all. And did your Goat take the blame? Oh, no, it's the poor harmless spirits, searching for a homelike atmosphere, a little conviviality with friends—"

"Ah, we're here." Farren broke in, thankfully. "Thanks so much, Aunt Nan, I'll just wait here for a while, and see if Riss turns up." The spiraling paths opened into a wide moonlit lawn with a curved stone bench under a broad maple tree. The autumn-drenched leaves shone a dark bronze in the light of the full moon.

"Shall I wait with you, dear? What if she doesn't come?"

"No, no. I'm fine. I'll just stay until the night watchman's next call. How's that?"

"I'll go check on her," Aunt Nan decided. "You stay right here, dear boy, I'm sure you won't mind being alone."

"No, no." *Not at all, in fact.* He dropped onto the stone seat. Aunt Nan had considerably more energy than she'd had a couple of weeks before. The contrast with her ailing body of the last few years was stunning. Farren blinked, trying to keep his eyes open. He rested his head in his hands, remembering the now familiar image of a crippled man wedged into a hell pit. He'd barely set foot in the Great Hall for dinner tonight when the sharp scent of wine forced the vivid memory to the fore. He'd fled and vomited behind the main storehouse. Last night had been sleepless, and now Aunt Nan insisted that tonight should be as well.

His master had been equally distraught, although less obvious about it. He wondered what Mistress Catherine thought of Master Pardell's behavior. Today, the Master had been unusually quiet, but finally lost himself in an intricate bit of inlay work. Farren tried to involve himself in dovetailing the corners of an oak chest, but for once, his nimble hands fumbled the tools. Rather than risk scratching the surface, he let Drellford take over, and checked the supply inventory instead.

Perhaps the maimed man wasn't Master Orino. Perhaps it was someone else, a criminal with a score of murders to his credit. He clung to the hope for an instant, and sank into despair. It made no difference. No matter what the man had done, this was not justice. He understood harsh punishments such as cutting off a hand for repeated theft, imprisonment in the mines for rape or piracy, but torture revolted him. It was deliberate cruelty, for no purpose but vengeance.

A scuffling sound drew his attention. A dark figure appeared between the last two yew trees of the hedge maze.

"Riss?" Farren ventured. He stood.

"Farren? How did you know I'd be here?"

She darted towards him, but stopped a couple of paces away. He jerked his hands back to his sides. "You sent Aunt Nan with a message, didn't you?"

Her faint laugh ruffled the stillness. "I felt like such a fool, talking to the air. I didn't think it would work. Farren, I'm *so* glad you came."

"Aunt Nan's as real as Caprio, and you've seen him. Come sit down. It's a long way to walk with a hurt knee. I could have met you closer. I got into the dungeon—"

She waved off his words, and he paused, confused. "Wait a minute." She turned and called softly. "Come on. He's here." She ducked into the maze for a moment and returned, tugging someone behind her. "Come on."

Farren's jaw dropped. Two girls stood side by side, both dressed in servant's clothes. Each wore a long braid of thick, black hair, caught back in a half-hood. One girl hung back, but the other gripped her hand tightly.

"You're twins," he said, amazed.

"I'm Riss," said the front one. With the smile, he knew her: Trissi of the kitchen, Denys' girl. The other was thinner, her face set like stone, as if she had never smiled in her life. Only her eyes glowed with life and determination.

Trissi drew the other girl forward. "And this is Riss, too. The first time I met you, Farren, was in the kitchen. I've never talked to Caprio, and I've never seen him. You rescued the other Riss in the garden. Mericia." He heard the nickname in the middle of the longer one. Mer-RISS-ee-ah. "Her mother connected us, kind of, a long time ago. Her mother's the Queen," she added. "Come on, Meriss, the bench is long enough for all of us."

Trissi's arm fell naturally around Mericia's shoulders, as the girls limped to the bench. Farren turned to face them. Unthinkingly, he sank to his knees, and crouched there staring at them.

"We've a story to tell you," said Trissi. "And we need your help."

"Sure," he said.

"You got into the dungeon. Did you find Master Orino?"

"Yes." He outlined the story, trying to gloss over the filth and cruelty he'd witnessed. The girls gave him identical looks of tolerance and he faltered.

"Don't protect us," Mericia said, her tone soft but incisive.

Her voice struck a chord in his memory. The whispered speech of the girl in the garden echoed in his dreams. Her eyes glowed with a rainbow of colors, each vibrant and sharply defined. Something in him, stirred into restlessness in the garden, and later in the kitchen with Trissi, now settled deeply into his heart and mind.

Mericia continued. "I have to deal with facts, not dreams. At least, not entirely dreams." At her side, Trissi tightened her grip on Mericia's hand.

Farren nodded and began again, leaving out nothing, from his visit to the Steward and Caprio's connivance, to his bargain with Master Pardell, the evidence in the dungeon, and his discovery in the Little Ease.

"...Enough drink to knock him out, and they left him, hidden behind the gate." His voice dried up, at the prospect of describing the indescribable. Mericia held out her hand, a small object cradled in the palm. He stared at the clay figure of a mangled face, flat in the wrong places, and lumpy in others.

"Exactly," he said.

The girls looked at each other, in perfect mirror image. Trissi caught his expression and grimaced. "We've a story to tell you too, but it goes back a long ways, about thirteen years ago."

Trissi's parents had drowned at sea when she was eight. A cousin sewed for the Queen in the Island palace, and took Trissi to live with her. Trissi ran with the other children through the laughing atmosphere of the Ailsandia palace, half a servant, and half a spoiled child. The Queen lived there six months out of the year. Mericia, as her heir, lived with her mother, but the King often rode down to stay for a week at a time, usually bringing the twins with him.

Queen Ailsa welcomed Trissi with loving arms, and soon the girls spent most of their waking hours together. Trissi shared lessons with Mericia, and in turn taught the young princess to sail a boat, climb trees, and scramble onto mountain ledges.

"Your Majesty," Minister Sendillon protested, after Mericia's sailing skiff had capsized for the third time in as many days. "Her Highness is taking unacceptable risks."

"Mother, I'm not—"

Queen Ailsa waved off her protests. *"Sendillon,"* Queen Ailsa said, *"When one learns to sail a boat, one sometimes overturns it. I did so myself, as you no doubt remember."*

"But three times? Your Majesty never capsized a boat three times."

"The andisaille is a notoriously unstable design," agreed Queen Ailsa. *She picked up Mericia's hand in her right, and Trissi's in her left.* *"I believe my daughter intends to master the racing andisaille in time? Ah, I thought so. They're practicing, Sendillon, that's all. If they master the andisaille, they'll be virtually unsinkable."* *She smiled at him over the girls' shoulders.* *"Hush, Sendillon, old friend."*

Queen Ailsa raised both girls' hands to her lips, and pulled them close, dropping a light kiss on each head of wind-blown black hair. She shooed them off briskly. As they ran down the marble steps, they heard the Queen say, "I always know what they're about, Sendillon. I've linked all three of us together. Trust me."

Now, sitting in the evening stillness, Trissi pulled away, and folded her hands in her lap. Mericia's stiff posture never shifted. Farren watched the twin colors of pink and yellow, trust and affection, well from their eyes, circle the pair and embrace them. "My brothers are twins," Mericia told Farren, as she watched Trissi. "I always wanted a twin, and now I had one. Even our names were similar, so we called each other Riss. But it's more than love. My mother practiced sympathetic magic. It means that she creates a link between two similar things. Usually, it's an object and the thing it represents."

"Like the images in the garden," said Farren, with dawning comprehension. "The clay bat that summons the other bats?"

"Yes, like that. The gift runs in my mother's family. I

made the images, and I put them in the garden." Mericia looked at Farren directly for the first time. "Thank you for your help. It would have been hard getting back to the castle that night without you. Especially since Trissi was falling down the stairs at the same time." The wry comment made Trissi laugh.

"It's inconvenient," Trissi exclaimed, "that's for sure. When one of us gets hurt, the other does, too, just the same way. Her Majesty linked us together with those kisses. Every time she kissed us, the bond got stronger. Now it's permanent. I *like* it that way." Trissi's chin jutted mulishly.

"A link can be broken," said Mericia.

"You want to break it?" asked Farren. Their words said one thing, their voices a second, and their emotional colors a third. Some sort of impasse separated the girls.

"No, she doesn't," said Trissi. She grabbed Mericia's wrist and shook it. "You've got to listen to me now, Riss, I keep telling you! This is proof. *There is no curse.*"

"No curse?" Mericia shook the clay figure in front of Trissi's nose. "It's not much of a blessing, is it?" Her face crumpled and she fought for control. In a bare moment, her mask-like face had recomposed itself. Gently, she pried Trissi's fingers loose.

Farren looked up at her, keeping his hands firmly to himself. "It's not a curse, or a blessing," he said evenly. "Somebody wanted revenge on him, but wanted him alive." He thought of Master Pardell's suggestion that the vengeance taker didn't want a shade left behind to revolt. But that seemed pointless. Eventually, Master Orino *would* die, and his shade would seek its justice. "A real live person wanted revenge on an actual, physical man. This scar wasn't made by a curse." He pointed to the clay head. "It was caused by a dagger."

"See?" said Trissi. "And that poor man at the joust, that wasn't your curse either," she added bitterly. "Someone's persecuting you. They've been doing it for years, systematically, trying to drive you insane, like..."

"Like my mother."

Farren's heart hurt at the dreary note. Mericia looked like an ice princess, but she'd been tortured as Master Orino had. The beautiful statue was crippled inside, mutilated into a semblance of the earless, noseless Master Orino.

"Listen to me." Trissi leaned forward and rapidly outlined Mericia's life of the last seven years, the deaths, the illnesses, the dogs, and the horse. "As long as she pulls herself in like a turtle, everything's all right, but let her act human for a change, and right away, something dreadful happens. They're controlling you, Riss. Haven't I been telling you? And poor Master Orino is the proof."

"But if you're right," said Farren, "you'd have been the first victim. If someone's trying to control Her Highness, the first thing they'd do is go after you, Trissi."

Trissi slapped her hand against the bench. "There, Meriss! He sees it, too!"

Mericia remained frozen for a moment longer and nodded. "They did. At least, they tried. Time and again. But every time Trissi got sick or injured, the link ensured that I was injured, too."

"And they wanted you alive," said Farren.

"Yes. It seems so. After the horse—died—Trissi and I agreed. Well, I guess we agreed. Nothing was *said*."

"But I knew," said Trissi. "In public, she treats me like a servant. She thinks she's better than I am." A glint of mischief sparked.

"I do not."

"And even in private, we're careful. I've never told Denys, though I might have to, if we ever—but I can't leave Meriss."

Poor Denys. Farren's brother faced stiff competition if Trissi had to decide between her lover and her friend.

Trissi stretched a hand out to Farren, palm upward. "I'm sorry, Farren, about Terrell. I asked Meriss to find some excuse not to take Terrell as Captain of her Guard. I was so afraid he'd die, too. Last spring, Lord Ranilth almost died, just because she asked for his name. She had to pick someone who'd be safe. The King likes Irandis, so we figured that would protect him. Poor Denys," she said, echoing Farren's thought. "He just exploded, he was so mad. I couldn't even tell him why."

"You should marry him," said Mericia.

"I'm not leaving you!"

Farren's mind had run along a different track. "Who do you think is doing this? And why?"

"I've got my notions," said Trissi. "It's got to be her, Riss."

"But she's so calm, Trissi. I just can't picture her having a man tortured."

"She's not calm," Trissi snorted. "She's boiling with emotions. She just pretends she's not. How do you think you learned to hide yours? She's the perfect model."

Mericia shook her head. "Trissi insists it's Lady Lelori, but I can't see it. Why would she care? I mean, care enough to kill people and torture them? It doesn't make sense. Let's drop this. It's not why we're here, remember? We're here because of Master Orino. Farren, please, I need your advice. You were there in the dungeon. How can I best get inside?"

"Into the dungeon?"

"Both of us," clarified Trissi. "How can we get inside? Secretly. It can't be openly, because we have to do something, and Lady Lelori can't find out."

"You can't." Farren clamped his hands on his knees. The knuckles whitened. "There are dangerous men in there. Lots of them. They'd...attack you."

"Father said there were only four," murmured Mericia. "Obviously, he doesn't know everything that goes on."

"Why don't you just tell your father the story?" Farren asked.

Mericia looked at him as though he were daft. "Whether it's a curse or some maniac, I'm *not* putting my father in that danger. Why are you smiling at me? Do you think this is *funny*?"

"You sound like my dear Aunt Nan," he said, letting the words drift between them without challenge. "She talks the same way about you. Why do you want to get inside?"

The girls looked at each other. Farren watched their eyes, roiling with anger, resolution, and something blacker, red-black, like blood.

"I have something for Master Orino," said Mericia.

"You can't give him anything that will help." He knew what she planned. If he drove her intentions into the open, perhaps she'd retreat.

"Yes, I can." Her implacable stare did not attempt to hide the truth. Poison. And whether he helped or didn't, she would deliver the draught to Master Orino, regardless of the cost.

"All right, then. Give it to me. I'll pass it on to him."

"You have a contact there?" Trissi said. "Meriss, he knows one of the guards! Farren, will he help us? Do you think you can talk him into it? I've some money if you need a bribe."

"That's all right," he said. "He wouldn't want anything. We've been friends for years." At least that was true enough, he thought.

"Oh, Farren, are you sure he'll help us? It's such a risk."

"I should do this myself," Mericia said. "It's a sin. I can't put that burden on you, or on your friend."

"You're making the potion, Meriss. You're carrying most of the sin, if it is a sin, to put the poor man out of his misery."

"I'll make sure Master Orino knows what it is, before he drinks it. My friend will pass on the message," Farren said.

"So that leaves me," said Trissi. "I need to help. We're

linked." She held up her hand, and Mericia rested her own against it. "Can your friend do it during the daily routine? Or does he guard during the night?"

"Night would be best. There are fewer guards to see what he's doing. If he checks the prisoners by himself, you see, that'd be safest."

"Good. Tell me which night, and I'll make sure the prisoners are asleep, so they don't see him either."

"How on earth—?"

"Easy. I figure they save the worst food for the prisoners, right? So, I'll make some porridge, add a few things, and make sure it's the worst possible food for the guards. You can bet they'll feed it to the prisoners." Trissi grimaced. "Terrible, but true. And I'll give you more of the sleeping stuff for your friend. He can give out extra doses if he needs to."

Mericia stirred. "Are you sure, Farren?"

The sound of his name on her lips made him suddenly fierce. "I'm sure. No problem at all."

Chapter Ten

It's not a *nice* place, Farren, dear."

"Aunt Nan, don't be silly. I'm going alone." Farren barely breathed the words.

"But all by yourself? Are you sure that's wise?"

Farren huddled in the comforting shadow of the bake house, watching a night guard stride towards the tower. The guard glanced at the barracks, his yearning for a mug of ale and a few lusty jokes as plain as the crossbow hung over his shoulder. He delayed only a moment at the tower door and rapped sharply. Thud-thud, pause, thud, pause, thud. He dropped a small jug by the door and half-ran to the barracks, slinging off the crossbow as he went. Behind him a guard emerged, hooked his lantern on an iron bar stuck in the wall, and snatched up the jug. He upended it and took a swig. At length, he recalled himself, lowered the jug, and stood stiff-legged before the door.

"Aunt, please, just stay with the Princess."

"The Princess," his aunt reminded him acidly, "is not trying to break into a dungeon in the middle of the night. She's fast asleep in her bed."

The watchtower guard surveyed the surrounding territory between judicious swigs from the jug.

"No, she's not. She's wide-awake. I'd bet on it."

"She is?" Nan disappeared.

Maybe she'd distract herself, and forget to come back. It was the very devil of an inconvenience, this talking to shades, even when they were family. Strive as he might, he could never ignore them; never remember not to speak aloud.

He'd never forget his greatest fiasco during a casual conversation with Drellford. Regrettably, Master Pardell's dead grandfather had been hovering over Drellford's shoulder at the time, remarking caustically on the journeyman's use of shaping tools. Throughout their light discussion of the rival merits of town girls, Farren strove to ignore the grandfather's derision.

Drellford touched up the edges of a curlicue on a chair back. "Mirial's a great cook, but there's something about Sondra, and the way she moves. Have you seen her dance? She just—" He drew circles in the air, shook his head, and shrugged. He dropped the shaping tool, and picked up a blade. "She's bewitching. It's all I can do not to grab her around the waist, and never let go."

The ghostly grandfather howled, "Not the Corter's blade, you fool. Take the number six file for that. Idiot, imbecile—"

Farren snapped. He hurled a chisel onto the workbench and yelled at the shade. "Would you shut the hell up? It's the Master's opinion that counts, not yours."

The grandfather retreated in offended silence before Farren noticed Drellford's stunned look.

"I'm sorry, Drellford," Farren said earnestly, trying desperately to recall what they'd been talking about. "I didn't mean you, I was—" For the thousandth time in his life, the futility of explaining defeated him. "I'm sorry, I was thinking of something else. I'm really sorry."

"Well, if that's the way you feel," said Drellford, "I'll shut up. Personally, I don't give a damn about the Master's

opinion of Sondra." For the rest of the day, Drellford clamped his mouth shut, disregarding Farren's attempts to patch things up. Even now, a year later, Drellford kept him at arm's length.

The guard took half a step backward, prudently within range of the wall. By casual degrees, he leaned against it, his alert stance buckling into a slouch.

Farren patted the flask attached to his belt. Trissi's cider packed quite a punch. If any prisoners were awake, he'd no doubt they'd sink into a puddle of bliss within moments. Rowdy laughter burst from the barracks. The guard turned his head sharply and staggered. He caught the wall and found his way into the tower, his boots scuffing the threshold. He left the door ajar for the later delivery of his dinner. He'd have to wait a bit, though. The errand runner was snoozing behind the woodpile. Trissi had a quick hand with a sleeping draught.

At last, the patrolling guard paced the top of the perimeter wall and disappeared behind the guard post. Farren counted under his breath and reached for the pouch with the guard's dinner. He plodded up the hill in open view, an errand runner performing one last tiresome chore. He lengthened his stride at the end, slipping past the lantern's glow at the door to the guardroom. He pushed the door closed, dropping the dinner pouch with relief.

"He's sleeping like a baby," Aunt Nan said.

Farren jumped, smacking the overhead lantern with his head. It swung crazily, throwing weird shadows on the walls.

Aunt Nan beamed at him. "Trissi's a clever girl. I've never known her to misjudge seasonings, and that's all this is, isn't it? A seasoning for cider, with a useful side effect."

Farren started to speak, but Aunt Nan pressed a finger to his mouth. The overhead lantern lit every corner of the small guard chamber. Next to the stairway gate, the guard sprawled, half-sitting, with closed eyes and a slack-jawed grin.

"The keys are hooked to his belt," said Aunt Nan. "You were perfectly right, the Princess is up *way* past her bedtime, but she wouldn't hear a word I said. Such a stubborn little thing, she is. She's sitting at the window, staring at the watchtower."

The thought warmed him and his hands steadied. He knelt by the sleeping guard, twisting the key ring tied to the guard's belt with a leather strap. It was handy for a guard. It kept the hands free. He'd unlock the gates by swinging the ring upwards, then dropping it immediately. It was less handy for a thief. Farren bit his lip and got to work prying at the knot.

"Farren? Dear?" Aunt Nan's voice was tentative. "I'm most dreadfully sorry, but I can't go into the dungeon with you. I tried, yesterday, but I simply can't get in. There's some sort of shield there. It's like walking into a wall, instead of through one. I don't know why. That dreadful Goat prances in and out all the time."

And Caprio was never around when someone needed him, thought Farren.

"Even Maari can't get in," said Aunt Nan.

"You asked mother to go into the dungeon?"

The guard stirred and Farren edged towards the door.

"*You*," said Aunt Nan to the guard, "you go right back to sleep, do you hear me? We'll have none of this gallivanting around after your bedtime, young man."

The guard cringed with a little boy's guilt and settled into sleep.

"Your mother might not talk to you, Farren, dear, but she loves you. She's just very, er, occupied right now."

The memory of his mother dancing behind the Queen floated into his mind. *Very occupied, yes indeed. Catching stars.*

"But she couldn't get in either. Most peculiar. Farren dear, just *cut* the strap. I grant you, he'll be puzzled in the morning, but you'll give the keys back before he wakes, so there's no harm done."

And in all likelihood, the guard would mend the strap secretly. Otherwise, he'd have to admit he'd fallen asleep. Farren got up, keys in hand, and sheathed his belt knife. He stretched out a hand to his aunt's figure and traced the faint line of her jaw.

"I love you," he said.

She hugged him. The warmth of her affection offset the chill of her touch. "You're a good boy, Farren. Go take care of that poor man. I'll wait right out here, and help him when he arrives."

When he arrived. As a shade.

He shuddered as he ducked through the doorway. The invisible barrier clutched at him, as if he'd walked through a dozen shades at once.

The lantern's dull glimmer lit the edge of each step, but he could have found his way just from the stench. At the foot of the stairs, he raised the lantern to the gate's narrow grill. The bars painted black shadows over the disorderly heaps of arms and legs. Only ragged snorts and moans broke the silence. The third key twanged in the lock, followed by a heavy thunk. He lowered the keys, stilling them against his hip to prevent their jangle. He slid inside and eased the gate shut.

The poison weighed heavily in its innocuous flask. Trissi had laced the bitter tasting brew of poisonous yew berries with wine and sleeping herbs because yew, alone, made an unkind death.

A wreck of a man slumped at his feet. A gaping, glistening wound splayed down the side of his head, partially covered by matted hair. Farren picked his way across the room, avoiding hands and legs, and steeling himself against their misery. There were so many men, in so much pain, and there was so little time to do anything.

Farren had known murderers, rapists, and brutal thieves, some alive, but most dead. He'd seen their victims, too.

During endless nights, he'd crouched in the dark, listening to shades relive their agony, seen their injuries appear in ghastly exactness. Like the battered dogs of his childhood nightmares, they'd heal in an instant and caper with joy, only to face with dawning horror the onset of torture yet again. He'd plead with them, throw his arms around them, and urge them to let the memories go, to rise to heaven in gladness. But they slipped through his arms, unhearing, one after the other, experiencing their own private hells in endless cycles. Eventually, they left, perhaps to heaven, perhaps to another plane, to suffer there as they had in the woods, his workshop, his bedroom, the temple, and the marketplace. It was no surprise, really, that neighbors considered him strange. He'd put on more than one unwitting show for their entertainment.

Prisons were essential, to save those who would otherwise become victims. Some criminals worked in the mines. Others were lashed, castrated, or hanged, their souls snatched away by shade guards as they left the gallows. The public supported the justice system with heartiness verging on glee.

So, why the secrecy? Why the torture, when it couldn't deter those who saw it?

Farren's eye caught on a hunk of flesh so battered he could scarcely see the fingers in what had been a hand. He stepped over a breathing skeleton covered with skin, a man with scarred pits instead of eyes, and another, whose legs ended at his knees, the stumps partially sunk in an oozing puddle of blood and slime.

No one ever heard them scream. At least Trissi had given them a night of peace.

Farren unlocked an inner gate. Three occupants hung from chains on the wall, like slabs of meat in a butchers' shambles, ready for a cut off the rump. His horror and nausea had gone, stunned by an excess of cruelty. Unreality settled on him, like the flies drowsing lazily along the open gashes. He had to deal with Master Orino first, in his pit beyond the next gate. That came first. He'd promised.

The last gate yielded to the fifth key. Farren hoisted it open. It thudded into something and jerked in his hands.

"Lay off, you bastard." A fist pounded weakly on the gate. "...Got to bash me on the head, let me move, can't you? Well, you son-of-a-bitch, you coming, or isn't you?"

Farren pushed the gate further, and it dragged to a stop on the stone floor.

"Damned door, jammed again, think they'd fuckin' build a fuckin' dungeon right, wouldn't you." The hoarse voice rose. "Well, wouldn't you?"

Farren edged around the door. Blood-shot streaming brown eyes, befuddled but canny, gleamed at him from a forest of hair. The man raised a hand to shield his weak eyes from the light. Knife scars ridged the palm of his hand.

"Who the hell are you?" the man muttered. "Know all the guards, I do, and you isn't one of 'em." He blinked and displayed a twisted snaggle-toothed grin. "Come to get me out, did you? Fletcher send you? Fletcher ain't nothing without his skinner, huh? About shittin' time, sonny."

"No, sorry."

"You's a prisoner too, huh? Don't look like one. Shit." He scowled at the door, his drug-marred brain trying to piece together his thoughts. "Funny they left that door unlocked."

Farren stepped around the Skinner, stooping to look at Master Orino in the wall pit. Putting a name to the misshapen face turned his knees to water. Master Orino, celebrated musician, reduced to this. "I need to talk to the singer."

"Him?" Skinner snorted. "Waste of your time. He's beyond help. I shove some food at him, times." Skinner looked slightly defiant. "He sings a good song. Island songs, like my Mama sung. Poor fucker. He's been there since I come. Years, it's been. Looks a right carcass, don't he? Huh.

Right down my line of work. Sneak up on a critter, bash its head in, and rip off the skin. Wouldn't get much for his, though." He regarded his fellow prisoner dispassionately. "Too many rips and scars."

Farren watched the Skinner, hoping he'd drift off to sleep again.

The Skinner rubbed his head, his eyes wandering over, above and beyond Farren. "There's some critters, near the sea, you catch the babies when the mamas leave. Them skins is just as soft as soft. Best skins in the world, worth a mountain of gold. Ladies like it. What's left, after you pull the skin, looks a lot like that." He jerked a thumb at Master Orino. "You'd think he'd a died by now, but none of us do. More and more they shove in, like you. But isn't none of us ever dies. Spooky." He worked his mouth and tried to spit.

"None of you die?" Master Pardell had it right, then. Reflexively, he scanned the darkness. There was not a shade to be seen anywhere, despite the terrifying condition of the prisoners. The barrier he felt, that Aunt Nan couldn't pass, must be sorcery at work. "How long have you been here?"

"Two years, give or take a month. About that. No daylight here. Two years, no light, damned little food. Yesterday, we got out for a little. First daylight I've seen in ages," he said reminiscently. "Hurt like hell, would've heaved, but that takes food, don't it? Those stairs, damn it! They hauled us all up into a little room a few floors up. Some of the buggers tried to get away, but it's no good. Guards bashed 'em down, dragged them back here after, chained 'em up." He indicated the room behind the door. "Should've died, they should. But they didn't. And they won't, neither. You wait and see. Fools, they was. Should have known there was guards everywhere, like damned roaches, they are. Bash a few of 'em, more come piling out of the sinkholes. Not even worth skinning.

"'S like one of his songs, you know?" Skinner's voice wobbled. "*Then treachery seeks to ensnare.* Huh. Got that right. Treachery. You sure you's not from Fletcher?" The weak eyes settled on him. "Hey. You got keys." Skinner straightened, looked over his shoulder, and hissed threateningly. "You're getting out, ain't you? You'll damned well take me with you, boy. Hear me?"

The Skinner dragged himself to his feet. He fell, caught himself on the gate, and lurched upright. "You will, boy, or I'll yell, and wake up me mates. Hear me?"

Trissi's brew wasn't strong enough to survive a bash on the head, apparently. Farren pictured himself, one man inside with the keys, faced with a mob of waking, angry men. There'd be a mass escape. He almost welcomed the notion of getting the poor fellows into the light, where they could mend. And yet, if sorcery kept them alive, some of them might die when they crossed the barrier. Or would they? The guards had managed to get them upstairs alive.

Besides, he couldn't risk it. He might be loosing human demons on the town. He needed more facts. "Sure," said Farren.

The menace in Skinner's glare faded. "Aye, well, you just remember that. You do your talking now, so's we can get out of here." He wagged a hand at Orino.

Farren crouched by the pit. "Master Orino?" He fumbled for the flask at his belt, and opened it. He raised it to his own lips, and pretended to gulp, aware of the fascinated eyes behind him. "Master Orino, I need to talk to you." Farren wiped his mouth with the back of his hand.

"Whassat?" Skinner collapsed onto the floor and stretched out a shaking hand.

"Just cider."

"Gimme some, boy. I'm dry as a bone."

Farren shook the flask. "There's a good bit left," he said reluctantly. "Let me—"

Skinner snatched it out of his hand, and backed against the wall. "You'll live without it, boy. There's more outside. It's no hardship." He swigged it down, groaning with pleasure. "Gods, thass good. Bless you, boy." He took another gulp. "Maybe I'll give you a job, iffen we get out of this, whatcha think, boy? How's that for an offer. Teach you all about skins, where best to hunt. Nobody better nor Skinner, just ask. Ask Fletcher. The cretin finally sent you in for me, din't he? Knew he needed me. Nobody better'n Skinner."

"Not good enough, though," Farren said, deliberately provocative. "You got caught. Skinning the King's deer, were you? I don't need a job from a fool."

The piggy eyes looked at him resentfully. "I'm no poacher, boy. I'm an adventurer. New animals, new skins, best kind, thass what I'm good at. Unknown rivers, untouched coastlines, tops of the highest mountains, thass where you find the best stuff, where nobody goes huntin'. Thickest fur, softest skin, sell 'em for a fortune, I do. The Empress has the only cloak in the world made out of dou'uu, takes a couple hundred to make one, and who you think got 'em for her? Me, thass who. Flaky little beasts, damned sharp teeth."

"But you got caught, thrown in here. Criminals have to be smart enough to get away. You didn't."

"Ain't no criminal. 'Tain't illegal, not climbin' the Crest looking for sommat new. Hey, you're tryin' to trick me, ain't you? Well, I ain't gonna tell you whatsomever I was after. Thass my secret. You wanna know, you's gonna have to get me out, ain't you? I ain't no dumbass like Fletcher." He tilted the flask, draining the final drops, and shook the bottle. "Huh. All gone. Good stuff, gotta get more soon's we get out. You got more outside?"

Farren nodded. Skinner's eyes fell shut, opened with an effort, and sagged to half-mast.

"Best skinner inna world, thass me," he said. "You name

it, I got it. Seals, otters, muskrats, them antelope things from down south, then up to the north for them longhaired dayaks. Aye yeah, got me tons of skins. Gotta reputation. I'se skinned things there ain't no name for. Stuck here, two goddamned years, four shittin' months, helluva waste of a good man. On the trail of something big, I am. Said there was no such thing, Fletcher said. What does he know? Cussed fool." Skinner sagged sideways onto the rough floor. He patted it with a hand, trying to plump the stone into a pillow.

"You tell me, boy, when you're done talkin'. I'm ready, hear?" A massive yawn overtook him. "No such thing, huh. What's he know?" His voice faded off. Farren strained to hear him. "No such thing as a dragon. Huh. Fool." With a final snort, Skinner subsided into noisy slumber.

A dragon? Farren grinned. Who was the fool, Fletcher or Skinner? He tugged the flask of Trissi's cider out of Skinner's hand, restored its cap, and hooked it to his belt. He detached the other, the Princess' brew.

"Master Orino? Master?" He reached through the bars and shook the man's shoulder gently.

Even in the light of the lantern, Orino's eyes looked dull and lifeless. His colors had faded so badly they were scarcely discernible.

"Master? The Princess sent me."

The grotesque head moved. Farren flinched with pity.

"Master, I could try to get you out—" He tested the rusting bars, but the Master moved a hand, stopping him. "I'm sorry, Master." The sight of him wrung Farren's soul to limpness. "I thought— The Princess thought— Maybe..."

He held up the open flask. "It's yew berries. Poison. Master, please, isn't there anything I can do for you?" Futilely, he yanked on the bars, still solid despite their rust. "At least, I can get you out of there, so you can breathe the air again."

"No."

"Master, I'm so sorry. I can get you free. Let me go back for my tools."

"No." The breathy voice halted him in its tracks. "Either way, I'd die. I'd have died years ago but for the binding laid on this place."

"It's true then? You can't die? Then the poison won't work. Master, I can't leave you here."

"Trust the girl. Her magic will turn the trick. She wouldn't have sent it, if she weren't sure." The ragged voice gave a breath of a chuckle. "Don't let it trouble you. I look forward to being a shade. I can sing again, where others will hear me."

"I'll listen for you, Master. The shades are waiting for you on the other side of the wall. My Aunt Nan is there. You used to know her. She was the Princess' Nanny."

"Ah, Nan. A good friend." The exhausted face managed a trace of a smile. "If a trifle talkative."

Involuntarily, Farren choked out a laugh. "Just a trifle."

"Thank you, messenger of the Princess. Thank her for me." The skeletal hand clutched the flask. "Be sure to take the flask with you when you leave." The sound of a teacher's voice, kindly but authoritarian, was incongruous. "And be sure that you leave promptly."

"Aye," Farren said. He reached through the bars, and rested his fingers on the Master's shoulder.

"Dear Mericia. She made it palatable, even tasty. A sweet girl, to be the center of such conspiracy."

"Sir, what is the conspiracy? What can you tell me?"

"I *know* very little. I get snatches, that's all. Has the Progress taken place?"

"We start tomorrow. Should I warn her not to go?"

"No, no. She must return to the Island." A glint returned to the dying eyes. "She must. Seven years, seven years. So many things have limits, and magic is among them. Seven years to build and seven years to break. Seven years, to the day, boy, to the very day. Tell her."

"What happened seven years ago? What happens at the end?"

"Threads of insanity," murmured Orino, "twined with those of coldest logic."

"Please Master, who is the enemy? Tell me. For the Princess' sake."

"I'm sorry. I only see images. The Goat says you see shades. Is it useful?" The thin body shuddered. The pulse in his throat pumped wildly.

"Not very."

"Ah. That's how it is with me. I see only faint scraps tied to the wind and blown away." Farren strained to hear the words. "Perhaps afterwards, I'll see more clearly."

"If you can't see me when you die, just look for Aunt Nan. Master?"

The pulse in the Master's throat had stopped.

"Master." Farren busied himself retrieving the flask, and stowing it away. He sat back on his heels, wiped his eyes fiercely, and cleared his throat. "Master," he said to the unseen shade, "Aunt Nan is waiting outside." The presence at his shoulder faded.

Farren rose, passed the sleeping Skinner, and left the chamber, locking the door behind him. Perhaps Skinner would think it had all been a dream. At least he'd sleep well. They'd all sleep well, for an hour or two at least. That gave him a little time for a mission of his own.

He unhooked his emergency pouch, with medicines, needles, waxed thread, and a second heavier bottle of Trissi's cider. His emotions firmly in check, Farren tried key after key. The manacles unlocked, and he lifted the first man down to the floor.

☙

"He should be out by now," said Mericia. "It's been an hour already." Mericia sat on the window seat of her bedroom, straining her eyes in the darkness outside.

"Don't worry about Farren," Trissi said. She drew up the straight chair next to the window and sat down. "He's a stubborn ass like his brother, but he'll take care of himself. All that blather about a friend of his, just as if we'd never guess he'd go by himself."

The room was dark, the better to watch out the window. Trissi stretched her sore knee to the side and rubbed it. It only twinged now and then, but she'd been running all day, up and down stairs, out to gather the yew for Meriss' potion, and still manage enough work that Bonnara hadn't noticed her absences.

"Trissi," Mericia gasped. Her face lit with sudden joy. "Trissi, look. He did it, Farren did it! Master Orino, thank the gods, you're here, you're free!" She turned from the window, and stretched out her hands.

Trissi stared intently. "I'll have to take your word for it. I can't see him at all, but I'm glad you do." She patted her friend's knee, also stuck out an awkward angle. Good, then. Meriss had one worry off her mind, at least.

Mericia stared into space for a long time, apparently entranced by the shade's conversation. At last, she blinked, and managed a watery smile.

"Trissi, he's so happy to be free. He's singing a sea chantey, the one your uncle sang about the great fish towing the ship to sea. Can't you hear him?"

" No. And I must say, I think it's totally unfair after all I've done," she added tartly. She waited until Mericia lost her blind look. "Is he gone already?"

"Yes, he's left. He's going to the Island, he says."

"Ah, good. Then you'll see him there. Come along, dear friend. It's been a long day. It's time for you to go dream about your dragon. Time to get to bed. And me, too!" she added fervently, pulling herself to her feet.

"I think I'll stay up for a while yet, Trissi. You go to bed."

"Why stay up?" Trissi raised an eyebrow, and rested a hand on one hip. "Surely you're not interested in our Farren, now are you, Meriss?"

"Of course not," said Mericia.

Trissi grimaced, watching the ice flow back into Mericia's face. Years of habit, of not daring to care, would be hard to overcome. And besides, the enemy, whether the Lady or someone else, was still out there, watching. It was safer for Farren if the princess' interest remained hidden. "I'm sorry, Meriss. I shouldn't tease you about something like that. It was cruel. Look, can't you think in bed? I'm going downstairs. I'll watch for Farren, and make sure he gets out safely. If I need to, I'll go rescue him, swinging a skillet over my head. He'll get out, Meriss. He's no fool." Trissi clenched a fist and waved it under Mericia's nose. "Get to bed, Riss, or I'll put you out myself."

A tiny smile stole over Mericia's face as she pushed the fist away. "Okay, Riss, you win."

At last, Trissi headed down the stairs, favoring her sore leg. So Master Orino was a shade, free to wander as shades wandered, doing whatever shades did. Or, so Mericia said, and she had no reason to lie. Oh, how infuriating, to listen to Meriss and Farren go on about Nanny and the Goat and Orino. Listening to them was like watching a juggler with your eyes shut. You missed all the best parts. Trissi yearned to see shades herself. At least sometimes, like now. After all her hard work, it was difficult not to feel let down at such circumstantial proof of success.

"I'm glad you're free, Master Orino," she said, testing the silence. "I always liked you. You were good to us both. I loved your songs."

Faintly, a breeze stirred in the dark corridor, where no draft should be. Faintly, but tunefully, the thread of a tenor voice traveled to her ears. She stood and listened, transfixed.

> *"When the wings of the mountains brush the soul*
> *of the sea,*
> *When the two and the many are one.*
> *When illusions of freedom encircle and flee*
> *Then the threads of the challenge are spun."*

She leaned against the wall, and closed her eyes, letting the words capture her as they had years before. Oh, that melody. She'd never heard anything to match it. It was like a spell winding her heart around the words. She'd never forget a single note.

> *"No matter the dream, or the steps you may stray*
> *Our lives entangle your net*
> *As you leap to the skies, or dive to the sea,*
> *Our hearts must follow you yet.*
>
> *When the wool and the flax meet madder and weld*
> *When the stars cease their tumble to flare*
> *When hidden desires refuse to be quelled*
> *Then treachery seeks to ensnare.*
>
> *No matter the captive, or the heart that now sleeps*
> *The world is caught in your net*
> *As you soar to the clouds, or plunge to the deeps,*
> *Our hearts are torn with regret.*
>
> *When the souls in bondage are freed at the last*
> *When the waves of the hurricane cease*
> *When a nation of chaos meets the sins of its past*

Then the world at last may know peace."

In the bedroom at the top of the stairs, Princess Mericia crept from under the covers and settled into the window seat. She breathed lightly on something cupped in her hands, and gazed out the window, preparing for the second part of her lengthy vigil.

And up a few stairs, down a corridor, and down some other stairs, a single candle lighted a tapestry. A pair of hands set a last stitch, and from the border of the cloth, Master Orino's face shone. His head tilted at a jaunty angle, and his mouth was open to sing. The hands rerolled the tapestry, and his face disappeared among others.

Chapter Eleven

D avid loitered by the barn. He studied the corner of the pasture, now thronged with great black mules. The Shadebinder hunched in the midst of them, barely visible over the long flicking ears. He must be picking stones from a mule's hoof. So, that was one more mark in the tally of the Shadebinder's curious actions during the first week of the Progress.

David's heady excitement about the Progress had dimmed by the second day. The King's retinue included knights, lords and ladies, artisans, craft masters, and merchants. They were attended by huntsmen, carters, coachmen, and grooms, as well as servants for cooking, laundry, dressing, cleaning, and sewing. Moving the lot of them south, an inch at a time, was backbreaking work. Scores of voices yelled, admonished, and ordered, while hundreds of hands poised to grab him by the ear.

Here boy, haul this box to milady in the fourth coach behind the Queen. You there, boy, fill this feedbag for the knight's courser, and be snappy about it.

Day by day, the retinue wrangled its way south, inundating manors and small castles along the way. Sometimes the overflow deluged neighboring towns. Officious stewards commandeered shops and cottages for their masters, while the original owners slept uncomfortably in outbuildings. David, after a few attempts to acquire bed space in cramped quarters, gave it up and slept in the straw next to his horses. Most of his mates followed his example.

Snobbish attitudes worsened matters. Lofty craftsmen and haughty upper servants with tiptilted noses scorned to lift a finger beyond their own particular specialties. Wolton exploded when the wheelwright conscripted David and Thom to prop up a cart. Wolton would thank him very much to keep his thieving hands off Wolton's cavalry juniors. Otherwise, the Horse Master would have a thing or two to say to the Wright Master, and so would the Captain of the King's Guard. Each man to his own calling, Wolton declared. David's gleeful appreciation died a rapid death as he mucked out years' worth of dung from neglected barns. The Progress' carriage horses were unaccustomed to such quarters, their offended irritability a perfect mirror image of the prevailing human attitudes.

David kept to his own calling. He rubbed down horses, kept them fit in substandard stables, shot dummy cross bolts at hastily erected targets, and helped maintain security. Guard captains relied on the eyes and ears of cavalry juniors. David spent hours in the saddle scouting the periphery of the plodding Progress. He saw Wolton's pronouncement proved again and again: each to his own calling. The wheelwright scorned to help a carpenter repair the front end of a coach. The huntsmen, to a man, refused to assist carters with vehicles fallen into ditches. The stonemasons snorted their disdain when entertainers pleaded for space and quiet to practice their routines.

The Shadebinder fascinated David. In the midst of the hubbub, he stood out like a bashed thumb. The Shadebinder held heated arguments with his carthorses as he walked with them. Sometimes he grinned like a lunatic, flailed the air with clenched fists, or bowed to an empty spot in the road. He conversed with a donkey, a refugee from several carts back. The master retrieved the donkey three times, then threw up his hands. After all, the donkey still carried his burden. He just chose to amble, untethered, next to the Shadebinder as he did so.

Despite the crowds crammed onto the bumpy roads, the Shadebinder's cart traveled in a large buffer of open space. People stepped off the road when passing him, as if the man had smallpox. Yet, for all the suspicious glares, an odd double standard permeated the Progress. Just when David accepted the man's pariah status, some little event occurred, and the Shadebinder's oddities were temporarily forgiven.

Last evening they'd lodged at Lord Ylnori's manor, which boasted a hall large enough to accommodate two-thirds of the travelers at a time. The royal family and highest nobility dined upstairs, but the rank and file elbowed their way into the hall. David squeezed into place at the lowest table. Bickering voices and childish wails filled the air. Two tables over, a woman jiggled a cranky baby over her shoulder. She wore the sleep-starved look of David's mother after the twins' birth.

David spotted the Shadebinder approaching. He weaved and ducked through the aisles, even stepping up on a bench for two steps to avoid something invisible. He halted suddenly, as though hauled up short by a leash, his head seemingly dragged towards the baby. The Shadebinder reached for the child, snatched back his hands, and leaned forward, whispering into the mother's ear. The mother started violently, hugging her child to her breast. The Shadebinder nodded and backed up a pace. Before he could leave, she thrust the child to him, her face pleading.

The clamor hushed as people stared at the Shadebinder. The baby's miserable wail captured all ears. The Shadebinder lifted the child over his head, his big hands wrapped around its chest.

"And what's the matter with you, little thing?" The mellow voice was rich with tolerant affection. "Really? You don't say. Well, we can't have that, can we?"

The Shadebinder danced down the aisle again, spinning in circles, his laughing face turned up to the baby's. The wail petered out, was replaced with hiccups, and finally a watery chuckle.

"Good for you," he crowed. "You've a tough spirit, little one. You'll make it. Just take it easy on your Mam, all right? She's exhausted. She doesn't always have time to play." He lowered the child until they were nose to nose. "We'd all be better off if we played more, that's what I think! Ha! You agree, don't you? I can see it clearly." He rubbed noses with the laughing child, held it close, and walked down the aisle. "See, little one, they're all moving out of the way, just for you! Thank you, all of you," he said, smiling. He nodded to the right and left, sometimes at a person on the bench, and sometimes to nothing at all.

By the time he reached the mother, he'd extracted a packet from the leather pouch at his waist. "Well, she's got quite a tummy ache, seems she can't handle beef broth very well. She's got the squits, too, but I'm sure you know that as well as I do. Here now, if you steep this in a bit of hot water—" He looked to the left and right, abruptly aware of his audience. "Could someone find hot water for this little girl? I'm afraid I don't know her name, as she can't talk yet. Gerita? Oh, thank you, dame, I appreciate it." He handed the bowl to the mother, jiggling Gerita with his other hand. "My Aunt Nan swears by this. It's good enough for the princess herself, she says, and she should know. She's the princess' Nanny, you know."

A muttering rose through those nearby, but he didn't seem to notice. "Now, Gerita," the Shadebinder murmured, "it tastes nasty, but it'll help your tummy. Drink it all down, now won't you?" He gave the baby to her mother and leaned on the table, bringing the cup to the baby's lips. "Sometimes we have to resort to the old wet cloth routine, but I think you'll manage. Yes, indeed. A fine girl. She'll feel better in a little bit." And with a pat and a nod, he traipsed down the aisle again, oblivious to the stares.

In the evenings, when travel halted, David had seen him rebuilding a footbridge, helping a one-armed man roof his cottage, shoveling out a latrine, and sharpening needles for Lady Siree. In a world of people jealously guarding their prerogatives, the Shadebinder was an adventurer, living everyone's lives but his own.

And now, the Shadebinder tended mules. All the merchants were supposed to tend their own beasts. Actually, they brought servants to coddle the horses, and left the mules to fend for themselves in the common pasture. Mules were tough beasts, everyone said. Everyone except the Shadebinder.

David vaulted the fence and walked towards the mules. The big, long-eared beasts stood slack-hipped and relaxed, clumped within a few lengths of the Shadebinder. A large black mule stood contentedly on three legs, one ear cocked forward and the other back, submitting his left forehoof to the Shadebinder's pick. David leaned against the fence, keeping his distance from the powerful hind legs. The drovers bragged about the mules' legendary kicks.

It was stupid to hang around the Shadebinder. There must be some substance to the sorcery rumors. Could the Shadebinder trap his soul? Could he mesmerize David as easily as these mules? But curiosity had grown to a fevered pitch, mingled with incoherent yearning. Was it all magic? Or something else, something more?

Several days ago, journey-horseman Wolton had sent David on a trial run with a new courser on a lead rein. David's pride at Wolton's trust soured with resentment at riding a Patrol extra while leading the courser. David might be only twelve, but he'd been a horseman since he could walk. His father'd seen to that. David cantered several miles through the surrounding hills, pressing the new horse as hard as he could without exhausting his own mount. He'd run another training loop two days ago, but this time David switched horses once out of sight. Without his weight, David's erstwhile mount made better speed. It caught the courser's enthusiasm and they'd had a great run.

That night, he'd scoffed to his friends. What was Wolton thinking about, prating on and on about this horse's strong will and vicious temper. The courser had a wonderful mile-eating stride, and a sunny temperament.

Thom's mouth dropped open. Their words tumbling over each other, Thom and Janos set him straight. David had been on scouting patrol when Western First Guard Terrell brought the horse in, months ago. The horse savaged a groom almost immediately. Even Vorest couldn't stick to his back for more than a few minutes. And the sudden change in temperament? Cavalryman Denys, now a Second, asked his brother to bewitch it and he had!

Watch your step around that horse, they warned. What if the Shadebinder released the spell? The horse would go crazy. And who'd be tending it? Not the Shadebinder or his brother, not by a long shot.

The Shadebinder. David's eyes flew to Usal and Thom. They'd hidden in the loft when David snuck into the stable to the haunted stall. He'd never told them the full story. They wouldn't have believed him.

"Aren't you tired of following me?"

David jumped. The Shadebinder's glance caught him, held him, and released him, smiling faintly. "David, isn't it?"

David nodded.

"Look, if you're here, then help. Otherwise, get away. I

don't need more people staring at me. I get enough of that already." Behind him, a mule shoved its nose into the crook of his arm. The Shadebinder settled his arm around the mule's neck. "After all," said the Shadebinder in a deep, threatening voice, "you're breathing my air."

David flinched before the words registered. A laugh escaped him. The Shadebinder grinned. He ran his fingers around the mule's ear, tugging gently. "Give me a hand, why don't you? I'm checking hooves, looking for pack galls, things like that." He pushed on a mule's rump. It ambled to David and butted his chest with its bony head.

David pushed the nose aside and ran his hands down its neck. Mechanically, he looked for swollen hocks and examined patches in the hide. The proportions seemed subtly wrong. He'd never dealt with mules. The cavalry lived and breathed horses. They scarcely considered other four-footed creatures alive.

"Thanks. Here, catch." The Shadebinder tossed him a small pot of ointment. His head disappeared behind a mule's substantial flank.

"Why do you bother with them?" David ventured. "They're not yours."

"Just helping my friends."

"Friends?" The Shadebinder didn't seem to have any friends, except the black-haired servant girl who walked alongside his cart sometimes.

"These friends." The Shadebinder slapped the mule on the flank. "A man can't have enough friends, and I've got plenty right here, can't you see?" He looked across the pasture. "Hmm." He pointed at the stable. "Is he looking for you?"

Wolton strode towards them. Instantly, David checked off his duties in his mind. Had he skipped one? He couldn't think of any. Of course, on Progress, that meant nothing. Work was endless.

"Hey," Wolton greeted the Shadebinder. "I brought your dinner." Wolton dropped a packet of food and a small jug on the ground on his side of the fence, well out of reach of inquisitive noses. He rested a foot on the lower bar of the fence, and propped his elbows on the top one. David relaxed, but his ears pricked up. The lead journey-horseman on the Progress, delivering a packet of food? In a pig's eye.

"Thanks," the Shadebinder said on an inquiring note.

"Vorest took that horse of Denys' out on a test run today. Brolin, you call him. Good horse, he says."

The Shadebinder nodded. His eyes traveled past Wolton. He chuckled. Reflexively, Wolton turned to look at the vacant yard and let out an exasperated sigh. "Gods, I *hate* it when you do that, Farren."

"Sorry." The Shadebinder looked amused. "I'm glad he adjusted well. Thanks for telling me."

"Yeah, well. Denys will be glad. You did good work."

"I didn't do anything much."

"Yeah, right." Wolton drummed his fingers on the fence top. His tentative attitude baffled David. Wolton shot off decisions as if they were arrows from a crossbow. He rapped out orders to apprentices and cavalry juniors, assigning tasks and kicking butt as needed. "Look, I need a favor."

"Name it." The Shadebinder moved up to the fence. His long-eared admirers followed.

Wolton scowled at David and waved him back to the barn. David's feet moved without conscious volition.

"Let him stay," said the Shadebinder.

Wolton scowled. "Huh. Keep your mouth shut, boy, you hear me?"

"He will," the Shadebinder said. "His name's David."

"David," said Wolton, automatically. "I *know* what his name is."

"Just thought I'd mention it," said the Shadebinder, with

a merry look in his eyes. "What's the favor?"

"Look, I've got this mare. Beautiful thing, nice gaits. Irandis picked her out for the King. She's a gift for the Princess' birthday."

David sucked in his breath. Wolton jerked a thumb towards him. "Even David could tell you. Superb little horse, but I wouldn't have said she'd suit the princess. I'm a bit worried. I thought maybe you'd take her on, calm her down."

"I can't ride for two feet without falling off. I'm not a horseman."

Wolton laughed. "I don't know what you are, friend. I've never known. But I saw Denys' horse when Terrell first brought him in, and now he's so gentle a child could ride him." He threw an ironic look at David. "Listen, we've got a week before we get to the Island. As she is, the mare'd never manage the boat without killing herself. Keep her with you for a while. Let me know what you think." He added deliberately, "The girl doesn't have the best luck with horses."

The men traded a long look. The Shadebinder looked into the distance, listening to something inaudible. Wolton waited. "All right. I'll be in when I'm done here."

Wolton clapped the other man on the shoulder roughly, and nodded his thanks.

David watched him go, and burst out, "Why do you do it? It's not your job to tame the horse, it's his. These mules aren't your job either. Why do you bother?"

The Shadebinder slapped the nearest mule lightly on the flank. It shook itself and wandered off to graze. Another pushed up in its place.

"How do you *do* that? The drovers say they're mean. Is it—is it magic? Do you bewitch them?"

The Shadebinder smiled in a flash of white teeth. "There's no magic to it."

"It *could* be magic." David shot him a glance and added daringly, "My mother says you're Sighted."

"Kind of her. Most people use other words," he said. "It's not magic. I see souls, that's all. Alive or dead, human or animal."

"Animals have souls? I mean, can you talk to them?" Suddenly he felt very young, like the twins begging for a puppy. He swallowed hard, and stared into a mule's ear. "Can you teach me?" His voice broke on the last word.

The Shadebinder picked at the mud on the mule's scarred hide. "Why?"

Hot and tangled thoughts tumbled through David's mind. The guards treasured horses. Farmers tended domestic beasts, and scarcely spared glances for birds overhead, or scampering squirrels. If they couldn't be eaten, ridden, or sheared, animals were only tales for children. David, however, had grown up on his mother's stories: of the great Island bird that hid in the cavern depths of the Crest; the thickly-pelted dou'uu, tiny enough to cup in two hands; the legendary kraaken, the sea creature so vast men sometimes mistook it for an island; great shaggy ox-like beasts on the plains of the southern continent, with horns larger than the greatest mountain goat ever found.

David's soul soared and cringed at every tale, every animal. Oh yes, David loved horses, but their part in the world felt immeasurably small.

"I found a hawk once," he said in a low voice. "Its wing was broken, and I could feel it hurting. I bound it up as best I could, and took it to the falconer." He'd been on a training run, two miles out. He felt the bird's throbbing pain in his own head, felt the jolting it would take if he rode back with it. He tied the horse's reins to his belt, and walked back to the castle as fast as he could. Wolton had been livid with fury. David's duty had been to the horse he rode, not to a damned bundle of feathers. "I got it there all right, but the falconer said it would never fly again. He killed it." All through that long walk, the bird had been in agony. David should have killed it himself. He'd thought about it, again and again on the road home, but he'd clung to hope. In his mind's eye, the bird had soared overhead, commanding the skies.

His vision blurred. Unthinkingly, David threw his arms around the mule's neck, comforted by the pulsing heat of the blood under its skin. He opened his mouth, and the words poured out in a torrent.

Rage drove Trissi's fingers through the complicated leather knots. Meriss didn't permit herself to get angry. Meriss crippled herself with 'rules for royalty' and 'honorable behavior' and 'Whether His Majesty Would Approve.' He wouldn't approve of this, but Trissi wasn't royal, and besides, honor shouldn't get in the way of common sense. Trissi was just protecting her friend. Mericia kept dragging her feet. She wouldn't confront Lady Lelori without proof of her treachery. Well then, fine. She wanted proof? Trissi would find it, probably right here in the luggage wagon.

Trissi peered through the cracks in the front wall of the enclosed cart. The carter, lackadaisically chewing on straw, hadn't the faintest idea about his stowaway. In fact, without Bonnara, the entire Progress was clueless about Trissi's activities, and that suited her right down to the ground. Bonnara'd stayed at Castle Ramsvalt, sinking her hands deeply into the crevices of the Ramsvalt castle kitchen, delighted to get everyone out of her hair. The other servants minded their dignity in wagons, or flirted along the wayside. Poor Meriss was trapped in the Queen's traveling carriage with the Queen, Lady Siree, and the Lady.

The wagon lurched violently as the horses struggled

to pull it free of another hole. Trissi fumbled the strap, swore, and started again. It felt *good* be angry, to be mad clear through to her bones. Her hands flew with ruthless efficiency. The strap loosened. She yanked the box off the stack, tipping it into the narrow aisle with a subdued thud. She braced herself against the wagon's sway, and shoved the crate onto another stack. She spared a moment to strap it into place. Loose crates in a moving wagon could tilt, fall, and knock her unconscious. She didn't have *time* to be unconscious. Her mercurial spirits rose at the absurdity, and she squirreled away at the next box.

Poor Meriss was caged in the traveling carriage, with no one but the Lady for company. The Queen would be fast asleep in her corner of the coach, wedged into place with blankets and cushions, her hands still moving restlessly at invisible stitchery. Lady Siree would be trying to sleep, insisting loudly that she *had* to sleep, right *now* while she had the chance. She was quite right, too. The instant the Queen alighted, she always reached for the rolls of tapestry stowed safely under her seat, with no thought of food or rest. She'd brought all six completed panels, as well as the current one. Every night, Siree and Trissi reassembled the blasted tapestry frame, and the Queen spent every nighttime moment stitching. After the first forty-eight hours, during which the Queen neither slept nor ate, Trissi packed food, pillows, and blankets into the coach.

Trissi jerked out a second crate, smashing her fingertips under the corner. She stifled an exclamation and listened for the wagon driver. Good, maybe he was deaf. She sucked on her wounded fingers for a moment, and kicked the crate down the aisle. Trust Lady Lelori to pack her own case at the absolute bottom, in the most awkward possible spot.

Meriss still half-believed in the mythical curse, but after old Brother Lawrence died, Trissi knew better. Slowly, feeling her way, she collected gossip and innuendo. She tracked the movements of her narrowing band of suspects with quick wits and sly questions. She was rock-solid sure of her information. Lady Lelori, under the veil of sophistication, persecuted the princess, methodically maiming or killing anyone she feared might gain influence with her. Quite apart from the little telltales Trissi picked up, who else controlled every detail of Mericia's life and also had access to the dungeon?

They had to move fast. Whatever the Lady's plans, she wouldn't kill Mericia, at least not yet. She wanted Mericia alive and unmarried. A living Princess Regent would need a chief advisor, and no doubt the Lady would elect herself. Perhaps she planned to marry Mericia off to a fellow conspirator, but more likely, she'd poison Queen Ailsa to force a coronation. Once the Progress retreated to Ramsvalt, the Lady could kill the new Queen, and seize power for herself. Neither Prince Kellian nor Prince Randall could inherit. On the island, power always went from woman to woman. It had been so long before Elizar's aborted reign, many generations ago. After Meriss died, there'd be no other logical choice than Lady Lelori, who was probably the Emperor's puppet.

Trissi loved Meriss and admired her courage. But faced with treachery, she'd study it to death, and never act. Meanwhile, the forces ranged against her would mass to crush her. Well, Trissi had her own plans. The Queen had done her job well, binding the girls' hearts and souls into an inextricable plait. For a fleeting moment, she grieved. Dear Denys. Even if Trissi wanted to leave Meriss, she couldn't. Meriss needed her. Riss needed Riss. Even if sisterly love didn't demand the sacrifice, Queen Ailsa's magic would.

Trissi wriggled between two stacks of crates, onto a leather-bound trunk. She dragged Lady Lelori's crate into the aisle and extracted a pry bar from her bag. She'd swiped it from Farren's wagon while he murmured to a bright brown horse tethered to his belt. He'd have loaned her the pry bar, but she didn't want to involve him. She half-wondered where he'd gotten the horse. He didn't have it yesterday.

The wood creaked as she pried the lid off the crate. The sound put her teeth on edge. She set it aside, revealing Lady Lelori's private travel case, securely enmeshed in blankets. She'd gone through the Lady's clothes and scanned the books already, though the filtering light made reading a trial. The travel case was about the size of a Valtiris' history volume. Mother-of-pearl and abalone shell decorated the light southern woods. The Lady had locked it.

Trissi balanced the box in her lap, holding over it a twiddle of clay shaped like a box: Trissi's idea, but Mericia's construction. She held it to her mouth, breathed on it, tapped the top of the clay box and lifted its tiny cover. She bent over the Lady's travel case. A breath on the case, a tap on the top, and the travel case opened obediently.

With difficulty, Trissi managed not to cheer out loud. *Way to go, Meriss!*

A brooch of pearls; an agate pin; hairpins; a scarf; small pots, sealed with wax. Trissi twisted one open to investigate. Ink? Green ink. A faint tinge of pink stained an identical pot. Trissi stared at the virtually empty case. Ink and a few baubles, no better than Bonnara's, and a letter or two. With a distinct feeling of letdown, Trissi picked up the small stack of letters.

It was only sensible to read them, she thought. Denys' face flitted through her mind, and she dropped the letters back into the case. Stupid, stupid, stupid, she scolded herself, but there it was, she wouldn't read private letters. But even Denys wouldn't argue about looking at the envelopes, would he? Well, would he? One, two, three—

And there it was, plain as day.

A letter in Prince Randall's broad boyish hand, addressed to his sister, Princess Mericia of Ramsvalt.

෧

Mericia sat by the window in the borrowed manor, the letter open inside a book.

> *To the Princess Mericia of Valtiris, Heir to Ailsandia, and our Elder Sister, Greetings,*
>
> *Oh good, he's gone. Sorry, Riss, our tutor was hanging around, and he's into all these foreign protocols. Well, you know how it is, like you with Lady Lelori. Anyway, we're really, really sorry we can't come to your birthday, especially since we'll miss the coronation and everything. The Island Progress celebrations are supposed to be fabulous, food and music, and gorgeous girls...*

Mericia glanced up from the book which hid the letter. Her mother sat stitching, and Lady Siree hovered over her. How strange. Instead of embroidering, her mother was joining two panels together, with white thread and nearly invisible stitches.

The letter changed into Randall's handwriting, still exuberant, but more legible.

> *Sorry, Riss, you know what Kell's like. But we were looking forward to it a lot, and to seeing you and Mom and Dad. We want to explore the volcano now we're old enough for some serious rock climbing. We were supposed to ship out in July, but a storm blew up, and after that our ship's mast just shattered, right there in the harbor.*

A blot marred the page, as if one brother had snatched the pen from the other.

Kellian: And then—you're not going to believe this. The Emperor planned to send a routine patrol down the coast, all the way to Catiffar, so we talked him into letting us go, too. Then we'd just ship across to the Island, because Catiffar's nearly as close to the Island as the Valtiris Coast on the other side. But it snowed, it damned well snowed in the summer. It was heaviest snowfall in generations, and the mountains were impassible. They had to send the Patrol around to the Eastern Pass, and they said we couldn't come. Besides, it would be too late. It's like we're cursed.

Mericia's stomach took a sickening dip.

Randall: Kell's joking. Just quirks of nature, but really badly timed, you know? Hey, do us a favor? Measure the width of the Island harbor, or maybe make us one of those relief maps Dad says you're so good at? The maps here are really out of date. Kell and me, we've got a bet going with our tutor. No way the harbor's as small as he says.

Seriously, Riss, we're sorry not to be there. It must be scary, having to take over for Mom already. How is she?

Mericia glanced at her mother. She was glad the boys weren't there to see her.

Kell: We wanted to hike right around the Island rim, from watchtower to watchtower, all ten of them. We'd figured to

*do it in two days, and stay overnight at the
southern tip. We're going to try to talk Dad
into letting us join the Sea Patrol for a six-
month hitch. Do you think he'd let us do it?
A southern Minister came to the audience
yesterday, and he told about pirates, and
towns laid waste, ships looted, charred
embers floating up on the tides. Just think
of it, all that, just south of you. I wish we
could be there to help. Besides, Valtiris is in
danger, too. We should help protect it.*

*Randall: We'll see you as soon as we
can. These storms can't go on forever. And
if they do, if the climate's changed like the
weather forecasters say, we'll just hike the
mountains and head down Catiffar Coast.
Somehow or other, we'll see you in the next
year or two. I promise. Word of a prince.*

*Kell: Me, too. Randall's got that right.
Take care of yourself, Riss. Write to us. We
haven't heard from you in ages. And tell us
how mother is, really. Dad just says she's
the same. He won't tell us anything, and
what the envoys say is really bad.*

*Brothers forever,
Kellian and Randall*

Mericia shook off a tear and forced herself to analyze the
letter, with all its shreds of news. Which piece, exactly, was
so important that Lady Lelori decided to steal the letter—
but not destroy it?

Chapter Twelve

The clouded bronze eyes blinked in the cave's depths. A breeze tickled the flaring nostrils, teasing the creature with the smell of fish, and the sharp piping cries of seabirds. Its empty belly growled. It shambled towards the cliff edge, squinting in the dusky half-light. Waves roiled on the rocks below, their turbulence split by sharp dropoffs and jagged outcroppings. The swells lofted the charred remnant of a ship's mast. For a brief moment, the mast stood upright, before crashing on the rocks, demolished by the mindless violence of the sea.

The dragon unfurled its wings, rose on its haunches, and shrieked its lament. The sea wind swallowed its keening. It strained its ears, but there was no answer. Low flying gulls beat the air with their wings as they escaped to other cliffs. It let them go. It hungered, but not for food. In this magnificent home, with a secluded cavern, fish by the school, and limitless sky, it craved the company of another creature, to patch the gaping hole inside itself. It had searched for companionship as long as it could remember, perhaps forever.

It spoke to the mountain goats and the sour-tasting gulls, but they rarely answered. It tried speaking to the two-legged men in their stone nests on the cliff tops, but they only ducked for cover and loosed sharp sticks in the air. After several tries, it avoided men, flying beneath the level of the cliffs.

It dropped its forelegs to the cave floor and folded its wings, stiff with disuse. It dragged its thinning body to the farthest reaches of the cave. It dared not fly. Its heavy heart dragged it down, its talons flicking the waves below. It feared the magnetic pull of the storms pounding the coast, fighting off the desire to seek death and its release. Hope endured, though shredded by time.

One night in the dark of the moon, it had discovered a stone nest, long since abandoned by men. Resting its jaw on the ramparts, it had watched the lights flicker in the buildings below, and the wooden ships bob safely in the arms of the harbor. Half-recalled thoughts and emotions slithered through its mind, of exhilaration, pride, loss, and despair. Torn with sudden grief, it launched into the sky in disordered flight. Grief for what? It didn't know. It strove far out to sea, trying to divert its mind from its agony.

And there it found a ship, with the fluttering cloth that spoke of evil deeds, and ghoulish pleasure in others' misery. Fragmented memories heaved themselves to the surface, bearing cries of anguish and images of bloodied heaps of dead flesh plastered on red-soaked ground.

A frenzied need to destroy seized it. Such evil must be fought. It swooped out of the sun, trumpeting its vengeance. Its talons splintered the mast, and its fiery breath reduced the sails to ash. Howling men shot their puny weapons as their vessel disintegrated beneath their feet. In triumph, the dragon summoned its undersea friends, and they glutted themselves on blood, flesh, and dying screams.

At last, cinders floated on the breeze over an empty sea, while bits of charred wood tossed idly on the waves. Victory! It had vanquished evil! Yet, guilt tore at it. Stricken with shame at its animal lust, it fled to cower in its cave.

Those ships were evil; their men were ravening monsters. The ships preyed on small coastal villages, spawning plagues of terror and grief among the men who lived there. It knew these things, but how? And why did it care?

For a full moon's span of days, and then another, it stole out only to catch fish, and then slunk into its cave again. At last, the iron grip of desire compelled it to venture forth. Once again, it crept to the empty stone nest, and lay there, mysteriously absorbing new knowledge of the place and the people below.

This nest, this tower, had not always been abandoned. Once in some years, others lived here. The span of years was nearly done. Then others would appear again, and with them would come the one for whom it longed. And its heart would be full, as it had been once before. A note swelled in the dragon's throat, deep, throbbing, and insistent.

Far below the tower, the townspeople shivered and cuddled their children. *It's only the wind*, they insisted. *Only the wind.*

The Master Weaver snagged the wine jug from the Master Cabinetmaker, and topped her wine cup before passing the jug to Master Carver. After a brief scuffle with the Master Carver, the Master Saddler gained control of the jug and filled his, too. He slapped the jug on the table with a resounding thwack.

The four erstwhile combatants sat glumly at the table in an upstairs room. The innkeeper reserved it for his better-paying customers. The table didn't attack the fingers with splinters, had chairs instead of benches, and the windows overlooked the mountain rather than the fish-gutting edifice to the rear.

"The wine's drinkable," remarked Saddler.

"It damned well better be," snarled the Carver, "the price

we paid that pert servant girl. No manners at all, that girl."

Weaver governed her expression, but Saddler smothered a laugh behind his hand. Carver glared at them.

Cabinetmaker heaved a sigh. "Well, I feel a right fool, and that's a fact."

"And so you should!" retorted Weaver, waving her finger at him. "All those fulsome compliments to the princess, as if she were a little niece that you'd dandled on your knee."

"That's fine talk," snorted Cabinetmaker. "At least I didn't send her a bribe!" He raised an eyebrow at Weaver and Saddler.

Saddler was unembarrassed. "It wasn't a bribe. More like a sample. You just wish you'd thought of it."

"No, he doesn't," said Carver with a sneer.

Cabinetmaker flinched. "I still say it was Pardell's work," he muttered.

"Her Highness said it was his journeyman," said Saddler. He leaned back in his chair, grinning. "You're not calling our Regent-to-be a liar, now are you?"

"She's misinformed," Cabinetmaker said, but his voice held no conviction. "Give me that, you're hogging it." The gurgle of the wine calmed him. "Well. Hmm. She's changed a bit, you've got to admit it."

Weaver smiled. "I remember once—oh, she must have been about ten or so. She scampered up the rocks behind the palace, her skirt hiked up above her knees. She climbed like a mountain goat."

Carver grunted. "Noisy rascal, she was. She and that kitchen girl—"

"Yani's daughter," corrected Saddler.

"Oh all right, Yani's daughter, Trissi. Into everything they were. Imps straight from hell." Carver's mouth shut in a grim line.

Cabinetmaker blinked. "That's a bit over the line, Carver, even for you."

Carver sank his head into his hands. The others conferred and opened the second jug. Leathermaker filled Carver's cup. "Drink up," he said kindly. "It's not such a disaster. We each went in, figuring to get our own way, and none of us got it. So, she's not just a malleable bit of fluff. Maybe she will be, once her father's gone. Had you thought of that? We could all have another go in a few weeks." He winked at Weaver.

Weaver threw back her head and laughed. "It won't work. She's got a mind of her own, that one. Steel under sugar and froth."

"Just like her mother," said Carver heavily.

"And what's wrong with that?" said Cabinetmaker, slightly owl-eyed. "Remember Queen Ailsa, in her heyday? And Mereni III, my word, you couldn't put a thing past her. Might be just what our fair land needs, eh?"

Carver lifted his head. "Her mother, the princess Ailsa, was just the same as a little girl, headstrong just like that! Well, don't you get it?" he barked. "What happened to her? She went and snapped, didn't she? One little illness and all her wits go flying. This one, Princess Mericia, she's half-gone already. You can see it in her eyes. She's cold as ice. That's a helluva thing for a girl just turned twenty-one. She'll snap sooner than her mother did. You just wait and see."

The others fell silent, remembering the thin, rigid girl with the frozen smile. She barely filled a third of the white marble throne. The jug passed from hand to hand.

Cabinetmaker slammed his hand on the table, and they all jumped. "I think you're full of it, Carver. She's a diamond, that girl." He swayed in his chair.

"You know," said Saddler, "if we can't budge her, none of the others can. Not like her father."

Weaver nodded. "True. How do you suppose the fishermen are making out in their audience?" Even Carver joined in the general chuckle.

Cabinetmaker sagged sideways in his chair, waving his hand in loose circles. "She's a diamond," he proclaimed. "You can't mold a diamond, but oh, it casts a wondrous light. Like a rainbow."

"Go home, to bed, you idiot," said Leathermaker. "And promise me you'll never write poetry."

"Right." Cabinetmaker held up his glass. "To our princess, our very own diamond." Weaver and Saddler held up their glasses.

Carver gripped his glass in both hands. "She'll break, I'm telling you. A few riots when ships dock, a plague or two, and she'll break. And when she does, there's no one to take her place. The Emperor will be in here with his iron boots. Don't you get it, you fools? The monarchy's done for. And so's the island. She'll never manage."

Princess Mericia sat on the Queen's throne of Ailsandia, a half-smile on her face, and a throbbing in her skull fit to break the glacier of which she'd been crafted. Her father sat beside her in the smaller throne, his fingers tapping restlessly on the arm. Tomorrow was the coronation. After that, she must sit alone in the throne room. But not today. Praise the One, not today.

Her face a mask of polite attention, she rested her eyes on the mural behind the cluster of merchants. Their superfine wool coats and gaudy braid trim spoke more of haughty self-importance than of economic reality. The murals, in contrast, swept joyously down the white marble walls and encircled each pillar, splashing images of island life throughout the bright, airy throne room. Girls spun in dance, their skirts whirling and their faces alight. Fishing boat crews hauled their nets, now filled with the silvery sparkle of moving fish. Scraggly trees bent double in the storm, while the southern watchtowers blinked their warning through the dusk.

Merchant Trandle stepped forward. Perhaps her expression had shifted and he'd taken it for interest. And she was fascinated, actually. The painted towers illustrated the merchants' plight more than he knew. It was only his shortsightedness that irritated her beyond measure. To listen to him pontificate, the Princess Mericia could wave a magic wand, and instantly construct thoroughfares up the coasts of Valtiris and Catiffar. All very well in theory, but she hadn't managed to trap a genie in a bottle yet.

She extended a graceful hand towards the map mural to her left. Silence fell.

"A fairly accurate map of the coastlines, even today," she said. Queen Ailsa had ordered it updated just before her illness. "Catiffar to the east, and Valtiris to the west. Quite rugged coastlines." How silly people could be. If she followed their advice, Ailsandia's treasury would hemorrhage to death, and their island would become a vassal of the Empire, instead of a member nation. "You'd need tunnels, bridges, and roads, as well as permanent staff to maintain them. Can the guilds afford it? Perhaps you should consider faster ships, or shipping convoys. If, however, you prefer to underwrite roads for Catiffar and Valtiris, I'm sure they'd be pleased. It just seems like an expensive solution, monetarily."

"Of course, the guilds couldn't afford it," huffed the lead merchant. "Roads are permanent improvements. They're the nations' business, not the guilds'."

"Ah. So, you prefer a tariff system, a pay-as-you-go scheme? Or perhaps a flat tax on each guild to cover the expense?"

A merchant stepped forward. His beard bristled like an outraged porcupine. "That would drive up prices," he exclaimed, his loose jowls wobbling with agitation. "It would ruin us!"

King Gerritt leaned forward and opened his mouth. He shot a glance at Mericia and sat back again clasping his hands tightly together.

The spokesman shouldered his way to the front. He shook his head, regarding the princess with paternal compassion. "The guilds, Your Highness," he explained carefully, "can't be held responsible for improvements to other nations' road systems. The expense would be prohibitive."

"More than hiring guard ships?" she asked, apparently surprised. "But yes, a tariff would be a nuisance. An outright tax on each guild would probably be easier." If only her head didn't hurt so much. If only she could laugh at their expressions. What sort of novice did they think her to be? "It appears you are undecided. The court suggests that the guilds confer on this matter, and present their wise and unified counsel at a later date."

Minister Sendillon's glance brimmed with appreciation as he hustled the merchants out of the audience chamber. Their conversation floated over their shoulders.

"I'm sending overland," a woman announced. "Ships aren't safe, especially to the south. Not just the damned weather either."

"You've got the bandits to deal with either way," said the spokesman. "But ships sink—"

"And caravans get burned," said a third, "no matter how many escorts you hire."

So, unhappy or not, they'd accepted her refusal. Princess Mericia relaxed, her gaze lingering on Minister Sendillon's stork-like form. He'd changed little in the last fifteen years, from his angular face to his shrewd eyes. Although only in his thirties, he'd served Ailsandia as Minister for over ten years, following his family's tradition. Sendillon's advice had smoothed a few wrinkles in the last week, as her father initiated her into Court duties. Soon, her father would leave, but at least she'd have Sendillon, Rogitas, and Jonsel to bolster her fledgling efforts.

"Well done, daughter," King Gerritt said. He sat on the consort's throne, which had been his since he'd married her mother twenty-three years before. "I'm quite superfluous. I could have gone sailing today, for all you've needed me."

Mericia twinkled at him. "They did seem a little surprised, didn't they?"

"Most definitely." He sounded worried and tense.

"But you see a problem?"

"Well, yes. Are you sure you want to relieve the Harbor Master of his post? In a time of change, a certain stability is highly desireable."

"But he was pocketing bribes for preferential docking privileges. You saw the accounts. He was clearly guilty."

"It still amazes me. He's given sterling service for five or six years now. Of course, I don't doubt your information at all..." A questioning note lifted his voice.

She felt a pang of guilt. She couldn't answer him directly, not yet. Until she'd flushed the Lady into the open, she didn't dare acknowledge Farren's help. She evaded, watching his face. "Lady Lelori has been a good teacher."

"Indeed, she's most fortunate to have my daughter as her student."

Mericia stifled a sigh. He'd be devastated to learn her suspicions. Her terror-filled nightmares weren't proof, but the stolen letter was, as were Master Orino's mutilation, and the dungeon prisoners. She couldn't bear to disillusion her father. She'd deal with the Lady in her own time.

"Father, I'm afraid he's been taking bribes from pirates, too. They're certainly getting their information from somewhere. Has piracy always been such an issue?"

His face sagged. "Well, it's a matter of degree." He stared at the map mural, absently. "The problem does appear to have worsened of late."

The light dawned. "Since mother's illness?"

He clenched his jaw, relaxed it, and at last nodded. Heaviness settled on her heart. Yesterday, the captain from the Island's Sea Patrol had brought survivors of a deadly attack two days sail southeast of the island. The dozen or so survivors huddled near a throne room pillar. One vacant-eyed girl stood with them, moving only when a hand on her elbow guided her. An ancient man testified, his quavering voice bearing witness to the acrid scent of burning thatch, the wails of women dragged onto ships, and heart-wrenching splashes of babies thrown into the sea.

The pirates' cut and run tactic was all too effective. Pirates struck, looted and enslaved in a single day, ran to sea, changed flags, disposed of overused captives, and arrived primly in other ports as bona fide merchants. Some of them, possibly, were merchants Ailsandia had served for years. Pirates dealt out gold and vengeance with lavish hands. A rebellious town risked being laid waste. Most locals chose to grit their teeth and outwait the pirates, hoping the thin veneer of civility would remain intact. Self-serving men like the Harbormaster didn't help matters.

Ideally, the Empire should combine its resources and pool information from all member nations. The risks to each individual nation, however, were too great. Even as they waved their fists and demanded action, they turned their heads as evidence of piracy paraded past them. As with the merchants, they wanted the problem solved—if someone else would do it.

She became aware of her father's stare. She blinked her thoughts away and smiled.

He touched her hand. "Don't pretend with me, daughter. You've serious thoughts in that smooth head of yours." He leaned forward, his eyes aglow. "Remember, we're allies of the most permanent kind. Father and daughter, as well as neighboring monarchs. We'll plan a punitive action very soon, you and I. If we drive piracy towards the Emperor, he'll have to react. Just keep your shipbuilders busy and those quarries active on your uninhabited islands. We'll need all the stone our masons can dress for fortifications." The King patted her arm and excused himself.

Princess Mericia retreated to her suite, changed into looser clothing, and walked to the famed plaza-like Palace balcony that overlooked the harbor. The darting andisailles wove a comforting counterpoint about the ponderous movement of the merchant ships. With their brightly colored sails, the andisailles looked like threaded needles stitching the harbor together.

The simile reminded her of her mother, and her endless swift, neat stitches. It was ironic, dragging a Queen to her land, and then watching her ignore the bright colors, invigorating scents, stiff breezes, and clamor of everything she'd loved in years past. The moment they'd arrived, her mother had made a beeline for the keep, a third of the way up the mountain from the main palace, and accessible only by the tunneled stairway. A bevy of servants trailed after the exhausted Lady Siree as she set herself to the climb. Her mother hadn't descended in the two weeks since, though she'd walked the rooftop a number of times, mostly after dark.

Mericia had never cared for the keep, or for the caves extending from its inner side. The windowless rooms left her shivering with claustrophobia. The white stone palace's open layout was far more inviting. Its extensive balcony could have engulfed Ramsvalt's Great Hall three times, and still leave ambling room on the outside. In her youth, she'd often slept out here, with Trissi, Kellian, and Randall sprawled nearby. She'd memorized the star-scapes, even those of cold, biting winters, and the way the mountain cut sharp outlines into the rising moon.

It wasn't fair to Trissi, penning her up on the Island. Of course, she couldn't travel with Denys on Patrol, and she might as well set up their home on the Island as anywhere else. But what kind of life was that? What kind of marriage could she have when her health and spirit were bound to Mericia? Loyalty shouldn't be forced. Somehow, somewhere, there must be a way to break the binding and free Trissi. Mericia refused to cling to her friend like a parasitic vine.

Mericia would be alone. Completely alone. With this damned headache. She touched the back of her neck, remembering.

During her third sleepless night on the Island, her splitting headache marked the passage of every tedious minute. Seeking distraction, she'd crept out of the palace and climbed to Master Eolin's terrace to investigate his juvenile orchard. She removed a tiny charm from her kitchen maid apron pocket, and stooped to bury it next to a citrus sapling. Agony lanced through her temple. She gasped, grabbing the sapling for balance, and jerking back as it bent under her hand. A hand caught her elbow and brought her upright. Without thinking, she leaned against Farren, her hand to her head, fighting back the pain. When the throbbing eased, she pulled away.

"I'm surprised to see you," she managed.

"No you're not." The gleaming eyes held a rueful look. "Here, let me bury those for you. You can't bend over with a pounding headache."

"Thank you," she said. "That's suddenly become obvious to me."

He grinned at her, took the charms and moved from tree to tree, burying each with careful precision. Twice he stopped, murmured to the tree—or to something—and waited for an answer before proceeding.

She walked towards him and paced alongside. "How did you know I'd be here? Caprio?"

"Oh, no, not him. The first day on the island, he leaped onto a ship. With luck, he'll haunt them for a while, and leave us be. Aunt Nan told me." He laughed, stretched out an arm, and wrapped it around an empty space in front of him. "My dear Aunt Nan, bringing her nurslings together. She says it's easier to watch over us if we stick together. Besides," he added, "I've missed our visits."

Mericia flushed slightly. On Progress, the royal carriages arrived at their destinations long before the rest of the procession. She'd borrowed one of Trissi's gowns, doubled back, and walked along with Farren as he led his horses. The half-hour's normalcy had gone a long way towards relieving the stress of cramped conditions.

"The Harbor Master caved in," she told him. "Jonsel took him off to explain his accounting methods."

"Are you going to remove him from his position?"

"I'll have to, I suppose. His subordinate seems competent."

"Right, I'll check him out."

She rested a hand on his sleeve. "That wasn't what I meant, Farren. I don't want you to spy for me. It's just—" She lifted her hand to her head. "It's this headache. It never lets up for long. It's like there's a demon inside, chiseling away with an ice pick." He'd stopped moving. She turned. "What is it? Why are you staring at me?"

"It's not a demon exactly." His eyes were thoughtful. "But there is something. Hold still." He held her chin in one hand, while the fingers of the other slid under her hair. She stiffened. "I said hold still!"

The words were hardly lover-like. Nor was his fierce glare at a spot just past her left ear. She felt ashamed of her suspicion, and waited while his fingers explored the base of her skull.

"Got it!"

She cried out and leaped away, one hand to her neck. "You burned me! With your fingers!" He cocked his head and raised an eyebrow. She rubbed the back of her neck, anger fading as realization bloomed. "The headache's gone.

How did you do that?"

"Hmm. The cure's as bad as the ailment, I'm afraid."

"Oh, I feel so much better. Thank you, Farren. It's completely gone."

"No, I'm afraid it's not. There's a warp in your colors there. I can't fix that until we know the cause. I've seen it a time or two. One poor woman got it every time she touched a cat. And a farmer I know gets it whenever the ragweed blooms. The warp, I mean. It looks the same. But don't worry. It must be something here on the island. I never saw it—" He shot her a quick look. "—er, before."

"Ah," she said lightly. "So as long as I'm on the island, I'll have to see you on a regular basis, so you can cure my headaches. Is that it?"

"Um. Well."

She laughed, daring a smile in the dark. "It sounds like a good bargain to me."

Now, gripping the balcony rail, her cheeks burned at the memory. No, she mustn't toy with him. She had to ally herself with someone of proven political worth to secure Ailsandia's future. In the limelight of a palace, Farren would shrivel away, shrunk by the constant disrespect others showed him. She couldn't subject him to that.

However, she agreed with the Emperor on one thing. If she refused to marry, Ailsandia's throne might come into contention as eligible bachelors from throughout the Empire vied for power. She didn't want to follow her mother's example and marry an outsider. Her father had done his best for Ailsandia, but undeniably, his loyalty was bound to Valtiris. But the choices were so few, once she'd ruled out non-islanders. Minister Sendillon, perhaps. She wished he weren't so fond of that yapping little dog. No, that was envy speaking. The devoted dog trailed after Sendillon even into the throne room and council chamber. A nice little dog, really. Loyal. And she mustn't love it, either, or it faced the same threat as her own dogs. In fact, she'd forget about Sendillon entirely, and concentrate on someone else, maybe in the Sea Guard. Someone safely unknown.

She'd forget about Farren in time, about his exasperating habits of laughing at serious matters, seeing through secrets, and ignoring the obvious. No matter what she expected of him, he was the opposite. And yet, somehow, he was more constant than any man she'd ever known.

Just as soon as she was crowned, she'd have to get down to work. She'd have to punish whoever was illegally overfishing the northern coast, negotiate with the ministers of Catiffar Coast about roads, talk to shipbuilders about possible enhancements in patrol vessels, and find some decent weather forecasters. And deal with Lady Lelori.

Oh yes, and find someone sensible to marry.

"Nanny," she said, unthinking. "I'm so tired of being alone," she murmured. Perhaps Nanny heard her. Farren said she could. Unbidden, a pair of brown eyes twinkling with irrepressible humor flashed into her mind. "Oh Nanny, please, could you just—"

But she didn't know what to ask.

"Hi," David whispered. Black-slitted yellow eyes studied him from the fence post. "Farren says you have a soul."

The cat lost interest, licked its paw, and rubbed its face.

"If Farren were here, he'd talk to you, and you'd understand him. You'd like him. All animals do." David scratched one pointed ear. The cat leaned into his hand with a brief purr before returning to its bath.

"Do you suppose I could ever be like that?" David bent close to the fence, angling his head to face the cat, eyes to eyes. The cat paused, its paw lifted. It rose to its feet. With slow grace and a twitching tail, it stalked along the fence and slipped onto the roof of the pavilion. David straightened, staring after it.

The gods made cats, Farren said. They made all animals, but cats know it. Just watch them move, and you'll see.

David got back to work, breaking open a bale of straw in the empty sheep's pen. Its sheep would arrive tomorrow, along with the rest of the livestock, in time for the Coronation ceremony. The pavilion's luxuriant display of gifts for Princess Mericia smacked of wholesale advertising for the guilds, farmers, and herdsmen. Farren had sighted the pavilion yesterday when he stepped out of his workshop. Wolton had commandeered an empty outbuilding near the palace stables for him.

"Damn," Farren said. "I'd better get down there." He slammed the workshop door and stormed off down the hill. With a wild look at the stables, David hurried after him, catching up as he reached the workers at the pavilion. "Hey, you! What's this pen for? Pigs? Where's their shelter? You know they sunburn, don't you? Especially when you scrub them up to heck and gone, and I'll bet that's the plan, isn't it?"

The workers shrugged. They'd followed orders, that was all. The Master of Ceremony was already yelling about risers, and they had to get moving. If the nitwit carpenter had time to spare putting up shelters for pigs, it was no skin off their noses.

"Damned idiots," Farren muttered. He walked to the lumber pile, snatched several boards, and headed back to the pen. The Master of Ceremonies scowled at him, hauling in breath for a blistering reprimand. A worker grabbed him by the arm and whispered urgently, pointing at Farren. The Master's glare dimmed, and he found someone else to scold.

"Um, Farren? What'll I do?" David anchored a board while Farren pounded it viciously.

Three weeks ago, Wolton had assigned David to Farren, ostensibly to help with the princess' mare. David yearned for Farren's knowledge, but he hadn't bargained for ostracism. His friends avoided him. Conversations hushed as he walked by them. Griffin, the worst bully in the cavalry juniors, tossed off snide remarks about apprentice Shadebinders. David, however, took the bull by the horns, and resolved matters to his satisfaction. A few fights, and a strategically placed bucket of mucky water had worked wonders. Finally, David concocted an elaborate scheme to lure a veritable anthill to Griffin's pallet. The sight of Griffin hopping out of bed, frantically slapping his clothes, reduced the other boys to raucous hilarity. Thom slapped David on the back and his friends took him back into the fold. Except for Griffin, of course, but he'd get over it. The others might look at David sidelong, but they accepted him. It reminded him of Wolton's attitude towards Farren.

"First off," Farren said, "get a cart down here with a load of straw. There's not enough bedding. The herdsmen don't want to muck up the fleeces, probably. Either that or they're just stingy brutes. Then we've got to get higher sides on the corral. Can you imagine keeping Firefly penned up in here? She'd be out in jig time. I don't know how you stick on her back." He grinned. "Myself, I'd rather walk beside her than ride her. She's quite a conversationalist."

David flushed, remembering his most recent ride on Firefly, and the sight of Wolton and Farren, side by side, nodding at him solemnly like puppets on strings. He'd learned a few tricks from Farren already, though he'd a long ways to go.

At last Farren returned to the workshop, satisfied that David had things well in hand. As David worked, he watched construction on the great barge. Tomorrow, it would slide ponderously into place in mid-harbor, lashed to the permanent stone mooring. The greatest part of the mooring sank beneath the lapping waters. For generations, it had served as an anchor for ceremonial barges, and ships too large to dock.

And tomorrow, David would be here. Right here on the southern spit, which split the harbor into its lopsided figure eight. The Princess' Guard would stand to attention opposite him, around the east spit's watchtower. The Lady Lelori would head the nobility assembled there, who'd traveled from throughout Valtiris and Catiffar. Here on the south side, the Queen's Guard would line the road from pavilion to the palace. The King's Guard would surround the watchtower poised on the west spit. Near the King, Ministers Jonsel and Sendillon would head the guildsmen and master fishermen, herdsmen, and farmers. David's father, High Captain Vance Heronlys, would oversee the King's Guard and the Southern Guard from the west watchtower.

The High Captain disapproved of his son's present assignment. His father had plans for him. Once David got through the cavalry juniors, he'd earn his way into the Guard in record time, and then possibly climb to emissary status, for detached duty with the Emperor. As far as the cavalry juniors were concerned, however, Wolton outranked even the High Captain, and his stubbornness rivaled the cussed black mules. Wolton had assigned David to Farren, and there he would stay. David's father protested, swore, and stalked away.

David gazed past the city and up the mountain. Perhaps after the celebration, he and his friends would merit a few days of vacation. The mountains called to him, hinting at the presence of wondrous secrets, just awaiting his discovery: something living, magical, mysterious, that only David could fathom. Something aching with hurt, that only David could heal.

If only, if *only*, his father would set him free.

Chapter Thirteen

A nd so," droned the High Guardian, "seven, and seven, and seven times eleven, we hail the advent of a new era with this most auspicious event, the coronation of our own beloved Princess Mericia. For it was precisely seventy-seven years ago, on this precise day, that the coronation of our illustrious Queen Mereni III took place, ushering in an age of prosperity unequalled in the history of our beloved Island."

For the first time in Mericia's memory, every boat clung to the dock, like little piglets nursing a sow. Not a single sailor ruffled the calm flow of the harbor waters. The barge barely moved beneath her feet. Flutters of color exulted from the extensive edge of the harbor where her subjects were stacked five deep. The canopy over the gift pavilion glittered with metal medallions turning in the breeze, with Minister Rogitas standing guard.

The beloved Princess Mericia stood on the highest level of the great barge, itself anchored to the mid-harbor mooring. The sun's heat drenched her shoulders and sank deeply into her loose black hair, burning her head. Its light bounced off the canopy spangles and dove through her eyes. The headache demon roused itself, and played drums on her brain. Ah well, she thought, if she passed out, at least Trissi could prop her back up again. Couldn't the man stop talking?

"For, upon her ascension—"

No, he still had two generations to go. Sweat trickled down her neck, gluing the gown to her back and breast. The people didn't have canopies either, she reminded herself. Moving only her eyes, she looked at the faceless blur of the people lining the harbor. She couldn't pick out faces, though she could guess a few. Farren and his apprentice must be the pair of figures in front of the horse by the pavilion. Vinita and Celli, her maidservants, planned to watch from the Weaver's guild rooftop, but there was quite a crowd up there.

Even in the dock area, people crowded onto the boats, the better to see her, to be a part of the ceremony that would bind her to them forever. In spite of the throbbing pain, her heart warmed towards them. For three days, people had flooded the city from every part of the island. They'd packed themselves like herring in a barrel, carpeting the docks, rooftops, towers, and shorelines all the way to the twin land spits by the harbor mouth. The dignitaries and visitors from Valtiris and Catiffar were speckled among them, like peppercorns in a huge stew.

If her people could bear such inconvenience and discomfort for her sake, she could certainly tolerate a little sun for theirs.

Lady Lelori's overzealous reproduction of Queen Mereni III's coronation irked Mericia. The Lady insisted that every detail conform, from the location of nobility, to the posting of the traditional Guards manning each promontory, just as they had stood for Queens Mereni II, Mereni III, Merellia, and Ailsa. Why on earth did it matter? She wasn't being crowned Queen, only Princess Regent.

"...Carried on through the able hands of her daughter, Queen Ailsa, to whom her subjects have declared their steadfast devotion, yea these many years..."

Lower guardians, brimming with self-importance, occupied each corner of the barge. On the lowest step stood her 'handmaiden.' Trissi's alert, constantly shifting gaze constituted a breach of protocol, but the Lady was on the western spit, and could do nothing about it. Besides, it comforted Mericia. Whatever happened, Trissi would notice.

The 'correct' positioning of Queen Ailsa had concerned the Lady considerably. Queens, she appeared to feel, should have the grace to die before their successors took the throne. It saved so much trouble. However, her cogitations proved unnecessary. Queen Ailsa had fainted, with one foot on the keep's stairway to descend for the festivities. Lady Siree leaped to her side and saved her from a serious fall. Now, Siree hovered over her bed, measuring Her Majesty's breaths, patting pillows, covers, and the Queen's hair in a way that would have driven Her Majesty mad, if she weren't already. The Lady, with spectacular insensitivity, remarked that if the Queen should die, the transition of power would be seamless.

As soon as the coronation was over and Mericia got out of the sun, she'd begin loosening the Lady's stifling grip. Trissi's vehemence notwithstanding, Mericia doubted the Lady's villainy. Lady Lelori had devoted too much time and intellect to Mericia's tutelage. In the few short days at court, Mericia had developed a passionate gratitude for the Lady's careful training, which permitted her to see a larger picture from the presentation of scattered scenes. The Lady, however, was not the monarch.

The High Guardian straightened. Mericia restored her polite attention. Beyond the High Guardian, two attending guardians advanced in rigid lockstep, and ascended the seven steps. One bore the royal crown, and the other, the seer's globe. None of the royal house had used the globe in four generations. Even its purpose had been lost. As gifts went, the dull globe attracted little notice, but its presentation to the ruler was, of course, 'traditional.'

By the time the High Guardian placed the crown on her head, Mericia was long since drained of exhilaration. She smiled, bowed, and honored the One and the Many through practiced gesture, but her mind had moved onwards. She passed the globe to Trissi, and set her hand on the High Guardian's arm for the final salutation. In a solemn promenade, the High Guardian escorted Princess Regent Mericia from station to station on the ceremonial circuit of the barge. Mericia raised her scepter in her right hand, touched her lips with the left, and stretched it towards the Queen's Guard near the pavilion. As one man, they sheathed weapons, bowed, and stepped back, forming an aisle for her eventual procession to the Palace.

In defiance of the Lady's dictums, Mericia offered her tribute again with every step, blessing the crowds as she passed. Like a multi-colored sea wave, the crowds knelt before her, in unscripted reverence. The sight stunned her. With tears in her eyes, she faced the eastern promontory. Her father's bright scarlet robes stood out before the ranked assemblage of the King's Guard. She bowed to her father, and watched through a haze of tears as he bowed to her, more deeply. Lady Lelori had been adamant. On the Island, the Queen or Princess Regent outranked King Gerritt of Valtiris. On Ailsandia, he remained only Prince Consort to the now retired Queen.

To the King's right, Minister Sendillon bowed again and again with almost unseemly enthusiasm. His loose brown robes wrapped around his legs, and he staggered, before bowing yet again. Behind her, Trissi chuckled, and Mericia let her half-smile warm. Minister Jonsel bowed also, ignoring his companion's awkwardness.

One more station and the ceremony was complete. She faced the western spit. The Lady Lelori, in a brilliant green gown, stood on the highest point of the promontory next to the Emperor's envoy. Reflexively, Mericia checked the watchtower for the distinctive helmet of Captain Irandis, but didn't find him. The newly renamed Regents' Guard raised their spears in exuberant salute.

Trissi hissed at her. "The Lady's not *bowing* to you."

Mericia froze. Far from bowing, Lady Lelori spun on one foot, swinging her hands up over her head to snap an invisible bar between them. She cast away the unseen pieces, and threw her arms wide, her fingers splayed. Wind gusted out of nowhere and whipped the gauzy drape off her head, and tossed it to the sea. The Lady's bright green locks bubbled through the air, like kelp on the sea tide. The Lady threw back her head, and a wordless song pumped the air into a whirlwind of fury. Even halfway across the harbor, Mericia heard every piercing note.

Beneath the Lady's feet, the ground heaved and broke free, shattering the watchtower, and spilling people into the water. The Lady's triumphant laughter sounded through the ageless siren's melody of the legendary Lorelei.

And the mouth of the Lady's trap snapped shut.

Trissi sidestepped decorously behind the Princess, keeping her place midway down the steps, bearing the seer's globe on the red cushion. Proudly, she noted her friends in the crowds. Farren stood poised by the rust-red horse at the pavilion. So that's why he'd spent so much time on it. The King must have bought it as a gift for the Princess. She spotted the palace servants standing in a clump, all agog for times to change, for the palace to return to its former prominence as the Princess Regent took up permanent residence. Further into the crowds, she saw her uncle and aunt, with all their children. With an effort, she quelled her flashing eyes, and sent them a smile of surpassing sweetness. When she'd been orphaned, they hadn't wanted her, hadn't gotten her, and she'd done just fine without them. Let them *try* to get any influence out of her.

Her eyes roamed the eastern promontory, settling unerringly on Denys in the brown uniform of the Southern Patrol. She let out a small contented sigh. Perhaps seeing her here, the only attendant on the Princess Regent, he'd understand that she couldn't possibly leave Meriss.

The princess had turned west. Trissi hop-skipped to recover her place. Contentment fled, and a simmering burn took its place as she located Lady Lelori. The bitch. Her total disrespect was unbelievable.

"She's not *bowing* to you," Trissi hissed to her friend.

Mericia gasped, and stepped forward suddenly, hand outstretched.

The western promontory thrust upwards, rearing from the water like an enraged ogre, suddenly awakened from a centuries-long sleep. People screamed as they hurtled into the sea. The Princess' guards were flung through the air like so many stones ejected from a catapult, only to sink instantly under the weight of their armor. A massive tentacle lashed out from what had once been land, snatched up a sinking guard, stuffed him into a gaping maw, and ravenously grabbed for another.

"A kraaken," screamed Princess Mericia. She jumped for the edge of the barge. Trissi recovered her wits and dragged her backwards.

"You can't swim in that gown." Trissi discarded the globe and cushion like a basket of meat scraps, and thrust her hand into a deep pocket. "Here! Call for help!"

As Mericia fumbled with the clay, Trissi heard a splash, then another, and another. The guardians threw themselves into the water, and flailed clumsily towards the kraaken.

"What are you doing?" she shouted. "Go the other way, get weapons! At least get a boat, you dolts. You'll die!"

A fourth splash answered her. The High Guardian brushed past her, his face slack, his arms swinging loosely as he marched towards the side of the barge. Trissi grabbed his arm, and hung on him.

"Stop," she pleaded. "Pray for us right here. We need you!"

"I must go to her," he said, his cultured voice ragged and unrecognizable. "Let me go, you fiend." He raised his fist and struck Trissi a heavy blow. She fell to the deck, stunned. "I'm coming, Lady," he called, and dove off the side of the barge.

"She's bewitched them," Trissi said. From every side of the harbor, men threw themselves into sailboats, skiffs, or the water. The arrows that should have flown from the eastern tower never took wing. The guards, like all the other men, were throwing themselves into the sea.

"She's the Lorelei," said Mericia, her voice grim and certain, "the immortal Siren of the sea. Men wreck ships and kill themselves, because of her spells." She brought a figure to her mouth, blew on it, and held it aloft. "All who may, come to the aid of the Island!"

Trissi cupped her mouth, screaming to every woman on shore. "Stop them! Cover their ears. She's a witch!" Belatedly, women grabbed for their husbands and sons. Men went down under the wave of women, but many escaped, dove into the harbor, and swam to their doom, rapt with desire.

The monstrous kraaken was a squid, octopus, ogre, and spouting mountain all rolled into one. Tons of shuddering water shifted in the monster's wake, sending waves crashing onto the shoreline, dragging down the hapless scrambling figures. The kraaken freed its last tentacle from the sucking quicksand of the island, and clutched greedily at the human fodder schooling towards it. Two-thirds of the land spit was gone, the tower crumbled into the seas, and bushes and trees shrugged off like a dirty coat to be kicked into the corner.

Standing on the beast's back, Lorelei shrieked with laughter and song, the wild trills of which Master Orino had tried in vain to copy.

"Meriss!" Trissi whirled her friend around, and pointed towards the keep. A vast golden creature launched itself from the ramparts.

"My dragon!" Mericia gasped.

Like an arrow streaking through the sky, the dragon soared across the city and the harbor, and darted towards the Lorelei.

A ragged volley of arrows issued from the eastern watchtower. They bounced off the Lorelei as though she were ringed with an invisible wall of iron. On a barked command, the volley rose higher, aiming at the dragon. It snaked its neck around, shot out a jet of flame, and the arrows fell, charred lumps of stick, and nothing more.

Who still lived, to fire those arrows? Sick with hope, Trissi combed the promontory. The King fired grimly; Minister Sendillon waved his arms to someone in the tower; High Captain Heronlys harried his men into formation to fire with crossbows. Nearly half of the King's Guard remained, and two-thirds of the Southern reinforcements. How had they defied the Lorelei? Mericia held aloft a clay helmet and Trissi understood. Meriss had deafened the men to the Siren's call.

The dragon dove, banked sharply, and caught the Lorelei in his talons. With a triumphant cry, it curved away, and streaked towards the keep. The High Captain barked a command. The crossbows fired. The dragon hissed, flamed, and reduced the arrows to ashes once more. All except one, one arrow, shot straight and true like a bolt out of hell. The dragon screamed, dropped the Lorelei into the water, and careened through the air. Splashes of blood fell across the sea and the barge. Trissi felt the fevered warmth of it splash across her cheek. Valiantly, the dragon steadied its flight, and streaked to the palace.

The Lorelei swam for the barge, churning a path through the water. Behind her, the kraaken flailed its way free of the swarms of men, through the bloodied waters, crashing through the waves after the Lorelei.

Mericia fumbled frantically with her clay. Trissi's legs failed her, and she fell to the deck staring in horror as long fingers, a shark-like smile, and flying green hair reached for her, to entangle her, and pull her down into the depths of the bay. Trissi screamed.

Suddenly, the stretching hand disappeared. The Lorelei flew backwards in a snarling clump of arms and legs, to be caught in the flailing tentacle of the kraaken.

Above her, Mericia's fingers flew, forming the kraaken itself, dashed from her mouth towards the sky. With a final flicking of her fingers, the clay image shot into the air, shattered into bits, and scattered over the harbor.

The kraaken and the Lorelei vanished.

In the sudden stillness, Trissi dragged in a shaky breath, and drew herself to her feet. At the same moment, Mericia subsided to the deck, in a puddle of white skirts and dragon's blood.

Swirls of ocean-green beauty, whirlpools of tumultuous song engulfed him. He had to reach her, give her his heart, his devotion. Finally, he knew what he'd waited for all his life.

"Farren, dear, stop this! You will *not* do this, do you hear me?"

If only it weren't for that buzzing noise, insistent and shrill. He shook himself, and shoved his way doggedly through the masses of men on the dock.

"Get back to your place this instant, young man!"

Instinctively he paused, the habit of obedience too deeply engrained. "You don't understand," he grated in gasping breaths. An armor-plated guard jostled him and pushed ahead. His temper flared, and he dove into the fray.

"No, no, *no*, NO!" Aunt Nan's shrieking wail pierced his eardrums. He shivered in pain.

"Aunt, please..."

"She's evil. She's the Siren!"

It didn't *matter* who she was. That deep-throated throbbing voice entreated and commanded him. He had to go to her, or he'd die of desire.

"Mericia. My little love, she'll *die*, Farren." An icy wind clutched his head. The music chilled, became brittle, and then shattered in the cold safety of his aunt's embrace. He threw his hands up in protest, and as he struck his aunt's shade, some sense returned.

"Don't leave me, Aunt," he breathed in pain. The freezing cold wrapped his head like a blanket, effectively deafening him.

"No, dear, I won't leave you. Catch the boy!"

His sight cleared. He lunged sideways, grappled with David, and yanked him close. The boy struggled, trying to join the mass migration of men into the harbor. Farren fought his way through the crowd to Firefly's miniature corral. He braced the boy against the fence, catching David's blows on his shoulders.

"To the right, dear, on the ground."

Farren groped with his foot, leaned sideways, and snatched up a coil of rope. He captured first one hand, then the other, and lashed David's wrists to the fence rail.

"Now get a skiff, dear. There's one on this side."

"What if David gets loose?"

"He'll never think to untie the rope. Farren, Mericia *needs* you."

Spurred by his aunt's desperation, Farren jumped into the skiff. All around him, the water bobbed with bodies of men swimming, intent on a single goal. He looked over his shoulder, and saw David straining mindlessly against the rope, totally enthralled by the Siren's song.

"Aunt Nan," he said, his voice sharp with fear, "Denys. He's closer to the Siren. Save him!"

The icy film disappeared and sound crashed into his brain, overturning rational thought. He had to get to the Siren. His hands plied the paddle urgently. The paddle jarred, and he yanked it back, bashing at the obstruction. A man cried out, but he didn't care. The obstruction was gone and his path was clear. Nothing else mattered.

A snow storm struck him in the face, damping sound, and clearing his other senses. He cried out in relief.

"Maari's got him," said Aunt Nan. "Denys is a good boy. He'll obey his mother."

Her certainty warmed him. He turned the skiff, and stroked clumsily but steadily towards the barge in what remained of the harbor. The guardians were gone. Mericia stood, her hands in the air.

"Hang onto your paddle, dear." The barge rocked violently. The waves hit the skiff, drove it into the air, and slapped it into a trough. Aunt Nan's determined pillar of frigid air held him solidly to the skiff. Water surged around the monstrous nightmare creature. To the west, first one dock and then another crumpled, shards of wood impaling people as they fell. Farren clung to his paddle, ramming it into the water.

A vast shadow raced over the harbor and disappeared into the raging chaos. It emerged, carrying something in its talons. An inhuman screech split the air as something splashed and the shadow fled.

Almost there, almost there...

"Here's the barge, dear. Grab onto the side."

There was a savage stillness in the air, as though a hurricane paused to consider its course. Mericia collapsed.

He threw himself to the deck, grabbing her hands, and pulling her into his arms.

David's shoulders stabbed him, as he jerked to awareness. His wrists were tied to a fence. What was he doing here? What happened? A single small boat maneuvered through a sea of heads plastering the harbor. A memory surfaced, of a fleeting gold image ripping through the clouds, and a cry of pain that sliced through his nerves, like the shriek of a dying hawk.

David jerked his head around, searching the skies. There. Over the palace, slower now, dripping gore, wobbling through the air. He stepped away, but the rope held him. Frenzied, he bent his head, and yanked on the knot with his teeth. He had to get to the dragon first! They'd kill it. He knew they would. He didn't know who "they" were, and didn't try to name them. He only knew that the most wondrous living creature in the world was on the palace roof, that it hurt, and was in deadly danger.

With a sob, he ripped the rope loose, heedless of the burns on his wrists, or the blood streaking his arms. He jumped the fence and forced himself into a moment's calm.

"Firefly, please, I need you." The horse pranced away, confined by the narrow pen. "Come on, girl, best horse in the world, bravest, most gallant..." For a wonder, she stood still. He threw himself on her bare back, one hand on her mane, and unlatched the gate with the other.

Firefly nearly unseated him as she leaped to avoid men strewn along the dock edge like so many netted fish. The staccato beat of her hooves on the cobblestones echoed his racing heart. Like a centaur, one brain and two bodies welded in frantic harmony, they tore through alleys, up avenues lined with fine houses, and down the service roads of rich craftsmen.

The Palace gates rushed towards him. A guard raised a spear, but Firefly ducked around him without pause, her rider's balance steadying her own. They veered to the left, across a broad lawn, jumping flowerbeds and low hedges. Right over there, up on the balcony. The dragon had to be there, it *had* to be.

Firefly jarred to a halt, her nose just short of the stone wall of the palace balcony. David flew off and scrabbled at the wall, grabbing toeholds and handfuls of whatever strayed into his path. He threw himself over the railing onto the balcony, dragging air into his lungs. Two men in bright red livery spun towards him. One held a dagger, and the other an upraised chair.

"No, boy!" yelled the chair-holder. "Keep away, it's dangerous!"

David danced out of his reach, and ran for the end of the balcony. And there, to the left, wedged into the far corner away from the railing—there it was!

With a glad cry, he bolted pell-mell to the gold dragon, hands yanking at a leather pouch on his belt as he skidded to a stop. He yanked out handfuls of cloth and grabbed the bloody wing, blessing Farren for forcing him to carry an emergency pouch. He grabbed the wing bone, his expert fingers finding an artery he never knew existed. How in the hell did you put a tourniquet on a wing? The pumping flow of dark purple blood slowed under his tensed hand. Impatiently, he dashed away his tears with a free purple-smeared hand, before exploring the wingsail with gentle fingers. He remembered the dead hawk, limp in his hands after the falconer killed it. Did a dragon's wing flex the same way?

He had to stop the blood loss until help arrived, until Farren could get here. He turned his head to explain, and stopped with his mouth open. Only then was he truly aware of the dragon. Eyes as large as David's head alternately sparkled and faded. Its head alone outweighed David.

He cleared his throat. "You're going to be okay." The head tilted to one side, stretched out on a long snake-like neck, and slumped its chin on the floor. "Don't you die on me," he shouted. "You *stay* here, with me, and you'll be fine. Do you understand?"

The huge eyelids blinked once slowly, deliberately, and opened again.

"All right, then." He laughed shakily. "Everything will be okay, as soon as Farren gets here. It will, really." His right hand cramped, but he didn't feel it. With the left, he continued his search for other injuries. His tears rained steadily onto the wingsail.

Chapter Fourteen

"Thank you, Vinita," said Trissi.

Vinita curtsied and stepped back from the bed, her eyes wide. Farren laid Mericia on the ornate bed of the Princess' chamber.

"Perhaps, if I brought warm water and cloth, Her Highness might find it refreshing..." Vinita's voice trailed off at Trissi's glare. Vinita gestured dismally at the dragon blood staining the bedcovers.

"Her Highness is exhausted," said Trissi, biting off her words. She closed her eyes briefly, and her expression lightened. "I'm sorry about the blood, Vinita. I'll give you a hand with it later, all right?"

"That's all right, I'll manage." Vinita's smile faded. "Will she be all right? Did the monster hurt her?"

"It never touched her. She's just very tired right now. Could you get her some food, and then sit with her a while?"

The words touched a chord in Mericia's tired mind. "Vinita? How is Her Majesty, the Queen? Have you spoken with Lady Siree?"

"Oh yes. She's no worse, but she's no better either. She just lies there, hour after hour." Vinita caught Trissi's glare again, and backed up several steps, clamping her mouth shut hurriedly.

"I'll go check on her, Your Highness," said Trissi.

Mericia clamped a hand on Trissi's wrist, preventing her from leaving. She closed her eyes. Her face looked bloodless. The sharp cheekbones stood out sharply.

"What would Your Highness care to eat?" Trissi asked.

Mericia winced. "Whatever there is." The Palace kitchen staff, long attuned to the tastes of the King during his visits, had served red meat almost exclusively during the last two weeks. With no gardens to rob, she'd been more than ordinarily hungry.

Farren cleared his throat. "You're the Regent of this Island," he said sternly. "You outrank everyone on it, including His Majesty. You can damn well order whatever you want to eat."

Vinita gasped and plastered herself against the wall near the door. Mericia's face relaxed slightly, curving into a faint smile. "Seafood," she whispered.

Trissi's face lit with sparkling satisfaction, and as quickly fell into lines of meek subservience. "Yes, Your Highness." She curtsied deeply, and turned to Vinita. "Her Highness has greatly missed the delicacies available only in Ailsandia. Please serve a selection of shellfish and one of the chowders for which the Palace cook is so rightly esteemed. And any other Island specialties, such as the exotic fruits she's seen growing on the terraces. Her Highness is delighted to have come home at last."

From the beaming look on Vinita's face, the Palace cook would be overjoyed with this command. Her quick steps rattled down the corridor. Behind her, the atmosphere relaxed.

"Rest, Meriss," Trissi said. "I'll check on your mother, and let you know how she is."

"No." Mericia fought for breath. "People were *killed* out there. They were trampled, drowned, maimed, and eaten. Get hold of the Ministers, and Guild Masters, especially the Physicians Guild. Make them get out there and *work*. There'll be none of this nonsense about payment either. This is a national emergency, and they are required to assist the throne. I'd better get out there." She tried to sit up, but a single finger from Trissi pushed her back down.

"All right. I'll relay that. What else?"

"Send engineers to the docks, and make sure the structures are stable. Check to see what buildings might be in the flood zone, once the water levels stabilize. I'm sure there's more, but I can't think of it. Get the Ministers on it."

"Should I have them attend you here?"

"If they argue, yes. Otherwise, just Jonsel and Rogitas. Minister Rogitas gets better compliance from the guilds than Sendillon does. She's got that demanding motherly air about her." She sighed. "She's good with numbers too. It's a pity I can't use her in political negotiations, but she's too easy-going with strangers. They can talk her into anything."

"The dragon," Farren said. "Don't let them kill the dragon. It's trapped on the balcony, and they're all waiting for someone higher up to make the decision."

"Is it so important?" Mericia said. "We've just had a monster and a Siren wreck our nation's primary asset."

She waited, but Farren didn't speak. She could never predict him. He wasn't contrary, exactly. He just took actions from angles people didn't expect. He cared about living things intensely, every living thing, and a lot of dead ones as well. Thinking of all the living things she'd lost because of her 'curse', she couldn't blame him.

"Trissi," she said with an effort. "The dragon is under the Crown's protection. Feed it, water it, and bandage it, whatever Farren says."

He still didn't speak, but his eyes glowed with warmth.

"Tell Nanny to take care of the dragon," she murmured, and dropped out of consciousness like a boulder to the floor.

☾

Farren hit the balcony at a run. He zigzagged through the crowd of shades and slid to a stop in front of the dragon. The snake-bodied creature lay coiled in a ball, now loosening as its life ebbed. Armor plating extended from the reptilian head. A few back scales flickered with sunlight, but others hung from its flanks, dull and lifeless. The half-dozen spikes down the long neck shuddered with each labored breath. Shades clustered around the dragon, patting it, murmuring to it, even singing lullabies.

He slipped a hand under the armored plate on the dragon's head, finding the softer scaled hide beneath. The fevered heat might be normal for a dragon, but that limpness of the hide always meant trouble. "Aunt Nan! Tell the shades not to touch it. They're too cold. And if any of them have any bright ideas about healing a dragon, tell me!"

David looked up at him with painful relief. One hand clutched the leading sail edge, while the other supported a narrow section of wing over his lap. Purple blood oozed hotly around his hands. "Farren! Thank the gods you got here. It's lost rivers of blood. I can't stop the bleeding!"

"It needs stitching. That must be the artery for the whole wing." He gripped David's shoulder. "That was nice fast work. Just clamp it, right there." He needed more hands! The poor beast needed water, but if David let go of the artery, the dragon would bleed to death. There were all these shades, avid to help, but not one of them could fetch a pail of water.

Farren turned, hunting the length of the balcony. Two heads peeked through the doorway. "Hey, help us out! This poor thing needs water." The heads disappeared, turtle-like. "Hey," he roared. "Help me! Somebody help me, or this beast is going to die."

Trissi emerged from the door, shoving two liveried men

in front of her. "You heard him, Bodi, Gareth. There are tubs in the garden. Go!" She leaned over the balcony yelling after them, "And don't you run away, either. The princess wants the dragon alive!" She turned her head, noticed something, and sucked in her breath. "Peter! Grab that poor horse and take her to the stable."

David's head jerked around. "Oh my God, I forgot all about Firefly."

"Get Wolton to check her," Farren said.

"Peter, get her to Wolton! Then grab as many helpers as you can find and get back here!"

"...Merchants...harbor..."

"I don't care about the merchant fleet! Find Wolton yourself, and get the stable lads up here. The princess wants this dragon alive, and if it dies, Peter, you can bet I'll remember your name!" She snorted. "Gods, can you believe that! The harbor's wrecked, hundreds of men are dead, and some idiot thinks a merchant fleet's on the way in. There's no way they could get into the harbor right now."

"...Watchtowers...signal..."

"That's the King's problem! The princess asked him to take over the harbor situation. Take that horse to Wolton!" She glowered over the balcony, then nodded in approval. "Farren, everybody's heading to the harbor to help with the dead and wounded, but I've got some boys coming. Bodi and Gareth have got the water. What else do you need?"

Farren took another stitch as David eased his thumb back. "Thanks, David, I think I can get it from here. Slowly now, try moving your hand back. Great. I'll get the rest of this. Get the water over here. Tell Trissi we need ladles, cooking oil, molasses, broth, whatever she can think of that's liquid and nourishing."

"Farren, dear," said Aunt Nan. "This nice fisherman says to get seaweed, too." "Trissi? Get seaweed, too."

The fisherman shade nodded complacently. "Best thing in the world for propping up dragon wings."

"How does he know that?" Farren asked. "There hasn't been another dragon since Elizar's!" But the fisherman shade drifted away, his place taken by an old woman shade holding an embroidery frame.

"Farren, dear, this lady says to remember not to stretch the fabric too much, or the stitches pull on it."

"Right," he said through tight lips.

"What's up with the fleet?" a sailor shade asked.

"Oh, they're all fussed because there's a four ship merchant fleet coming in," said a guard shade. "And there's something funny going on with the watchtower signals. They insist two of the ships are galleys."

"Nonsense," scoffed the sailor shade. "Two galleys never sail with less than five merchanters."

"Sweetheart, check the wingtip." A shade floated next to Aunt Nan, with a shade falcon perched on his gauntlet. "The falconer says it's the only way to be sure the blood flow gets all the way through the wing.

Farren set the final stitch and tied it off. With hands suddenly expert, he traced a line down the golden wing to the wing tip, checking the color as the blood rushed to the starved tissues. Booted feet scuffled out of his way, but he didn't notice. He extended the wing tip, and was relieved to feel the heat in the sail membrane.

Tubs arrived, dragged over the pavement to the sound of frightened exclamations. Farren saw David prying open the dragon's mouth. He leaped over to help. The dragon's upper jaw lay in his hands like the lid of an unwieldy box, without muscle or brain behind it.

"Somebody give us a hand," he exclaimed. "I've got to deal with that gash in his side."

"Let me." A pair of gauntleted hands fitted themselves

between the largest fangs, while David poured water, a careful tankard at a time, onto the banner-sized forked tongue.

"And keep his head up or he'll choke on the water," Farren commanded. "If he gags, he could take your arms off, and David's head, too."

"He? It's male?"

"Of course he's male," said a farmer shade, seeming grossly insulted.

"They must have lost some ships along the way," the guard shade said. "Pirate attack, maybe? You, boy, did they say anything about pirates?"

"I don't care about the ships!" Farren yelled. "Shut up, will you! If it's not about the dragon, shut up!" Farren threw his hair back out of his eyes, and glared about wildly. "I appreciate the help, but would you please get the hell out of my way! Keep the subject on the dragon, or get out of here!"

"He's just talking to shades," said David. "Don't worry about it."

"Ah. Farren? Is the dragon a weapon for the sorceress?"

"A weapon?" snapped Farren, crawling headfirst under the wing close to the dragon's body. "Of course not," he said, his voice muffled. He found the gash. The cross bolt had struck the wing, and then, its force spent, glanced off the side. He thumped the dragon's side. "Hang in there, little one." The hide shuddered under his touch. "Good for you. Wake up and drink. You need the fluid!"

Farren turned onto his side, trying to get at the footlong gash. "Just a few stitches, little one. Talk to me, okay?" How did a dragon talk? "We're just trying to help. David, toss me some rags. I can't see what I'm doing under here. He retrieved a wad of cloth from David's hand and mopped up the gash. He set his first stitch, but the dragon didn't flinch.

"Is the dragon a friend to the sorceress? To pirates?"

Muscle tension returned to the wing stretched over

Farren's body. He could feel a rumbling protest in the great body beside him. Pain? Or was the dragon trying to answer the question. "I doubt it." The rumbling lessened. "In fact, no, I'm sure of it." The dragon relaxed. *Hmm*, thought Farren. *That answers that question.*

"Are there other dragons nearby?"

The dragon shivered. Farren could almost feel its mournfulness. "No. He has no friends." Farren backed out and scrambled to his feet.

David stepped back, saying, "We need to close his mouth, and keep the head level so Farren can check his eyes." David ducked under the head, setting his shoulder under the neck, and crooning into the flattened ear.

Farren examined the dragon's right eye. He raised the green-scaled lid, and then a cloudy white second lid, revealing a many-faceted emerald-green eye.

"How do you *know* he has no friends? Does he talk to you?"

Farren looked up involuntarily, meeting a pair of inquisitive eyes across the dragon's snout. Farren gasped, "Who the *hell* are you? You're *alive*, aren't you?" He shook his head. "Sorry, stupid question. I've been shoving shades out of my way since the moment I got off the barge. I didn't see you. It's like you popped out of nowhere, like a genie out of a bottle. Who the—who are you?"

"David's father. I'm Heronlys."

Distractedly, Farren scratched the dragon behind the flat nub of an ear. "Oh damn it, I'm sorry. I thought you were Trissi, or else a shade. They've been swarming like bees. Or maggots to a bleeding wound," he finished. "Sorry, Aunt Nan, I don't mean you. But you, and you, and those three..." He stabbed his finger at the sailors and guards.

"Farren," said Heronlys, "may I ask you some questions? Perhaps these, er, shades have information, which would be useful to us in our present crisis."

"Oh, they won't talk to me," Farren said bitterly. "They talk to Aunt Nan, and she relays information. They only see the people who are important to them. David, that's enough, we'll set the head down. Go get a bag of salt, and see about the fish oil for his hide. It's drying out. See where the molasses went, and grab anything else that looks good for an injured dragon. Some sort of tarp, too. He's not used to direct sunlight."

David tallied the list on his fingers. "Fish oil's most important?"

"Right." Farren helped Heronlys release the dragon's chin onto the stone floor. "Go on, David. You've done miraculous work here. He won't die."

David ducked his head with embarrassed pleasure. Heronlys' eye trailed him as he ran to the door.

"You're sure he won't die."

"Not until they kill him." Farren's mouth twisted. He buried his face in the scaled hide of the dragon's neck, inhaling the sharp, smoky odor. The shades closed in around him, poking at the dragon, patting it, crooning in its ears. He could barely hear the dragon's breathing for all the noise. He pulled away, whirled, and screamed, "Get away from him. Bother some one else for a change!"

"Farren," Heronlys gripped his shoulder and shook it. "Perhaps there's a *reason* they're interested. He could be a key to the sorceress, or the kraaken. We don't know where they got to, remember. They could be anywhere, controlling him. Farren, please. Help me. Tell me about the shades."

Farren closed his eyes, and sank to the floor against the dragon's neck. Absently, he stroked the huge knobby forefoot. The curving talons that had held the Lorelei now lay quiescent under Farren's hand. Heronlys crouched next to him.

"Who are they all? Dead warriors?" he persisted.

"No, they're everybody. There's no rhyme or reason to it,"

Farren said wearily. "I've seen shades since I was a baby. I didn't know it for a long time, what they were, that I wasn't supposed to see them. They were just always there: the neighbor dead of the fever, the guard killed in a brawl, or a dog beaten to death. They never stayed. They'd be there for a week or two, maybe as long as a year, and then they'd drift off."

"Farren," warned Aunt Nan, "we're not all shades!"

A faint smile crossed Farren's face. "Yes, Aunt Nan, of course. Aunt Nan wants me to tell you that she's not a shade. She's a spirit, on her way to heaven, but delayed because she's not done taking care of me. She does a good job of that, even now. The Siren's song trapped me, but Aunt Nan screamed in my ear, so I came out of it. She's very hard to ignore. So anyway, that's the way it was. At any given time, there were maybe five or ten around the castle. Not everyone becomes a shade. Most animals don't bother. Sorry, I'm rambling."

"That's fine. Just go on. There seem to be more than five or ten around just at present, from what you're saying."

Farren nodded. "Several hundred, maybe a thousand or so. I can't sleep any more. They're everywhere, crowding in, talking, and gossiping. But they never seem to *do* anything. They don't tell stories to living family members, or go around touching familiar objects, or making sudden noises to frighten people they hate. They just gather, more and more of them, every day, merchants, farmers, servants, nobles, members of every guild, children, horses, dogs. I even saw a pig yesterday. Since we've hit the Island, I can't take two steps without running into someone, literally. I hate walking through them, but it's impossible to avoid."

"When did this gathering begin?"

"A few years. Five or six, maybe."

"Or seven," exclaimed Heronlys. "Since the last Progress! Farren, it's all related. The Lady Lelori turned up just before the last Progress. Illness and death all through castle, the Queen's instability. Now, seven years later, the Queen is ill again, Lady Lelori has worked her spell, released the sea creature, and this dragon appears out of nowhere. They're all tied together. Farren, is it possible that a sorcerer *bound* these spirits?"

"I'm *not* a Shadebinder," Farren cried.

Heronlys looked guilt-stricken. "No, you're not a Shadebinder. But someone is. And you are the only one who can help us catch that person."

David bounded up with Trissi, followed slowly by several nervous boys and girls. Trissi organized two boys into setting up a canopy over the dragon. A girl piled wet seaweed along the front of the wounded wing, while David slathered fish oil on the dragon's hide with a mop. Absently, Farren patted the dragon's snout, which obediently opened to let Trissi to pour ladlefuls of a sweetish mixture onto the flicking tongue.

Farren stared at Heronlys. If only, just for once, his Sight could be useful instead of a nuisance.

"First," said Heronlys, "are these shades dangerous?"

"I don't think so. They're just *people*, you know. Like you'd meet on the street any day. They're just dead, that's all."

"Right. In themselves, they're not evil. But could an evil person force them into actions they wouldn't normally choose?"

"I suppose so," Farren said unwillingly.

"Would the shades remember these actions, if they had performed them? If they'd brought illness, or scared some one off a cliff?"

Farren looked around, watching Aunt Nan as she scolded one of the stable lads for his slowness. The colors around the shades overlapped. It was like living in a rainbow. As he took in the significance, relief swept through him. "They might not remember, but their colors would have changed." Farren spoke with new certainty. "I'd have noticed it. *Thank you*, sir, I hadn't thought of that. I think I was afraid to think it through."

"Then if a sorcerer has bound them, his intent is not yet accomplished. Would that be a true statement?"

"Yes, I suppose so."

"So their purpose is still to come. The events we've seen are not the end of the problem. Either the Lorelei wasn't the Shadebinder, or she plans to return. If it were she, and if she's dead, they'd be released from the spell, wouldn't they?"

"Yes. Elizar's were, according to legend." Farren paced in a tight circle, his hands clamped together behind his back. "Oh gods, I thought it was over when the Siren vanished, but it's not. They're still here! No one would bind this many shades to service without a reason. Who could need them all, from all walks of life?"

He threw out his arms, heedless of the workers around the dragon, or the curious eyes turned his way. "Who are you?" he shouted. "Who commands you?" He wove across the balcony, waving his arms in front of one shade after another. None of them noticed him.

"Quit making a fool of yourself, boy," Caprio snorted.

Farren jumped and turned, staring down at the Goat. "NO! You're back again? I thought I was rid of you, Caprio! This is crazy. Look at them all, just milling around. Something terrible's going to happen. I can *feel* it."

"Well, good." The Goat looked about him with a self-satisfied air. "The Shadebinder's about to move. It's about time we scared up some excitement around here."

"Shadebinder?"

"Of course there's a Shadebinder," Caprio said scornfully. "Open your eyes."

"Well then, who is it? Answer me, Caprio. For once in your shade's existence, give me a straight answer."

The Goat gave him a shifty look. "Haven't got a clue."

Farren slammed his fist through the Goat, but Caprio pranced away. Farren pursued him. "I'm telling you, Caprio, it's beyond fun and games. The Lorelei and her kraaken took out scores of good people today."

"The more the merrier! We could use a few more shades to brighten up the place!"

"Don't you talk to my nephew like that! Where's Brother Lawrence?" Aunt Nan cried. "*He'll* shake the nonsense out of this demon-Goat!" She flew at Caprio, clinging to his horns. He spun in circles trying to throw her off of him.

"Aunt Nan, don't! He's just causing more trouble." He swung his arm between them. She allowed herself be coaxed free, and primly straightened her gown. "Get away from us, Caprio, you devil."

Farren turned to Heronlys, his eyes haunted. "The trouble is, to Caprio, death doesn't matter. So, what if a few men switch from live souls to shades? They're still around, aren't they?"

"Let's look at it another way." Heronlys said. "What powers do shades have? What kinds of things could their Shadebinder expect of them?"

"It's all right, Aunt Nan," Farren murmured. His hands shook as he hugged her irate figure. "It'll be all right. Take it easy." He looked at Heronlys. "Mostly, they can haunt the people they're attached to, give them dreams, good or bad. Rattle things in cupboards, make babies laugh. If vengeance binds them, they'll startle people and cause accidents. Like making a horse shy, and throw someone, or an archer slip up and shoot an arrow that kills the wrong person. That's what Aunt Nan tells me."

"Do they work with animals directly? Control them?"

"Like the dragon? No, no, he *chose* to do what he did, but he can't explain why. He's a friend."

A bellowed shout from the courtyard caught their attention. "Sir, Sir? Captain?" A lathered bay horse stood splay-legged on the grass, head hanging. Its rider looked blown, as though he'd run the distance on his own two legs and dragged his horse along behind him.

"Report," Heronlys said curtly.

"Those ships, Sir. They're approaching the harbor. Two merchanters and two galleys. The merchanter's flag is from the House of Fedron." At Heronlys' glower, the Runner hurried on. "The new Harbor Master's journeyman came from the South, sir. He's in contact with his family there. They said the House of Fedron lost its entire fleet of merchant ships to a hurricane. And these ships, sir? They're in formation, sir."

"How are the ships riding?"

"Low, sir, but not as low as a full cargo hold would pull them. It doesn't smell right. Begging your pardon, sir, but the Sea Patrol Captain's called for your help manning the catapults, in case."

"Right. I'll advise the Princess Regent. Call for fresh horses."

He strode down the balcony, but Farren caught his shoulder, and pulled him back from the doorway. His face flushed with feverish excitement.

"The dragon, sir. He can help lead an attack on the ships if needed." Farren's face fell absurdly. "Oh no, he can't fly, can he?"

"Of course he can fly," Caprio exclaimed. "Shake those flies out of your brain and use it! Have the girl do one of her twiddles and fix his wing."

"She can't heal," Farren objected. "She couldn't even heal her own knee, or Trissi's."

"She might not be able to heal it, but she can strengthen it, can't she? Enough to fly!"

A dawning hope spread over Farren's face. "You could be right."

"Harruff! Of course I'm right. I'm always right." The Goat

pranced in tight circles. "In fact, she can make *me* fly, too!"

Farren gave a short laugh and ran to Trissi. She knelt in front of the damaged wing, now supported on a neat bed of seaweed. David was squirting gooey stuff into the dragon's mouth. Farren dropped beside Trissi.

"Let me have some clay, Trissi. Caprio thinks Meriss can make the dragon fly. He could actually help us, for once!"

Farren took the clay, fumbled it, and swore. He rolled it out again, snatched his knife from his belt, and carved the clay as if it were wood. It took on the semblance of a wing, outspread and undamaged. Wordlessly, he handed it to Trissi, who dashed into the Palace.

Caprio bolted after her, running right through Heronlys. The man clutched his stomach.

"Get back here," yelled Farren, and then rolled his eyes. "Sorry, Sir. He knows people hate that. Caprio's exasperating. Now he's going to go bother Meriss, blast him."

Heronlys halted in mid-step, and stared at him. "Meriss?" he said faintly.

Farren wrapped his arms around the dragon's head and spoke into its ear. "Listen, we need your help. I know you feel awful right now, but we've got a big problem. There's a bunch of ships headed in, and we're not sure if they're friendly. They might be coming to attack, especially if they knew the Siren planned all this. We've got no real defenses. If you'll fly me out there, we can look. Meriss can help, I think, if you're willing to do it. Are you?"

The dragon lifted its head and turned one eye to Farren. It blinked twice, and nudged him in the chest.

"Thanks so much," Farren said gratefully. "It's probably nothing to worry about. We'll get back here as soon as we can, and let you rest."

Trissi ran back out, gasping for breath. She held the clay figure over the injured wing, blew on it, touched it, and then the wing. "She says it's worth a try, if you're willing, but be careful. Don't do anything until you're sure. Surveillance only. If they are pirates, accept surrenders. Farren, she thinks maybe you and Denys can communicate long-range?"

Farren's eyes lit up. "Aunt Nan! You can talk to mother, and she can talk to you! Will she help?"

"Of course, dear," Aunt Nan said reprovingly. "Maari's been busy, but she'll certainly help keep her boys safe. She proved that already, hasn't she? Keeping Denys free of the Siren?"

"Thanks, Aunt Nan. If anyone can make my knuckleheaded brother listen, it's mother."

"And me," Trissi added.

"Good idea." The dragon shifted, flexed his wing, and his eyes brightened. Farren grinned at him. "The dragon says he's glad to help! Captain Heronlys, would you plant my brother Denys somewhere useful for long-range communications. Trissi will explain it to you!"

"Denys," said Heronlys. "Terrell's brother. He's in Southern, right? I'll put him on one of the ships."

Heronlys seemed to have adapted to the change of events very readily. Farren hesitated, staring into Heronlys' eyes. He hunted for the light of integrity, but read only firm resolve, wariness, and secrecy. Heronlys, he realized, was used to hiding his intent from others. A High Captain needed his secrets, but Farren resented it all the same. He and the dragon, he determined, would not be anyone's weapons, not the sorcerer's, not Heronlys', and not even the princess'. He, Farren, would act on what he saw, and what he knew, and that was all.

"Right, let's get moving," he said abruptly. He released the dragon's head and moved away to give him room. The stable lads scattered. Shades clustered around the dragon as if helping him rise. A small shade child clung to his tail, shrieking in delight as it swung from side to side. "I guess the shades are going with us. They're just massing all over him."

"Can a dragon can be a Shadebinder?"

Farren shrugged and laughed. "It almost looks that way, doesn't it? But they sure don't seem to mind."

The dragon ducked out from under the canopy. He furled his wings, and spread them again, flexing them lightly.

"Still hurts, but strong as iron, he says," Farren said. "She even took care of some of the blood loss."

Heronlys' mouth hung agape. He shut it.

"David," ordered Farren. "Stay with your father. Trissi'll stay with Denys. Listen and watch, hear me? And all of you, don't let *anyone* shoot our dragon."

David nodded so hard his head seemed in danger of falling off. He stepped to his father's side with alacrity.

"Move aside," yelled Farren, sweeping people and shades out of his way with both arms. He vaulted onto the dragon's back, where the neck joined the wings. "You know, these spikes are really in the way," he remarked, patting the dragon on the neck. "I'm going to skewer myself if I don't watch out. Can you launch from the balcony edge? We can knock it down if we have to, but I'd rather not."

The dragon clutched the top of the wall with the talons of his forefeet, and stretched his neck, seeking a balance point. Heronlys stepped back hastily as it unfurled both wings, which now stretched nearly the full length of the balcony.

Trissi waved to Farren. "I'll explain it to the captain," she yelled.

Farren nodded. With a tremendous sweep, the dragon took off, buffeting the air past their ears like a gale force. Farren crouched over the dragon's neck and clung tight, half-afraid he'd fall. Caprio zoomed up beside him and flipped through the air in a loop-the-loop.

"Ha, boy! You should've learned to ride a horse when you

had the chance!"

Farren laughed in spite of himself. "Come on, shades. With us! Make yourselves useful. Don't you disappear, Caprio. You owe her one! You'd never have been able to fly without her."

"Why would I leave? The fun's just starting!"

Chapter Fifteen

David scrambled out of the harbormaster's sailboat, rounded Trissi on the dock, and raced after his father. Men crowded the eastern spit, wearing the shocked looks of hurricane survivors. Wet and bedraggled, they hauled casualties from small boats and lined them up along the shore. Some bodies bore gaping holes, or the deep compression marks of the kraaken's tentacles. Other corpses bore no conspicuous mark. The lost look in the half-opened eyes resembled the dazed look of men diving towards the Siren.

Further up the slope, a ragged line of archers formed a loose, scattered group under the lashing fury of a Patrol Second. The Second turned, looking for someone. His eye settled on David.

"You, boy, tell the—"

"Sorry," called David, wearing the harried look of boy-on-urgent-errand. "I'm with the..." He let the words trail over his shoulder as he leaped the final gap to the watchtower door. He scaled the ladder-like stairs, and burst onto the top floor of watchtower, only to flatten himself against the wall.

Two men hauled on cables, turning the huge base of the catapult. Another guard operated the crane swinging a heavy sling over the ramparts. His father conferred with a

Sea Guard Second, gesturing to the sea beyond the spit. The Second shook his head dubiously, pointing to the other side of the inlet. Of course, David thought. Usually, there were two catapults, one on each side of the inlet. Pinned between the twin catapults, most attacking ships would think twice before entering the harbor.

Drawn by equal parts dread and ghoulish curiosity, David leaned through an archer's hole, staring at the vast expanse of water, fully half a mile across. He tried to visualize the kraaken, a creature a thousand feet long, frozen in the sands for decades or centuries. Trees and bushes sprouted on its back. Islanders built a watchtower on it, and a catapult, and barracks for guards. All of it had tumbled into the harbor like so many pebbles, along with scores of people. Others swam to their doom, to drown or feed the kraaken, who wakened at last from countless years of paralysis and starvation.

David shivered with sudden sympathy for the freed beast. Like fire leaping from flint to tinder, his mind flicked to the dragon and Farren. They'd head to the Sea Patrol's warships first. There were three warships nearby, patrolling the north ends of the straits on either side of the Island, and the near waters of the Merolian Sea. The Watchword was closest, then the Southern Sentinel. The third, Her Majesty's Own, was barely a fleck on the horizon. David looked over his father's shoulder and glimpsed a gold spark far out to sea.

The merchantmen's convoy approached from the eastern strait. The two merchant ships were like others David had seen docked. Fat-bellied, with an expanse of sail rigged out from the single mast, they reminded David strongly of certain guildsmen, puffed with their dignity, and chronically overfed. A maneuvering sail angled down to the bow. They weren't fast unless the winds were right, but they stored masses of cargo. Once moving, they were ponderously slow to stop. The guards had dubbed them Pelican One and Pelican Two.

Two sleek galleys flanked them. David's eyes widened slightly. He'd heard of galleys, quick to maneuver, fast to slice through waves, while others wallowed helplessly. Their stair-stepped seating arrangement put forty rowers on each side, an incredible use of manpower. On open sea, they used a sail as well, but David didn't see one. His eyes lingered on the prow of the closer galley. Its front was carved into a double point. He frowned. He hadn't seen many ships until the Progress, but most of them carried flags rather than carvings on the front. Each merchant ship bore a long banner from the bowsprit, matching the one that sailed from the top of the mast: the banner of the far-south House of Fedron, of legendary artistry in glassware.

"...Took the long boat, with some of the Regent's guard," the Second told the High Captain. He pointed to the Watchword. Southern Sentinel approached from the west. It must have come in from the strait, probably timed to arrive as the Coronation barge retreated from its mooring.

His father scowled at the Watchword. David puzzled over it. It seemed fit enough, and well placed. The merchant convoy couldn't very well bypass it. If they were honest merchants, they wouldn't anyway, since it carried the King's banners. Besides, they'd see at a glance that the harbor couldn't possibly receive them. If they were pirates, they'd never risk getting penned in the harbor, given the presence of two Patrol warships.

His father grunted, clapped the Second on the shoulder, and jumped onto the ladder. David kept right behind him. Farren had ordered him to stay with his father, and Farren was officially his master. Farren also seemed to be in charge of defense, in some peculiar way. Surely, his father wouldn't send him back? Nevertheless, David let a pace or two stretch between himself and his father. There was no point in calling attention to himself.

Denys, Trissi, and the Regent's Captain Irandis waited next to a beached longboat. The High Captain broke into a run and climbed onboard. David jumped in behind him, avoiding the dozen oarsmen.

"Sir. His Majesty sent a party to the Watchword," Denys told the High Captain. The longboat jerked sharply as the oarsmen sped the boat towards the Southern Sentinel. "He left the Sentinel for you. Further away, but better strategic position."

Trissi cradled a roll of fabric in her lap. After a moment's peering, David deduced that these were the Regent's banners. The thought cheered him. The Regent's ship, the King's ship, and Her Majesty's Own, further fortified by a dragon and hundreds of shades. The world had never seen such an army. He, David Heronlys, cavalry junior, had saved the dragon's life. The thought filled him with a great, secret satisfaction. He exulted, watching the gold speck grow to thumb size, then hand-sized, and almost instantly, it seemed, into an air-borne marvel whose length rivaled that of the Pelicans.

The longboat jarred, and latched onto the side of the Southern Sentinel. A ladder fell over the side of the warship, dangling by their heads. His father climbed up first, then Denys with the banner rolls, and then Trissi, who swarmed up the side as easily as Denys did. Irandis stood in front of him, mouth agape as he stared avidly after the girl. David curled a lip in disgust. Irandis was captain of the Regent's Guard? He'd forget a war for the sake of a girl's ankle! David faked a stumble, and bumped against Captain Irandis. Irandis let fly with the back of his hand, staggered, and missed. David snorted quietly. Wolton would have boxed both ears, and never lost his balance, despite being a complete landsman.

A gust of wind set the small boat rocking violently. David waited for Irandis to heave himself up the ladder, and swung up behind him. He gave a quick wave to the longboat seamen.

His father, Irandis, and Denys were deluged with questions. Was the convoy attacking? What the *hell* had happened to the harbor? What *was* this weather, with a sudden flood, and strangely frigid winds that cut across the normal breezes? David, watching Farren circle the ships, waving his arms to his invisible companions, had his own ideas about that whirlwind pattern.

David elbowed his way forward to the forecastle. Trissi grabbed his arm as he started up the deck ladder.

"Good, it's you. Wriggle out there on the bowsprit, and hook this banner on it."

David shinnied out on the pole, clinging tightly to the bowsprit as it bucked over the choppy sea waves. The banner flipped up over his head, and he yanked it back down again, nearly losing his grip. He hooked it onto the damp iron rings, and felt Trissi's hands on his ankles guiding him back the moment he'd finished.

"I can't climb the rigging to put the top one on," he said, forestalling the request at the tip of Trissi's tongue. "They wouldn't let me. They wouldn't let you either," he warned. "Besides, you're wearing skirts."

"Of course I'm—," she snapped, and then paused. "Oh. Well, not that I care." Her eyes trailed Denys along the main deck. "Humph. I'll catch one of the sailors, and get him to do it."

David didn't doubt it in the slightest. He hunted for a useful task to do, but after a doubtful glance at men climbing the ropes, and the synchronized motions of the Sentinel's oarsmen, he decided to stay out of the way until called. He leaned against the railing and stared at the dragon, now circling the Pelicans and their galleys. One galley's prow was carved into the shape of a fish's open mouth, while the other was shaped like vast chicken's beak. He pictured their sailors' terror. Imagine seeing a dragon over your ship, a menace from fireside stories, flying, in the flesh, breathing fire!

This was going to be *great*.

⌒

"Lower down!" The wind whipped the words from Farren's mouth, along with most of his spit, and tossed them behind him. The dragon's body dropped out from under him. He clutched the neck spikes, caught between terror and laughter. This whole thing was so insane, so utterly unreal. What would Master Pardell say? He grinned at the thought of his testy master's probable reply. *Put your heart into your work, boy. Lose yourself in it, and you'll never be sorry.* Now, instead of files, clamps, and knives, he corralled shades to investigate ships. The Shade Patrol!

"Farren, dear, I don't quite understand what we're doing here."

Farren looked at his Aunt, soaring easily alongside the dragon. She was the very picture of a kindly adult curbing the antics of boisterous youngsters.

"We're spying, Aunt Nan."

"Surely, the Patrol Captains could deal with nasty things like that."

"Exactly," said Farren, moderating his voice into serious tones. "That's why I dropped the message to the High Captain of the Sea Patrol. He's bringing in Her Majesty's Own so he can deal with the problem. Since our dragon has wings, and the shades can fly, they've asked us to help."

The Sea Patrol Captain and his crew, aboard Her Majesty's Own, had been noticeably upset by the approach of a dragon. Farren and the dragon evaded the arrows, and dropped a piece of wood on the forecastle. On it he'd carved the word HELP and the rough outline of a pirate flag. It was fairly legible for someone writing on dragonback. A few more arrows shot in their direction, falling lamentably short, and then ceased altogether as a truce flag whipped the air. In a remarkably short time, he'd been able to fly near enough to shout the basic facts.

"But what," persisted Aunt Nan, "exactly, are we supposed to do?"

"Ah." Farren wondered that himself. The air groaned with the weight of a thousand shades, flying in confused patterns. Well, they weren't flying, exactly. They walked, rowed, ran, eyed the weather, sat in ghostly rocking chairs, or pointed out the fish swimming below them. They resembled an audience on the castle green, enthusiastically awaiting entertainment of a high order. The 'green' in this case was the airspace around Farren and the dragon.

With every powerful swing of its strong but aching wings, the dragon drove the air behind it. The shades eddied along behind, engulfing Farren in a heedless camaraderie of freezing puffs, and the tumult of a thousand voices.

"Hey," he shouted. "All of you! We need a plan."

"My dear, there's no need to shout."

There was no point to it, either. No one could hear him except Aunt Nan and the dragon.

The cluster of ships near the Island grew larger. What was he supposed to do? The harbor lay ahead with the intact eastern watchtower and the pile of wreckage, remains of docks, and shattered fishing boats. A beehive of activity spoke of intensive efforts to recover the dead and near dead from the waters.

The Watchword and Sentinel lay ahead, and Her Majesty's Own behind him. He hoped to heaven that three warships would be enough. The island's other two ships were far north. He had no time to reach them. Maybe these weren't pirates. Maybe they were just the merchants they claimed to be. Even as he dismissed his fears, he studied the galleys. The sleek galleys sported heavy ornaments on the bow. He'd heard Terrell talk about boats like these. They were built for ramming, for attacking ships at sea, splintering the structure, and leaving men to drown. If he could see the danger, the High Captain, the High Sea Captain, and the King would, too.

"Aunt Nan, look below the decks on those galleys, will you? See what they're hiding?"

"Now, dear, you know I get seasick—"

The dragon swerved, driving his head through a knot of shades wearing Patrol gear. A burly shade with a Second's badge turned on them huffily, hands on his hips, ignoring the fact that the wind shoved him along with the others, willy-nilly.

"What do you mean by that, eh boy?" the Second bawled. "If you were in my Guard, I'd soon learn you some respect."

Farren stifled his impulse to apologize, and saluted with a free hand. "Sir. I have a message for you, sir. From High Captain Heronlys."

"Humph." The Second glowered at him. "Out with it, boy."

"The ships before us might be pirates in disguise. Sir, the Captain requests that you mount a mission to determine the contents of the holds, whether they be merchandise, arms, or troops."

Interest kindled in Second's face. "Hah. About time he had a mission for us. You'd think we were past it, for all the attention we get these days. Proud to assist. You tell the High Captain that we're on it."

"Yes, sir."

"Hey, you lot, we've got orders. To the ships. Bernie, you take a squad to the front galley; Alf, the second..."

A deep rumbling noise startled Farren. The huge snakelike head whipped back and looked him through sparkling eyes.

"You understood all that?" Farren said.

The dragon tucked in one wing, and spun in midair, frightening a gasp out of his rider. A casual stretch of the long neck threw Farren back into his seat as the dragon soared through another cluster of Guard shades. Farren gasped out instructions to look over the crews of the two Pelicans, and asked a third group to distract the oarsmen. By then, the ships were nearly beneath them. Several knots of shades flew on their missions, but the vast majority hovered alertly, as though watching a puppet show.

If the situation weren't so urgent, he'd have found the sight ridiculous. Several farmers plowed the clouds with misty tools; women tended babies, chattering amiably among themselves; a guardian led a small congregation in rousing songs; eight or ten youngsters played tag, ducking behind weavers at their looms, and a long-faced doctor studying the bleeding stump of a guard's arm.

A jolt slammed Farren against the neck-spikes. He cried out in pain, but the dragon's bellow of rage drowned his cry. Farren grabbed the neck spikes, and pulled himself down to lie alongside. Something spat past him, and the dragon reared back on his tail. Farren's scream choked in his throat as he saw three archers on the merchant ship the guard had dubbed Pelican One, crossbows held steady against the rocking of the waves.

The dragon screamed defiance, and streaked towards Pelican One. Behind him, an ugly murmur spread through the shades, who exploded into a roar of fury. Winds tore past them, sucking them onwards, engulfing them in icy whistling winds and deafening shouts. Disbelieving, Farren saw a townswoman shooting like an arrow at the lead archer, her knitting needles held forward to stab. Small children waved sticks and stones, while a guardian intoned curses, and a blacksmith wielded an anvil in one hand and fiery tongs in the other.

What good were their weapons? They were made of mists and clouds, as insubstantial as the shades themselves.

However, the wind they made, *that* was a weapon indeed. So was a dragon, plummeting towards the ship, his sheet of flame licking the air.

"NO!" screamed Farren. "Don't kill, don't kill." He dragged on the neck spikes, nearly dislodging himself. He pounded on the neck, twisted the spikes, but the enraged creature beneath him didn't respond. Flames shot ahead of them, and Farren saw the looks of horror on the archers, the round mouths growing larger and larger...

"No!" As the vastly expanding ship filled his vision, he scrambled along the dragon's neck, seeking footholds among the spikes. Then he shot past them, on the sinuous snake-like upper neck, now spear-straight, as its flame lashed the archers. He wrapped an arm around the dragon's throat, and with his other fist, pounded on the flat head between the armor plates. "Stop! Let them surrender!"

A shriek of frustration accompanied a writhing movement, which sent him sliding onto the shelf-like top of the first spike. The dragon lurched upwards, and flamed the ship's sails instead. They puffed into cinders, splattering small burning fragments across the deck, singeing the shocked faces of those below. Farren risked a look backwards. The archers recovered, turning to aim again just as a horde of shades attacked. The frigid winds swept the archers onto the decking like so many rag dolls.

"Thanks," Farren said. "The Princess says they should have a chance to surrender. We might need to attack later." He patted the dragon's neck. The scaled hide shuddered, like a horse trying to rid itself of a pesky fly.

"Farren, dear," Aunt Nan said urgently. "Maari says stop. Denys says these ships are legitimate merchants." The dragon peered back over its shoulder, and snorted derisively. Aunt Nan patted its nose. "Now, now," she warned it firmly. "You just *listen* for a change, do you hear me?"

"But they fired on us." The dragon hovered, bending its neck in a backwards 'C' to peer at her.

"Most people fire at dragons," Aunt Nan said primly. "It's to be expected. Dear heart, Denys told your mother, and Maari told me. The House of Fedron borrowed these ships and sent them north for essential supplies for the hurricane victims. It's been confirmed. You know the winter storms did them a great deal of damage. Of course, they need supplies. It makes sense, doesn't it?"

"I guess so," said Farren, but he shook his head. "Aunt Nan, I saw their eyes, the archers' eyes. I don't think they're merchants. Their colors are totally wrong."

"Of course not the *archers*, dear. Most guards are a little bloodthirsty. Think of Denys, when he gets in a fight—or Terrell. Are you going to tell me they're all sweetness and light? Come now, I know Maari's boys better than that."

Farren chuckled involuntarily. "When the Second comes back, we'll know better. How's that? Depending on what they're carrying, we'll know if they're friends or not."

"What are you two doing up here?" demanded Caprio. "Scared, are you?"

Aunt Nan puffed up instantly, "I'll have you know, Goat, that my nephew—"

"We've gotten the signal that they're friends," said Farren. "We're waiting for the report from the Shade Patrol." A grin slipped over his face and disappeared.

"Friends. Haruff. What the hell kind of evidence do you sons-of—"

"Such language."

"Lady, you can take your 'language' and stuff it up a pheasant for all I care. That's an invading force. Look at the galleys, fool."

Farren stared at the galleys. If they were obviously pirates, the High Captain would know, wouldn't he? "What about them? They're fast, I'll admit. They'd have to be, with eighty oarsmen each."

"Eighty oarsmen, my sainted hoof. They're triremes, you fool. Look!"

Chapter Sixteen

Holes sprouted down the side of the fish-head galley. David's jaw dropped. It looked like a giant hand had punched it to bits. Had the Watchword fired on it?

Just a moment before the tower had semaphored, advising that these were honest merchants. A collective sigh of relief sounded throughout the deck, as tense muscles relaxed. The battle was over before it had begun. No doubt, the King would apologize for the misunderstanding, and offer to replace Pelican One's burned sails. No one could blame the archers for shooting at the dragon. Captain Irandis had done so himself, when he'd thought it was the Siren's weapon.

"Holy Brotherhood, it's a trireme!" someone yelled. David puzzled over the word. As if in a ghastly dance, oars leaped through the new holes along the galleys, striking the water beneath the other oars. His stomach gave a sickening lurch. Not eighty oarsmen per ship, creating lightning speed in time of emergency, but one hundred and twenty in each galley, in stair-stepped ranks of forty. David paled as understanding dawned. No one in the Empire owned a trireme, because no one needed that kind of speed. Not until pirates showed up with galleys of their own.

Behind him, men darted into new positions. Fresh oarsmen fell into place as exhausted ones peeled off the benches. A rough hand grabbed David's shoulder.

"Help with grapples, boy. All hands on deck." The sea guard jumped down to the main deck, and David leaped after him.

"Farren dear, look at these odd ships. They've got way too many people rowing." Sixty oarsmen on each side dug into the water, shoving it rapidly behind them. "Maari says that's a trireme, but I'm not sure what she means exactly. Farren, dear, perhaps you're right after all. They don't look like very nice men."

Farren threw a look at the Southern Sentinel. Denys was in the forecastle, waving a red flag, one, two, three, pause, one, two, three. "Damn," he breathed. He rubbed the dragon's head between the armor plating. "Okay, you've got your way. Lead the attack!"

The dragon bugled and flew through small knots of shades. Shades mobbed all four ships, their voices ringing across the water.

The Shade Patrol Second swooped on the captain of the fish-head galley. "Surrender," he bellowed. "High Captain says surrender or die! Last warning, you son-of-a-bitch."

The captain cuffed a sailor out of his way and strode to the forecastle, oblivious to the shade's warning.

"Oh, you would, would you?" exclaimed the Second, incensed. "Take that. And that! Oh, to hell with it." The shade hurled away his useless sword. He grappled the man around the neck, and chortled as the captain jerked back. "Aha. That got you, did it? Men, listen up. Hand to hand, that's the way to get these buggers!"

"Guess who!" crowed a child, leaping onto an archer's

back, wrapping her arms around his throat. The archer spun away, clawing at his neck.

"Repent," intoned a line of guardians, weaving through the scrambling fighters, spattering incense at them. Fighters scrubbed their eyes feverishly as their vision blurred.

"The mast," yelled Farren into the dragon's ear.

The dragon curvetted over Pelican One, snatching the mast with the curve of his tail. The earsplitting screech of splintering wood sounded, followed by a resounding crash. The ship rocked violently, throwing three sailors overboard.

"Gods, I love flying!" shouted the Goat, his shaggy body leaping through the air in mighty bounds. "It's magnificent. All of you follow me! Wind will stop them!" The air groaned with the sudden weight of shades circling the ships in ever-tightening circles, a hurricane in the making. "Surrender!" the Goat roared, and his followers picked up the chant.

"Surrender, surrender, surrender—"

Farren clung to the dragon as it tore out Pelican Two's mast. Collapsing sails and rigging ensnared half-a-dozen seamen as the mast thundered into the sea, ripping the railing as it went. Two men scrambled to a line thrown by their mates, but the others drifted, unconscious, like flotsam upon the waves.

"The lead galley," said Farren into the golden dragon's ear. Scores of shades clustered around the dragon, as though shielding him from danger. Their blustering enthusiasm reminded him strongly of boys braving the horrors of a "haunted" stable. Wind whistled past his ears. Only a flat reptilian head and a hundred feet of air separated him from the galley's deck. Archers lined up on a catwalk strung from end to end above the oarsmen. As one, their aim swiveled, and the cross bolts turned his way. Farren tensed, exultation and terror mingled in painful ecstasy.

"Farren, be careful. They've got slaves!" Aunt Nan clung to

his shoulder. "The men underneath the deck, the oarsmen, they're manacled! If the ship sinks, they'll drown."

Farren freed an arm from his stranglehold on the dragon's throat and waved frantically. To his astonishment, the shades followed his orders, and split into three rivers, one to the front of the galley, one to the back, and the third through the belly where the shackled oarsmen lived their darkened lives.

The dragon rumbled from deep in its chest. "Don't kill the archers," Farren shouted, divining the dragon's intent.

The dragon screamed its rebellion. A sudden turn nearly dislodged Farren altogether. A face beneath a metal helmet loomed large, its mouth a terrified O. It disappeared beneath him as talons and tail swept him and his comrades into the sea. Farren pounded on the dragon's head with both fists.

"Up! Up higher! We've got to see what's going on." A wild veer jarred him to one side, before the dragon rose with obvious reluctance.

The shades' windstorms rocked the enemy ships, snapping oars like toothpicks. The Island's Patrol longboats and warships, in contrast, slipped through calm waters, smooth and invincible as they approached the enemy. Farren spotted King Gerritt on the Watchword's forecastle as it approached Pelican One, grappling irons at the ready. The king's flags waved their insistent message, surrender, surrender. A flag answered from Pelican One.

"They're going to do it, they're going to surrender—"

A stunning jolt pitched them backwards. A shimmering sparkle, as hard and cold as iron, blocked their progress. The dragon evaded, dropped, and slipped to the side, but a bone-shaking collision against an invisible barrier tossed them back. The dragon screamed a protest, as a suffocating pressure shoved them down, like a mountainous avalanche.

෩

Hesselin slipped into the captain's cabin and pulled the door shut. His cheeks were flushed with anger. Gods, to be so close! What the hell was Kogyr thinking, calling in the ships so soon? If only he'd waited a month or so, to let the furor settle down. Even a day would have been enough. Given a single day's grace, the seven-year spell would be complete. Kogyr could throw off his shackles, loose his horde on Valtiris, and pillage the country at his leisure, just as long as he left Ailsandia alone. Ailsandia was Hesselin's. He'd inherited it, worked for it, and fought for it. It was his by right.

"Durgas! Serpe!" he snapped.

Serpe's fluttering figure appeared before him.

"Kogyr," he said. "Tell me about Kogyr. You've been watching him."

"Yes, Master, of course," she said, pointing through the wall hesitantly. "He's out there."

Hesselin stifled a curse. "He must have called in these ships somehow. When did he send the message? Who carried it?"

"Message?" she faltered. "Well, he was always talking to the guards, and he sends little notes with carriers." Her figure turned watery. "I'm sorry, Master. It's hard to keep track of people with two faces. I mean, he talks with one face, and scowls with the other. I've always told you, when he hurts people, but I can never tell when he's talking if it's really him..."

The woman was as brainless dead as she had been alive. Sometimes he wondered why Elizar had bothered to bind six different shades. Hesselin's two were enough to drive him mad. Ah well, Durgas was a good tool, and Serpe's uselessness was his own fault. He'd chosen badly. A seamstress wasn't much good as a spy.

"All right, Serpe," he said through gritted teeth. "Go find him now. Tell him to disengage. If he starts hurting our people, stop him. Is that clear?"

"But, Master!"

He cut off her shrill voice. "I didn't say to kill him. I said to stop him. Grab him by the throat or something, make him trip. Use your imagination for once!"

Serpe bobbed in dismal agreement, and swooped through the wall. Hesselin stood by the edge of the window, keeping his face out of sight. He could barely see the fish-head galley through the small opening.

"Durgas!" He made a snatching gesture with his hand. Durgas appeared, emerging through the wall, back-end first. "Get in here."

Durgas faced him, wearing his strange open-mouthed grin. "Yeah?" His head turned automatically to the window, and he stared at the havoc as if mesmerized.

"Control yourself," Hesselin snapped. "You follow Kogyr's lead again, and I'll bind to you to the sphere for a month. We're not letting those ships land. Serpe's telling him to disengage, and you'll enforce that order."

"He's not going to give up now," protested Durgas. "The rest of the oars are out!"

Hesselin's eyes flew open wide. "Triremes," he exploded. "The idiot brought in triremes. Gods, we're stuck with a pitched battle, now." Damn, he'd have to change his strategy. Did he have the power left to transport the ships? Even if he did, Kogyr was probably on one of those ships right now. Much as he hated the man, he needed him.

"Lookit that!" Durgas breathed.

The gold dragon dove onto the fish-head galley, pulling up at the last minute, pounding the sky with his wings.

"I never killed a dragon before," mused Durgas, a greedy

smile edging onto his face.

"You're not going to kill one now! You keep your hands off that dragon, hear me? I need it alive." *At least until tomorrow...*

"Well, what about the boy, then?" said Durgas, sulkily.

The ship lurched, throwing Hesselin against a table bolted to the floor. "You get out there and deal with Kogyr," he snarled. "I'll deal with the dragon. And its rider!"

As the shade vanished, Hesselin braced himself into a corner. He raised his hands before him, visualizing a frozen column of air trapping a dragon, holding it like an insect in a tumbler made of glass.

The shades howled in rage. A thousand strong, they mobbed the ships indiscriminately, setting merchant ships, galleys, longboats, and Patrol ships alike rocking in frenzied animation, puppet ships bobbing helplessly in the tidal wave of the shades' fury. Small eddies of calm disrupted the waves around a favored few. Maari threw her arms around Denys and Trissi, while Aunt Nan protected David.

"No, not our ships," yelled Farren, but the shades didn't listen. From every ship, men were hurled overboard. The Watchword's sails ripped and tattered in the storm. The Sentinel's rigging snapped loose, and the cables lashed with peerless aim leaving streams of blood in their wake.

Suddenly, the crushing pressure eased. Like the tip of a sapling released from its strap, the dragon sprang to safety, hauling the shades with him.

All was still.

Farren and the dragon circled. In fluttering confusion, the shades stared intently at the six ships, the three longboats, the scattered oars and splintered timbers, and the bobbing heads on the water, as men struggled to their ships.

"In the One's name, what *happened*?" Farren said.

"Haruff," snorted the Goat. "A *sorcerer* happened, you fool. Or maybe that Siren of yours. A sorcerer attacked you, and the Shade Patrol countered and saved your feeble little lives. They were led by the best, I might add," said the Goat insufferably, tapping Farren's leg with a frozen hoof.

"But did someone *kill* the sorcerer, or did he give up?"

"Who knows? You're just damned lucky I was here to help. You'd never have survived without me. Mortals!"

A scream cut through the windstorm, drawing David's gaze into the sky where a dragon hurtled downwards. Farren huddled along its neck. The dragon flailed its wings helplessly, shrieking its dismay. As if in answer, a whirlwind seized the Sentinel, battering it with invisible forces, slamming men into the decks, rails, and sea.

A wall of water crashed over the side, snatched three men, and flung them overboard. Men clung to railings, hatches, and cleats. A sailor lashed himself to a mast, ducking his head into his hands to save his face from flying debris. Amid them all, David stood in the middle of the deck, sheltered in a bubble of calm. A thick invisible bandage wound around David, paralyzing him with its chilly comfort. A man careened past him. David tried to grab him, but his hands wouldn't move.

An abrupt silence swallowed sound. No, it wasn't silence, not exactly. The punished Sentinel creaked as its violent rocking eased. Men groaned from the deck, and called faintly from the waters beyond. The whistling whirlwind, forcing them under the waves, simply stopped. The eye of the storm? Once again, the dragon soared over the waves. The wintry enveloping blanket loosened and let David go free.

David staggered to the railing of the ship, where a man lay inert. David reached out to touch him and jerked his hand back. What if the fellow was dead? He forced himself to touch the man's throat. The pulse leaped under his fingers. He hadn't the least idea what to do for the man. Once, he'd known what to do, his hands swift and sure even when a dragon collapsed on a balcony. He hadn't thought about it. He'd just done it, and somehow he'd been right. But a man? David swallowed hard.

"Boy!"

David turned, ludicrously grateful for an order. "Yes, sir?"

A Second threw him a coil of rope. "Start casting. We've got to pull these poor buggers in before they drown. Leave the seamen for last. They can swim."

David looped the line to the rail, found a pair of flailing arms in the waves, and cast his line to the poor wretch. If he hit the man by mistake, he could take out an eye with the rope. His shoulders aching, he helped a man over the railing, hoping he hadn't rescued an enemy by mistake. The man tumbled onto the deck, gasped his thanks, and turned to the unconscious man lying nearby. David drew a shaky breath and searched for another bobbing head among the scattering of small boats. Trissi and Denys had found a dinghy and launched it to hunt for survivors further away from the ships.

A muffled shout diverted him. Thrashing arms beat the surface of the water, barely keeping the man's head afloat. "Over here." David shouted. "You're almost there." His line fell short, but the man floundered towards it, his courage renewed.

The thunk of metal on wood carried across the water. David stared in amazement. One of the longboats had grappled onto Pelican One. A dozen Patrol Guards swarmed aboard and laid about with swords. Yes! He searched in vain for his father's unmistakable figure. He was probably in a boat on the other side, coordinating the attack. It made sense, but his heart fell.

"Sharks!" From the top of the mast, a Sea Patrol guard pointed a rigid arm. He snatched up a red flag, and waved with frenzied motions. "Shark, shark!"

"Frickin' idiot," grunted a sailor. "There ain't no sharks in these waters."

The rope jerked in David's hands as a man hauled himself to the ship. David reeled him in. He'd heard of sharks, as he'd heard of witches and zombies. Guards loved to terrify their juniors with lurid stories that the juniors repeated, often with gruesome additions. David choked back a scream as a triangular fin cut the water. The man clinging to the rope glanced behind, and doubled his speed. The rope burned David's hands.

"Help," David gasped.

Heavy boots hit the deck behind him. Hands gripped the rope and yanked. The man skidded over the top of the water, the shark only a dozen feet behind. With a glad cry, the man hit the ship and ran up the side, clinging to his rope. David and his helper pulled him under the railing. A heavy thud hit the boat, and David shivered.

"You're safe, boy," said the dripping man. "It's an Island ship, you know. An oversized fish ain't gonna sink one of these." The man gave him a gap-toothed grin. "Thanks, boy. Thanks, Captain. More sharks out there? Or just the one, do you think?"

David glanced up, hoping to see his father, but it was Captain Irandis of the Regent's Guard.

"I wouldn't know. I'm no seaman," said Irandis. He cuffed the man's shoulder roughly. "Glad you're all right, Clark." He paused, tracking the dragon in its flight overhead. "Sea monsters and dragons. Dear gods, what's next?" He shook his head, and muttered to himself. "A man's got to *do* something. I can't let this go on."

"Sir? Can I help?" Clark asked.

"Huh? Oh." Irandis stared at him, apparently flummoxed. "Ah. Help the boy."

"Right, sir. You're sure?"

"Huh," said Captain Irandis. His face fell into deep lines, a man who'd seen too much, and didn't know what to make of most of it. "You can see it, can't you?" he pleaded. He clawed his hands through his thinning hair. "It's insane, all of it."

"Sir?" Clark said uncertainly.

"Kraaken," said Irandis in deep disgust. "A kraaken, for godssake! And a siren, a dragon, and now the damned sharks. I'm done with it, that's all. To hell with him and his plots." He seemed to wake from his trance. "You, Clark. Help the boy, pull in the survivors, heh?" He slapped Clark on the back and stalked towards the cabin.

"Damn it all," Clark exploded. "There *are* more sharks. Where's a boat? I've got to get out there, help my mates!"

"The boats are out already, sir," David said. "The seamen took them out first thing. The longboats are out, too." He waved towards Pelican One. "Look, we've boarded a merchantship."

Clark glanced over at the battle, unbelieving. "Who ordered that? He reacted damned fast, whoever it was."

Screams from the water brought them back to duty as a man struggled below the surface, leaving a spreading red stain behind him. Sickened, David leaned over the rail, calling the scattered men. "Hurry," he screamed. "This way, move it."

Clark pointed to the left. "That poor bugger's never going to make it."

"That boat's close enough to get him. Hey, HEY!"

Clark waved his arms, and bellowed in a deep, carrying voice. "Boat, ahoy, boat! That way! Ah, good, they see him."

The slicing sound of a cross bolt split the air behind them. David ducked instinctively. Irandis stood on the forecastle, crossbow raised.

"What's he think he's doing?" Clark gasped. "Can't shoot fish with a crossbow, and we're too far from the other ships. He'll never reach them from here."

"He's aiming up," said David. "Maybe..." His voice trailed off as he followed the likely arc of the bolt. "No!" He ran for the forecastle. "No, don't shoot him!" His mind conjured a memory, of a dragon in mid-flight, charring arrows and evading bolts with effortless ease—all but one. One bolt flew straight and true, as though guided to its target. Perhaps the rocking of the ship disturbed Irandis' aim on this shot, but the second would go true.

He scaled the ladder, scarcely touching it, and lunged at Irandis. "Don't! The dragon's on our side. He's helping us, can't you see it?"

Irandis shook him off, but David clung like a burr, like a cavalry junior to a rearing horse. Irandis struck him with end of the crossbow. David's ears rang but he hung on, trying to throw the bolts overboard.

"...Goddamned kraaken, sharks, and now a dragon, it's not right, not right—"

"Irandis!" The sharp, commanding tone filled David with relief. At last, his father had come! "Drop your bow, Irandis. The dragon's an ally."

"Ally?" cried Irandis. "You're insane." He yanked David to his feet and grappled him around the chest.

High Captain Vance Heronlys paused at the top of the ladder. "Let him go, Irandis," he warned.

David kicked, but Irandis' other hand, slung through the bow, grabbed his hair and dragged his head back. The bow knocked into him from behind. The thick arm around David's chest drove the air from his lungs, and he hung there, limp.

"Irandis. Everything's all right," Heronlys said, his voice strained. "You don't understand the situation. I should have explained more fully."

"Oh yeah. Explain! I'm sure you can, High Captain," he sneered. "Explaining is what you're best at, aren't you?"

"Irandis, the situation is this. The dragon is flying overhead with one of our men. It's conducting a survey, and relaying information below. I assure you, the dragon has never acted against our interest. You'll recall, in the harbor, it only attacked the Siren."

"Come off it, Vance. Tell the truth for a change. You're all in it, you and the Siren, and the sea monsters, and dragons, and even the damned sharks. You and all your precious Firsts, with their noses in the air."

"Irandis, I'm not sure what you think—"

"What I think? What I know! Got your little pets in every Patrol, haven't you? All except the Regent's Guard. That's where the King was too smart for you, putting me in there. Hurt, didn't it? Knowing you couldn't pull your little tricks there."

David stared at his father, wide-eyed. Heronlys' face set sternly. "You're mistaken, Irandis. Let the boy go. We'll discuss this later, over a glass of wine, eh?"

"Oh, you're afraid, are you? Afraid I'll throw your boy overboard?" A sudden jerk backwards terrified David. "Let your pet sharks at him. Or are you afraid he'll finally hear the truth about you? Tell him about Rampton Vale, did you? A thriving little town, until your precious Rimlands Patrol ripped right through it."

"Irandis," snapped Heronlys.

"Dad?" breathed David. Rampton Vale was a mountain

town. His mother had valued their fleeces more than any other, until the town's destruction by bandits three years before. Neighboring towns hunted down the errant sheep, and rescued them from starvation. Two-thirds vanished, either eaten or smuggled out of Valtiris.

"And Southern Patrol's taken care of those coastal towns, haven't they? Oh yeah, took care of them *real* good. Those pirate ships out there." A violent jerk towards the ships dangled David halfway over the rail. David tried to snag his feet around a post, but Irandis hauled him back as a shield. "You called them in," said Irandis with grim certainty. "The King's onto you, Vance. Why'd you think he took off without you? Why'd you think he's leading the boarding party, all on his lonesome? He knows you're a traitor, and so do I. No dragon's gonna roast my King into a scrap of charred meat. You want to save your boy? You can damn well shoot that dragon yourself." He hooked a long pouch with his foot and slung it towards Heronlys. "Only, you gotta use my bolts. Special ones, they are. Got a spell on them, against supernatural creatures. I coulda taken out the damned Siren myself, if I'd known about her ahead of time and blocked my ears."

Heronlys pulled the pouch towards him with his foot. David's eyes stung. His father hadn't denied anything. It couldn't be true, it couldn't be! David stared at his father, and felt his pride shatter into a thousand fragments.

"No, Dad." His plea barely stirred the air.

Heronlys' gaze flicked beyond Irandis. The man scoffed at him. "Don't try that old trick, Vance. Nothing out there but air, water, and sharks."

"And a dragon," said Heronlys evenly.

Irandis threw a glance backwards. Straight as a crossbow bolt, the dragon shot towards them. Irandis cried out hoarsely, as Heronlys tackled him.

"Take the boy," screamed Irandis, and with a mighty heave, he swung David's body over the rail and dropped him into the water.

David screamed. His mouth and nose filled with water as he plunged. He beat the water with his hands and feet. *Sharks, please no! Don't let them eat me.* Darkness enveloped him. Which way was up? If he surfaced under the ship, he was dead for sure. He'd never get out from underneath in time to breathe. And the sharks—*Gods, oh gods, please, one of you—*

A shadow above him—or was it below? Oh hell, it *was* a shark. Every thought streaked out of David's head, as the sleek gray killing machine flashed towards him. His lungs burned with terror. Another shadow bore down on him from the other side, and he gave himself up for lost.

A huge creature snaked past him. A hand snagged him, and shoved him hard against a scaled hide. David found himself clutching two huge spikes, while a dragon's head and Farren's body blocked the shark's attack. The water boiled as flame poured forth, splashing the water in red and orange. David shut his eyes against the shark, now writhing in super-heated steam. Waves of scalding water backwashed over him as the dragon coursed upwards, and broke through the surface like a geyser.

David sat on the dragon's shoulders, numbly clinging to the lowest spikes. The wind whipped his drenched clothing around him. He shivered, but not from the cold or wind.

Two hours ago, he'd have given his life for the chance to ride a dragon. He nearly *had* given his life. Now he soared over sea, ships, and men on the mythical winged beast, but his dreams lay tattered like the beleaguered ships beneath him. The battle, the sorceries, and destruction paled before the image of his father's face, closed and unrevealing.

The dragon swept low over the Southern Sentinel. Trissi

and Denys' boat docked at its side, letting soaked men climb up toeholds on the side of the ship. David's father, once again, had disappeared from view. Irresistibly, David's eyes latched onto the bobbing figure of half a man, the whiteness of his face testifying to blood loss and death.

It was Irandis.

David's last vestige of terror faded, replaced by a lard-like ball of grief deep in his gut.

As they approached the eastern watchtower, Farren's glance sharpened. A familiar white-robed figure waved to him. The dragon cupped his wings, landing on the ramparts to one side of the readied catapult. The sudden draft sent Mericia's hair flying. A guard grabbed David and eased him onto the rooftop, throwing a cloak over him with rough kindness.

The fighting had spread through all the ships. Her Majesty's Own, finally in range, grappled onto the fish-head galley. Sea Patrol guards swung a scaffold from their mast over the deck of the galley's catwalk. From the scaffold, arrows shot into the midst of the fighting, taking out oarsmen and archers. On Pelican One, the King's attack force gained steady advantage, assisted by sudden cold spikes of air that unaccountably acted only on the enemy. The shades were back in action.

Mericia rushed to Farren, ignoring the dragon entirely. A second guard stepped in close, his hands poised behind her. She grabbed Farren's arm, holding out a wad of clay.

"Here, carve one for me, one of those water beasts. I don't know what they look like." The lump of clay held a triangular fin on top of a formless mass. "I tried to throw the ships away, like the Siren and kraaken, but I couldn't do it." She swayed. Matter-of-factly, the guard caught her under the elbow and set her upright. So that was why he hovered so close. "I just don't have the power left, Farren, I'm sorry. I've been throwing men back on board as fast as I can. But I think those sea monsters are small enough, I can get rid of them."

Farren pinched the clay into the fish-like shape with the undershot jaw and soulless eyes that would haunt his dreams for years to come.

"Ah," said the guard, enlightened. "Shark. Couldn't tell from here. We hardly get two in a decade, and it looks like there's dozens."

"There are." Farren addressed the Princess Regent. "Your Highness, Caprio says a sorcerer brought them, unless it was the Siren. I haven't seen her, though, or heard her."

"Us neither," agreed the guard, with an islander's disregard for formality.

"If a sorcerer brought them, I can get rid of them," Mericia said. She gestured to the guard. "Tell him what you told me." She raised the shark figure from lips to sky, and stared out to the sea.

The guard eyed the dragon with cautious respect, and took up his position behind the princess, ready to catch her if she collapsed. He looked squarely at Farren. "My buddies and me, we don't understand half of what's going on, but if you can stir up magic winds like you're doing—. Well, we've got a notion for you, might speed things up a little. Throw us a wind around Pelican Two and shove it over here, like. Then we can take it out with the catapult. That just leaves the last galley, the chicken-beak, right? It's trying to pick up position to ram. We thought maybe if you took out the oars with your friend here, that'd slow 'em down. We think their leader's on chicken-beak, not on a Pelican. There's been flags a-going steady from back there, and other ships just reading 'em. Could be your sorcerer's back there, too."

A wave of relief washed over Farren. Aunt Nan's relayed instructions were diffident and often, he suspected, edited. Caprio romped through the forays happily, but Farren didn't trust his regard for human life. Thank the One, someone could see the larger picture and advise him on it.

"Thank you!"

"Er," said the second guard. "You look a mite damp." He held out a leather jerkin.

With a nod of gratitude, Farren stripped off his shirt, and shrugged into the jerkin. "Fortunately, dragon hide's warm," he said, indicating his pants.

The dragon shook out his wings, craning his head towards the action on the waves. "Well, we're off then." Farren glanced at the boy huddled against the turret wall. The terror had knocked David for a loop, and he didn't seem to be recovering. "Take care of the boy?"

"Sure thing," said the second guard. "High Captain's son, ain't he?" He stirred the boy gently with his boot. "I know the Captain's right proud of him."

David shivered.

"He'll be fine. Off with you, now. Great job, Farren. Terrell'd be proud. He'll be mad as hell he missed it, too."

Caprio, as it happened, was only too delighted to lead several hundred shades in a whirlwind tour around Pelican Two. As the ship pitched and yawed towards the catapult, Farren and the dragon flew for the chicken-beak galley, keeping a sharp eye out for well-aimed crossbows.

"Aunt Nan? See if you can trick someone into unlocking the chains from the lower oarsmen." Once released, the prisoners would add to the confusion, and possibly turn the tide.

"Excellent idea, dear," she said warmly. "Slavery is an abhorrent practice. I will attempt to educate the relevant person."

The chicken-beak galley had gathered up most of its oars.

The oarsmen dug into the waves, trying to pick up speed to ram the Sentinel. The mysterious sorcerer didn't seem to be present. If they were all very lucky, a shark had gotten him. A ragged line of nervous archers manned the catwalk until the dragon winged over them. The archers scrambled below with record speed.

Farren was dead-tired, and sick of the whole bloody mess. The guard's recommendation seemed like child's play compared with the rest of this day's events. He conferred wordlessly with the dragon, a process that now seemed second nature. The dragon swooped down to the wreckage on the waters and grabbed the end of a broken mast in his talons. He aligned all four feet along it as though he were riding a gigantic broomstick.

With horrific precision, they flew alongside the galley. The mast, dragging behind, shattered oars and ripped others from clutching fists. Another pass up the other side, and the galley lay dead in the water, inert and powerless, without a single casualty. The dragon settled along the empty catwalk.

In the deep stillness that followed, Aunt Nan proclaimed to the captain, "You, sir, are a bad man. Your mother would be ashamed of you. Unlock those manacles instantly."

Sweat and salt water streaked the captain's strained face. He looked stunned by the defeat. Farren almost felt sorry for him. The captain drew his short sword and brandished it at his men. "Get to your posts, you bastards, get this ship moving." The crouching oarsmen stared at the dragon, and didn't move.

"Stop threatening these poor men," said Aunt Nan, with icy dignity. "The very idea. Such language, and you in a position of authority!"

The captain lunged through her, raising his sword over the nearest oarsman. Aunt Nan gasped in outrage, hurtled in front of him, and slapped him briskly across the face.

"Now, *that* is enough of that. Down on your *knees*, villain, before the One smites you!"

A blast of discordant music raised the hackles on every man's neck. The piercing sound rose relentlessly to a teeth-jarring shriek. The captain dropped his sword, clapped his hands over his ears, and fell to his knees. Behind Aunt Nan, the Goat tilted his head, and winked at Farren.

"There now," said Aunt Nan approvingly. "Submission is good for the soul. Don't you feel better now?"

Oblivious to the Goat, Aunt Nan bent to retrieve the captain's keys. She pursed her lips as her hand slipped through the keys. She nodded regally to Farren. "Dear, I believe I've subdued the captain for you. If you would be so kind as to convey him to the Palace for the Regent's justice?"

"Of course," said Farren gravely. "Let me give you a hand with those keys."

"Most kind of you. You might send Denys over, with a squadron or two. Until he gets here, I'll keep matters under control."

Farren held the keys out to a ship's boy. "Unlock those men down below. Otherwise," he said, "you'll regret it. Got that?" The boy took the keys with nerveless fingers. "Thank you very much, Aunt Nan. We couldn't have handled this without you."

Aunt Nan gestured graciously towards the prostrate captain, still trying vainly to block out the Goat's discordance. The dragon plucked the captain from the deck in his front talons. As they flew away, Farren heard Aunt Nan holding forth sternly.

"Now, there will be order here, young men. Sit down, fold your hands, and keep them in your laps..."

Chapter Seventeen

"Execution is the only answer," King Gerritt exclaimed. He slammed his fist into his open hand. "They took arms against the royal house!"

Mericia looked at him, puzzled. "But Father, what about the assassin? The young man who tried to kill you? You only kept him in the dungeon..." She blinked, recalling Farren's description of the dungeon. Still, the Lady had been responsible for those conditions. The dungeon prisoners' suffering hadn't meant a thing to the Lorelei. Neither had Maari's death, or Nanny's, or any of the agonies Mericia's 'curse' had caused.

Mericia tried to force her tired mind back on track. Execution, that was the subject. Whether they should execute the leaders of the attacking ships. "At least, you said—"

"A totally different matter. That was a private dispute, with a nobleman's son, not at all the same thing. This is treason!"

Minister Rogitas raised a warning hand. "Only if they're citizens of Ailsandia or Valtiris," she said. "If they come from the south, it's not treason."

"Your Highness, Your Majesty," Minister Jonsel said, bowing to each, "perhaps this matter should be deferred until a later time. We're all exhausted." He rubbed a sizeable knot on the side of his head. "The Guard has the men under restraint—"

"In warehouses!" said Vance Heronlys. "Hardly a secure location for several hundred pirates. They could break out again at any moment."

He paced back and forth on the palace balcony, oblivious to the sprawled dragon and rider only a few feet away.

"Watch out for the dragon wings," said Mericia lightly. "Trampling our heroes is hardly an appropriate expression of gratitude." The balcony felt packed with shades. She knew they were there. They had to be. Their fantastic performance during the sea battle proved their interest in current events. She tried in vain to see them, but there was nothing, not even a prancing Goat. Nevertheless, she sensed a hushed expectancy in the air, as though every unseen listener waited with drawn breath. As though, any minute now, something important would happen.

"I suppose," said the King, glancing at the corner of the Palace balcony, "you don't want any advice on them either." One side of his mouth turned up in a grin. "So I won't give any. On either subject. All right, Vance? We'll leave the pirates and dragons until tomorrow."

Mericia smiled. "Thanks, father."

"Any time, my dear." He shook his head, chuckling. "Dragon wings are quite the decorative touch. Starting a fashion?"

When the fighting petered out, the dragon had returned to the balcony bearing his rider. Admiring servants plied the two adventurers with water and a pile of fish, both raw and cooked, while clamoring for a firsthand account. To their intense disappointment, both man and dragon collapsed into a profound sleep. Even now, as dusk arrived, Farren lay against the dragon's neck, a sprawling arm draped over the nearest spike. The dragon, half-awake, curled protectively around his rider.

Vance Heronlys paced in rapid circles, staring at the floor. Mericia glanced from him to David. The boy unnerved her. Considering the stories Trissi told, she'd expected him to leap onto the dragon heap in delighted abandon. Instead, he sat on a stool near the balcony railing, his head bowed, and his hands pinned between his knees. His mother, Chandra Heronlys, stood nearby, her hands thrust in her skirt pockets in a way most unlike the graceful Master Weaver. Her frequent darting glances at her son spoke eloquently of her desire to reassure him, and equally of her determination not to humiliate him. Perhaps David was less resilient than Mericia had thought.

"Perhaps we could tackle a different problem," she suggested. "My mother used to tell us about Sorcerer Elizar— an object lesson against shadebinding. She said he had a green dragon, but I don't remember where it came from."

"One of the southern countries, wasn't it?" Rogitas said. "Jonsel, you're the one with the import connections to the south. Didn't the dragon come from Rubia, or somewhere?"

"I don't think so," Jonsel said doubtfully. "They've got incense trees there, but I've never heard a thing about dragons. Always thought they were fairy tales, myself."

"Elizar conjured his," said Sendillon. "I remember Her Majesty telling you the story. I believe I was patching a skinned knee at the time." He flashed Mericia a rueful grin, somewhat distorted by the darkening bruises on his face. She hid a smile at the alert look of Sendillon's small dog, sitting under his chair. "There was something about a girl he'd seized, and a fired-up mob of angry fishermen."

"I remember that part," Rogitas agreed. "He tried to enchant the dragon to incinerate them, but it didn't work right. Shortly after that, your ancestor, er, took care of him."

"Executed him," said the King, with a glint of humor. "For treason."

Mericia tensed. Hadn't her father agreed to leave the treason issue until morning? "What happened to the dragon afterwards?" She glanced from Rogitas to Sendillon.

"I don't know," confessed Sendillon. "If he conjured it, it probably disappeared when he died. Wouldn't you think so?"

"Excuse me." Chandra Heronlys stepped forward. Mericia looked at her in surprise. "I work with tapestries, you know, all sorts of them," she said, with a faint questioning note.

"Yes, of course. Lady Siree has often remarked on your helpfulness to the Queen," Mericia said.

"Since we've arrived here, I've been studying the ones at the guild hall, here on the Island. Customers often commission weavers to commemorate an important scene, like great battles, celebrations, or treaty signings. They're fascinating historical records. One of them showed the green dragon."

"That's wonderful. You must show me," Mericia said warmly. "Can you spare the time tomorrow? I'd love to see it. I'm sure Farren would, too."

The King's head jerked upwards. Minister Jonsel and Vance Heronlys glanced at her sharply. So, Mericia noted, the notion of Farren raised a few hackles, did it? Well, they'd better get used to it. She'd take their advice on many things, but not on the man and his dragon. The long-term complications of *that* relationship had yet to sink in, but she would adjust. She caught herself, and tested the thought. Yes, she'd adjust. She'd made her decision, without knowing it. Now, as long as Farren's decision was the same...

"Well," Chandra shot a quick look at her son. "Of course, Your Highness. There was something else, though, stitched under the dragon's wing. It was a sort of feathery silver line fading away from it. I thought at it first it was an arrow, but it was too long for that."

Minister Jonsel stared at her intently. "Did the line lead to Elizar?"

"No, nowhere near him. I think it went towards the keep, but I'm not sure."

"The dragon wasn't conjured," stated Jonsel. "It was a displacement sorcery. A seven-year displacement. Gods, I wonder who Elizar ensorcelled? Must have been someone in the keep!"

"Nonsense, Jonsel," exclaimed Rogitas. "Talk about fairy tales! Conjuring a human soul into a dragon, just to disguise someone else? What a waste of power! Why not a simple illusion?"

"You've got to watch what you're doing, to set an illusion. No one can watch the same person forever, just to make the illusion stick," said Jonsel fiercely. "After seven years, if the imposter and victim live, the transformation is permanent. This dragon here, he's part of a displacement sorcery. He's got to be. A seven-year displacement, probably. My granny told us it's always in sevens. Seven, fourteen, twenty-one, like that." He shook his finger under Rogitas' nose. "Seven years ago, this whole mess started. All those people died, the Queen fell ill, and the Siren showed up, all of it, seven years ago! I'd bet that's when the dragon appeared, too. If so, we've got to break the enchantment tonight, or he'll be a dragon forever!"

The palace door opened. The Queen stood in the doorway looking dazed, her gloved hand on the doorframe. Mericia jumped to her feet, and the King leaped forward. They spoke simultaneously.

"Mother, are you feeling better?"

"My dear, should you be up? Come sit down."

Lady Siree bustled in, unaware that a Goat tripped along behind her. "It comes and goes, this illness. She walked on the roof of the keep for a while today. Isn't that nice? Then she took a little nap, and just now, she insisted on coming down to visit. She's still not speaking, but at least she's calm."

"Girl," snapped Caprio. He shoved his nose into Mericia's

face, and rapped her on the knee with his hoof. It felt as though a sharp icicle was batting her. "Get the damned tapestry down here."

The Queen, comfortably disposed in a chair, glanced around at the assembled company. Mericia ignored Caprio. For once, her mother seemed at least partly normal, and she didn't want to disrupt the mood.

Lady Siree whispered, "So nice to see her without a *needle* in hand, don't you agree?" Like a proud Nanny, she pulled up a chair behind the Queen, and beamed at the company.

"Mother, I'm so glad you're feeling better." The Queen was staring at Chandra Heronlys. "That's Chandra. Do you remember Chandra?" said Mericia. "You used to trade weaving patterns with her."

"Listen to me, you idiot!" bellowed Caprio.

Mericia flinched, covering the movement by rising from her seat. She stifled an urge to hit the Goat, recalling everyone's likely reaction if she did so. She couldn't deal with another of his commotions. The dragon watched the Goat with interest. Farren roused himself, rubbing his eyes. To Mericia's relief, the Goat bounded over to him. Farren could deal with Caprio.

"Mother," she said brightly, "Chandra's son, David, was quite the hero today. He helped on the Patrol ship, saved several men from drowning, got kidnapped, thrown to the sharks—," Oh dear One, what *was* she saying? She must sound insane. She persevered, drowning out Farren's conversation with the Goat. "—Got rescued by a fire-breathing dragon, and finally helped fire a catapult that took out one of the four enemy vessels. That's an amazing performance for a young man, isn't it?"

"You're *both* idiots!" the Goat exploded. With stiff-legged rage, he disappeared through the wall into the Palace.

Mericia was delighted to see him go. Everyone was staring

at her. The still, marble face copied from Lady Lelori stood her in good stead. Trying to turn her rambling speech into something constructive, she turned to the High Captain.

"You must be exceptionally proud of your son, Captain Heronlys. He owes a great deal to your good example and teaching, I am sure."

Vance Heronlys ceased his pacing, one foot still raised. Whisker stubs bristled from an abnormally pale face. "Thank you, Your Highness," he said. "I am indeed proud of my son. We have much to discuss this evening, David." His voice sounded oddly stressed. Chandra Heronlys threw an anxious look from her husband to her son.

David met his father's look, his face blank and uncommunicative. Vance Heronlys held out his hand, and let it drop. "David—"

"Harruff!" The Goat pranced onto the balcony, shoving Trissi ahead of him. Trissi looked utterly confused, and well she might, Mericia thought. Trissi had never seen Caprio, or heard him, and by the looks of her baffled face, she still couldn't. Nonetheless, she marched ahead of the Goat, bearing in her arms a heavy roll of cloth.

"First," said the Goat in biting accents, "I have to go lure in the pirate ships, a job which took weeks, mind you. But did I complain? Not a word! Now you reduce me to fetching your damned tapestry. Do I have to do everything myself?"

"You brought in the pirate ships?" shouted Farren, lunging at the Goat, fist raised. Mericia shouldered past him and took the tapestry from Trissi. The weight of it startled her. It felt like all the panels, bundled together. Lady Siree lifted the bulky roll from her arms with the ease of long practice.

"Why the hell did you haul in the pirate ships?" Farren said. "You could have killed us all!"

"I had to do something," the Goat said, rolling his eyes. "It was getting a bit boring around here."

"Oh dear," Siree exclaimed, "did you have to bring it down, Trissi? What *were* you thinking! When I'd finally gotten her away from it? She spent all last night stitching the final panel onto the others, and hadn't started a new one yet, so I thought we'd have a little peace. Don't let her see it. Let's just put it on this table over here."

"I'll give you a hand with that," said Sendillon, clearing the small table.

"No," bellowed the Goat, jabbing at Sendillon with his hooves. "No!" The Goat leaped at Lady Siree, unleashing his 'music'. They clapped their hands over their ears. Lady Siree dropped the tapestry to the ground where it rolled, partially unwinding, against the Queen's feet.

Farren sprang at the Goat. "Caprio, you demon!" Behind him, the dragon shifted slowly to its haunches.

"Pick up the tapestry," the Goat thundered.

The balcony air thickened with unseen figures, holding their breath. Every creature, living, and dead, stared at the Queen. She stripped off her gloves and cast them away, revealing hands deeply scarred by starfire.

She bent shakily, and touched the edge of the loose panel. The tapestry roll leaped into Queen Ailsa's hands. For a hushed instant, the Queen flashed a glance at her daughter, alight with love, awareness, promise, and joy. She blew a kiss to Mericia, and a radiant smile wreathed her face as she threw the tapestry into the air. Like a bird taking wing, the tapestry unfurled in an endless ribbon.

Chapter Eighteen

The First Tapestry Panel: Witness, The Mariner

From the crowds of shades surrounding the captive audience, a man emerged. His thin expressive face darkened as he clawed a hand through his mop of curly black hair. "I am Stavros, and that is my ship. I am the sailor in the rigging." He touched the first panel of the tapestry, and it rippled to life before them.

On the broad sea, a single ship strove through the waves, its triple sails billowing. A sailor clung to the rigging, his agile figure swaying with the ropes, sometimes suspended directly over the water as the ship tossed from side to side in the huge troughs. The sailor freed a hand, signaling to those below. His words were lost to the wind. The ship shifted its heading, approaching the gray line of a distant shore.

A snarl of black tapestry yarn squirmed to life. Its fluid tentacles changed color, the upper ones turning into the yellow-green of kelp floating on the waves, while the others hid in the green-black water below. With a quick rippling motion, the kraaken lofted the Siren onto the rocky crags offshore.

From the rocks, a lilting melody caught the wind, the enchanting trill freezing the hands of all men on deck. A clamor of voices rose, hushed instantly as every hand grappled the sheets, turning the ship into the wind on its slow, inexorable path towards destruction.

The man in the rigging hurled himself into the sea, bronzed arms flashing through the waves. A powerful tentacle lashed out, and seized its prey. The water heaved, teeth flashed, and the kraaken swallowed Stavros whole. From the beast's belly, a shade emerged, floating in the breeze in stunned shock as every man aboard became fodder for the great beast.

At last, nothing remained but the hulk of a ghost ship, bobbing on the waves towards the island's rocky shore. The only sound was of the ocean itself, capped by the Lorelei's shrieking laughter.

The sun rose and fell in an endless stream. The siren and kraaken wandered through the waters, pursued by an ever-changing host of shades. At length, the partners separated, and the kraaken swam north. The seas grew strange, colder, the fish fatter and more sluggish. The kraaken itself slowed, seeming to drift with the currents. Finally, it reached an island in the midst of a narrow strait.

The kraaken strayed into the harbor, settled itself on the underwater ledge, stretched out its tentacles one last time, and withdrew them to slumber beneath the water. In the morning, the sea rolled differently over the undersea shelf. Sailors blinked and nodded to themselves, pleased by the added protection of the new sandbar. They gathered stone by the boatload, and dumped it into the water, stabilizing this gift of the gods. Most of the shades dissolved, but Stavros remained.

The shade sighed. "The old queen died and her daughter, Mereni III, took her place. The Empire sent its banner ships south to honor her coronation." His tense face relaxed in a moment's pleasure. "A beautiful sight. I felt peaceful at last, ready to leave the Island. But then, I saw him." He pointed at the kraaken-spit.

A man wearing the Emperor's insignia moved in a sideways spiral, his hands echoing the movement. As he closed the spiral, he spun on one foot, as though anchoring the ground to its underpinnings. He drew his fists apart, stretching an invisible bar between them. He was a sorcerer, secretly binding the kraaken into the structure of the Island, safeguarding the most perfect harbor the Empire had ever discovered.

"I felt the binding, like fishing lines of steel anchoring the beast to the island for all time. I laughed at this perfect end, this perfect revenge. At last, the sorcerer left, and I launched myself into the skies, determined to seek out my gods at last. A wrenching pain shot through me, and I fell to the earth. As I cowered on the spit, I knew he'd trapped me. The kraaken was bound to the island for eternity, and so was I."

The Second Tapestry Panel: Witness, The Seer

The second panel of the tapestry wound around them, over the sea to the seat of the Dannevalt Empire, the city of Dannerald. A tamed river coursed in through a vast watergate on the north, looped through the city center and out again, making a moat for a man-made island in the middle of town. The Emperor's castle crowned the island, commanding the view of city, river, and countryside. Scores of towers reached for the sky, almost pricking the passing clouds with their spires.

The lines of gray wool expanded, each small square of stitching growing into the stones of a large building tucked into the warren of the castle grounds. A diffident young man with mild blue eyes looked out of the third story window. His hand rested familiarly on a scarred crystal ball on the table by his side.

"I'm not a sorcerer," said a shade, regarding his image. "Just Orbri, the seer. I hunted people in my glass, to see what they were doing, or read the papers on their desks. I became moderately useful to my emperor." He smiled ruefully. "But there were other things in my glass, creatures of magic and mystery. That was how I found her. The Lorelei."

His eyes fell to the crystal. It flickered with images, of nobles, craftsmen, kings, and princes, but again and again, a laughing vision with eyes of green glass filled the sphere. Orbri's dark hair thinned and faded. His face lost its youthful firmness and fell into slack wrinkles.

His gnarled hands cradled the ball. He watched mesmerized, as the Lorelei swam to the Great Island's land spit. With teasing nudges, and then frantic thumping, she sought to wake her friend, the kraaken. Her face grew dark with rage. In an instant, the laughter fell away from her face as if it had never existed. She swam to the Emperor's coastline. Shrouding her lovely form in linen, she walked through the Emperor's capital city, alone and unmolested, surrounded by a nameless shield.

A bit of gray wool fuzzed out of the tapestry tower: Orbri's hair, as disordered as a half-blown dandelion. The old man sat in his heavy wooden chair, cradling his crystal in his hands. He hunched away from the arrogant young man standing over him. The young man rolled a bottle of wine in his hands, displaying it, and then gestured towards the crystal. Orbri ignored him.

"That man," Orbri told them, "that is Hesselin, the King's sorcerer."

With an exclamation of disgust, Hesselin set the wine bottle on the table, and laid a heavy hand on Orbri's shoulder. Orbri flinched, but his gaze remained fixed on an image in the ball. A vein in Hesselin's temple pulsed, and his face flushed with anger. He dug his fingers into the old man's shoulder.

As if in a trance, Orbri looked up at the empty doorway, his face alight with painful anticipation. Hesselin scowled, finally hearing the footsteps on the stairs. He strode to the window and leaned against it. He leaned there, tense with bridled impatience until the intruder should finish his business and leave.

The door opened and a woman entered. A green gown covered her from head to toe, hiding her hair. Her chalk-white face seemed carved of stone. Only her eyes were alive, moving, assessing, and rejecting Hesselin in less than a heartbeat.

Orbri spoke, his eyes bright and eager. He stretched out a hand and let it fall. The Lorelei raised a questioning eyebrow, considering his request. At length, she inclined her regal head, agreeing to the bargain.

Orbri blinked the tears from his eyes. "I told her all I knew. And before I died, she sang for me." A tear streaked his cheek. "It was most beautiful moment of my life."

The Third Tapestry Panel: Witness, The Lady's Maid

The second panel rolled away, drawing the third in its wake. Red, blue, and yellow stitches draped Ailsandia's harbor city in banners, while the harbor danced with colorful sails. The seven-year Progress had arrived. Queen Ailsa stepped onto the platform in the town square. King Gerritt stood on her left, the fourteen-year old Mericia on the right. Behind them stood Ministers Sendillon, Jonsel, and Rogitas. Dignitaries flanked the sides of the platform, including the Lady Lelori.

A shade detached itself from the first ranks of observers. As she moved to the fore, she glanced briefly at each member of the audience, lingering wistfully on her son. She cleared her throat. "I am Maari, lady's maid to Queen Ailsa. I stood right there when the horror began."

Queen Ailsa smiled at her people, opened her mouth to speak, and dropped like a stone to the platform. King Gerritt clutched his heart, stumbled, and fell by his wife's side. Maari ran to the Queen and knelt to cradle her head. Minister Sendillon yelled for the carriage, while Minister Jonsel felt King Gerritt's throat for a pulse. The platform swarmed with attendants. The milling crowd ebbed and flowed as within its midst people fell, struck down as suddenly as the Queen and King.

"Hundreds of people were felled, as invisible hands clutched their hearts and stopped their beating. Fourteen people died. I was only one."

Thirteen other shades ranged around her: two ship's captains, a master merchant, two craft masters, a groom, two of the Queen's advisors on commerce, two maidservants, a guard from the northernmost watchtower, an herbal physician, and a small boy with his thumb in his mouth. As one, they touched the tapestry. Fourteen stitched figures took on life and clustered around the queen's bed.

The Queen spread her arms. A flurry of sparks flew from her fingertips, arched through the shades and crackled through the tapestry. Each of the shades quivered and fell towards the tapestry, as though sucked through a reed into its own stitched figure. Silence blanketed the watchers and splintered with the sound of voices. One by one the moving figures on the tapestry spoke, their words breaking the silence of seven years.

The shade of Marthe, the herbal woman, turned to the others. "She's in a coma, poor love. There's not a thing I can do, nor my daughter, neither. I can tell you this, though. It ain't natural. I never seen a sickness hit like this, sudden like, not so many at once."

Captain Twyldis slammed a fist into his open hand.

"We were all felled, as surely as if an enemy stood in a watchtower, and shot us, one after the other."

"Then our island is under attack!" growled Merchant Reece. "It's those Catiffar nobles, I'll swear it. They've had an eye on Ailsandia for generations."

Timmy pulled his thumb from his mouth. "She's not from Catiffar."

"Who?" Captain Twyldis put his hand on Timmy's shoulder.

"Her, the Lady. She swam here, she did. Stole my Mam's clothes off the line. I seen her."

"Hush," Marthe said. "Her Majesty's waking. Where's that Jacasin? She went for soup ten minutes ago."

Captain Twyldis scowled. "If only we could talk to Her Majesty! Tell her what we suspect!"

Maari hesitated, then nodded. "She'll hear us."

The others watched her, stunned, as she touched the Queen's cheek and then her lips.

"Silence, Your Majesty. Pretend you can't see me. We don't know who might be watching."

The Queen opened her eyes slowly. Grief touched her face as she scanned the shades hovering over her. She schooled her expression into blankness. "You've stayed to take leave of me?" she asked silently, as she always spoke to shades. "Thank you, dear friends, but you must seek your peace."

Captain Twyldis shook his head. "Your Majesty, we cannot leave you. This was sorcery, not illness."

"Please, Your Majesty," Maari pleaded. "Someone has very deep plans. They endanger our families. We want to fight this. We must fight it. Accept our service, let us fight those who've orphaned our children, who murder our people."

"Maari..."

"It's within your power," Maari argued. "We were slain, but who's next? The King? Your children and ours? We *must hunt down the truth. Bind us to your service."*

"Maari! I'm not a Shadebinder!"

Merchant Reece touched the Queen's hand. "Help us, Your Majesty, or we will lose our sense of purpose and fade away. We are the strongest witnesses to this evil. You need us. Let us help."

In disbelief, Queen Ailsa turned her eyes from one to another of her servants, advisors, and old friends. One by one, they nodded. Tears filled her eyes. With difficulty, she formed the words. "You won't regret it, my friends. If you choose to leave me, ask, and I'll release you. We'll fight this evil together. I take my oath on that."

The sparks in the tapestry flared out with a faint hiss as the figures grew still. Fourteen shades emerged from the linen panel, silent once more. Maari stepped forward, holding out her hands in entreaty.

"And so," Maari said, "it began. In the next year alone, dozens of shades sought her out with their demands. They would stay, watch, and gather information, but most of all they would bear witness to evil."

Maari looked at Farren steadily, the tears streaming down her cheeks. She curtseyed to her Queen with the most profound reverence.

The Fourth Tapestry Panel: Witness, The Seamstress

A woman shade urged another forward, but the second crumpled at her feet.

"Serpe, it's all right. You're safe now, you can tell what you know."

"No, no, no," cried Serpe. "He's alive, he's here!"

"Who? Tell us! The Queen will protect you. She has the power."

"No," Serpe moaned. "I can't, Helain. He'll hurt me. You

don't know, can't guess..."

Helain brushed Serpe's hair out of her eyes. "It's all right," she sighed. "You needn't tell. Master Orino, if you would tend her?"

"Gladly." Master Orino ushered Serpe into the crowd of shades behind the Queen."My sister and I," began Helain, "were apprenticed to a seamstress in Dannerald. The work was hard, the hours long, and the food little. When the sweating sickness took the city, as it does every few years, she died. A few days later, I did as well.

"As a shade, I hunted for my sister, but she'd vanished. Strange things began to happen, snowstorms out of season, huge tidal waves that kept ships in port. Shades of every description were flocking to the sea, and over it, to Valtiris. Perhaps Serpe had followed them. I crossed the sea, and walked through Ramsvalt. At last, I found her, in the oddest of places.

Helain paused in the stable, astounded. She saw Serpe, hovering before a stall. Inside it, a dappled gray horse sidled nervously. Helain exclaimed in delight and rushed forward to delight to greet her sister.

Startled, Serpe screamed. The horse leaped in its stall and backed into a corner, shivering. With a sudden cry, Serpe rushed at him, beating him with her fists. The horse reared and shied away in the close quarters, his eyes rolling in frenzy.

Helain grabbed at Serpe, her hands slipping through the insubstantial stuff of her sister's body. She tore at her sister, but Serpe slipped through her hands and flew at the horse once more.

The horse neighed in terror, his sharp hooves pounding the walls and floor. An anguished cry came from the floor of the stall, as the groom struggled to escape. Serpe recoiled, staring at the bloody body still moving on the floor. She covered her face, sobbing, and vanished before Helain could catch her.

Grooms rushed from all corners of the stable, but it was too late to save either the groom or the horse.

THE FIFTH TAPESTRY PANEL: WITNESS, THE MINSTREL

The tapestry shifted to the greens and grays of Ramsvalt Castle. Master Orino stepped forward, resting his hand on the prickling wool of the yew hedge.

"Your Highness, I wish I were worth the tears you've shed for me. Dear ladies, I deceived you all. You thought me a singer, a dancer, a true minstrel, but alas but I served another in your stead. Several years ago, Emperor Theomedon took a sudden fright. Orbri died, and Hesselin vanished. Thus, the emperor lost his visionary and his sorcerer at a single blow. He dispatched us, a dozen or more, to every court and hall.

"Traveling minstrels find welcome anywhere, and their information trickles back steadily to their masters. We're a nosy lot, we minstrels. I ingratiated myself at Ramsvalt, and installed myself as Your Highness' dance master. I sang my trivial songs, leaped about the dance floor, and jotted a few small notes. But one of those notes went astray."

Orino touched the tapestry on the stitched image of the Ramsvalt watchtower. The Queen stretched out a hand, and a spark flew to Orino's fingers. The tapestry watchtower glowed and expanded. With a writhe and a wriggle, the fabric drew in the shade's form and puffed to life.

The Ramsvalt watchtower expanded and split in two, exposing a dark dungeon chamber. With a sudden sharp sense of disorientation, the watchers shivered in the dampness and blinked their eyes against the darkness. They heard the scuttle of a rat as it scurried across the floor. A figure lay bound on the floor. Wordless cries of protest emerged from the watchers as their thoughts were overcome by those of the prisoner.

Orino's head was splitting. He opened his eyes, but the room was pitch black. He started to sit up, but something clanked. He fell back onto the floor, his arms and legs contorted backwards. He was wearing manacles, he realized dimly. He shifted his hips to ease his legs, nearly jerking his shoulders loose from their sockets. He turned the other way, and his knees twisted painfully. He settled on an awkward slump, flexing his muscles to relieve the ache, swallowing against the dryness of his throat.

He filtered through his memories, trying to assemble them into some sort of order. He'd given himself away. Which of his discoveries had they known? There was the banditry near Khonsvalt. He'd thought bandits belonged to the Patrol Guards, but he couldn't find a pattern. Besides, that wouldn't account for those sudden changes in guild leadership in Selefrevalt. All was confusion, disconnection, and unrest, that same mélange of feelings that had sparked his prophecy song. He knew that there was a pattern somewhere, if he could see his way clear to the end of it.

Somehow, the little song linked the whole thing together. He couldn't get that melody out of his head.

A key clanked in a lock, and a door swung open, just past his head. He craned his neck, but all he could see was light, and a partial silhouette. A boot prodded his head.

"Who are you? Why am I here?" Orino cried. "I'm just a minstrel."

"The ship was boarded. We found a message on it, from you."

"Message? What message? It must have been a song," he said. "I trade songs with guild friends!" The boot slammed into his head, jolting him against the chains. His shoulders burned, and he cried out.

A second shadowy figure moved into the doorway.

"Make him talk."

The boot slammed into his leg, again and again, methodically destroying his right knee. Orino screamed. He was dead already, he knew. There was no point in his silence. He might as well tell his tale, and meet his death. At least his shade could wander, singing his saga to those would hear. Perhaps then, he'd have the answers.

However...He knew that voice, from the second man. Where had he heard it before? His mind racing, he gabbled out a meaningless stream of words, trying to delay his captors until he'd winkled out at least one bit of the puzzle.

"Kogyr," Orino gasped. He cursed himself. Gods, what a slip! If he wasn't dead before, he was now. Kogyr, the ship's captain who'd swaggered onto Ailsandian docks, his hands dripping with gold. His men had flanked him, big, bluff, and hearty, but others remained on the ship, lean and sullen-eyed. Curious, Orino had followed for a while, but Kogyr merely stopped at the harbormaster's office, and proceeded to the nearest inn, humming all the while.

Kogyr, humming the tune that haunted Orino's dreams.

Dazed with pain, Orino ceased his babbling, and twisted his neck again, trying to see the figure in the hallway.

"Whose song is it?" Orino whispered.

There was sudden silence. His torturer drew in a sharp breath and glanced into the hallway where Kogyr stood hidden.

"The song," Orino insisted. "Where did you hear it?" There was no answer. Orino took a deep breath and uttered the first sweet notes.

Kogyr's bellowed curse filled the air as he drew his knife and stormed into the prison cell. Orino's song cut short.

The watchers gasped in blessed relief as the spell ended, releasing them from Orino's pain and despair.

"The other prisoners lie there still, captive in the dungeon where Hesselin has trapped them. When Your Highness' draught released me, I took their tales to Her Majesty. The Queen will hold them in safety and comfort until she can safely release each one to life or death. My gratitude, dear sirs, and madams, for your listening ears." Orino bowed, and moved away.

THE SIXTH TAPESTRY PANEL: WITNESS, THE GUARD

"I'm Brandt, Second in the Ramsvalt Castle Guard." Brandt stood with his feet apart, hands clasped behind his back. "I've been hunting down information for Queen Ailsa these last seven years. I'm not much of a storyteller. I leave that to my wife and the minstrels. But I know what I saw. "

The small village of Rampton Vale nestled into its cranny above the mountain foothills. The tapestry surface shifted with the movements of men and horses, jingling with harness and swords. On the shoulders of their jackets lay the shield-shaped insignia of the Western Patrol. The Captain shook hands with a well-dressed farmer, and mounted his horse. He waved to his men and they headed for the mountain pass. Night came, and passed peacefully.

At last, morning light filtered over the ridges, though the sun wouldn't rise for an hour or two. Drowsy youngsters herded their sheep up onto the slopes for a day's grazing.

A boy crossed the ridge, seeking fresh pasture for his small flock of a dozen sheep. He settled his sheep and propped himself against a boulder, keeping a lazy eye on them. A man rushed him from behind the boulder, cut his throat, and dropped him to the ground. Two others herded the sheep on down the hills to a rock walled dead-end in the foothills. One by one, they waylaid other children, and other herds.

When sheep filled the rock-walled corral, the leader raised his arm and shouted to his men. Raucous laughter met his command. As one, they descended on the village. Thatched roofs blazed like beacons, while screaming villagers dodged greedy hands. Knives flashed, clothing ripped, and blood puddled in the dirt roads.

Grumbling, the bandits dug the burial pits expected in plague towns. They tumbled the dead into them. Small wails and flopping limbs showed life, but the graves were covered, and feet stomped them down.

Life faded from the tapestry, the colors dulling to red-brown mud. The cloth jerked sharply, brightening another section of the mountains fifty miles north of Khonsvalt.

A dozen people exclaimed excitedly over a handful of gold nuggets. They slapped a young man on the back. He grabbed a light pack, and ran down the trail. Ten miles further on, the runner rounded a bend and caught his step, surprised to find six men breaking camp. His cautious look faded into relief as he noted the uniform of the Rimlands Patrol.

A bearded fellow laughed and held out a flask. With a grateful look the runner drank deeply. He rested, bent slightly, his hands on his knees, catching his breath.

The guard glanced at the miner's insignia on the boy's right shoulder. He exchanged glances with the others, over the boy's head. He pointed down the mountain in the direction of Khonsvalt, and posed a casual question.

The boy stiffened, a wary look crossing his face. He waved a hand, denying Khonsvalt, but his voice faltered as he answered. He coughed, and attempted an easy smile as he straightened up again.

A few minutes later, the young man's body bounced on the rocks on its way down the cliff. A few hours later, the bandits picked off the miners, one at a time, followed by their sons, and their women.

Deep lines scored Brandt's face. "We tried, the fellows and me. But it's a hell of a lot easier to kill someone than it is to stop 'em from killin'."

Figures came to life, all over the tapestry. Pirates boarded ships in southern waters, to torture and drown the crews while pillaging the ship. Caravans moved from one city to another, through Valtiris and beyond. Raids picked off the stragglers, and the carts resumed their trek with stolen goods. Lines of manacled slaves marched from the outskirts of Catiffar, out of the Empire.

On Ramsvalt's keep, the Queen kept watch, capturing a shooting star for every shade she bound. With each star, a grimace of pain crossed her face, and her hands earned another scar of valor. Shades streamed to the roof, their faces urgent, their arms waving. Time and again, the Queen raised her hands, calling up storms, avalanches, and earthquakes, delaying and hampering the enemy's advance.

"The rest of us, the shades, we kept as busy as we could. Started a lot of fights among the bandits, scared their horses off, things like that. Thank the gods we finally got into the thick of the battle out there, at last. With my own boy, leading the fight, too. Beat those pirates to hell and gone, didn't we? Did my heart good."

The Seventh Tapestry Panel: Witness, The Goat

The tapestry made its final turn, displaying Ailsandia's harbor, the surrounding city, the white palace, and the keep tucked into the mountain above.

The shades shifted, looking at each other. No one moved forward. They turned towards Queen Ailsa with questioning looks. She gazed steadily at a single figure. Gradually, everyone else, living and dead followed her stare.

Caprio shifted uncomfortably. "So, what are you all looking at me for?" He trotted in a tight circle. "Is the show over already? You're a dour lot, all gloom and doom. It's over now, don't you see it?"

Despite his words, he lingered, staring at the Queen with a peculiar mix of resentment and speculation. "Well get on with it, woman! There's only one thing left to do! Take care of the damned dragon!"

"Tell the story as you know it," said Master Orino softly. "Give us the last pieces of the puzzle."

"There's no puzzle! She's got 'em all right here in her hand. Crush 'em!"

"Tell the story. The tapestry waits."

"You're just going to stand there, aren't you," fumed the Goat. He trotted to the Queen, reared up, and set his fore hooves on her shoulders. She stood like a statue, carved of white marble. "You can't force me. I'm a *Being*, not a shade. You never bound me. You can't lay a finger on me, not with every star in the sky!"

"The story," said Orino.

"Not until she admits it! I'm not her servant, and she couldn't bind me if she tried. Admit it!"

The Queen dipped her chin once.

"Harruff! Well. All right then." Caprio launched himself into the air and zoomed over their heads. "In a nutshell, here's how it goes." The tapestry came to life, every threaded figure moving as Caprio glared at it. "We're up to the last month now, okay? The Progress comes to Ailsandia. Hesselin latches onto Ailsa and Mericia. He's stretched too thin already, trying to keep his grip on Kogyr until the Siren makes her move. Girl gets headaches, but keeps moving. Queen does her stuff and falls apart."

The Queen set down the tapestry and fell to the floor. Dragging in one breath at a time, she crawled up the keep stairs to the roof. She hung onto the rampart as night fell and the moon rose. Through the darkness, a golden dragon flew to her, landing on the roof. The Queen staggered a step or two, and collapsed against its neck. She slept through the night, kept warm by dragon coils.

"Quite a touching picture, isn't it?" Caprio said, eyeing the tapestry moodily. "She sent him off in the morning. As long as the kraaken was a boulder, he was safe enough, but after the woman freed it, the need for displacement was over. Kogyr would've headed off on a dragon hunt as soon as he had a chance. That's the thing about those displacement spells. Got to keep your opposite safe until seven years have passed, or you're toast.

"The dragon, though, he couldn't stand it. When he saw Siren out there, menacing the girl, there was nothing for it. He had to be a stupid hero, get shot up by Irandis' charmed cross bolts. He should've let her alone. Our Riss is no fool. She threw the Siren and the kraaken both five hundred miles south. Hmm. I wonder what they think of all this. I think I'll go look them up when we're done here. Now, the ships—" Caprio's eyes lit with sudden enthusiasm. "Now they livened things up no end! Glad I brought 'em in. Got the timing down perfect, didn't I? If I left things alone, Kogyr wouldn't have brought them in until the winter storms. By then he and Hesselin would have taken control for certain, leaving the girl and her mother both dead. So you're damned lucky I took a hoof in the matter." He tossed his head, his beard spiraling impressively. "No need to thank me. I was just tying up loose ends.

"I thought Hesselin would pull it off for a bit. The frozen air column to trap the dragon was pretty good, and the sharks were inspired. He couldn't beat the Shade Army, though, not with *me* leading the way. Knocked him out, good and proper, when we tossed the ship around like that. The Queen woke up for a bit then, but unfortunately, he wasn't dead. Once he came to, he started throwing sharks around, and grappled the Queen tight with his sorcery and wouldn't let go.

"You know, if hadn't been for me, that tapestry'd *still* be at the top of the keep, and the dragon would stay a dragon forever. Or until Kogyr killed it, of course," said the Goat, fairly. "And gods know *when* you'd have figured out Hesselin's disguise. I have to hand it to him, he's pretty good for a mortal."

"So," he concluded. "That's the story. Your turn." He wheeled and glared at the Queen.

The Queen gestured at the tapestry. It shrank and fell to the floor in crumpled heaps. A line of shades passed before them, a thousand strong: nobles and muckrakers, smiths and stable boys, ladies and tavern wenches, each bearing witness to evil. Each bowed to the Queen, brushed her hand, smiled, and stood aside, waiting, and watching. Last of all came Master Orino, the notes of his lute shifting into the music of his song, the Siren's song.

Mercia shook herself out of her trance. She remembered a chair crashing to the floor, Lelori's fingers tight on the table, and felt the Lorelei's torment over the seven-year loss of her music.

Master Orino's clear tenor cut through the stillness.

> *"When the wings of the mountains brush the soul*
> *of the sea,*
> *When the two and the many are one,*
> *When illusions of freedom encircle and flee*
> *Then the threads of the challenge are spun."*

Mercia heard the words of his song transform into images of Farren and the dragon joining the Shade Patrol, so instrumental in defeating the imposter's aims.

> *"No matter the dream, or the steps you may stray*
> *Our lives entangle your net*

> *As you leap to the skies, or dive to the sea,*
> *Our hearts must follow you yet."*

She and the Siren entangled each other's lives. The Siren only sought to rescue her immortal friend. Yet, she'd been the best possible tutor for a girl to become Queen. Her frozen exterior was a perfect model for Mericia, as she strove to survive the torture inflicted on her by the imposter the Siren had put in place.

> *"When the wool and the flax meet madder and*
> *weld*
> *When the stars cease their tumble to flare*
> *When hidden desires refuse to be quelled*
> *Then treachery seeks to ensnare.*
>
> *No matter the captive, or the heart that now sleeps*
> *The world is caught in your net*
> *As you soar to the clouds, or plunge to the deeps,*
> *Our hearts are torn with regret.*
>
> *When souls in slavery are freed at the last*
> *When the waves of the hurricane cease*
> *When a nation of chaos meets the sins of its past*
> *Then the world at last may know peace."*

Master Orino bowed deeply. "The truth is spoken. It remains, Your Majesty, only to reverse two transformations and we've finished our work. Let us assist you, one last time."

The Queen nodded. She laid a hand on the dragon's neck, and stretched the other out to her daughter. As if impelled, Trissi leaped forward and took Mericia's hand. A cold flame leaped from Mericia and sparked to Trissi, expanding into a ring of fire surrounding them both. The Queen smiled lovingly and crooked her finger. The ring snapped open and flew to its mistress. Mericia and Trissi slipped their arms around each other's waists. Their eyes met, in mingled delight and sorrow. The magical link between them was gone, leaving only love behind.

The Queen cupped the fireball in her hand, then shot it into the seer's ball, lying forgotten on the chair. Sparkling lights soared from the crystal, as the shooting stars released their hosts and coursed into the Queen's hand, engulfing it in flame and blood.

The dragon shrieked, its writhing coils thrashing a chair into splinters. Farren leaped forward, arms outstretched. Beyond the trio of dragon, Queen, and woodworker, a man crashed to the floor, echoing the agonized scream. Before the horrified eyes of the beholders, the two went still, staring upwards sightlessly. Farren clutched the dragon's neck as the form in his arms blurred, changed, and shrank. The fire spluttered and died. The shade army exulted, as half of them shed the burden of the Shadebinder's spell.

At the Queen's feet lay two men. Alone, crumpled in a heap, was the imposter Kogyr, the pirate. In Farren's arms lay King Gerritt, formerly the golden dragon.

Chapter Nineteen

A t the dragon's scream, Farren leaped forward. He skidded beneath the arching flames, and hugged the dragon tightly around the neck, striving to lessen the pain by sharing it. Above him, the dragon's neck and head froze in a column of agony, while his tail thrashed convulsively and his feet scrabbled at the floor.

"Little one," he cried, tears streaking his cheeks and catching in the stubble of his whiskers, "it's almost over. Whatever's happening, it's nearly done. Little one..." Meaningless, pointless words, but he couldn't bear the creature's pain. Gods, please, let it be over soon.

The dragon's head fell to the floor. Within the circle of his arms, the scaly flesh melted away. The wings shriveled and dissolved. "Little one!" He grieved with the loss, blinded with tears, still gripping the remnants of his friend.

Behind him came a jumble of voices.

"Father?"

"My lady, your hand!"

"Your Majesty?"

A sharp gasp from David: "It was *him*?"

Within his arms, the figure stirred. Farren let go and helped him up. "Little one, are you all right?" he choked, shaking off the blinding tears.

The ghost of a chuckle, and then the deep, resonant voice, "Yes, my friend. The pain is gone. Come, help me stand up, —or should I help you?"

Farren scrambled up, tugging the other's arm. His vision cleared and he stared in bewilderment at his King. Hot blood flushed his cheeks, and he backed away in confusion.

The King caught and held his hand, while pulling the Queen into his embrace with the other. He rested his cheek against her hair, whispering, "My love." He cleared his throat. "You are a true friend, Farren. I will not forget."

Farren stared into his eyes, and sudden joy swept over him. "That's it! That's why your eyes, I mean the other King—" He raked his hand through his hair. "I only saw his eyes today, for the first time, and it seemed so odd, the colors were so mixed. They didn't match what everyone said, what I expected. There was so much going on, with the dragon— I mean, with you. Sir. Your Majesty."

"And what other mixed colors have you seen, good friend? Point out the sorcerer to us. I'm sure my good Queen knows, but independent verification is always preferred."

Farren whirled. Three men stood stock-still: Vance Heronlys, Minister Sendillon, and Minister Jonsel. Minister Rogitas hovered nearby. David stood stiffly next to his mother, his face a mask of dread.

"That one," Farren said, pointing at Sendillon.

"Ah. And Vance? Rogitas? Jonsel? Chandra? Siree?"

"Their colors are true."

The Queen turned her head from her husband's shoulder and nodded. Her glance transfixed Sendillon, holding him motionless.

"Vance," said King Gerritt, "if you would take charge of the prisoners?"

"Gladly, Your Majesty," said Heronlys. He clamped a hand

around the dazed Sendillon's wrist, and stirred the limp pirate with the toe of his boot. "For the moment they seem safe enough."

"They'd have been safe enough, tomorrow. The enchantment would have been permanent. Then he merely needed to mount a dragon hunt, slay me, my wife, and deal with my children. He might have found that a little more difficult than he anticipated." He grinned at his daughter. "However, I don't see another dragon. My love, where was our Sendillon's soul transferred to?"

Mericia, leaning against her father's side, spoke eagerly. "Caprio! It must be Caprio. Don't you think so, Farren?"

"Nonsense," snorted the Goat, outraged. "Me, a mortal?"

Farren eyed the Goat doubtfully. "Aunt Nan? You others? What do you think?" The shades returned varying shades of bewilderment. "If he were Sendillon, wouldn't he know?"

"I didn't know who I was," said the King. "I thought I'd lived forever, and been a dragon since the beginning, whenever that was. I only knew I was lonely, and that someone I loved was missing." He hugged the Queen tightly. "I thought it was another dragon, and in a way, I was right."

"I am not," stated Caprio frostily, "a mortal. I was *never* a mortal. I am a Being." He stamped his foot and snorted at Sendillon. "If you're going to turn me into *that* thing, I'm off!" He darted to the edge of the balcony.

"But—" said Mericia.

"Wait," thundered Farren. "You owe this lady, remember? You've lived forever, and never been able to fly, until now. The princess gave you the power to fly."

Caprio skidded to a halt, and shook his beard. "Harrumph. She did not! It was just a matter of—"

"Are Beings dishonorable?"

"Honor is a meaningless concept, when considered between mortals and immortals."

"How about gratitude, appreciation, common courtesy?"

"I am *not* a mortal!" bellowed the Goat.

"Then it won't hurt you to stick around, will it? If you're not Sendillon, there won't be a transfer. Besides, would you dare leave a sorcerer unmasked? One that can affect Beings?"

"Mortal sorcerers cannot affect Beings!"

"Ha. He blinded you, didn't he? When the dragon fell out of the sky, did you know who did it? When you called in the pirate ships, was that your idea, or his? He hid from you, in plain sight. He *tricked* a Being."

"He did not!" Caprio pranced in rage. He charged through Sendillon, and the man shivered.

"What do *you* call it?" said Farren, scathingly. "It's a good thing for you the Queen's got him entranced. Otherwise, he'd hold you off with a raised finger. How do you know he didn't ensorcel you to begin with? Create you out of thin air to hold Sendillon's soul?"

"No!" Caprio stood stiff with insult.

"Prove it." Farren's voice was heavy with irony. "Stick around, and let's see."

With slow steps of martyrdom, Caprio stepped next to Sendillon. "Do your worst, woman," he snorted at the Queen.

Farren turned to the Queen. "Your Majesty?"

"No, Your Majesty," protested Lady Siree. "Your hand. Let us tend to it!"

The Queen raised her good hand to fend off Lady Siree. She stepped next to Sendillon, the King close behind her. She placed her wounded hand, charred flesh and white bone, on Sendillon's forehead, and stretched the other out to the host of shades.

The arc of fire struck, as virulent as before, searing the Queen's remaining hand. Sendillon howled, the howl mingling with another, as man and dog fell to the floor in spasms. Caprio stepped back with a snort of distaste.

The small dog swelled, its legs expanding into the long legged stork-like figure of Minister Sendillon. Next to him, the imposter's body shriveled, becoming a one-eyed man with a neat triangular beard.

The Queen staggered, falling into a chair that Lady Siree shoved behind her. Queen Ailsa swayed in her seat. "Thank you," she said softly.

Mericia knelt next to her, cradling the bloody hands. "Mother," she breathed. "I haven't heard your voice in seven years."

"It's over, my daughter. I despaired many a time, but at last it's over." She leaned her head back into her husband's gentle hands.

"Your Majesty? I grieve to intrude," said Heronlys, "but this sorcerer. He's unconscious now, but when he wakes, what should I do to secure him?"

"He is secure," murmured the Queen. "The souls of his victims achieved their revenge. Serpe and Durgas are free. Hesselin will be mindless, ever more, as will the other villain."

"I'll call the guards," said Trissi, "if, er..." She stumbled to a halt, glancing uncertainly between the King, Queen, and Princess.

"My daughter is Regent," said Queen Ailsa with a ghost of a chuckle. "Soon to be Queen. I've a mind to retire, I believe." The King dropped a kiss on her hair.

"Please do, Trissi," said Mericia. "And call the physicians to tend my mother, father, and poor Sendillon." She stifled a chuckle at the sight of Minister Rogitas, solicitously assisting the new confused Sendillon into a chair. "Are you all right, Minister Sendillon?"

"Much better, thank you." His voice wavered. "Exceedingly tired of raw meat, and trailing this varlet." He rubbed his nose reflectively. "I won't be sorry to lose that sense of smell, even if it did make him easy to track."

Farren eased back against the balcony railing, fighting a crushing depression. He'd lost his dragon, and Mericia was completely absorbed in her family. Even David was totally wrapped up in his father.

He forced himself to look away. At least he had Denys. Wouldn't they have tales to share tomorrow! With a weak chuckle, he took note of his surroundings. The shades were gone, and the balcony clear for the first time since he'd seen it. Only a shade, a spirit, and a Being remained: Brandt, Aunt Nan, and Caprio.

"Aunt Nan?" He reached out and brushed the transparent cheek. "You can ascend to heaven, now. You've waited long enough."

"Oh my dear, it was never the Queen who bound me. It was you."

" Me? Aunt Nan, I never did. I wouldn't, and besides I haven't a clue how to catch stars."

She chuckled warmly. "Love works just as well."

"I'm sorry, Aunt Nan. I never meant to hold you back."

"I'm saying this badly, dear. You didn't bind me. I bound myself, through my love of you. Just as your father did. He'll traipse after all three of you until you're Master, Captain, and Captain. One day, he'll leave, and I will, too." She gave him a roguish look. "But not until I've a grand-niece or nephew, I think."

"Aunt Nan!" Someone pulled on his elbow, and guided him to a seat.

"Oh, hush your mouth," she said. "I've years to spare. There's no hurry. I suspect Denys and Trissi will oblige me soon, even if you don't."

"Oh." Belatedly, he realized who had pushed him into a chair. "I'm sorry, Sire."

The King waved off his protests, and pulled a chair up next to him. "You've got the right of it, Farren. It's best to stay out of the ladies' way when they're like this. Or were you talking to that aunt of yours?"

"Er, yes."

Across the balcony two physicians, Lady Siree, Trissi, and Chandra directed a flurry of activity around the Queen's chair. Mericia conferred with Vance Heronlys, her hand resting on her mother's shoulder. David stood at his father's elbow, glowing with pride. Four guards held the two unsteady prisoners between them.

"I've had a thought or two about that boy," ruminated the King, eyeing David. "It's been brought home to me that helping wild animals is extremely important. In fact, a personal priority." A grin flickered. "Perhaps David would accept a royal commission to search out wildlife populations and advise the king regarding their treatment. When he's a little older. What do you think?"

"A wonderful idea," said Farren.

"Hmm. I've an idea or two about you as well, young man." King Gerritt gave him a sidelong glance.

"Thank you, Sire. I plan to prove mastery of my craft, and work with Master Pardell. He's been after me for years to seek my master's pin, and I've come to see he's right. I owe him that. He was a kind friend to me when I had very few."

"Ah. Perhaps he'd consider moving to the Island, he and his family. I'll be sorry to lose him at Ramsvalt, but things being what they are, I'd best look ahead."

"Sir?"

Mericia rushed over to her father.

"Ah, my dear daughter. Draw up a chair and join us. Meriss, I can't begin to tell you how horrified I am by the torment you've suffered. How can I make it up to you?"

"It wasn't your doing, father. It was *his*." Mericia gestured implacably towards the disappearing prisoner. She threw her arms around her father. "But everything's all right now.

I can hardly believe it. Mother is well again, truly well!"

"She was never ill, Meriss. She was pretending, the whole time."

Mericia shuddered. "Like Lady Lelori."

"That woman. That soulless excuse for a governess."

"No, father. It wasn't the Lorelei. She didn't hurt me. All those things, the dogs, the horse, the knights who were injured when they spoke to me, even Father Lawrence's death, and Master Orino's torture, —Hesselin ordered those. He wanted me in his power, unmarried, when the Siren broke the kraaken's spell. Either he'd marry me himself, or he'd kill me then, but in either case, control of the Island would pass to him. I'm not cursed, you're alive, and mother is well. And above all, our nations are safe from the horror that might have been." The calm planes of her face broke, and a radiant smile burst forth. The next moment, the smile disappeared, and the cool mask-like exterior of the Princess returned.

Farren watched her eyes contentedly. The radiance remained. It did not matter, now or ever, what expression her face wore. He would always know her feelings as clearly as if she trumpeted them across the city.

"But the woman still troubles you," suggested King Gerritt.

"Yes. But I don't know," her words slowed, "if I meant anything to her. It shouldn't matter. She lured scores of our men to their doom, and destroyed whatever got in her way. I learned a great deal from her, nonetheless. I wish I knew—" She broke off and fell silent, remembering the clawed fingers groping at Trissi on the barge. Would the Siren have killed both of them, if she'd had the chance? Or had she another plan?

"It doesn't make the shade of a difference," said Farren. "She was good and evil both, like everyone else, mortal and immortal."

Mericia looked at him. "I learned a great deal from her. I just hope it was good, and not evil."

"Intentions matter as much as knowledge. Her intentions don't matter any longer. Yours do."

Mericia's eyes warmed. A slow smile spread over her face. "And yours, too," she teased.

"I've been meaning to ask him about his intentions," King Gerritt remarked.

"Oh hush, father." Mericia caught Farren's hand, and they walked to the edge of the balcony. Down in the harbor, lantern light flickered, as people worked into the night. Farren's arm stole around her waist. Side by side, they watched the activity below, murmuring ideas for tomorrow.

"Haruff," snorted the Goat, as he trotted across the balcony to view the wrecked harbor before him. "Mortals. They can't do a thing without making a mess. If they didn't have such good food, I wouldn't bother with them." He scowled to himself, staring at the empty stretch of the bay, where the kraaken had lain for so long. "Funny," he muttered. "That kraaken seems familiar somehow. The sorcerer who bound him, too. In fact, Mereni III's whole coronation strikes a chord. I wonder—" He cocked his head for a moment and shrugged.

The Goat leaped onto the balcony railing, poised there for a moment, and took off, flying through the night sky of Ailsandia, to parts unknown.